SOME FANATICS
PREDICT THE END.

THIS ONE
CAN BRING IT OFF.

He's just unleashed a
20,000-foot tidal wave
on Los Angeles to prove
it. Next, California's
last earthquake—in a
cracking good suspense story
that could only have been
written by the world's
undisputed master of
adventure . . .

ALISTAIR MACLEAN

GOODBYE CALIFORNIA

ALISTAIR MACLEAN

FAWCETT CREST • NEW YORK

GOODBYE CALIFORNIA

THIS BOOK CONTAINS THE COMPLETE TEXT OF
THE ORIGINAL HARDCOVER EDITION.

Published by Fawcett Crest Books, a unit of CBS Publica-
tions, the Consumer Publishing Division of CBS Inc., by arrangement with Doubleday and Company, Inc.

ISBN: 0-449-23834-2

Selection of the Book-of-the-Month Club

Printed in the United States of America

10 9 8 7 6 5 4 3 2 1

Gisela

Foreword

IT was at twenty seconds to six o'clock on the morning of February 9, 1972, that the earth shook. As such tremors go, it could hardly even be called noteworthy; it was certainly no more remarkable than those that afflict the citizens of Tokyo and its surrounding countryside scores of times a year. Pendant lamps oscillated briefly, some precariously balanced objects fell from their shelves, but those were the only discernible effects of the passing of the earth ripple. The aftershock, considerably weaker, came twenty seconds later. It was learned afterward that there had been four more aftershocks but those were of so low a magnitude that they registered only on the seismographs. Altogether a rather inconsequential affair but memorable for me, at least, inasmuch as it was the first tremor I had experienced: having the ground move beneath your feet provides a distinctly disquieting sensation.

The area where the maximum damage had occurred lay only a few miles to the north and I drove out to see it the following day. The township of Sylmar, which had borne the brunt of the earthquake, lies in the San Fernando Valley in California, some miles north of Los Angeles. Damage to buildings was widespread but not severe, except in one very localized area: the Veterans Administration Hospital. Before the earthquake it had consisted of three parallel blocks of buildings. The two outer blocks had remained virtually intact; the central one had collapsed like a house of cards. Destruction was total: no part of it was left standing. More than sixty patients died.

It had been destroyed by an earthquake the epicenter of which had been eight miles distant to the northeast. But what was important—and significant—about the earthquake that had caused this considerable damage was

7

the factor of its power—or lack of it. The magnitude of an earthquake is registered on an arbitrarily chosen Richter scale which ranges from 0 to 12. And what is important to bear in mind is that the Richter scale progresses not arithmetically but logarithmically. Thus, a 6 on the Richter scale is ten times as powerful as a 5 or a hundred times as powerful as a 4. The earthquake that leveled this hospital in Sylmar registered 6.3 on the Richter scale; the one that wreaked havoc on San Francisco in 1906 registered 8.3 in the former estimate (7.9 according to the recent modifications of the Richter scale). Thus, the earthquake that caused this damage in Sylmar was possessed of only 1 per cent of the effective power of the San Francisco one. It is a sobering thought and, to those burdened with an overactive imagination, a fearful one.

What is even more sobering and frightening is the fact that, to the best of our knowledge, no great earthquake— "great" is arbitrarily taken to be anything 8 and above on the Richter scale— has ever occurred beneath or in the immediate vicinity of any major city, except apparently for that awesome North Chinese earthquake of July 1976 when two thirds of a million people in and around Taugshan are reported to have died, although the Chinese have not officially confirmed any statistics. But the law of averages would indicate strongly that major earthquakes will occur in places not conveniently uninhabited or, at least, sparsely populated. There is reason to imagine, unless one chooses to take refuge behind I-don't-want-to-know mental blinders, that this possibility may even today be a probability.

The word "probability" is used because the law of averages is strengthened by the fact that earthquakes largely tend to take place in coastal areas, whether those coastal areas be of land masses or islands; and it is in these coastal areas, for the purposes of trade and because they are the points of ingress to the hinterland, that many of the world's great cities have been built. Tokyo, Los Angeles and San Francisco are three such examples.

That earthquakes should be largely confined to those areas is in no way fortuitous: their cause, as well as that of volcanoes, is now a matter of almost universal agreement among geologists. The theory is simply that in the unimaginably distant past when land first appeared, it was in the form of one gigantic supercontinent surrounded by—inevitably—one massive ocean. With the passage of time and for reasons not yet definitely ascertained this supercontinent broke up into several different continental masses which, borne on what are called their tectonic plates—which float on the still molten magma layer of the earth—drifted apart. Those tectonic plates occasionally bang or rub against one another; the effects of the collisions are transmitted either to the land above or the ocean floor and appear in the form of earthquakes or volcanoes.

Most of California lies on the North American plate, which, while tending to move westward, is not the real villain of the piece. That unhappy distinction belongs to that same North Pacific plate which deals so hardly with China, Japan and the Philippines and on which that section of California lying to the west of the San Andreas fault so unhappily lies. Although the North Pacific plate appears to be rotating slightly, its movement in California is still roughly to the northwest and, now and then, when the pressure between the two plates becomes too much, the North Pacific plate eases this pressure by jerking northwest along the San Andreas fault and so producing one of those earthquakes that Californians don't care so much about.

The extent of the dislocation along this right-slip fault—so-called because if you stand on either side of the fault after an earthquake the other side appears to have moved to the right—is crucial in relation to the magnitude of the shock. Occasionally, there may be no lateral slip at all. Sometimes, it may be only a foot or two. But, even though its consequences are not to be contemplated lightly, a lateral slip of forty feet is eminently possible.

In fact, and in this context, all things are possible. The active earthquake and volcanic belt that circumgirdles the Pacific is commonly—and appropriately—known as the ring of fire. The San Andreas fault is an integral

9

part of this and it is on this ring of fire that the two greatest monster earthquakes (in Japan and South America) ever recorded have occurred. They were on the order of 8.9 on the old Richter scale. California can lay no more claim to divine protection than any other part of the ring of fire and there is no compelling reason why the next monster, about six times as powerful as the great San Francisco one, shouldn't occur, say, in San Bernardino, thus effectively dumping Los Angeles into the Pacific. And the Richter scale goes up to 12!

Earthquakes on the ring of fire can show another disadvantageous aspect—they can occur offshore as well as under land. When this occurs, huge tidal waves result. In 1976 Mindanao in the southern Philippines was inundated and all but destroyed and thousands of lives were lost when an undersea earthquake at the mouth of the crescent-shaped Moro Gulf caused a fifteen-foot tidal wave that engulfed the shores of the bay. Such an ocean earthquake off San·Francisco would devastate the Bay area and, in all probability, wouldn't do any good to the Sacramento and San Joaquin valleys.

As it is said, it is the wandering nature of those tectonic plates that is the prime cause of earthquakes. But there are two other imponderable possibilities that could well act as triggering factors which could conceivably cause earthquakes.

The first of those is emissions from the sun. It is known that the strength and content of solar winds alter considerably and wholly unpredictably. It is also known that they can produce considerable alterations in the chemical structure of our atmosphere which in turn can have the effect of either accelerating or braking the rotation of the earth; an effect which, because it would be measurable in terms of only hundredths of a second, would be wholly undetected by many but could have (and may have had in the past) an influence ranging from the considerable to the profound on the unanchored tectonic plates.

There is a respectable body of scientific opinion that holds that the gravitational influences of the planets act on
10

the Sun to modulate the strength of these solar winds. This is of immediate concern since a rare alignment of all the planets of the Solar System is due in 1982. If this theory, known as *The Jupiter Effect* from the title of a book by Drs. John Gribbin and Stephen Plagemann, is correct that alignment will be the trigger for unprecedented solar activity, with repercussions on the stability of planet Earth. So scientists are waiting for 1982 with considerable interest, and not a little trepidation.

The second potential trigger is man. He has gratuitously and haphazardly interfered with due natural processes since the dawn of recorded time and there appears no logical reason why he shouldn't extend his unwanted tinkering to the realm of earthquakes. A species that is capable of prying into and eventually exploiting the ultimate secrets of nature and coming up with the hydrogen bomb is capable of anything. That man should consider the regulation of earthquakes, either by staged triggering or inhibition, is not a new idea. Experiments along those lines have already been carried out for peaceful purposes. Unfortunately (if inevitably), the idea has also occurred that the triggering of earthquakes might be an interesting innovation in the next nuclear war and, indeed, has occurred to such a marked extent that there already exists a multinational agreement, duly signed and solemnly sworn to, prohibiting the use of nuclear weapons that could endanger the environment by causing such things as atmospheric pollution and the creation of tidal waves.

The existence of this sacred treaty will, of course, only serve to incite the signatories, especially the nuclear powers, to intensify their frenzied research into exploiting the capacities of this hitherto unthought-of weapon to its fullest possible extent. One has only to think of the similarly sacred SALT treaties—the Strategic Arms Limitation Talks—signed by America and Russia in Helsinki which resulted in the immediate redoubling of activities of the scientists on both sides in their quest for the golden grail, the speedy development of new and more dreadful means for annihilating large sections of mankind. The

11

signing of worthless pieces of paper does not remove the spots from the coat of the leopard.

And, apart from war, this concept can be employed for a variety of other interesting purposes, which is what this book is about.

ONE

■ RYDER opened his tired eyelids and reached for the telephone without enthusiasm. "Yes?"

"Lieutenant Mahler. Get down here right away. And bring your son."

"What's wrong?" The lieutenant customarily made a point of having his subordinates call him "sir," but in Sergeant Ryder's case he'd given up years ago. Ryder reserved that term for those he held in respect; no friends or acquaintances, to the best of their knowledge, had ever heard him use it.

"Not over the phone." The receiver clicked and Ryder rose reluctantly to his feet, pulled on his sports coat and fastened the central button, effectively concealing the .38 Smith & Wesson strapped to the left-hand side of what had once been his waist. Still reluctantly, as became a man who had just finished a twelve-hour nonstop duty stint, he glanced around the room, all chintzy curtains and chair covers, ornaments and vasefuls of flowers: Sergeant Ryder, clearly, was no bachelor. He went into the kitchen, sniffed sorrowfully at the aroma coming from the contents of a simmering casserole, turned off the oven and wrote "Gone downtown" at the foot of a note instructing him when and to what temperature he should turn a certain switch, which was as near to cooking as Ryder had ever come in his twenty-seven years of marriage.

His car was parked in the driveway. It was a car that no self-respecting police officer would care to have been found shot in. That Ryder was just such a policeman was beyond doubt, but he was attached to the Detective Division and had little use for gleaming sedans equipped with illuminated "Police" signs, flashing lights and sirens. The car, for want of a better word, was an elderly and battered Peugeot of the type much favored by Parisians

13

of a sadistic bent of mind whose great pleasure it was to observe the drivers of shining limousines slow down and pull into the curb whenever they caught sight of those vintage chariots in their rearview mirrors.

Four blocks from his own home Ryder parked his car, walked up a flagged pathway and rang the front doorbell. A young man opened the door.

Ryder said: "Dress uniform, Jeff. We're wanted downtown."

"Both of us? Why?"

"Your guess. Mahler wouldn't say."

"It's all those TV cop series he keeps watching. You've got to be mysterious or you're nothing." Jeff Ryder left and returned in twenty seconds, tie in position and buttoning up his uniform. Together they walked down the flagged path.

They made an odd contrast, father and son. Sergeant Ryder was built along the general lines of a Mack truck that had seen better days. His crumpled coat and creaseless trousers looked as if they had been slept in for a week: Ryder could buy a new suit in the morning and by evenfall a second-hand clothes dealer would have crossed the street to avoid meeting him. He had thick dark hair, a dark mustache and a worn, lined, lived-in face that held a pair of eyes, dark as the rest of him, that had looked at too many things in the course of a lifetime and had liked little of what they had seen. It was also a face that didn't go in for much in the way of expressions. Jeff Ryder was two inches taller and thirty-five pounds lighter than his father. His immaculately pressed California Highway Patrolman's uniform looked like a custom-built job by Saks. He had fair hair, blue eyes—both inherited from his mother—and a lively, mobile, intelligent face. Only a clairvoyant could have deduced that he was Sergeant Ryder's son.

On the way, they spoke only once. Jeff said: "Mother's late on the road tonight—something to do with our summons to the presence?"

"Your guess again."

Central Office was a forbidding brownstone edifice overdue for demolition. It looked as if it had been specifically designed to further depress the spirits of the many miscreants who passed or were hauled through its doorway. The desk officer, Sergeant Dickson, looked at them gravely but that was of no significance: the very nature of his calling inhibits any desk sergeant's latent tendency toward levity. He waved a discouraged arm and said: "His Eminence awaits."

Lieutenant Mahler looked no less forbidding than the building he inhabited. He was a tall thin man with grizzled hair at the temples, thin unsmiling lips, a thin beaky nose and unsentimental eyes. No one liked him, for his reputation as a martinet had not been easily come by: on the other hand, no one actively disliked him for he was a fair cop and a fairly competent one. "Fairly" was the operative and accurate word. Although no fool, he was not overburdened with intelligence and had reached his present position partly because he was the very model of the strict upholder of justice, partly because his transparent honesty offered no threat to his superiors.

For once, and rarely for him, he looked ill at ease. Ryder produced a crumpled packet of his favored Gauloises, lit a forbidden cigarette—Mahler's aversion to wine, women, song and tobacco was almost pathological—and helped him out.

"Something wrong at San Ruffino?"

Mahler looked at him in sharp suspicion. "How do you know? Who told you?"

"So it's true. Nobody told me. We haven't committed any violations of the law recently. At least, my son hasn't. Me, I don't remember."

Mahler allowed acidity to overcome his unease. "You surprise me."

"First time the two of us have ever been called in here together. We have a couple of things in common. First, we're father and son, which is no concern of the police department. Second, my wife—Jeff's mother—is employed at the nuclear reactor plant in San Ruffino. There hasn't been an accident there or the whole town would have known in minutes. An armed break-in, perhaps?"

15

"Yes." Mahler's tone was almost grudging. He hadn't relished the role of being the bearer of bad news but a man doesn't like having his lines taken from him.

"Who's surprised?" Ryder was very matter-of-fact. For any sign of reaction he showed Mahler could well have remarked that it looked as if it might rain soon. "Security up there is lousy. I filed a report on it. Remember?"

"Which was duly turned over to the proper authorities. Power-plant security is not police business. That's IAEA's responsibility." He was referring to the International Atomic Energy Agency, one of the responsibilities of which was to supervise the safeguard system for the protection of power plants, specifically against the theft of nuclear fuels.

"For God's sake!" Not only had Jeff failed to inherit his father's physical characteristics, he was also noticeably lacking in his parent's massive calm. "Let's get our priorities right, Lieutenant Mahler. My mother. Is she all right?"

"I think so. Let's say I have no reason to think otherwise."

"What the hell is that supposed to mean?"

Mahler's features tightened into the preliminary for a reprimand but Sergeant Ryder got in first. "Abduction?"

"I'm afraid so."

"Kidnap?" Jeff stared his disbelief. "Kidnap? Mother is the director's secretary. She doesn't know a damn thing about what goes on there. She's not even security classified."

"True. But remember she was picked for the job; she didn't apply. Cops' wives are supposed to be like Caesar's wife—beyond suspicion."

"But why pick on her?"

"They didn't just pick on her. They took about six others, or so I gather—the deputy director, deputy security chief, a secretary and a control-room operator. More importantly—although not, of course, from your point of view—they took two visiting university professors. Both are highly qualified specialists in nuclear physics."

16

Ryder said: "That makes five nuclear scientists to have disappeared in the past two months."

"Five it is." Mahler looked acutely unhappy.

Ryder said: "Where did those scientists come from?"

"San Diego and U.C.L.A., I believe. Does it matter?"

"I don't know. It may be too late already."

"What's that supposed to mean, Sergeant?"

"It means that if those two men have families they should be under immediate police guard." Mahler, Ryder could see, wasn't quite with him so he went on: "If those two men have been kidnapped then it's with a special purpose in mind. Their co-operation will be required. Wouldn't you co-operate a damn sight faster if you saw someone with a pair of pliers removing your wife's fingernails one by one?"

Possibly because he didn't have a wife the thought had clearly not occurred to Lieutenant Mahler, but then thinking was not his forte. To his credit, once the thought had been implanted he wasted no time. He spent the next two minutes on the telephone.

Jeff was grim-faced, edgy, his voice soft but urgent. "Let's get out there fast."

"Easy. Don't go off half-cocked. The time for hurry is past. It may come again but right now it's not going to help any."

They waited in silence until Mahler replaced his phone. Ryder said: "Who reported the break-in?"

"Ferguson. Security chief. Day off, but his house is wired into the San Ruffino alarm system. He came straight down."

"He did what? Ferguson lives thirty miles out in the hills in the back of nowhere. Why didn't he use his phone?"

"His phone had been cut, that's why."

"But he has a police band car radio—"

"That had been attended to also. So had the only phones on the way in. One was at a garage—owner and his mechanic had been locked up."

"But there's an alarm tie-in to this office."

"There was."

"An inside job?"

"Look, Ferguson called only two minutes after he got there."

"Anybody hurt?"

"No violence. All the staff locked up in the same room."

"The sixty-four-dollar question . . ."

"Theft of nuclear fuel? That'll take time to establish, according to Ferguson."

"You going out there?"

"I'm expecting company." Mahler looked unhappy.

"I'll bet you are. Who's out there now?"

"Parker and Davidson."

"We'd like to go out and join them."

Mahler hesitated, still unhappy. He said, defensively: "What do you expect to find that they won't? They're good detectives. You've said so yourself."

"Four pairs of eyes are better than two. And because she's my wife and Jeff's mother and we know how she might have behaved and reacted we might be able to pick up something that Parker and Davidson might miss."

Mahler, his chin in the heels of his hands, gazed morosely at his desk. Whatever decision he took the chances were high that his superiors would say it was the wrong one. He compromised by saying nothing. With a nod from Ryder both men left the room.

The evening was fine and clear and windless and a setting sun was laying a path of burnished gold across the Pacific as Ryder and his son drove through the main gates of San Ruffino. The nuclear station was built on the very edge of the San Ruffino cove—like all such stations it required an immense amount of water, some 1,800,000 gallons of sea water a minute, to cool the reactor cores down to their optimum operating temperatures: no domestic utility supply could hope to cope with the tiniest fraction of this amount.

The two massive, gleamingly white and domed containment structures that housed the reactor cores were at once

18

beautiful—in the pure simplicity of their external design—and also sinister and threatening, if one chose to view them that way. They were certainly awe-inspiring. Each was about the height of a twenty-five-story building with a diameter of about 150 feet. The three-and-a-half-feet-thick concrete walls were hugely reinforced by the largest steel bars in the United States. Between those containment structures—which also held the four steam generators that produced the actual electricity—was a squat and undeniably ugly building of absolutely no architectural merit. This was the Turbine Generator Building, which, apart from its two turbogenerators, also housed two condensers and two sea-water evaporators.

On the seaward side of those buildings was the rather inaptly named auxiliary building, a six-story structure, some 240 feet in length, which held the control centers for both reactor units, the monitoring and instrumentation centers and the vastly complicated control system, which ensured the plant's safe operation and public protection.

Extending from each end of the auxiliary building were the two wings, each about half the size of the main building. These in their own ways were areas as delicate and sensitive as the reactor units themselves for it was in these that all the nuclear fuels were handled and stored. In all, the building of the complex had called for something like a third of a million cubic yards of concrete and some fifty thousand tons of steel. What was equally remarkable was that it required only eight people, including a good proportion of security staff, to run this massive complex twenty-four hours a day.

Twenty yards beyond the gate Ryder was stopped by a security guard wearing an irregular uniform and a machine carbine that was far from menacing inasmuch as the guard had made no move to unsling it from his shoulder. Ryder leaned out.

"What's this, open-house day? Public free to come and go?"

"Sergeant Ryder." The little man with the strong

19

Irish accent tried to smile and succeeded only in looking morose. "Fine time now to lock the stable door. Besides, we're expecting lawmen. Droves of them."

"And all of them asking the same stupid questions over and over again just as I'm going to do. Cheer up, John. I'll see they don't get you for high treason. Were you on duty at the time?"

"For my sins. Sorry about your wife, Sergeant. This'll be your son?" Ryder nodded. "My sympathies. For what they're worth. But don't waste any sympathy on me. I broke regulations. If it's the old cottonwood tree for me I've got it coming. I shouldn't have left my box."

Jeff said: "Why?"

"See that glass there? Not even the Bank of America has armored plate like that. Maybe a Magnum .44 could get through. I doubt it. There's a two-way speaker system. There's an alarm buzzer by my hand and a foot switch to trigger off a ten-pound charge of gelignite that would discourage anything short of a tank. It's buried under the asphalt just where the vehicles pull up. But no, old smarty-pants McCafferty had to unlock the door and go outside."

"Why?"

"No fool like an old fool. The van was expected at just that time—I had the note on my desk. Standard fuel pickup from San Diego. Same color, same lettering, driver and guard with the same uniforms, even the same license plates."

"Same van, in other words. Hijack. If they could hijack it when it was empty why not on the return journey when it was full?"

"They came for more than fuel."

"That's so. Recognize the driver?"

"No. But the pass was in order, so was the photograph."

"Well, would you recognize *that* driver again?"

McCafferty scowled in bitter recollection. "I'd recognize that damned great black beard and mustache again. Probably lying in some ditch by this time."

"The guard?"

"Didn't have time even to see the old shotgun, just the one glance and then the van gate—they're side loaders—fell down. The only uniform the guys inside were wearing were stocking masks. God knows how many of them there were, I was too busy looking at what they were carrying—pistols, sawed-off twelve gauges, even one guy with a bazooka."

"For blasting open any electronically locked steel doors, I suppose."

"I suppose. Fact of the matter is, there wasn't one shot fired from beginning to end. Professionals, if ever I saw any. They knew exactly what they were doing, where to go, where to look. Anyway, I was grabbed into that van and had hand and leg cuffs on before I had time to close my mouth."

Ryder was sympathetic. "I can see it must have been a bit of a shock. Then?"

"One of them jumped down and went into the box. Bastard had an Irish accent, I could have been listening to myself talking. He picked up the phone, got through to Carlton—he's the number two man in security, if you recollect, Ferguson was off today—told him the transport van was here and asked for permission to open the gate. He pressed the button, the gates opened, he waited until the van had passed through, closed the door, came out through the other door and climbed into the van that had stopped for him."

"And that's all?"

. "All I know. I stayed in there—I didn't have much option, did I?—until the raid was over, then they locked me up with the others."

"Where's Ferguson?"

"In the north wing."

"Checking on missing articles, no doubt? Tell him I'm here."

McCafferty went to his guard box, spoke briefly on the phone and returned. "It's O.K."

"No comments?"

"Funny you should ask that. He said: 'Dear God, as if we haven't got enough trouble here.' "

Ryder half-smiled a very rare half-smile and drove off.

Ferguson, the security chief, greeted them in his office with civility but a marked lack of enthusiasm. Although it was some months since he had read Ryder's acerbic report on the state of security at San Ruffino, Ferguson had a long memory. The fact that Ryder had been all too accurate in his report and that Ferguson had neither the authority nor the available funds to carry out all the report's recommendations hadn't helped matters any. He was a short stocky man with wary eyes and a habitually worried expression. He replaced a telephone and made no attempt to rise from behind his desk.

"Come to write another report, Sergeant?" He tried to sound acid but all he did was sound defensive. "Create a little more trouble for me?"

Ryder was mild. "Neither. If you don't get support from your blinkered superiors with their rose-colored glasses then the fault is theirs, not yours."

"Ah." The tone was surprised but the face still wary. Jeff said: "We have a personal interest in this, Mr. Ferguson."

"You the sergeant's son?" Jeff nodded. "Sorry about your mother. I guess saying that doesn't help very much."

"You were thirty miles away at the time," Ryder said reasonably. Jeff looked at his father in some apprehension; he knew that a mild-mannered Ryder was potentially the most dangerous Ryder of all, but in this case there seemed no undue cause for alarm. Ryder went on: "I'd expect to find you down in the vaults assessing the amount of loot our friends have made off with."

"Not my job at all. Never go near their damned storage facilities except to check the alarm systems. I wouldn't even begin to know what to look for. The director himself is down there with a couple of assistants finding what the score is."

"Could we see him?"

"Why? Two of your men, I forget their names—"

"Parker and Davidson."

22

"Whatever. They've already talked to him."

"My point. He was still making his count then."

Ferguson reached a grudging hand for the telephone, spoke to someone in tones of quiet respect, then said to Ryder: "He's just finishing. Here in a moment, he says."

"Thanks. Any way this could have been an inside job?"

"An inside job. You mean, one of my men involved?" Ferguson looked at him suspiciously. He himself had been thirty miles away at the time, which should have put himself, personally, beyond suspicion: but equally well, if he had been involved he'd have made good and certain that he was thirty miles away on the day that the break-in had occurred. "I don't follow. Ten heavily armed men don't need assistance from inside."

"How could they have walked through your electronically controlled doors and crisscross of electric eyes undetected?"

Ferguson sighed. He was on safer ground here. "The pickup was expected and on schedule. When Carlton heard from the gate guard about its arrival he would automatically have turned them off."

"Accepting that, how did they find their way to wherever they wanted to go? This place is a rabbits' warren, a maze."

Ferguson was on even surer ground now. "Nothing simpler. I thought you would know about that."

"A man never stops learning. Tell me."

"You don't have to bribe an employee to find out the precise layout of any atomic plant. No need to infiltrate or wear false uniforms, get hold of copies of badges or use any violence whatsoever. You don't have to come within a thousand miles of any damned atomic plant to know all about it, what the layout is, the precise location of where uranium and plutonium are stored, even when nuclear fuel shipments might be expected to arrive or depart as the case may be. All you have to do is to go to a public reading room run by the Atomic Energy Commission at 1717 H Street in Washington, D.C. You'd find it most instructive, Sergeant Ryder—especially if you were bent on breaking into a nuclear plant."

23

"This some kind of a sick joke?"

"Very sick. Especially if, like me, you happen to be the head of security in a nuclear plant. There are card indexes there containing dockets on all nuclear facilities in the country in private hands. There's always a very friendly clerk at hand—I've been there—who on request will give you a stack of more papers than you can handle giving you what I and many others would regard as being top-secret and classified information on any nuclear facility you want—except governmental ones, of course. Sure it's a joke, but it doesn't make me and lots of others laugh out loud."

"They must be out of their tiny minds." It would be an exaggeration to say that Sergeant Ryder was stunned; though facial and verbal over-reactions were alien to him, he was unquestionably taken aback.

Ferguson assumed the expression of one who was buttoning his hair shirt really tight. "They even provide a Xerox machine for copying any documents you choose."

"Jesus! And the government permits all this?"

"Permits? It authorized it. Atomic Energy Act, amended 1954, states that citizen John Doe—undiscovered nut case or not—has the right to know about the private use of nuclear materials. I think you'll have to revise your insider theory, Sergeant."

"It wasn't a theory, just a question. In either case, consider it revised."

Dr. Jablonsky, the director of the reactor plant, came into the room. He was a burly, sun-tanned and white-haired man in his mid-sixties but looking about ten years younger, a man who normally radiated bonhomie and good cheer. At the moment he was radiating nothing of the kind.

"Damnable, damnable, damnable," he said to no one in particular. "Evening, Sergeant. It would have been nice to meet again in happier circumstances for both of us." He looked at Jeff interrogatively. "Since when did they call C.H.P.s on an—"

"Jeff Ryder, Dr. Jablonsky. My son." Ryder smiled slightly. "I hope you don't subscribe to the general belief

24

that highway patrolmen only arrest on highways. They can arrest anyone, anywhere, in the state of California."

"My goodness, I hope he's not going to arrest me." He peered at Jeff over the top of rimless glasses. "You must be worried about your mother, young man, but I can't see any reason why she should come to any harm."

"And I can't see any reason why she shouldn't," Ryder interrupted. "Ever heard of any kidnapee who was not threatened with actual bodily harm? I haven't."

"Threats? Already?"

"Give them time. Wherever they're going they probably haven't got there yet. How is it with the inventory of stolen goods?"

"Bad. We have three types of nuclear fuel in storage here—uranium-238, uranium-235 and plutonium. U-238 is the prime source of all nuclear fuel and they didn't bother taking any of that. Understandably."

"Why understandably?"

"Harmless stuff." Absently, almost, Dr. Jablonsky fished in the pocket of his white coat and produced several small pellets, each no more than the size of a .38-caliber bullet. "That's U-238. Well, almost. Contains about three per cent U-235. Slightly enriched, as we call it. You have to get an awful lot of this stuff together before it starts to fission, giving off the heat that converts water to steam that spins the turbine blades that makes our electricity. Here in San Ruffino we crowd six and three quarter million of these, two hundred and forty into each of twenty-eight thousand twelve-foot rods, into the nuclear reactor core. This we figure to be the optimum critical mass for fissioning, a process controlled by huge supplies of cooling water and one that can be stopped altogether by dropping boron rods between the uranium tubes."

Jeff said: "What would happen if the water supply stopped and you couldn't activate the boron rods or whatever? Bang?"

"No. The results would be bad enough, clouds of radioactive gas that might cause some thousands of deaths and poison tens, perhaps thousands of square miles of

25

soil, but it's never happened yet, and the chances of it happening have been calculated at five billion to one so we don't worry too much about it. But a bang? A nuclear explosion? Impossible. For that you require U-235 over ninety per cent pure, the stuff we dropped on Hiroshima. Now that is nasty stuff. There were one hundred and thirty-two pounds of it in that bomb, but it was so crudely designed—it really belonged to the nuclear horse-and-buggy age—that only about twenty-five ounces of it fissioned, but was still enough to wipe out the city. We have progressed, if that's the word I want, since then. Now the Atomic Energy Commission reckons that a total of five kilograms—eleven pounds—is the so-called trigger quantity, enough for the detonation of a nuclear bomb. It's common knowledge among scientists that the AEC is most conservative in its estimate—it could be done with less."

Ryder said: "No U-238 was stolen. You used the word 'unfortunately.' Couldn't they have stolen it and converted it into U-235?"

"No. Natural uranium contains one hundred and forty atoms of U-238 to each atom of U-235. The task of leaching out the U-235 from the U-238 is probably the most difficult scientific task that man has ever overcome. We use a process called gaseous diffusion and the process is prohibitively expensive, enormously complicated and impossible to conceal. The going cost for a gaseous diffusion plant, at today's inflated rates, is in the region of three billion dollars. Even today only a very limited number of men know how the process works—I don't. All I know is that it involves thousands of incredibly fine membranes, thousands of miles of tubes, pipes and conduits and enough electric power to run a fair-sized city. Then those plants are so enormous that they couldn't possibly be built in secret. They cover so many hundreds of acres that you require a car or electric cart to get around one. No private group, however wealthy or criminally-minded, could ever hope to build one.

"We have three in this country, none located in this

26

state. The British and French have one apiece. The Russians aren't saying. China is reported to have one in Langchow in Kansu Province.

"It can be done by high-speed centrifuges, spinning at such a speed that the marginally heavier U-238 is flung to the outside. But this process would use hundreds of thousands of centrifuges and the cost would be mind-boggling. I don't know whether it's ever been done. The South Africans claim to have discovered an entirely new process but they aren't saying what and U.S. scientists are skeptical. The Australians say they've discovered a method by using laser beams. Again, we don't know—but if it were possible a small group—and they'd all have to be top-flight nuclear physicists—could make U-235 undetected. But why bother going to such impossible lengths when you can just go to the right place and steal the ready-made damned stuff just as they did here this afternoon?"

Ryder said: "How is this stuff stored?"

"In ten-liter steel bottles each containing seven kilograms of U-235, in the form of either an oxide or metal, the oxide in the form of a very fine brown powder, the metal in little lumps known as broken buttons. The bottles are placed in a cylinder five inches wide that's braced with welded struts in the center of a perfectly ordinary fifty-five-gallon steel drum. I needn't tell you why the bottles are held in suspension in the air space of the drum—stack them all together in a drum or box and you'd soon reach the critical mass where fissioning starts."

Jeff said: "This time it goes bang?"

"Not yet. Just a violent irradiation which would have a very nasty effect for miles around, especially on human beings. Drum plus bottle weighs about a hundred pounds so is easily movable. Those drums are called bird cages, Lord knows why, they don't look like any bird cage I've ever seen."

Ryder said: "How is this transported?"

"Long distance by plane. Shorter hauls by common carrier."

"Common carrier?"

"Any old truck you can lay hands on." Ferguson sounded bitter.

"How many of those cages go in the average truck shipment?"

"That hijacked San Diego truck carries twenty."

"One hundred and forty pounds of the stuff. Right?"

"Right."

"A man could make himself a fair collection of nuclear bombs from that. How many drums were actually taken?"

"Twenty."

"A full load for the van?"

"Yes."

"So they didn't touch your plutonium?"

"More bad news, I'm afraid. When they were being held at gunpoint but before they were locked up some of the staff heard the sound of another engine. A diesel. Heavy. Could have been big—no one saw it." The telephone on his desk rang. He reached for it and listened in silence except for the occasional "Who?" "Where?" and "When?" He hung up.

"Still more bad news?" Jablonsky asked.

"Don't see it makes any difference one way or another. The hijacked van's been found. Empty, of course, except for the driver and guard trussed up like turkeys in the back. They say they were following a furniture van around a blind corner when it braked so sharply that they almost ran into it. Back doors of the van opened and the driver and the guard decided to stay just where they were. They say they didn't feel like doing much else with two leveled machine guns and a bazooka six feet from their windshield."

"An understandable point of view," Jablonsky said. "Where were they found?"

"In a quarry, up an unused side road. By a couple of young kids."

"And the furniture van is still there?"

"As you say, Sergeant. How did you know?"

"Do you think they'd have transferred their cargo into an identifiable van and drive off with it? They'd have a second plain van." Ryder turned to Dr. Jablonsky. "As you were about to say about this plutonium—"

"Interesting stuff and if you're a nuclear bomb-making enthusiast it's far more suitable for making an atom bomb than uranium although it would call for greater expertise. Probably call for the services of a nuclear physicist."

"A captive physicist would do as well?"

"What do you mean?"

"They—the kidnapers—took a couple of visiting physicists with them this afternoon. From San Diego and Los Angeles, I believe they were."

"Professor Burnett and Schmidt? That's a ludicrous suggestion. I know both men well, intimately, you might say. They are men of probity, men of honor. They'd never co-operate with the criminals who stole this stuff."

Ryder sighed. "My regard for you is high, Doctor, so I'll only say that you lead a very sheltered life. Men of principle? Decent men?"

"Our regard is mutual so I'll just content myself with saying that I don't have to repeat myself."

"Men of compassion, no doubt?"

"Of course they are."

"They took my wife, and a stenographer—"

"Julie Johnson."

"Julie Johnson. When our hijacking thieves start feeding those ladies through a meat grinder, what do you think is going to win out—your friends' high principles or their compassion?"

Jablonsky said nothing. He just lost a little color.

Ferguson coughed in a skeptical fashion, which is a difficult thing to do, but in his line of business he'd had a lot of practice. "And I'd always thought you were devoid of imagination, Sergeant. That's stretching things a bit, surely."

"Is it? As security chief it's your job to vet everybody applying for a job here. This stenographer, Julie. What's her background?"

"Ordinary. Typist making a living. Shares a small flat,

29

nothing fancy, with two other girls. Drives a beat-up Volkswagen. Parents dead."

"Not a millionairess doing the job for kicks?"

"Millionairess! Her old man was a gardener."

Ryder looked at Jablonsky. "So. A stenographer's paycheck. A sergeant's paycheck. A patrolman's paycheck. Maybe you think they're going to hold those ladies for ransom of a million dollars each? Maybe just to rest their eyes on after a long day at the nuclear bench?" Jablonsky said nothing. "The meat grinder. You were talking about this plutonium."

"God, man, haven't you got any feelings?"

"Time and a place for everything. Right now, a little thinking, a little knowledge might help more."

"I suppose." Jablonsky spoke with the restrained effort of a man whose head is trying to make his heart see sense. "Plutonium—plutonium 239, to be precise. Stuff that destroyed Nagasaki. Synthetic—doesn't exist in nature. Man-made—we Californians had the privilege of creating it. Unbelievably toxic—a cobra's bite is a thing of joy compared to it. If you had it in an aerosol in liquid form with Freon under pressure—no one has as yet got around to figuring out how to do this but they will, they will—you'd have an indescribably lethal weapon on your hands. A couple of squirts of this into a crowded auditorium, say, with a couple of thousand people, and all you'd require would be a couple of thousand coffins.

"It's the inevitable by-product of the fissioning of uranium in a nuclear reactor. The plutonium, you understand, is still inside the uranium fuel rods. The rods are removed from the reactor and chopped up—"

"Who does the chopping? Not a job I'd want."

"I don't know whether you would or not. First chop and you'd be dead. Done by remote-controlled guillotines in a place we call the 'canyon.' Nice little place with five-foot walls and five-foot-thick windows. You wouldn't want to go inside. The cuttings are dissolved in nitric acid then washed with various reactive chemicals to separate the plutonium from the uranium and other unwanted radioactive fission products."

30

"How's this plutonium stored?"

"Plutonium nitrate, actually. About ten liters of it goes into a stainless-steel flask, about fifty inches high by five in diameter. That works out about two and a half kilograms of pure plutonium. Those flasks are even more easily handled than the uranium drums and quite safe if you're careful."

"How much of this stuff do you require to make a bomb?"

"No one knows for sure. It is believed that it is theoretically possible although at the moment practically impossible to make a nuclear device no bigger than a cigarette. The AEC puts the trigger quantity at two kilograms. It's probably an overestimate. But you could for sure carry enough plutonium in a lady's purse to make a nuclear bomb."

"I'll never look at a lady's purse with the same eyes again. So that's a bomb flask?"

"Easily."

"Is there much of this plutonium around?"

"Too much. Private companies have stock-piled more plutonium than there is in all the nuclear bombs in the world."

Ryder lit a Gauloise while he assimilated this. "You did say what I thought you said?"

"Yes."

"What are they going to do with this stuff?"

"That's what the private companies would like to know. The half-life of this plutonium is about twenty-six thousand years. Radioactively, it'll still be lethal in a hundred thousand years. Quite a legacy we're leaving to the unborn. If mankind is still around in a hundred thousand years, which no scientist, economist, environmentalist or philosopher seriously believes, can't you just see them cursing their ancestors some three thousand generations removed?"

"They'll have to handle that problem without me. It's this generation I'm concerned with. Is this the first time nuclear fuel has been stolen from a plant?"

"God, no. The first forced entry I know of, but others

may have been hushed up. We're touchy about those things, much more touchy than the Europeans, who admit to several terrorist attacks on their reactor stations."

"Tell the man straight out." Ferguson sounded weary. "Theft of plutonium goes on all the time. I know it, Dr. Jablonsky knows it. The Office of Nuclear Safeguards—that's the watchdog of the AEC—knows about it best of all, but gets very coy when questioned, even though their director did admit to a congressional energy subcommittee that perhaps one half of one per cent of fuel was unaccounted for. He didn't seem very worried about it. After all, what's one half of one per cent, especially when you say it quickly. Just enough to make enough bombs to wipe out the United States, that's all. The great trusting American public knows nothing about it—what they don't know can't frighten them. Do I sound rather bitter to you, Sergeant?"

"You do a bit. You have reason to?"

"I have. One of the reasons I resented your security report. There's not a security chief in the country that doesn't feel bitter about it. We spend billions every year preventing nuclear war, hundreds of millions for preventing accidents at the reactor plants but only about eight million on security. The probability of those occurrences are in the reverse order. The AEC says they have up to ten thousand people keeping track of material. I would laugh if I didn't feel like crying. The fact of the matter is they know where it is only about once a year. They come around, balance books, count cans, take samples and feed the figures into some luckless computer that usually comes up with the wrong answers. Not the computer's fault—not the inspector's. There're far too few of them and the system is ungovernable anyway.

"The AEC, for instance, says that theft by employees, because of the elaborate built-in protection and detection systems, is impossible. They say this in a loud voice for public consumption. It's rubbish. Sample pipes lead off from the plutonium runoff spigot from the canyon—for testing strength, purity and so forth. Nothing easier than to run off a little plutonium into a small flask. If you're not greedy and take only a small amount occasionally the chances are that you can get away with it almost indefinitely. If you can bribe two of the security guards—the one who monitors the TV screens of the cameras in the sensitive areas and the person who controls the metal-detector beam you pass through on leaving—you can get away with it forever."

"Has it ever been done?"

"The government doesn't believe in paying high salaries for what is basically an unskilled job. Why do you think there are so many corrupt and crooked cops? If you don't mind me saying so."

"I don't mind. This is the only way? Stealing the stuff in dribs and drabs. Hasn't been done on a large scale?"

"Sure it has. Again, nobody's talking. As far back as 1964, when the Chinese exploded their first nuclear bomb, it was taken for granted in this country that the Chinese just didn't have the scientific know-how to separate out U-235 from natural uranium. Ergo, they must have pinched it somewhere. They wouldn't have stolen it from Russia because Chinese, to say the least, are not welcome there. But they're welcome here, especially in California. In San Francisco you have the biggest Chinese community outside China. Their students are received with open arms in California's universities. It's no secret that that's how the Chinese came to have the secrets of making an atom bomb. Their students came over here, took a post-graduate course in physics, including nuclear physics, then hightailed it back to the mother country with the necessary information."

"You're digressing."

"That's what bitterness does for you. Shortly after they exploded their bomb it came to light, perhaps accidentally, that sixty kilos of U-235 had disappeared from a nuclear fuel fabricating plant in Appolo, Pennsylvania. Coincidence? Nobody's accusing anybody of anything. The stuff's showing up missing right and left. A security chief in the East once told me that a hundred and ten

33

kilos of U-235 somehow got lost from his plant." He broke off and shook his head dejectedly. "The whole thing is so damned stupid anyway."

"What's stupid?"

"Pilfering a few grams at a time from a plant or breaking into one to steal it on a grand scale. That's being stupid. It's stupid because it's unnecessary. If you'd wanted a king-size haul of U-235 or plutonium today what would you have done?"

"That's obvious. I'd have let the regular crew of that truck load up and hijack it on the way back."

"Exactly. One or two plants send out their enriched nuclear fuel in such massive steel and concrete drums— transported in big fifteen–twenty-ton trucks—that the necessity for a crane effectively rules out hijacking. Most don't. We don't. A strong man on his own would have no difficulty in handling our drums. More than one nuclear scientist has publicly suggested that we approach the Kremlin and contract the Red Army for the job. That's the way the Russians do it—a heavily armored truck with an escort armored vehicle in front and behind."

"Why don't we do that?"

"Not to be thought of. Same reason again—mustn't scare the pants off the public. Bad for the nuclear image. Atoms for peace, not war. In the whole fuel cycle, transportation is by so far the weakest link in security that it doesn't deserve to be called a link at all. The major road shippers—like Pacific Intermountain Express or Tri-state or MacCormack—are painfully aware of this—and are worried sick about it. But there's nothing they can do about it and, more importantly, there's nothing their drivers can do about it. In the trucking business—many would prefer the word 'racket'—theft and shortages are frequently the name of the game.

"Every day two per cent of goods being transported by road in this country just turn up missing—the figure may even be higher. The wise don't complain; in the minority cases where people do complain the insurers pay up quietly because their premiums are loaded against what they regard as an occupational hazard. 'Occupational' is

34

the key word. Eighty-five per cent of thefts are by people inside the trucking industry. Eighty-five per cent of hijackings involve collusion—which has to involve truck drivers."

"Has there ever been a case of nuclear hijack on the open road?"

"Hijacks don't happen on the open road. Well, hardly ever. They occur at transfer points and drivers' stopovers. Driver Jones visits the local locksmith and has a fresh set of keys for ignition and cab doors cut and hands it over to Smith. Next day he stops at a drivers' pull-over, carefully locks the door and goes—either himself or with his buddy—for his hamburger and french fries or whatever. When he comes out, he goes through the well-rehearsed routine of double-take, calling to heaven for vengeance and hot-footing it to the nearest phone box to call the cops, who know perfectly well what is going on but are completely incapable of proving anything. Those hijackings are rarely reported and pass virtually unnoticed because there are very rarely any crimes of violence involved."

Ryder was patient. "I've been a cop all my life. I know that. Nuclear hijack, I said."

"I don't know."

"You don't know or you aren't telling?"

"That's up to you to decide, Sergeant."

"Yes. Thank you." It was impossible for anyone to say whether Ryder had decided anything or not. He turned to Jablonsky.

"Okay, Doc, if we go and have a look at Susan's office?"

Jablonsky's voice was dry. "Unusual of you, Sergeant, to ask anybody's permission for anything."

"That's downright unkind. Fact is, we haven't been officially assigned to this investigation."

"I know that." He looked at Jeff. "That is hardly the stamping ground for a highway patrolman. Have you been expressly forbidden to come here?"

"No."

"Makes no difference. Heavens, man, in your place

I'd be worried to death. Search the whole damned building if you want." He paused briefly. "I suggest I come with you."

" 'The whole damned building,' as you call it, can be left to Parker and Davidson, who are already here, and the lawmen in their droves who will be here in any moment. Why do you want to come with us to my wife's office? I've never tampered with evidence in my life."

"Who says you did?" He looked at Jeff. "You know your father has a long-standing and well-justified reputation for taking the law into his own hands?"

"I've heard rumors, I have to admit. So you'd guarantee on the witness stand the good behavior of someone in need of care and protection?" It was the first time that Jeff had smiled since he'd heard of his mother's kidnaping.

Jablonsky said: "First time I ever heard anyone mention care and protection and Sergeant Ryder in the same breath."

"Jeff could be right." Ryder was unruffled. "I am getting on."

Jablonsky smiled his total disbelief.

TWO

■ THE office door, slightly ajar, had four splintered holes tightly grouped around the lock and handle. Ryder looked at them with no reaction, pushed open the door and walked inside. Sergeant Parker stopped what he was doing, which was pushing scraps of paper around a desk top with the rubber tip of a pencil, and turned around. He was a burly, pleasant-faced man in his late thirties who didn't look a bit like a cop, which was why his arrest record ranked second only to Ryder's.

"Been expecting you," he said. "A damnable business, just incredible." He smiled as if to alleviate the tension which Ryder didn't seem to be feeling at all. "Did you come to take over, to show the incompetents how a professional goes about it?"

"Just looking. I'm not on this and I'm sure old Fatso will take great pleasure in keeping me off it." "Fatso" referred to their far from revered police chief.

"The sadistic blubber of lard would love to do just that." He ignored the slight frown of Dr. Jablonsky, who had never had the privilege of making the police chief's acquaintance. "Why don't you and I break his neck someday?"

"Assuming he's got a neck inside that twenty-inch collar." Ryder looked at the bullet-ridden door. "McCafferty—the gate guard—told me there was no shooting. Termites?"

"Silencer."

"Why the gun at all?"

"Susan is why." Parker was a family friend of long standing. "They'd rounded up the staff and put them in the room across the hallway there. Susan just happened to look out of the door and saw them coming so she closed the door and locked it."

"So they blasted it open. Maybe they thought she was making a dive for the nearest telephone."

"You made the security report."

"That's so. I remember. Only Dr. Jablonsky here and Mr. Ferguson were permitted direct lines to the outside. All other calls have to be cleared through the switchboard. They'd have taken care of the girl there first. Maybe they thought she was leaving through a window."

"Not a chance. From all I've heard—I haven't had time to take statements yet—those guys would have been perfectly at home here with blindfolds on. They'd have known there was no fire escape outside. They'd have known that every room is air conditioned and that you can't very well jump through plate-glass windows sealed like those are."

"Then why?"

"Maybe in a hurry. Maybe just the impatient type. At least he gave warning. His words were: 'Stand well to one side, Mrs. Ryder, I'm going to blast open that door.'"

"Well, that seems to prove two things. The first is that they're not wanton killers. But I said 'seem.' A dead hostage isn't much good for bargaining purposes or as a lever to make reluctant physicists bend to their task. Second, they knew enough to be able to identify individual members of the staff."

"That they did."

"They seem to have been very well informed." Jeff tried to speak calmly, to emulate the monolithic calm of his father, but a rapidly beating pulse in his neck gave him away.

Ryder indicated the tabletop strewn with scraps of torn paper. "Man of your age should be beyond jigsaws."

"You know me, thorough, painstaking, the conscientious detective who leaves no stone unturned."

"You've got all the pieces the right way up, I'll say that for you. Make anything of it?"

38

"No. You?"

"No. Contents of Susan's wastepaper basket, I take it."

"Yes." Parker looked at the tiny scraps in irritation. "I know secretaries, typists, frequently tear up bits of papers destined for the wastepaper basket. But did she have to be so damned thorough about it?"

"You know Susan. Never does things by halves. Or quarters. Or eighths." He pushed some of the scraps around—remnants of letters, carbons, some pieces of shorthand. "Sixteenths, yes. Not halves." He turned away. "Any other clues you haven't come up with?"

"Nothing on her desk. She took her handbag and umbrella with her."

"How do you know she had an umbrella?"

"I asked," Parker said patiently. "Nothing but this left." He picked up a framed and unflattering picture of Ryder, replaced it on the desk and said apropos of nothing: "Some people can function efficiently under any circumstances. And that's it, I'm afraid."

Dr. Jablonsky escorted them to the battered Peugeot. "If there's anything I can do, Sergeant—"

"Two things, as a matter of fact. Without letting Ferguson know, can you get hold of the dossier on Carlton? You know, the details of his past career, references, that sort of thing."

"Jesus, man, he's number two in security."

"I know."

"Any reason to suspect him?"

"None. I'm just curious why they took him as a hostage. A senior security man is supposed to be tough and resourceful. Not the kind of man I'd have around. His record may show some reason why. Second thing, I'm still a pilgrim lost in this nuclear desert. If I need any more information, can I contact you?"

"You know where my office is."

"I may have to ask you to come to my place. Head office can put a stop order against my coming here."

"A cop?"

"A cop, no. An ex-cop, yes."

Jablonsky looked at him consideringly. "Expecting to

be fired? God knows it's been threatened often enough."

"It's an unjust world."

On the way back to the station Jeff said: "Three questions. Why Carlton?"

"Bad choice of hostage, like I said. Secondly, if the bastards could identify your mother they could probably identify anyone in the plant. No reason why they should be especially interested in our family. The best source of names and working locations of the staff is in the security files. Only Ferguson and Carlton—and, of course, Dr. Jablonsky—have access to them."

"Why kidnap him?"

"To make it look good? I don't know. Maybe he wasn't kidnaped. You heard what Ferguson said about the government not paying highly for unskilled jobs. Maybe greener fields were beckoning."

"Seargeant Ryder, you have an unpleasantly suspicious imagination. What's more, you're no better than a common thief." Ryder drew placidly on his cigarette and remained unmoved. "You told Jablonsky you never tampered with evidence. I saw you palm pieces of paper from the table where Sergeant Parker was trying to sort them out."

"Suspicious minds would seem to run in this family," Ryder said mildly. "I didn't tamper with evidence. I took it. If it is evidence, that is."

"Why did you take it if you don't know?"

"You saw what I took?"

"Didn't look much to me. Squiggles, doodles."

"Shorthand, you clown. Notice anything about the cut of Jablonsky's coat?"

"First thing any cop would notice. He should have his coat cut looser to conceal the bulge of his gun."

"It's not a gun. It's a cassette recorder. Jablonsky dictates all his letters and memos into that, wherever he is in the plant, as often as not when he's walking around."

"So?" Jeff thought for a bit, then looked properly chagrined. "Guess I'll just stick to my trusty bike and handing out tickets to traffic violators. That way my lack of intelligence doesn't show up so much. No shorthand required, is that it?"

"I would have thought so."

"But why tear it up into little bits?"

"Just goes to show that you can't believe half the experts who say that intelligence is hereditary." Ryder puffed on his cigarette with just a hint of complacency. "Think I would have married someone who panicked and lacked resource?"

"Like she runs from a room when she sees a spider? A message?"

"I would think. Know anyone who knows shorthand?"

"Sure. Marge."

"Who's Marge?"

"Goddamnit, Dad, your goddaughter. Ted's wife."

"Ah. Your fellow easy rider on the lonely trails of the freeways? Marjory, you mean? Ask them around for a drink when we get home."

"What did you mean back there by saying to Jablonsky that you expected to be fired?"

"He said it, not me. Let's say I sense premature retirement coming up. I have a feeling that Chief Donahure and I aren't going to be seeing very much eye to eye in a few minutes' time." Even the newest rookie in the police force knew of the police chief's enmity toward Ryder, a feeling exceeded only by the massive contempt in which Ryder held his superior.

Jeff said: "He doesn't much like me either."

"That's a fact." Ryder smiled reminiscently. Some time before her divorce from the chief of police, Mrs. Donahure had gotten a speeding ticket from Jeff although he had known perfectly well who she was. Donahure had first of all asked Jeff and then demanded that he tear up the citation. Jeff had refused, as Donahure must have known in advance he would. The California Highway Patrol had the reputation, of which it was justifiably proud, of being perhaps the only police force in the country that was wholly above corruption. Not too long ago a patrolman had handed out a speeding ticket to the governor. The governor had written a letter of commendation to police headquarters—but he still had to pay up.

Sergeant Dickson was still behind his desk. He said: "Where have you two been?"

"Detecting," Ryder said. "Why?"

"The brass have been trying to reach you at San Ruffino." He lifted a phone. "Sergeant Ryder, Patrolman Ryder, Lieutenant. They've just come in." He listened briefly and hung up. "The pleasure of your company, gentlemen."

"Who's with him?"

"Major Dunne." Dunne was the area head of the FBI. "A Dr. Durrer from Erda or something."

"Capitals," Ryder said. "E-R-D-A. Energy Research and Development Administration. I know him."

"And, of course, your soul mate, the chief."

Four men were seated in Mahler's office. Mahler, behind the desk, was wearing his official face to conceal his unhappiness. Two men sat in chairs: Dr. Durrer, an owlish-looking individual with a bottle-glass pince-nez that gave his eyes the appearance of those of a startled fawn, and Major Dunne, lean, graying, intelligent with the smiling eyes of one who didn't find too much in life to smile about. The standing figure was Donahure, chief of police. Although he wasn't very tall, his massively pear-shaped body took up a disproportionate amount of space. The layered fat above and below his eyes left very little space for them to peer out: he had a fleshy nose, fleshy lips and a formidable array of chins. He was eying Ryder with distaste.

"Case all sewn up, I suppose, Sergeant?"

Ryder ignored him. He said to Mahler: "You sent for us?"

Donahure's face had turned an instant purple; one had only to rile him enough and he'd be his own executioner. "I was speaking to you, Ryder. *I* sent for you. Where the hell have you been?"

"You just used the word 'case.' And you've been
42

phoning San Ruffino. If we must have questions do they have to be stupid ones?"

"By God, Ryder, no man talks to me—"

"Please." Dunne's voice was calm, quiet but incisive. "I'd be glad if you gentlemen would leave your bickering for another time. Sergeant Ryder, Patrolman, I've heard about Mrs. Ryder and I'm damned sorry. Find anything interesting up there?"

"No," Ryder said. Jeff kept his eyes carefully averted. "And I don't think anyone will. Too clean a job, too professional. No violence offered. The only established fact is that the bandits made off with enough weapons-grade material to blow up half the state."

"How much?" Dr. Durrer said.

"Twenty drums of U-235 and plutonium; I don't know how much. A truckload, I should think. A second truck arrived after they had taken over the building."

"Dear, dear." Durrer looked and sounded depressed. "Inevitably, the threats come next."

Ryder said: "You get many threats?"

"I wouldn't bother answering that," Donahure said. "Ryder has no official standing in this case."

"Dear, dear," Durrer said again. He removed his pince-nez and regarded Donahure with eyes that weren't owlish at all. "Are you curtailing my freedom of speech?" Donahure was clearly taken aback and looked at Dunne but found no support in the coldly smiling eyes. Durrer returned his attention to Ryder. "We get threats. It is the policy of the state of California not to disclose how many, which is really a rather stupid policy as it is known—the figures have been published and are in the public domain—that some two hundred and twenty threats have been made against federal and commercial facilities since 1969." He paused, as if expectantly, and Ryder accommodated him.

"That's a lot of threats." He appeared oblivious of the fact that the most immediate threat was an apoplectic one: Donahure was clenching and unclenching his big ham fists and his purpled complexion was shading into an odd tinge of puce.

"It is indeed. All of them, so far, have proved to be hoaxes. But someday the threat may prove to be real—that is, either the government or private industry may have to pay up or suffer the effects of a nuclear detonation or nuclear radiation. We list six types of threat—two as highly improbable, four reasonably credible. The highly improbable are the detonation of a home-made bomb made from stolen weapons-grade materials or the detonation of a ready-made nuclear bomb stolen from a military ordnance depot—the credible are the dispersion of radioactive material other than plutonium, the release of hijacked radioactive materials from a spent fuel shipment, the detonation of a conventional high explosive salted with strontium-90, krypton-85, cesium-137 or even plutonium itself or simply by the release of plutonium for contamination purposes."

"From the businesslike way those criminals behaved in San Ruffino it might be that they mean business."

"The time has to come. We know that. This may be the time we receive a threat that really is a threat. We have made preparations, formulated in 1975. 'Nuclear Blackmail Emergency Response Plan for the State of California' it's called. The FBI has the overall control of the investigation. They can call on as many federal, state and local agencies as they wish, including, of course, the police. They can call on nuclear experts from such places as Donner Lab in Berkeley and Lawrence at Livermore. Search and decontamination teams and medical teams, headed by doctors who specialize in radiology, are immediately available, as is the Air Force, to carry those teams anywhere in the state. We, at ERDA, have the responsibility of assessing the validity of the threat."

"How's that done?"

"Primarily by checking with the government's computerized system that determines very quickly if unexpected amounts of fissionable material are missing."

"Well, Dr. Durrer, in this case we know already how much is missing so we don't have to ask the computers.

Just as well. I believe the computers are useless anyway."

For the second time Durrer removed his pince-nez. "Who told you this?"

Ryder looked vague. "I don't remember. It was some time ago." Jeff kept his sardonic smile under cover. Sure, it was some time ago: must have been almost half an hour since Ferguson had told him. Durrer looked at him thoughtfully, then clearly decided there was no point in pursuing the subject. Ryder went on, addressing himself to Mahler. "I'd like to be assigned to this investigation. I'd look forward to working under Major Dunne."

Donahure smiled, not exactly an evil smile, just that of a man savoring the passing moment. His complexion had reverted to its customary mottled red. He said: "No way."

Ryder looked at him. His expression wasn't encouraging. "I have a very personal interest in this. "Forgotten?"

"There'll be no discussion, Sergeant. As a policeman, you take orders from only one person in this county and that's me."

"As a policeman." Donahure looked at him in sudden uncertainty.

Dunne said: "I'd appreciate having Sergeant Ryder working with me. Your most experienced man and your best in the Detective Division—and with the best arrest record in the county—any county, come to that."

"That's his trouble. Arrest-happy. Trigger-happy. Violent. Unstable if he was emotionally involved as he would be in a case like this." Donahure tried to assume the expression of pious respectability but he was attempting the impossible. "Can't have the good name of my force brought into disrepute."

"Jesus!" It was Ryder's only comment.

Dunne was mildly persistent. "I'd still like to have him."

"No. And with all due respect, I needn't remind you that the authority of the FBI stops on the other side of that door. It's for your own sake, Major Dunne. He's a dangerous man to have around in a delicate situation like this."

"Kidnaping innocent women is delilcate?" Durrer's dry voice made it apparent that he regarded Donahure as something less than a towering intelligence. "You might tell us how you arrive at that conclusion?"

"Yes. How about that, Chief?" Jeff could restrain himself no longer; he was visibly trembling with anger. Ryder observed him in mild surprise but said nothing. "My mother, Chief. And my father. Dangerous? Arrest-happy? Both of those things—but only to you, Chief, only to you. My father's trouble is that he goes around arresting all the wrong people—pimps, drug pushers, crooked politicians, honest, public-spirited members of the Mafia, respected businessmen who are no better than scofflaws, even—isn't it sad?—corrupt cops. Consult his records, Chief. The only time his arrests have failed to secure either a conviction or a probation order was when he came up against Judge Kendrick. You remember Judge Kendrick, don't you, Chief? Your frequent house guest who pocketed twenty-five thousand dollars from your buddies in City Hall and finished up in the penitentiary. Five years. There were quite a lot of people who were lucky not to join him behind bars, weren't there, Chief?"

Donahure made an indeterminate sound as if he were suffering from some constriction of the vocal cords. His hands were clenching and unclenching and his complexion was changing color with the speed and unpredictability of a chameleon crawling over tartan.

Dunne said: "You put him there, Sergeant?"

"Somebody had to. Old Fatso here had all the evidence but wouldn't use it. Can't blame a man for not incriminating himself." Donahure made the same strangled noise. Ryder took something from his coat pocket and held it hidden, glancing quizzically at his son.

Jeff was calm now. He said to Donahure: "You've also slandered my father in front of witnesses." He looked at Ryder. "Going to sue? Or just leave him alone with his conscience?"

"His what?"

"You'll never make a cop." Jeff sounded almost sad. "There are all those finer points that you've never mastered, like bribery, corruption, kickbacks and having a couple of bank accounts under false names." He looked
46

at Donahure. "It's true, isn't it, Chief? Some people have lots of accounts under false names?"

"You insolent young bastard." Donahure had his vocal cords working again, but only just. He tried to smile. "Kinda forgotten who you're talking to, haven't you?"

"Sorry to deprive you of the pleasure, Chief." Jeff laid gun and badge on Mahler's table. "Forward those to the Highway Patrol," he said, and looked at his father in no surprise as Ryder placed a second badge on the table.

Donahure said hoarsely: "Your gun."

"It's mine, not police property. Anyway, I've got others at home. All the licenses you want."

"I can have those revoked tomorrow, copper." The viciousness of his tone matched the expression on his porcine face.

"I'm not a copper." Ryder lit a Gauloise and drew on it with obvious satisfaction.

"Put that damned cigarette out!"

"You heard. I'm not a copper. Not anymore. I'm just a member of the public. The police are servants of the public. I don't care to have my servants talk to me that way. Revoke my licenses? You do just that and you'll have a photostat of a private dossier I have, complete with photostats of signed affidavits. Then you'll revoke the order revoking my licenses."

"What the devil's that mean?"

"Just that the original of the dossier should make very interesting reading up in Sacramento."

"You're bluffing." The contempt and certainty in Donahure's voice would have carried more conviction if he hadn't licked his lips immediately afterward.

"Could be." Ryder contemplated a smoke ring with a mildly surprised interest.

"I'm warning you, Ryder." Donahure's voice was shaking and it could have been with something else other than anger. "Get in the way of this investigation and I'll have you locked up for obstruction of justice."

"It's just as well you know me, Donahure. I don't have to threaten you. Besides, it gives me no pleasure to see fat blobs of lard shaking with fear."

Donahure dropped his hand to his gun. Ryder slowly unbuttoned his jacket and pushed it back to put a hand on each hip. His .38 was in full view but his hands were clear of it.

Donahure said to Lieutenant Mahler: "Arrest this man."

Dunne spoke in cold contempt. "Don't be more of a fool than you can help, Donahure, and don't put your lieutenant in an impossible position. Arrest him on what grounds, for heaven's sake?"

Ryder buttoned his jacket, turned and left the office, Jeff close behind him. They were about to climb into the Peugeot when Dunne caught up with them.

"Was that wise?"

Ryder shrugged. "Inevitable."

"He's a dangerous man, Ryder. Not face to face, we all know that. Different when your back's turned. He has powerful friends."

"I know his friends. A contemptible bunch, like himself. Half of them should be behind bars."

"Still doesn't make them any less dangerous on a moonless night. You're going ahead with this, of course?"

"My wife, in case you have forgotten. Think we're going to leave her to that big fat slob's tender care?"

"What happens if he comes up against you?"

Jeff said: "Don't tempt my father with such pleasant thoughts."

"Suppose I shouldn't. I said I'd like you to work with me, Ryder. You, too, if you wish, young man. The offer stands. Always room for enterprising and ambitious young in the FBI."

"Thanks. We'll think it over. If we need help, advice, can we contact you?"

Dunne looked at them consideringly, then nodded. "Sure. You have my number. Well, you have an option. I don't. Like it or not I've got to work with that big fat slob, as you so accurately call him. Carries a lot of political clout in the valley." He shook hands with the two men. "Don't turn your backs on him."

In the car, Jeff said: "Going to consider his offer?"

"Hell, no. That would be out of the frying pan into the fire. Not that Sassoon—he's the California head of the FBI—isn't honest. He is. But he's too strict, goes by the book all the time and frowns on free enterprise."

Marjory Hohner, a brown-haired girl who looked too young to be married, sat beside her uniformed C.H.P. husband and studied the scraps of paper she had arranged on the table in front of her. Ryder said: "Come on, goddaughter. A bright young girl like you—"

She lifted her head and smiled. "Easy. I suppose it will make sense to you. It says: 'Look at back of your photograph.' "

"Thank you, Marjory." Ryder reached for the phone and made two calls.

Ryder and his son had just finished the reheated contents of the casserole Susan had left in the oven when Dr. Jablonsky arrived an hour after the departure of the Hohners, brief case in hand. Without expression or inflection of voice, he said: "You must be psychic. The word's out that you've been fired. You and Jeff here."

"Not at all." Ryder assumed an aloof dignity. "We retired. Voluntarily. But only temporarily, of course."

"You did say 'temporarily'?"

"That's what I said. For the moment it doesn't suit me to be a cop. Restricts my spheres of activities."

Jeff said: "You *did* say temporarily?"

"Sure. Back to work when this blows over. I've got a wife to support."

"But Donahure—"

"Don't worry about Donahure. Let Donahure worry about himself. Drink, Doctor?"

"Scotch, if you have it." Ryder went behind the small wet bar and pulled back a sliding door to reveal an impressive array of different bottles. Jablonsky said: "You have it."

"Beer for me. That's for my friends. Lasts a long time," he added inconsequentially.

Jablonsky took a folder from his brief case. "This is the

49

file you wanted. Wasn't easy, Ferguson's like a cat on a hot tin roof. Jumpy."

"Ferguson's straight."

"I know he is. This is a photostat. I didn't want Ferguson or the FBI to find out that the original dossier is missing."

"Why's Ferguson so jumpy?"

"Hard to say. But he's being evasive, uncommunicative. Maybe he feels his job is in danger since his security defenses were so easily breached. Running scared, a little. I think we all are in the past few hours. Even goes for me." He looked gloomy. "I'm even worried that my presence here—" he smiled to rob his words of offense— "consorting with an ex-cop might be noted."

"You're too late. It has been noted."

Jablonsky stopped smiling. "What?"

"There's a closed van about fifty yards down the road on the other side. No driver in the cab—he's inside the van looking through a one-way window."

Jeff rose quickly and moved to a window. He said: "How long has he been there?"

"A few minutes. He arrived just as Dr. Jablonsky did. Too late for me to do anything about it then." He thought briefly, then said: "I don't much care to have those snoopers around my house. Go to my gun cupboard and take what you want. You'll find a few old police badges there, too."

"He'll know I'm no longer a cop."

"Sure he will. But d'you think he'd dare say so and put the finger on Donahure?"

"Hardly. What do you want me to do? Shoot him?"

"It's a tempting thought, but no. Smash his window open with the butt of your gun and tell him to open up. His name is Raminoff and he looks a bit like a weasel, which he is. He carries a gun. Donahure reckons he's his top undercover man. I've kept tabs on him for years. He's not a cop—he's a criminal with several sentences behind him. You'll find a police band radio transmitter. Ask him for his license. He won't have one. Ask him for his police

50

identification. He won't have that either. Make the usual threatening noises and tell him to push off."

Jeff smiled widely. "Retirement has its compensations."

Jablonsky looked after him doubtfully. "You sure got a lot of faith in that boy, Sergeant."

"Jeff can look after himself," Ryder said comfortably. "Now Doctor, I hope you're not going to be evasive about telling me why Ferguson was being evasive."

"Why should I?" He looked glum. "Seeing that I'm a marked man anyway."

"He *was* evasive with me?"

"Yes. I feel more upset about your wife than you realize. I think you have the right to know anything that can help you."

"And I think that deserves another drink." It was a measure of Jablonsky's preoccupation that he'd emptied his glass without being aware of it. Ryder went to the bar and returned. "What didn't he tell me?"

"You asked him if any nuclear material had been hijacked. He said he didn't know. Fact is, he knows far too much about it to be willing to talk about it. Take the recent Hematite Hangover business, so-called, I imagine, because it's given a headache to everybody in nuclear security. Hematite is in Missouri and is run by Gulf United Nuclear. They may have anything up to a thousand kilograms of U-235 on the premises at any given time. This comes to them, bottled, in the form of UF6, from Portsmouth, Ohio. This is converted into U-235 oxide. Much of this stuff, fully enriched and top weapons-grade material, goes from Hematite to Kansas City by truck, thence to Los Angeles as air cargo, then is again trucked a hundred and twenty miles down the freeways to General Atomic in San Diego. Three wide-open transits. Do you want the horrifying details?"

"I can imagine them. Why Ferguson's secretiveness?"

"No reason really. All security men are professional clams. There's literally tons of the damned stuff missing. That's no secret. The knowledge is in public domain."

"According to Dr. Durrer of ERDA—I spoke to him this evening—the government's computer system can tell you in nothing flat if any significant amount of weapons-grade material is missing."

Jablonsky scowled, a scowl which he removed by fortifying himself with some more scotch. "I wonder what he calls significant. Ten tons? Just enough to make a few hundred atom bombs, that's all. Dr. Durrer is either talking through his hat, which, knowing him as I do, is extremely unlikely, or he was just being coy. ERDA has been suffering from very sensitive feelings since the GAO gave them a black eye in, let me see, I think it was in July of '76."

"GAO?"

"General Accounting Office." Jablonsky broke off as Jeff entered and deposited some material on a table. He looked very pleased with himself.

"He's gone. Heading for the nearest swamp I'd guess." He indicated his haul. "One police radio—no license for it so I couldn't let him keep that, could I? One gun—clearly a criminal type so I couldn't let him keep that either, could I? One driver's license—identification in lieu of police authorization, which he didn't seem to have. And one pair of Zeiss binoculars stamped L.A.P.D.—he couldn't recall where he got that from and swore blind that he didn't know that the initials stood for Los Angeles Police Department."

"I've always wanted one of those," Ryder said. Jablonsky frowned in heavy disapproval but removed the frown in the same way he had removed his scowl.

"I also wrote down his license plate number, opened the hood and took down the engine and chassis numbers. I told him that all the numbers and confiscated articles would be delivered to the station tonight."

Ryder said: "You know what you've done, don't you? You've gone and upset Chief Donahure. Or he's going to be upset any minute now." He looked wistful. "I wish we had a tap on his private line. He's going to have to replace the equipment, which will hurt him enough but not half as much as replacing that van is going to hurt him."

Jablonsky said: "Why should he have to replace the van?"

"It's hot. If Raminoff were caught with that van he'd get laryngitis singing at the top of his voice to implicate Donahure. He's the kind of trusty henchman that Donahure surrounds himself with."

"Donahure could block the inquiry."

"No chance. John Aaron, the editor of the *Examiner*, has been campaigning for years against police corruption in general and Chief Donahure in particular. A letter to the editor asking why Donahure failed to act on information received would be transferred from the letters page to page one. The swamp, you say, Jeff? Me, I'd go for Cypress Bluff. Two hundred feet sheer into the Pacific, then sixty feet of water. Ocean bed's littered with cars past their best. Anyway, I want you to take your own car and go up there and drop all this confiscated stuff and the rest of those old police badges to join the rest of the hardware down there."

Jeff pursed his lips. "You don't think that old goat would have the nerve to come around here with a search warrant?"

"Sure I do. Trump up any old reason—he's done it often enough before."

Jeff said, wooden-faced: "He might even invent some charge about tampering with evidence at the reactor plant?"

"Man's capable of anything."

"There's some people you just can't faze." Jeff left to get his car.

Jablonsky said: "What was that supposed to mean?"

"Today's generation? Who can tell? You mentioned the GAO. What about the GAO?"

"Ah, yes. They produced a report on the loss of nuclear material for a government department with the memorable name of the House Small Business Subcommittee on Energy and Environment. The report was and is classified. The subcommittee made a summary of the report and declassified it. The GAO would appear to have a low opinion of ERDA. Says it doesn't know its job. Claims

53

that there are literally tons of nuclear material—number of tons unspecified—missing from the thirty-four uranium and plutonium processing plants in the country. GAO says they seriously question ERDA's accountability procedures and that they haven't really a clue as to whether stuff is missing or not."

"Dr. Durrer wouldn't have liked that?"

"ERDA was hopping. They said there was—and I know it's true—up to sixty miles of piping in the processing system of any given plant and if you multiply that by thirty-four you have a couple of thousand miles of piping and there could be a great deal of nuclear material stuck in those pipes. GAO completely agreed but rather spoiled things by pointing out that there was no way in which the contents of those two thousand miles could be checked."

Jablonsky peered gloomily at the base of his empty glass. Ryder rose obligingly and when he returned Jablonsky said accusingly but without heat: "Trying to loosen my tongue?"

"What else? What did ERDA say?"

"Practically nothing. They'd even less to say shortly afterward when the Nuclear Regulatory Commission compounded that attack on them. They said in effect two things—that practically any plant in the country could be taken by a handful of armed and determined men and that the theft-detection systems were defective."

"You believe that?"

"No silly questions, please—especially not after what happened today."

"So there could be tens of tons of the stuff cached around the country?"

"I could be quoted on my answer?"

"Now it's your turn for silly questions."

Jablonsky sighed. "What the hell. It's eminently possible and more than probable. Why are you asking these questions, Sergeant?"

"One more and I'll tell you. Could *you* make an atom bomb?"

"Sure. Any competent scientist—he doesn't have to be

a nuclear physicist—could. Thousands of them. There's a school of thought that says no one could make an atomic bomb without retracing the Manhattan Project—that extremely long, enormously complicated and billion-dollar program that led to the invention of the atom bomb in World War II. Rubbish. The information is freely available. Write to the Atomic Energy Commission, enclose three dollars and they'll be glad to let you have a copy of *The Los Alamos Primer*, which details the mathematical fundamentals of fission bombs. A bit more expensive is the book called *Manhattan District History, Project Y, the Los Alamos Project*. For this you have to approach the Office of Technical Services of the U.S. Department of Commerce, who will be delighted to let you have a copy by return mail. Tells you all about it. Most importantly, it tells you of all the problems that arose in the building of the first atomic bomb and how they were overcome. Stirring stuff. There's any amount of works in public print—just consult your local library—that consist of what used to be the supersecret information. All else failing, the Encyclopedia Americana will probably tell any intelligent person as much as he needs to know."

"We have a very helpful government."

"Very. Once the Russians had started exploding atom bombs they reckoned the need for secrecy was past. What they didn't reckon on was that some patriotic citizen or citizens would up and use this knowledge against them." He sighed. "It would be easy to call the government of the day a bunch of clowns but they lacked the gift of Nostradamus: 'Hindsight makes us all wise.' "

"Hydrogen bombs?"

"A nuclear physicist for that." He paused, then went on with some bitterness: "Provided, that is, he's fourteen years of age or over."

"Explain."

"Back in 1970 there was an attempted nuclear blackmail of a city in Florida. Police tried to hush it up but it came out all the same. Give me a million dollars and a safe-conduct out of America or I'll blast your city out of existence, the blackmailer said. Next day came the same threat, this time accompanied by a diagram of a hydrogen bomb—a cylinder filled with lithium hydride wrapped in cobalt, with an implosion system at one end."

"That how they make a hydrogen bomb?"

"I wouldn't know."

"Isn't that sad? And you a nuclear physicist. They nail the blackmailer?"

"Yes. A fourteen-year-old boy."

"It's an advance on fireworks." For almost a minute Ryder gazed into the far distance, which appeared to be located in the region of his toe caps, through a drifting cloud of blue-gray smoke, then said:

"It's a come-on. A con job. A gambit. A phony. Don't you agree?"

Jablonsky was guarded. "I might. If, that is to say, I had the faintest idea what you are talking about."

"Will this theft of the uranium and plutonium be made public?"

Jablonsky gave an exaggerated shrug. "No, sir. Not if we can help it. Mustn't give the shivers to the great American public."

"Not if you can help it. I'll take long odds that the bandits won't be so bashful and that the story will have banner headlines in every paper in the state tomorrow. Not to mention the rest of the country. It smells, Doc. The people responsible are obviously experts and must have known that the easiest way to get weapons-grade material is to hijack a shipment. With all that stuff already missing, it's long odds that they've got more than enough than they need already. And you know as well as I do that three nuclear physicists in the state have just vanished in the past couple of months. Would you care to guess who their captors were?[2]

"I don't think so. I mean, I don't think I have to."

"I didn't think so. You could have saved me all this thinking—I prefer to avoid it where possible. Let's assume they already had the fuel. Let's assume they already had the physicists to make the nuclear devices, quite possibly even hydrogen explosives. Let's even assume that they have already got one of those devices—and why

56

stop at one?—manufactured and tucked away at some safe place."

Jablonsky looked unhappy. "It's not an assumption I care to assume."

"I can understand that. But if something's there, wishing it wasn't won't make it go away. Some time back you described something as being eminently possible and more than probable. Would you describe this assumption in the same words?"

Jablonsky thought for some moments then said: "Yes."

"So. A smoke screen. They didn't really need the fuel or the physicists or the hostages. Why did they take something they didn't need? Because they needed them."

"That makes a lot of sense."

Ryder was patient. "They didn't need them to make bombs. I would think they needed them for three other reasons. The first would be to obtain maximum publicity, to convince people that they had means to make bombs and meant business. The second is to lull us into the belief that we have time to deal with the threat. I mean, you can't make a nuclear bomb in a day or a week, can you?"

"No."

"So. We have breathing space. But we haven't."

"Getting the hang of your double-talk takes time. If our assumption is correct, we haven't."

"And the third thing is to create the proper climate of terror. People don't behave rationally when they're scared out of their wits, do they? Behavior becomes no longer predictable. You don't think, you just react."

"And where does all this lead us?"

"That's as far as my thinking goes. How the hell should I know?"

Jablonsky peered into his scotch and found no inspiration there. He sighed again and said: "The only thing that makes sense out of all this is that it accounts for your behavior."

"Something odd about my behavior?"

"That's the point. There should be. Or there should have been. Worried stiff about Susan. But if you're right in your thinking—well, I understand."

57

"I'm afraid you don't. If I'm right in what you so kindly call my thinking she's in greater danger than she would have been if we'd accepted the facts at their face value. If the bandits are the kind of people that I think they are then they're not to be judged by ordinary standards. They're mavericks. They're power-mad, megalomaniacs if you like, people who will stop at nothing, people who will go all the way in ruthlessness, especially when thwarted or shoved into a corner."

Jablonsky digested this for some time, then said: "Then you ought to look worried."

"That would help a lot." The doorbell rang. Ryder rose and went to the hall. Sergeant Parker, a bachelor who looked on Ryder's house as a second home, had already let himself in. He, like Jablonsky, was carrying a brief case: unlike Jablonsky, he looked cheerful.

"Evening. Shouldn't be associating with a fired cop but in the sacred name of friendship—"

"I resigned."

"Comes to the same thing. Leaves the way clear for me to assume the mantle of the most detested and feared cop in town. Look on the bright side. After thirty years of terrifying the local populace, you deserve a break." He followed Ryder into the living room. "Ah! Dr. Jablonsky. I didn't expect to find you here."

"I didn't expect to be here."

"Lift up your spirits, Doc. Consorting with disgraced cops is not a statutory crime." He looked accusingly at Ryder. "Speaking of lifting—or lifting up spirits—this man's glass is almost empty. Imported London gin for me." A year on an exchange visit to Scotland Yard had left Parker with the profound conviction that American gin hadn't advanced since Prohibition days and was still made in bathtubs.

"Thanks for reminding me." Ryder looked at Jablonsky. "He's only consumed about a couple of hundred crates of the stuff here in the past fourteen years. Give or take a crate."

Parker smiled, delved into his brief case and came up with Ryder's photograph. "Sorry to be so late with this. Had to go back and report to our fat friend. Seemed to be recovering from some sort of heart attack. He was less interested in my report than in discussing you freely and at some length. Poor man was very upset so I congratulated him on his character analysis. This picture has some importance?"

"I hope so. What makes you think so?"

"You asked for it. And it seems Susan was going to take it with her then changed her mind. Seems she took it with her into the room where they were all locked up. She told the guard she felt sick. Guard checked the washroom for windows and telephone, I guess, then let her in. She came out in a few minutes looking, so I'm told, deathly pale."

"Morning Dawn," Ryder said.

"What's that?"

"Face powder she uses."

"Ah! Then—peace to the libbers—she exercised a woman's privilege of changing her mind and changed her mind about taking the picture with her."

"Have you opened it up?"

"I'm a virtuous honest cop and I wouldn't dream—"

"Stop dreaming."

Parker eased off the six spring-loaded clips at the back, removed the rectangle of white cardboard and peered with interest at the back of Ryder's photograph. "A clue, by heavens, a clue! I see the word 'Morro.' The rest, I'm afraid, is in shorthand."

"Figures. She'd be in a hurry." He crossed to the phone, dialed, then hung up in about thirty seconds. "Damn! She's not there."

"Who?"

"My shorthand translator. Marjory. She and Ted have gone to eat, drink, dance, go to a show or whatever. I've no idea what they do at night or where the young hang out these days. Jeff will know. We'll just have to wait till he returns."

"Where is your fellow ex-cop?"

"Up on Cypress Bluff throwing some of Chief Donahure's most treasured possessions into the Pacific."

"Not Chief Donahure himself? Too bad. I'm listening."

THREE

■ AMERICA, like England, has much more than its fair share of those people in the world who choose not to conform to the status quo. They are the individualists who pursue their own paths, their own beliefs, their own foibles and what are commonly regarded as their own irrational peculiarities with a splendid disregard, leavened only with a modicum of kindly pity and sorrow and benign resignation, for those unfortunates who are not as they are, the hordes of faceless conformists among whom they are forced to move and have their being. Some few of those individualists, confined principally to those who pursue the more esoteric forms of religions of their own inventions, try sporadically to lead the more gullible of the unenlightened along the road that leads to ultimate revelation: basically, however, they regard the unfortunate conformists as being sadly beyond redemption and are resigned to leaving them to wallow in the troughs of their ignorance while they follow the meandering highways and byways of their own chosen life-style, oblivious of the paralleling motorways that carry the vast majority of blinkered mankind. They are commonly known as eccentrics.

America, as said, has its fair share of such eccentrics—and more. But California, as both the inhabitants of that state and the rest of the union would agree, has vastly more than its fair share of American eccentrics: they are extremely thick upon the ground. They differ from your true English eccentric, who is almost invariably a loner. California eccentrics tend to polarize, and could equally well be categorized as cultists, whose beliefs range from the beatific to the cataclysmic, from the unassailable —because incapable of disproof—pontifications of the self-appointed gurus to the courageous resignation of those who have the day, hour and minute of the world's end or those who crouch on the summit of a high peak in the Sierras awaiting the next flood which will surely lap their ankles—but no higher—before sunset. In a less free, less open, less inhibited and less tolerant society than California's, they would be tidied away in those institutions reserved for imbalanced mavericks of the human race: the Golden State does not exactly cherish them but does regard them with an affectionate, if occasionally exasperated, amusement.

But they cannot be regarded as the true eccentrics. In England, on the eastern seaboard of the States, one can be poor and avoid all contact with like-minded deviants and still be recognized as an outstanding example of what the rest of mankind is glad it isn't. In the group-minded togetherness of California, such solitary peaks of eccentric achievement are almost impossible to reach, although there have been one or two notable examples, outstandingly the self-proclaimed Emperor of San Francisco and Defender of Mexico. Emperor Norton the First became so famous and cherished a figure that even the burial ceremony of his dog attracted such a vast concourse of tough and hard-headed nineteenth-century Franciscans that the entire business life of the city, saloons and bordellos apart, ground to a complete halt. But it was rare indeed for a penniless eccentric to scale the topmost heights.

To hope to be a successful eccentric in California one has to be a millionaire: being a millionaire brings with it a cast-iron guarantee. Von Streicher had been one of the latter, one of the favored few. Unlike the bloodless and desiccated calculating machines of the oil, manufacturing and marketing billionaires of today, Von Streicher had been one of the giants of the era of steamships, railways and steel. Both his vast fortune and his reputation as an eccentric had been made and consolidated by the early twentieth century and his status in both fields was unassailable. But every status requires its symbol: a symbol for your billionaire cannot be intangible: it has to be seen and the bigger the better: and all self-respecting eccentrics
61

with the proper monetary qualifications invariably settled on the same symbol: a home that would properly reflect the uniqueness of the owner. Kubla Khan had built his own Xanadu and, as he had been incomparably wealthier than any run-of-the-mill billionaire, what was good enough for him was good enough for them.

Von Streicher's choice of location had been governed by two very powerful phobias: one of tidal waves, the other of heights. The fear of tidal waves stemmed from his youth, when he had read of the volcanic eruption and destruction of the island of Thera, north of Crete, when a tidal wave, estimated at some 165 feet in height, destroyed much of the 'early Minoan, Grecian and Turkish civilizations. Since then he had lived with the conviction that he would be similarly engulfed someday. There was no known basis for his fear of heights but an eccentric of good standing does not require any reason for his whimsical beliefs and behavior. He had taken this fearful dilemma with him on his one and only return to his German birthplace, where he had spent two months examining the architectural monuments, almost exclusively castles, left behind by the mad Ludwig of Bavaria, and on his return had settled for what he regarded as the lesser of two evils—height.

He didn't, however, go too high. He selected a plateau some fifteen hundred feet high on a mountain range some fifty miles from the ocean and there proceeded to build his own Xanadu, which he later christened Adlerheim—the home of the eagle. The poet speaks of Kubla Khan's pied-à-terre as being a stately pleasure dome. Adlerheim wasn't like that at all. It was a castellated neo-Gothic horror, a Baroque monstrosity that came close to being awe-inspiring in its totally unredeemed vulgarity. Massively built of northern Italian marble, it was an incredible hodgepodge of turrets, onion towers, crenelated battlements and slit windows for the use of archers. All it lacked was a moat and drawbridge but Von Streicher had been more than satisfied with it as it was. For others, living in more modern and hopefully more enlightened times, the sole redeeming feature was to be seen from the battlements, looking west: the view across the broad valley to the distant coastal range, Von Streicher's first breakwater against the inevitable tidal wave, was quite splendid.

Fortunately for the eight captives in the rear of the second two vans grinding around the hairpins up to the castle, they were doubly unable to see what lay in store for them. Doubly, because in addition to the van body being wholly enclosed, they wore blindfolds as well as handcuffs. But they were to know the inside of Adlerheim more intimately than even the most besotted and aesthetically retarded admirer of all that was worst in nineteenth-century design would have cared to.

The prisoners' van jolted to a stop. Rear doors were opened, bandages removed and the eight still handcuffed passengers were helped to jump down onto the authentically cobbled surface of what proved to be a wholly enclosed courtyard. Two guards were closing two massive, iron-bound oak doors to seal off the archway through which they had just entered. There were two peculiarities about those guards. They were carrying Ingram submachine guns fitted with silencers, a favorite weapon of Britain's elite Special Air Service—despite its name, an Army regiment—which had two rare privileges: the first was that they had access to their own private armory, almost certainly the most comprehensively stocked in the world, the second being that any member of the unit had complete freedom to pick the weapon of his own particular choice. The popularity of the Ingram was testimony to its deadly effectiveness.

The second idiosyncrasy about the two guards was that, from top of burnous to sandal-brushing skirts of robe, they were dressed as Arabs, not the type of gleamingly white garb that one would normally look to find in the state of California but, nonetheless, eminently suitable for both the very warm weather and the instantaneous concealment of Ingrams in voluminous folds. Two other men, bent over colorful flower borders that paralleled all four walls of the courtyard, and two others carrying slung

63

rifles were all dressed similarly. All six had the sun-tanned swarthiness of an Eastern desert dweller but some of their facial bone structures were wrong.

The man who was obviously the leader of the abductors, and had been in the leading van, approached the captives and let them see his face for the first time—he had removed his stocking mask on leaving San Ruffino. He was a tall man, lean but broad-shouldered and, unlike the pudgy Von Streicher, who had habitually worn lederhosen and a Tyrolean hat with a pheasant's feather when in residence, he looked as if he belonged in an eagle's home. He had a lean, sun-tanned face, a hooked nose and a piercing light blue eye. One eye. His right eye was covered by a black patch.

He said: "My name is Morro. I am the leader of this community here." He waved at the white-robed figures. "Those are my followers, acolytes, you might almost call them, all faithful servants of Allah."

"That's what *you* would call them. I'd call them refugees from a chain gang." The tall thin man in the black alpaca suit had a pronounced stoop and bifocal glasses and looked the prototype of the absent-minded academic, which was half true. Professor Burnett of San Diego was anything but absent-minded: in his professional circle, he was justly famous for his extraordinarily acute intelligence and justly notorious for his extraordinarily short temper.

Morro smiled. "Chains can be literal or figurative, Professor. One way or another we are all slaves to something or other." He gestured to the two men with rifles. "Remove their handcuffs. Ladies and gentlemen, I have to apologize for a rather upsetting interruption of the even tenor of your ways. I trust none of you suffered discomfort on our journey here." His speech had the fluently correct precision of an educated man to whom English is not a native language. "I do not wish to sound alarming or threatening"—there is no way of sounding more alarming and threatening than to say you don't intend to—"but, before I take you inside, I would like you to have a look at the walls of this courtyard."

They had a look. The walls were about twenty feet

high and topped with a three-stranded barbed-wire fence. The wires were supported by but not attached to the L-shaped steel posts imbedded in the marble, but passed instead through insulated apertures.

Morro said: "Those walls and the gates are the only way to leave here. I do not advise that you try to use either. Especially the wall. The fence above is electrified."

"Has been for sixty years." Burnett sounded sour.

"You know this place, then?" Morro didn't seem surprised. "You've been here?"

"Thousands have. Von Streicher's Folly. Open to the public for about twenty years when the state ran it."

"Still open to the public, believe it or not. Tuesdays and Fridays. Who am I to deprive Californians of part of their cultural heritage. Von Streicher put fifty volts through it as a deterrent. It would only kill a person with a bad heart—and a person with a bad heart wouldn't try to scale that wall in the first place. I have increased the current to two thousand volts. Follow me, please."

He led the way through an archway directly opposite the entrance. Beyond lay a huge hall, some sixty feet by sixty. Three open fireplaces, of stone, not granite, were let into each of three walls, each fireplace large enough for a man to stand upright: the three crackling log fires were not for decorative purposes because even in the month of June the thick granite walls effectively insulated the interior from the heat outside. There were no windows, illumination being provided by four massive chandeliers that had come all the way from Prague. The gleaming floor was of inlaid redwood. Of the floor space, only half of the area was occupied, this by a row of refectory tables and benches: the other was empty except for a hand-carved oaken rostrum and, close by, a pile of very undistinguished mats.

"Von Streicher's banqueting hall," Morro said. He looked at the battered tables and benches. "I doubt whether he would have approved of the change."

Burnett said: "The Louis XIV chairs, the Empire period tables. All gone? They would have made excellent firewood."

"You must not equate non-Christian with being barbaric, Professor. The original furniture is intact. The Adlerheim has massive cellars. The castle, I'm afraid, its splendid isolation apart, is not as ideal as we would have wished for our religious purposes. The refectory half of this hall is profane. The other half"—he indicated the bare expanse—"is consecrated. We have to make do with what we have. Someday we hope to build a mosque adjoining here—for the present this has to serve. The rostrum is for the readings of the Koran—the mats, of course, are for prayers. For calling the faithful to prayer we have again been forced to make a most reluctant compromise. For Mohammedans, those onion towers, the grotesque architectural symbol of the Greek Orthodox Church, are anathema, but we have again consecrated one of them and it now serves as our minaret from which the muezzin summons the acolytes to prayer."

Dr. Schmidt, like Burnett an outstanding nuclear physicist and, like Burnett, renowned for his inability to suffer fools gladly, looked at Morro from under bushy white eyebrows that splendidly complemented his impossible mane of white hair—which had to be a wig but wasn't. His ruddy face held an expression of almost comical disbelief.

"This is what you tell your Tuesday and Friday visitors?"

"But of course."

"My God!"

"Allah, if you please."

"And I suppose you conduct those personal tours yourself? I mean, you must derive enormous pleasure from feeding this pack of lies to my gullible fellow citizens."

"May Allah send that you someday see the light." Morro was not patronizing, just kindly. "And this is a chore—what am I saying?—a sacred duty that is performed for me by my deputy Abraham."

"Abraham?" Burnett permitted himself a professional sneer. "A fitting name for a follower of Allah."

"You have not been in Palestine lately, have you, Professor?"

"Israel."

"Palestine. There are many Arabs there who profess the Jewish faith. Why take exception to a Jew practicing the Muslim faith? Come. I shall introduce you to him. I daresay you will find the surroundings more congenial there."

The very large study—for that it unquestionably was—into which he led them was not only more congenial, it was unashamedly sybaritic. Von Streicher had left the internal design and furnishings of the Adlerheim to his architects and interior designers and, for once, they had got something right. The study was clearly modeled on an English ducal library: book-lined walls on three sides of the room, each book expensively covered in the finest leather, deep-piled russet carpet, silk damask drapes, also russet, comfortable and enveloping leather arm-chairs, oak side tables and a leather-topped desk with a padded leather swivel chair behind it. A slightly incongruous note was struck by the three men already present in the room. All dressed in Arab clothes. Two were diminutive with unremarkable features not worth a second glance: but the third man was worth all the attention that the other two were spared. He looked as if he had started out to grow into a basketball player then changed his mind to become an American football player. He was immensely tall and had shoulders like a draft horse: he could have weighed anything up to three hundred pounds.

Morro said: "Abraham, our guests from San Ruffino. Ladies and gentlemen, Mr. Abraham Dubois, my deputy."

The giant bowed. "My pleasure, I assure you. Welcome to the Adlerheim. We hope your stay here will be a pleasant one." Both the voice and the tone of the voice came as a surprise. Like Morro, he spoke with the easy fluency of an educated man and, coming from that bleak impassive face, one would have expected any words to have either sinister or threatening overtones. But he sounded courteous and genuinely friendly. His speech did not betray his nationality but his features did. Here was no Arab, no Jew, no Levantine and, despite his surname, no Frenchman. He was unmistakably American. Not your

67

clean-cut All-American campus hero, but a native American aristocrat whose unbroken lineage was shrouded in the mists of time: Dubois was a full-blooded red Indian.

Morro said: "A pleasant stay and, we hope, a short one." He nodded to Dubois, who nodded to his two diminutive companions, who left. Morro moved behind the desk. "If you would be seated, please. This will not take long. Then you'll be shown to your quarters—after I have introduced you to some other guests." He pulled up his swivel chair, sat, and took some papers from a desk drawer. He uncapped a pen and looked up as the two small white-robed men, each bearing a silver tray filled with glasses, entered. "As you see, we are civilized. Refreshments?"

Professor Burnett was the first to be offered a tray. He glowered at it, looked at Morro and made no move. Morro smiled, rose from his seat and came toward him.

"If we had intended to dispose of you—and can you think of any earthly reason why we should—would I have brought you all the way here to do so? Hemlock we leave to Socrates, cyanide to professional assassins. We prefer our refreshments undiluted. Which one, my dear professor, would you care to have me select at random?"

Burnett, whose thirst was legendary, hesitated only briefly before pointing. Morro lifted the glass, lowered the amber level by almost a quarter and smiled appreciatively. "Glenfiddich. An excellent Scottish malt. I recommend it."

The professor did not hesitate. Malt was malt no matter what the moral standards of one's host. He drank, smacked his lips and sneered ungratefully. "Muslims don't drink."

"Breakaway Muslims do." Morro registered no offense. "We are a breakaway group. As for those who call themselves true Muslims, it's a rule honored in the breach. Ask the manager of any five-star hotel in London which, as the pilgrimage center of the upper echelons of Arabian society, is now taking over from Mecca. There was a time when the oil sheiks used to send out their servants daily to bring back large crates of suitably disguised refreshments until the managements discreetly pointed out that this was wholly unnecessary and all that was required was that they charge such expenses up to laundry, phones or stamps. I understand that various governments in the Gulf remained unmoved at stamp bills for a thousand pounds sterling."

"Breakaway Muslims." Burnett wasn't through with sneering yet. "Why the front?"

"Front?" Morro smilingly refused to take umbrage. "This is no front, Professor. You would be surprised how many Muslims there are in your state, Professor. You'd be surprised how highly placed a large number of them are. You'd be surprised how many of them come here to worship and to meditate—Adlerheim, and not slowly, is becoming a place of pilgrimage in the West. Above all, you'd be surprised how many influential citizens, who cannot afford to have their good names impugned, would vouch for our unassailable good name, dedication and honesty of purpose."

Dr. Schmidt said: "If they knew what your real purpose was I wouldn't be surprised, I'd be utterly incredulous."

Morro turned his hands palms upward and looked at his deputy. Dubois shrugged, then said: "We are respected, trusted and—I have to say this—even admired by the local authorities. And why not? Because Californians not only tolerate and even cherish their eccentrics, regarding them as a protected species? Certainly not. We are registered as a charitable organization and, unlike the vast majority of charities, we do not solicit money, we give it away. In the eight months we have been established, we have given over two million dollars to the poor, the crippled, the retarded and to deserving pension funds, regardless of race or creed."

"Including police pension funds?" Burnett wasn't through with being nasty for the evening.

"Including just that. There is no question of bribery and corruption." Dubois was so open and convincing that disbelief came hard. "A *quid pro quo* you may say for the security and protection that they offer us. Mr. Curragh, county chief of police, a man widely respected for his integrity, has the whole-hearted support of the

69

governor of the state in ensuring that we can carry out our good works, peaceful projects and selfless aims without let or hindrance. We even have a permanent police guard at the entrance to our private road down in the valley to ensure that we are not molested." Dubois shook his massive head and his face was grave. "You would not believe, gentlemen, the number of evilly intentioned people in this world who derive pleasure from harassing those who would do good."

"Sweet Jesus!" Burnett was clearly trying to fight against speechlessness. "Of all the cant and hypocrisy I've encountered in my life . . . You know, Morro, I believe you. I can quite believe that you have—not bribed, not subverted—you have conned or persuaded honest citizens, an honest chief of police and an honest police force into believing that you are what you claim to be. I can't see any reason why they shouldn't believe you—after all, they have two million good reasons, all green, to substantiate your claims. People don't throw around a fortune like that for amusement, do they?"

Morro smiled. "I'm glad you're coming around to our point of view."

"They don't throw it around like that unless they are playing for extremely high stakes. Speculate to accumulate. Isn't that it, Morro?" He shook his head in slow disbelief, remembered the glass in his hand and took further steps to fortify himself against unreality. "Out of context, one would be hard put not to believe you. In context, it is impossible."

"In context?"

"The theft of weapons-grade materials and mass kidnaping. Rather difficult to equate that with your alleged humanitarian purposes. Although I have no doubt you can equate anything with anything. All you have to have is a sick enough mind."

Morro returned to his seat and propped his chin on his fists. For some reason, he had not seen fit to remove the black leather gloves that he had worn throughout. "We are not sick. We are not zealots. We are not fanatics. We

70

have but one purpose in mind—the betterment of the human lot."

"Which human lot? Yours?"

Morro sighed. "I waste my time. Perhaps you think you are here for ransom? You are not. Perhaps you think it is our purpose to compel you and Dr. Schmidt to make some kind of crude atomic weapon for us? Ludicrous—no one can compel men of your stature and integrity to do what they do not wish to do. You might think—the world might think—that we might compel you to work by the threat of torturing the other hostages, particularly the ladies? Preposterous. I would remind you again that we are no barbarians. Professor Burnett, if I pointed a six-gun between your eyes and told you not to move, would you move?"

"I suppose not."

"Would you or wouldn't you?"

"Of course not."

"So, you see, the gun doesn't have to be loaded. You take my point?"

Burnett remained silent.

"I will not give you my word that no harm will come to any of you for clearly my word will carry no weight with any of you. We shall just have to wait and see, will we not?" He smoothed the sheet in front of him. "Professor Burnett and Dr. Schmidt I know. Mrs. Ryder I recognize." He looked at a bespectacled young girl with auburn hair and a rather scared expression. "You must, of course, be Miss Julie Johnson, stenographer."

He looked at the three remaining men. "Which of you is Mr. Haverford, deputy director?"

"I am." Haverford was a portly young man with sandy hair and a choleric expression who added as an afterthought: "Damn you anyway."

"Dear me. And Mr. Carlton? Security deputy?"

"Me." Carlton was in his mid-thirties, with black hair, permanently compressed lips and, at that moment, a disgusted expression.

"You mustn't reproach yourself." Morro was almost

71

kindly. "There never has been a security system that couldn't be breached." He looked at the eighth hostage, a thin pale young man with pale hair whose bobbing Adam's apple and twitching left eye were competing in sending distress signals. "And you are Mr. Rollins, from the control room." Rollins didn't say whether he was or not.

Morro folded the sheet. "I suggest that when you get to your rooms each of you should write a letter. Writing materials you will find in your quarters. To your nearest and dearest, just to let them know that you are alive and well, that—apart from the temporary curtailment of your liberty—you have no complaints of ill treatment and have not been and will not be threatened in any way. You will not, of course, mention anything about Adlerheim or Muslims or anything that could give an indication as to your whereabouts. Leave your envelopes unsealed—we shall do that."

"Censorship, eh?" Burnett's second scotch still had had no mellowing effect.

"Don't be naïve."

"And if we—or I—refuse to write?"

"If you'd rather not reassure your families that's your decision entirely." He looked at Dubois. "I think we could have Drs. Healey and Bramwell in now."

Dr. Schmidt said: "Two of the missing nuclear physicists!"

"I promised to introduce you to some guests."

"Where is Professor Aachen?"

"Professor Aachen?" Morro looked at Dubois, who pursed his lips and shook his head. "We know no one of that name."

"Professor Aachen was the most prestigious of the three nuclear physicists who disappeared some weeks ago." Schmidt could be very precise, even pedantic, in his speech.

"Well, he didn't disappear in our direction. I have never heard of him. I'm afraid that we cannot accept responsibility for every scientist who chooses to vanish. Or defect."

"Defect? Never. Impossible."

72

"I'm afraid that's been exactly the reaction of American and British colleagues of scientists who have found the attractions of state-subsidized flats in Moscow irresistible. Ah! Your nondefecting colleagues, gentlemen."

Apart from a six-inch difference in height, Healey and Bramwell were curiously alike. Dark, with thin intelligent faces and identical horn-rimmed glasses and wearing neat conservatively cut clothes, they would not have looked out of place in a Wall Street board room. Morro didn't have to make any introductions: top-ranking nuclear physicists form a very close community. Characteristically, it occurred to neither Burnett nor Schmidt to introduce their companions in distress.

After the customary hand shaking, gripping of upper arms and not-so-customary regrets that their acquaintance should be renewed in such deplorable circumstances, Healey said: "We were expecting you. Well, colleagues." Healey favored Morro with a look that lacked cordiality.

Burnett said: "Which was more than we did of you." By "we" he clearly referred only to Schmidt and himself. "But if you're here we expected Willi Aachen to be with you."

"I'd expected the same myself. But no Willi. Morro here is under the crackpot delusion that he may have defected. Man had never even heard of him, far less met him."

" 'Crackpot' is right," Schmidt said, then added grudgingly: "You two look pretty fit, I must say."

"No reason why not." It was Bramwell. "An enforced and unwanted holiday, but the seven most peaceful weeks I've had in years. Ever, I suppose. Walking, eating, sleeping, drinking and, best, no telephone. Splendid library, as you can see, and, in every suite, color TV for the weakminded."

"Suite?"

"You'll see. Those old-time billionaires didn't begrudge themselves anything. Any idea why you are here?"

"None," Schmidt said. "We were looking to you to tell us—"

"Seven weeks and we haven't a clue."

"He hasn't tried to make you work for him?"

"Like building a nuclear device? Frankly, that's what we thought would be demanded of us. But nothing." Healey permitted himself a humorless smile. "Almost disappointing, isn't it?"

Burnett looked at Morro. "The gun with the empty magazine, is that it?" Morro smiled politely.

"How's that?" Bramwell said.

"Psychological warfare. Against whomever the inevitable threat will ultimately be directed. Why kidnap a nuclear physicist if not to have him manufacture atom bombs under duress? That's what the world will think."

"That's what the world will think. The world does not know that you don't require a nuclear physicist for that. But the people who really matter are those who know that for a hydrogen bomb you do require a nuclear physicist. We figured that out our first evening here."

Morro was courteous as ever. "If I could interrupt your conversation, gentlemen. Plenty of time to discuss the past—and the present and future—later. A late supper will be available here in an hour. Meantime, I'm sure our new guests would like to see their quarters and attend to some—ah—optional correspondence."

Susan Ryder was forty-five and looked ten years younger. She had dark blond hair, laughing cornflower-blue eyes and a smile that could be bewitching or coolly disconcerting according to the company. Intelligent and blessed with a sense of humor, she was not, however, feeling particularly humorous at that moment. She had no reason to. She was sitting on her bed in the quarters that had been allocated to her. Julie Johnson, the stenographer, was standing in the middle of the room.

"They certainly know how to put up their guests," said Julie. "Or old Von Streicher did. Living and bedroom from the Beverly Wilshire. Bathroom with gold-plated taps—it's got everything."

"I might even try out some of these luxuries," said Susan in a loud voice. She rose, putting a warning finger
74

to her lips. "In fact I'm going to try a quick shower. Won't be long."

She passed through the bedroom into the bathroom, waited some prudent seconds, turned the shower on, returned to the living room and beckoned Julie, who followed her back to the bathroom. Susan smiled at the young girl's raised eyebrows and said in a soft voice: "I don't know whether these rooms are bugged or not."

"Of course they are."

"What makes you so sure?"

"I wouldn't put anything past that creep."

"Mr. Morro. I thought him quite charming, myself. But I agree. Running a shower gets a hidden mike all confused. Or so John told me once." Apart from herself and Parker, no one called Sergeant Ryder by his given name, probably because very few people knew it: Jeff invariably called her Susan but never got beyond "Dad" where his father was concerned. "I wish to heaven he was here now—though mind you, I've already written a note to him."

Julie looked at her blankly.

"Remember when I was overcome back in San Ruffino and had to retire to the powder room? I took John's picture with me, removed the backing, scribbled a few odds and ends on the back of the picture, replaced the backing and left the picture behind."

"Isn't it a pretty remote chance that it would ever occur to him to open up the picture?"

"Yes. So I scribbled a tiny note in shorthand, tore it up and dropped it in my wastepaper basket."

"Again, isn't it unlikely that that would occur to him? To check your basket? And even if he did, to guess that a scrap of shorthand would mean anything?"

"It's a slender chance. Well, a little better than slender. You can't know him as I do. Women have the traditional right of being unpredictable, and that's one of the things about him that does annoy me—ninety-nine point something per cent of the time he can predict precisely what I will do."

"Even if he does find what you left—well, you couldn't have been able to tell him much."

"Very little. A description—what little I could give of anybody with a stocking mask—his stupid remark about taking us to some place where we wouldn't get our feet wet and his name."

"Funny he didn't warn his thugs against calling him by name. Unless, of course, it wasn't his name."

"Sure it's not his name. Probably a twisted sense of humor. He broke into a power station, so it probably tickled him to call himself after another station, the one in Morro Bay. Though I don't know if that will help us much."

Julie smiled doubtfully and left. When the door closed behind her Susan turned around to locate the draft that had suddenly made her shoulders feel cold, but there was no place a draft could have come from.

Showers were in demand that evening. A little way along the hallway Professor Burnett had his running for precisely the same reason as Susan had. In this case the person he wanted to talk to was, inevitably, Dr. Schmidt. Bramwell, when listing the amenities of Adlerheim, had omitted to include what both Burnett and Schmidt regarded as by far the most important amenity of all: every suite was provided with its own wet bar. The two men silently toasted each other, Burnett with his scotch, Schmidt with his gin and tonic: unlike Sergeant Parker, Schmidt had no esoteric preferences as to the source of his gin. A gin was a gin was a gin.

Burnett said: "Do you make of all this what I make of all this?"

"Yes." Like Burnett, Schmidt had no idea whatsoever what to make of it.

"Is the man mad, a crackpot or just a cunning devil?"

"A cunning devil, that's quite obvious." Schmidt pondered. "Of course, there's nothing to prevent him from being all three at the same time."

"What do you reckon our chances are of getting out of here?"

"Zero."

"What do you reckon our chances are of getting out of here alive?"

"The same. He can't afford to let us live. We could identify them afterward."

"You honestly think he'd be prepared to kill all nine of us in cold blood?"

"He'd have to." Schmidt hesitated. "Can't be sure. Seems civilized enough in his own oddball way. Could be a veneer, of course—but he just possibly could be a man with a mission." Schmidt helped his meditation along by emptying his glass, left and returned with a refill. "Could even be prepared to bargain our lives against freedom from prosecution. Speaking no ill of the others, of course" —he clearly was—"but with four top-ranking nuclear physicists in his hands he holds pretty strong cards to deal with either state or government as the case may be."

"Government. No question. Dr. Durrer of ERDA would have called in the FBI hours ago. And while we may be important enough we mustn't overlook the tremendous emotional factor of having two innocent women as hostages. The nation will clamor for the release of all of us, irrespective of whether it means stopping the wheels of justice."

"It's a hope." Schmidt was glum. "We could be whistling in the dark. If only we knew what Morro was up to. All right, we suspect it's some form of nuclear blackmail because we can't see what else it could be but *what* form we can't even begin to guess."

"Healey and Bramwell could tell us. After all, we haven't had a chance to talk to them. They're mad, sure, but they seemed fairly relaxed and not running scared. Before we start jumping to conclusions perhaps we should talk to them. Odds are that they know something we don't."

"Too relaxed." Schmidt pondered some time. "I hesitate to suggest this, I'm no expert in the field, but could they have been brainwashed, subverted in some way?"

"No." Burnett was positive. "The thought occurred to

me while we were talking to them. Very long odds against it. I know them too well."

Burnett and Schmidt found the other two physicists in Healey's room. Soft music was playing. Burnett put a finger to his lips. Healey smiled and turned up the cassette volume.

"That's just to put your minds at rest. We haven't been here for seven weeks without knowing the rooms aren't bugged. But something's bugging you?"

"Yes. Bluntly, you're too casual by far. How do you know Morro isn't going to feed us to the lions when he gets whatever he wants?

"We don't. Maybe we're stir-happy. He's repeatedly told us that we will come to no harm and that he has no doubt about the outcome of his negotiations with the authorities when he's carried out whatever mad scheme he has in mind."

"That's roughly what *we* had in mind. It doesn't seem like much of a guarantee to us."

"It's all we have. Besides, we've had time to figure it out. He doesn't want us for any practical purposes. Therefore we're for psychological purposes, like the theft of uranium and plutonium—as you said, the pointed gun without bullets. If we were wanted for only psychological purposes then the very fact of our disappearance would have achieved all he wanted and he could have disposed of us on the spot. Why keep us around for seven weeks before disposing of us? For the pleasure of our company?"

"Well, there's no harm in looking on the bright side. Maybe Dr. Schmidt and I will come around to your way of thinking. I only hope it doesn't take another seven weeks." Healey pointed toward the bar and lifted an interrogative eyebrow, but Burnett shook his head, clear indication of how perturbed he was. "Something else still bugs me. Willi Aachen. Where has he disappeared to? Reason tells me that if four physicists have fallen into Morro's hands so would the fifth. Why should he be so favored? Or, depending on your point of view, so blessed?"

"Lord only knows. One thing for sure, he's no defector."

Schmidt said: "He could be an involuntary defector?"

Burnett said: "Such things have happened. But it's one thing to take a horse to water."

"I've never met him," Schmidt said. "He's the best, isn't he? From all I hear and all I read, that is."

Burnett smiled at Healey and Bramwell, then said to Schmidt: "We physicists are a jealous and self-opinionated lot who yield second place to no one. But well, yes, he's the best."

"I assume because I've been naturalized only six months and that he works in a supersensitive area is why I've been kept away from him. What's he like? I don't mean his work. His fame is international."

"Last seen at that symposium in Washington ten weeks ago. The three of us were there. Cheerful, happy-go-lucky type. Frizzled head of black hair. Tall as I am, and heavily built—about two hundred and ten pounds, I'd say. And stubborn as they come—the idea of the Russians or anybody making him work for them just isn't conceivable."

Unknown to Professor Burnett, unknown to any other person who had ever known Willi Aachen in his prime, Burnett was wrong on every count. Professor Aachen's face was drawn, haggard and etched with a hundred lines, none of which had existed three months previously. The mane of frizzled hair he still had but it had turned the color of snow. He was no longer tall because he had developed a severe stoop akin to that of an advanced sufferer from kyphoscoliosis. His clothes hung on a shrunken frame of 150 pounds. And Aachen would work for anybody, especially Lopez. If Lopez had asked him to step off the Golden Gate Bridge, Aachen would have done it unhesitatingly.

Lopez was the man who had worked this change on Aachen. Lopez—nobody knew his surname and his given name was probably fictitious anyway—had been a lieutenant in the Argentinian Army, where he had worked as an interrogator in the security forces. Iranians and Chileans are widely championed as being the most efficient torturers in the world, but the army of the Argentine, who are reluctant to talk about such matters, make all others specializing in the field of extracting information appear to be fumbling adolescents. It said a great deal for Lopez's unholy expertise that he had sickened his ruthless commanders to the extent that they had felt compelled to get rid of him.

Lopez was vastly amused at stories of World War heroes gallantly defying torture for weeks, even months, on end. It was Lopez's claim—no boast, for his claim had been substantiated a hundred times over—that he could have the toughest and most fanatical of terrorists screaming in unspeakable agony within five minutes and, within twenty minutes, have the name of every member of his cell.

It had taken him forty minutes to break Aachen and he had to repeat the process several times in the following three weeks. For the past month, Aachen had given no trouble. It was a tribute and testimony to Lopez's evil skill that, although Aachen was a physically shattered man with the last vestiges of pride, will and independence gone forever, his mind and memory remained unimpaired.

Aachen gripped the bars of his cell and gazed through them with lack-luster eyes veined with blood, at the immaculate laboratory-cum-workshop that had been his home and his hell for the previous seven weeks. He stared unblinkingly, interminably, as if in a hypnotic trance, at the rack against the opposite wall. It held twelve cylinders. Each had a lifting ring welded to the top. Eleven of those were about twelve feet high and, in diameter, no more than the barrel of a 4.5-inch naval gun, to which they bore a strong resemblance. The twelfth was of the same diameter but less than half the height.

The workshop, hewn out of solid rock, lay forty feet beneath the banqueting hall of the Adlerheim.

FOUR

■ RYDER, Dr. Jablonsky, Sergeant Parker and Jeff waited with varying degrees of patience as Marjory transcribed Susan's shorthand, a task that took her less than two minutes. She handed her notepad to Ryder.

"Thank you. This is what she says: 'The leader is called Morro. Odd.' "

Jablonsky said: "What's odd about that? Lot of unusual names around."

"Not the name. The fact that he should permit one—or more—of his men to identify him by his name."

"Bogus," Jeff said.

"Sure. 'Six foot, lean, broad-shouldered, educated voice. American? Wears black gloves. Only one with gloves. Think I see black patch over his right eye. Stocking mask makes it difficult to be certain. Other men nondescript. Says no harm will come to us. Just regard the next few days as a holiday. Bracing vacation resort. Not the sea. Can't have anyone getting their feet wet. Meaningless chatter? Don't know. Turn the oven off.' That's all."

"It's not much." Jeff's disappointment showed.

"What did you expect? Addresses and telephone numbers? Susan wouldn't have missed anything so that was all she had to go on. Two things. This Morro may have something wrong with both hands—disfigurement, scarring, amputation of fingers—and with one eye—could be a result of an accident, car crash, explosion, even a shoot-out. Then, like all criminals, he may occasionally be so sure of himself that he talks too much. Not the sea, but bracing. Could have been telling lies to mislead but why mention it at all? Bracing. Hills. Mountains."

"Lots of hills and mountains in California." Parker

sounded less than encouraging. "Maybe two thirds. Just leaves an area about the size of Britain to search. And for what?"

There was a brief silence, then Ryder said: "Maybe it's not what. Maybe it's not where. Maybe we should be asking ourselves why."

The front doorbell rang for an unnecessary length of time. Jeff left and returned with the chief of police, who appeared to be in his customary foul mood, and an unhappy young detective called Kramer. Donahure looked around him with the thunderously proprietorial air of a house owner whose premises have been invaded by a hippie commune. His glare settled on Jablonsky.

"What are you doing here?"

"Funny you should ask that." Jablonsky spoke in a cold voice and removed his glasses so that Donahure could see that those were cold too. "I was about to ask you the same."

Donahure let him have some more of the glare, then switched it to Parker. "And what the hell are you doing here?"

Parker took a slow sip of his gin, an action that had a predictable effect on Donahure's complexion. "An old friend visiting an old friend. Maybe for the thousandth time. Talking over old times." Parker took another leisurely sip. "Not that it's any of your goddamned business."

"Report to me first thing in the morning." Donahure's larynx was giving him trouble again. "I know what you're talking about—the break-in. Ryder is not only not on the case, he's not a cop anymore. You don't discuss police business with the public. Now, get out. I want to talk to Ryder privately."

Ryder was on his feet with surprising ease for a man of his bulk. "You'll be getting me a reputation for downright lack of hospitality. I can't have that."

"Out!" A difficult word to snarl but Donahure made a creditable attempt. Parker ignored him. Donahure swung around, crossed the room, lifted a telephone and yelped in agony as Ryder's left hand closed over his arm.

The ulnar nerve in the elbow is the most exposed and sensitive of all peripheral nerves and Ryder had powerful fingers. Donahure dropped the telephone on the table to free his right hand for the purpose of massaging his left elbow: Ryder replaced the phone on its rest.

"What the hell was that for?" Donahure rubbed his elbow industriously. "Right. Kramer. Book Ryder for assault and obstruction of justice."

"What?" Ryder looked around. "Anyone here see me assault Fatso?" Nobody, apparently, had seen anything. "A Californian's home is his castle. Nobody touches anything without my say-so."

"Is that so?" Triumph overcame the throbbing nerve. He dug into a pocket and produced a piece of paper which he flourished at Ryder. "I'll touch anything I like in this house. Know what that is?"

"Sure. A search warrant with LeWinter's name on it."

"It's a warrant, mister."

Ryder took the warrant. "Law says I've the right to read it. Or didn't you know?" Ryder glanced at it for all of a second. "Judge LeWinter it is. Your poker-playing pal at City Hall. Next to only yourself the most corrupt official in town, the only judge in town who would issue you with a warrant on a trumped-up charge." He looked at the four seated people. "Now please watch the reactions of this upholder of public morality, especially his complexion. Jeff, would you have any idea what this trumped-up charge might be?"

"Well, now," Jeff thought. "A theft trumped-up charge, I'd think. A stolen driver's license? A missing police radio? Or something really ridiculous, like harboring a set of binoculars with an L.A.P.D. stamp."

"Observe the complexion," Ryder said. "An interesting clinical study. Violet with overtones of purple. I'll bet a good psychologist could make something of that. A guilt complex, perhaps?"

"I've got it," Jeff said happily. "He's come to search the place for evidence stolen from the scene of the crime."

Ryder studied the warrant. "I don't know how you do it."

Donahure snatched the warrant back. "Too damn right. And when I do find it—"

"Find what? That's why it's a put-up job—you've no idea what you're looking for. You haven't even been out to San Ruffino."

"*I* know what I'm looking for." He marched off to an adjacent bedroom, then halted as he became aware that Ryder was following him. He turned. "I don't need you, Ryder."

"I know. But my wife does."

"What do you mean?"

"She's got some pretty nice jewelry in there."

Donahure balled his fists, looked at Ryder's eyes, changed his mind and stalked—if a hippopotamus could ever be said to stalk—into the bedroom, Ryder at his heels.

He started with a dressing-table drawer, riffled through a pile of blouses, left them in an untidy heap, slammed the drawer shut, moved to the next drawer and repeated his cry of pain as Ryder found the ulnar nerve again. In the living room, Parker rolled up his eyes, rose, picked up his own glass and that of Jablonsky and headed purposefully for the bar.

Ryder said: "I don't like untidy people. Especially, I don't want filthy fingers touching my wife's clothing. *I'll* go through her clothing and you can watch. As I've no idea what the hell you're looking for I can't very well hide it, can I?" Ryder made a meticulous search of his wife's clothing, then allowed Donahure to take over.

Jeff brought a drink into the kitchen. Kramer, leaning against the sink with his arms folded, looked glum and unhappy. Jeff said: "You look like a man who could do with a morale booster. Gin. Donahure is loaded up with Bourbon. He'll never smell it." Kramer took the drink gratefully. "What are you supposed to be doing?"

"Thanks. You can see what I'm doing. I'm searching the kitchen."

"Found anything yet?"

"I will when I start looking. Pots and pans, plates and saucers, knives and forks—all sorts of things." He gulped some of his drink. "Don't know what the hell I'm supposed to be looking for. I'm damned sorry about this, Jeff. What can I do?"

"Just what you're doing. Nothing. Inactivity becomes you. Any idea what our fat friend is looking for?"

"No. You?"

"No."

"Your father?"

"It's possible. If he knows, he hasn't told me. Not that he's had a chance to."

"Must be something important. Something that makes Donahure pretty close to desperate."

"How come?"

"Sergeant Ryder is how come. Or maybe you don't know the reputation of the bogeyman?"

"Ah."

"Yes. Takes a desperate man to provoke your old man."

"Like a man playing for high stakes. Well, now. You interest me."

"I interest myself."

"Looking for incriminating evidence, perhaps."

"Incriminating whom, I wonder?"

"I wonder."

Footsteps and voices approached. Jeff plucked the glass from Kramer, who had a drawer open before Donahure entered. Ryder was close behind him. Donahure gave Jeff the benefit of his customary glare.

"What are you doing here?"

Jeff lowered the glass from his lips. "Keeping an eye on the cutlery."

Donahure jerked a thumb. "Out." Jeff glanced at his father.

"Stay," Ryder said. "Fatso's the one who leaves."

Donahure breathed heavily. "By God, Ryder, push me any more and I'll—"

"You'll do what? Give yourself a heart attack by picking up your teeth?"

Donahure took it out on Kramer. "What did you find? Nothing?"

"Nothing that shouldn't be here."

"Sure you searched properly?"

"Never mind," Ryder said. "If there was an elephant in this house Donahure would miss it. He never tapped a wall, lifted a rug, tried to find a loose tile, didn't even look under a mattress. They couldn't have had police schools in his days." He ignored Donahure's apoplectic splutterings and led the way back to the living room. He said to no one in particular: "Whoever made this jerk a chief of police was either mentally deficient or a victim of blackmail. Fatso, I'm now looking at you with what is known as undisguised contempt. You better go make a fast report to your boss. Tell him you've made a classic blunder. Two blunders. One psychological, one tactical. I'll bet for once you acted on your own—no one with an IQ above fifty would have tipped his hand in that stupid way."

"Boss? Boss? What the hell do you mean boss?"

"You'd make as good an actor as you are a police chief. You know, I do believe I'm right. Bluster—your only stock in trade, of course, but beneath the bluster you're running scared. Boss I said, boss I meant. Every puppet needs his puppet master. Next time you're thinking of making any independent move I suggest you first consult someone with intelligence. One assumes your boss must have a little intelligence."

Donahure tried out his basilisk stare, realized it was the wrong fit, turned on his heel and left. Ryder followed him to the front door. "It's not your day, Donahure. But then it wasn't quite Raminoff's day either, was it? But I hope his had a better ending. I mean, I hope he managed to jump clear before he dumped your van in the Pacific." He clapped Kramer on the shoulder. "Don't look so perplexed, young man. I'm sure the chief will tell you all about it on the way back to the station."

He went back into the living room. Parker said: "What was all that about?"

"I'm not quite sure. I talked about his blunders and I'm sure I was right. He'd never play the lead in *The Great Stone Face*. I blundered myself, but in a different way. I blundered into what seemed to be a sensitive area. I wonder what that area could be."

"You said it yourself. He's taking orders from some-one."

"That crook's been taking orders all his life. Don't look so shocked, Dr. Jablonsky. He's a crook and has been for as long as I've known him, which is far too long. Sure, the California police forces are no better than the other states in the country as far as the three P's are concerned—power, politics and promotion. But it is remarkably free from genuine corruption—Donahure is the exception that proves the rule."

"You have proof?" Jablonsky said.

"Just look at him. He's living proof. But you mean documented proof. That I have. What I'm going to say you can't quote me on, because I didn't say it."

Jablonsky smiled. "You can't faze me anymore. As I said, I've got the hang of your double-talk now."

"Not for repetition. Ah! Something else." He picked up the picture with the shorthand. "Not for repetition either."

"I can tell Ted?" Marjory said.

"I'd rather not."

"Wait till I tell Susan you keep secrets from her."

"Okay. But a secret shared is no longer a secret." He caught her interrogative glance at Jablonsky and Parker. "My dear child, the first thing nuclear physicists and intelligence cops learn is how to hold their tongues."

"I won't talk. Ted won't talk. We just want to help."

"I don't want your help."

She made a *moue*. "You're a rotten old godparent."

"Sorry." He took her hand in apology. "That wasn't nice. If I need you, I'll ask. I just don't want to involve you in what may be a messy business."

She smiled. "Thank you." Both of them knew that he would never ask.

"Chief of Police Donahure. He has a rather special house, Spanish-Moroccan, swimming pool, wet bars everywhere, expensive furniture in aweful taste, no mortgage. Mexican couple. Late-model Lincoln, full payment on delivery. Twenty thousand dollars on bank deposit.

Living high off the hog, you might say, but then Donahure doesn't have a wife to spend all his money for him— understandably, he's a bachelor. An acceptable life-style —he doesn't get paid in pennies. What's not so acceptable is that in seven different banks under seven different names he has just over half a million dollars salted away. He might have some difficulty in accounting for that."

"Nothing that goes on or is said in this house is going to surprise me anymore." Jablonsky nevertheless managed to look surprised. "Proof?"

"Sure he's got proof," Jeff said. As Ryder didn't seem disposed to deny this, he carried on: "I didn't know until this evening. My father has a dossier on him, complete with signed affidavits, which would make very interesting reading in Sacramento."

Jablonsky said: "This true?"

"You don't have to believe it," Ryder said.

"I'm sorry. But why don't you lower the boom on him? Repercussions wouldn't matter a damn to you."

"They wouldn't. But they'd matter to others. Nearly half of our friend's ill-gotten gains come from blackmail. Three prominent citizens of this town, basically as clean and innocent as most of us are, which doesn't say a very great deal, have been badly compromised. They could also be badly hurt. I'll use this document if my hand is forced, of course."

"And what would it take to force your hand?"

"State secrets, Doc." Parker smiled as he said it and rose to his feet.

"So state secrets." Jablonsky rose also, nodded toward the file he'd brought. "Hope that's of some use to you."

"Thank you. Thank you both very much."

Jablonsky and Parker walked together to their cars. Jablonsky said: "You know him better than I do, Sergeant. Ryder really cares about his family? He doesn't seem terribly upset to me."

"He cares. He's just not much for the emotional scene, he'll probably be just as relaxed when he kills the man who took Susan."

88

"He would do that?" Jablonsky seemed unhappy.

"Sure. Wouldn't be the first time. Not in cold blood, of course—he'd have to have a reason. And if he has no reason, he'll just leave a nice challenging case for the plastic surgeon. And either of those two things could happen to anyone who gets in his way when he's trying to get next to Morro or whatever his name is. I'm afraid the kidnapers made a big mistake—they kidnaped the wrong person."

"What do you think he's going to do?"

"Don't know. I'm just guessing when I say I know what I'm going to do, something I never thought I would. I'm going right home and say a prayer for the health of our chief of police."

Jeff nodded toward the file Jablonsky had brought. "How about your homework? I always had to do it first thing when I came home."

"I need uninterrupted thought for that one."

"I suppose he thinks that's a gentle hint. Come on, Marge, take you home. See you when I see you."

"Half an hour."

"Ha!" Jeff looked pleased. "So you're not going to sit there all night and do nothing?"

"No, I'm not going to sit here all night and do nothing."

For some time after they had left it seemed as if he intended to do just that. After some minutes he put his photograph back in the frame, rose and placed it between two others on the upright piano. The one to the left was that of his wife: the other, that of Peggy, his daughter, a sophomore in arts at San Diego. She was a laughing girl with dancing eyes who had inherited her father's coloring in eyes and hair but, fortunately, neither his features nor build, both of which belonged strictly to her mother. It was common knowledge that she was the only person who could wrap the formidable Sergeant Ryder around her little finger, a state of affairs of which Ryder was well aware and by which he appeared completely untroubled. He looked at the little photographs for some seconds, shook his head, sighed, removed his own and placed it in a drawer. He made a call to San Diego, listened for a full half minute and hung up. The next call he made was to Major Dunne of the FBI. After the first ring Ryder suddenly replaced the receiver. Some thought had evidently occurred to make him change his mind. Instead, he poured himself an unaccustomed scotch, picked up the file on Carlton, sat and began to leaf through it, making neat, precise notes as he reached the foot of each page. He had just gone through a second time when Jeff returned. Ryder rose.

"Let's go take a little ride in your car."

"Sure. Where?"

"Anywhere."

"Anywhere? I can manage that," Jeff thought. "Donahure might be more persistent than one would give him credit for?"

"Yes."

They drove off in Jeff's Ford. After half a mile Jeff said: "I don't know how you do it. There was a stake-out. We're being followed."

"Make sure."

Jeff made sure. Another half mile and he said: "I'm sure."

"You know what to do."

Jeff nodded. He turned left at the first intersection, turned right up a poorly lit lane, passed the entrance of a builder's yard and came to a stop opposite a second entrance, turning his lights off. Both men got out and walked unhurriedly into the yard.

The car following drew up about fifty yards behind. A lean man of medium height, his face shadowed by a fedora that had become passé in the thirties, emerged and walked quickly toward the Ford. He had just passed the first entrance when something told him that all was not well. He swung around, reached inside his coat, then lost all interest in what he was doing when a heavy toe cap caught him just below the knee: in any event it is difficult to reach for a gun when hopping around on one leg and clutching the other with both hands.

"Stop that noise," Ryder said. He reached inside the

man's coat, pulled out an automatic, transferred his grip to the barrel and struck the man squarely in the face with the butt. This time the man screamed. Jeff flashed a torch in his face and said in a voice that could have been steadier: "His nose is gone. Some of his top teeth, too."

"So's your mother." The tone of the voice made Jeff flinch and he looked at a man that he'd never seen before. "You rode your luck too far, Raminoff. If I catch you within a mile of my house again you'll be a month in Belvedere." Belvedere was the city hospital. "Then after that I'll go and attend to your boss. Tell him that. Who is your boss, Raminoff?" He lifted the gun. "You have two seconds."

"Donahure." It was a peculiar gurgling sound and one for which Raminoff could hardly be blamed. Blood was pumping steadily from mouth and nose. Ryder watched him for a couple of dispassionate seconds, then turned on his heel.

Back in the Ford, Ryder said: "Stop at the first phone booth." Jeff glanced at him questioningly but Ryder wasn't looking at him.

Ryder spent three minutes in the booth and made two calls. He returned to the car, lit a Gauloise and said: "Drive home."

"We've got a phone there. Tapped?"

"Would you put anything past Donahure? Two things. I've just made a call to John Aaron. Editor of the *Examiner*. No word yet from the kidnapers. He'll let me know as soon as anything comes through. I've also made a call to Major Dunne of the FBI. I'll be seeing him shortly. After you've dropped me off home I want you to come inside, pick up a gun and something that will serve as a mask and go out to Donahure's place and find out whether he's at home or not. Discreetly, of course."

"He's having visitors tonight?"

"Two. You and me. If he's there, call me at this number." He switched on a map light and wrote on a notepad, tearing the page off. "The Redox in Bay Street. Know it?"

"By reputation." Jeff sounded severe. "A singles, full of gays and drug pushers, not to mention addicts. Hardly your scene, I would have thought."

"That's why I'm going there. Must say Dunne didn't sound too happy about it either."

Jeff hesitated. "Going to give Donahure the Raminoff treatment?"

"It's a tempting thought, but no. He'd have nothing to tell us. Anyone smart enough to pull off this raid would be smart enough not to establish any direct contact with a clown like Donahure. He would certainly use an intermediary, maybe even two. I would."

"Then what would you be looking for?"

"I wouldn't know until I have looked."

Ryder was in disguise—he was wearing a freshly pressed business suit which only his family knew he possessed. Dunne, too, was in disguise: he wore a beret, dark glasses and a pencil mustache, none of which suited him and made him, as he was uncomfortably aware, look slightly ridiculous. But the gray eyes were as intelligent and watchful as ever. He looked in distaste at the oddly attired clientele, mainly teen-agers and those in their early twenties, and sniffed the air in nose-wrinkling disgust.

"Place smells like a damn bordello."

"You frequent those places?"

"Only in the line of duty." Dunne smiled. "Okay, so no one would look for us here. Certainly I wouldn't." He broke off as a creature dressed in pink pantaloons deposited two drinks on their booth table and left. Ryder poured both into a convenient potted plant.

"Can't do it any harm. Teaspoonful of blend topped with water." He produced a flask from an inside pocket and poured generous measures. "Scotch. Always prepared. Your health."

"Excellent. And now?"

"Four things. One, our chief of police. For your information only. Donahure and I are not seeing eye to eye."

"You surprise me."

"Probably not half as surprised as Donahure is right now. I've been upsetting him. I've been the cause of his losing a van of his this evening—it fell off a cliff into the Pacific. I've confiscated some of his personal goods and interviewed a tail he set on me."

"The tail in the hospital?"

"He'll need medical care. Right now I'd guess he's reporting to Donahure on the failure of a mission."

"How did you link him to Donahure?"

"He told me."

"Naturally. Well, can't say I'm sorry. But I did warn you—he's dangerous. Rather, his friends are. And you know how cornered rats behave. You have a tie-in between him and San Ruffino?"

"Things point that way. I'll look through his house later on tonight, see what I can find."

"He might be at home."

"What difference does that make? Then I think I'll go have a word with Judge LeWinter."

"You will? He's a different kettle of fish from Donahure. Spoken of as the next chief justice of the state supreme court."

"He's still tarred with the same brush. What do you know of him?"

"We have a file on him." Dunne peered at his glass.

"That means he's poison?"

"I'm being noncommittal."

"Yes. Well, something else for your file. Donahure called tonight with a search warrant on such an obviously trumped-up charge that only a crooked judge would have signed it."

"Any prizes for guessing?"

"No. Number two. I'd appreciate your help in this and the next couple of matters." He drew Carlton's file and the notes he had made on it from a large envelope. "Security deputy. One of the eight snatched this afternoon. His curriculum vitae or whatever you call it. Seems aboveboard."

"All the best villains are."

"Yes. Army, intelligence, two security jobs before coming to San Ruffino. As he's always worked for the Army or the AEC his past should be an open book. However, I'd like an answer to those few questions I've noted, especially his past contacts. The contacts, no matter how unimportant, are the important things."

"You have reason to suspect this man Carlton?"

"I've no reason not to, which is the same thing to me."

"Routine. Number three?"

Ryder produced another paper, Marjory's transcription of Susan's shorthand, and explained how he had come by it. Dunne read through it several times. Ryder said: "You seem to find this interesting?"

"Odd. This bit about not getting feet wet. About once a year since the turn of the century some people in this state have been confidently expecting the second flood. Cranks, of course."

"Cranks and highly organized criminals like this Morro or whoever don't go together?"

"They're not mutually exclusive either."

"Does the FBI have their names?"

"Of course. Thousands of them."

"Forget it. If you were to lock up all the nonconformists in this state you'd have half the population behind bars."

"And maybe the wrong half at that." Dunne was pensive. "You mentioned the word 'organized.' We do have groups of what you might call organized and successful cranks."

"Subversives?"

"Weirdos. But weirdos who have managed to put it together in an acceptable and comprehensive fashion. Acceptable and comprehensive to them, that is."

"Are there many of those so-called organized groups?"

"Haven't seen the list lately. Couple of hundred perhaps."

"Just a handful. No stone unturned, is that it?"

"And no avenue unexplored. I'll get a list. But that's not what you're interested in. This Morro character. Fictitious name, of course. *May* have disfigurement or damage to hands and right eye. That's easy. Number four?"

"Bit more personal, Major." Ryder slid a photograph and piece of paper across the table. "I want this person taken care of."

Dunne looked at the photograph with appreciation. "Lovely young lady. Obviously no relation of yours so what's the connection?"

"Peggy. My daughter."

"Ah!" Dunne was not an easy man to knock off stride. "Mrs. Ryder must be a beautiful person."

"Well, thank you very much." Ryder smiled and was quickly his old impassive self. "She's a sophomore at San Diego. The address is the flat she shares with three other girls. Tried to phone her—that's her number there—but no reply. I'm sure one of your men could find out where she is in no time. I'd like her to know what's happened before she finds out on the radio or TV in some crowded discotheque."

"No problem. But that's not all, is it. You said 'taken care of.'"

"They already have my wife. If Donahure is tied into this—and I'll know within an hour—Morro and his friends might not like me."

"The request is unusual."

"So are the circumstances." Dunne was hesitating. "You have children, Major."

"Damn it, yes. I mean, damn you, yes. How old is your Peggy?"

"Eighteen."

"So's my Jane. Blackmail, Sergeant, downright blackmail. All right. But you know I'm supposed to be cooperating closely with Donahure. Putting me in a difficult position."

"What kind of position do you think I'm in?" He looked up as pink pantaloons approached their table and looked at Ryder.

"You Mr. Green?"

"Yes. How did you know?"

"Caller said a wide man in a dark suit. You're the

only wide man in a dark suit here. Phone's this way."

Ryder followed and picked up the phone. "Well-built, son, not 'wide.' What's new?"

"Raminoff's been and left. Houseboy drove him. Still bleeding. Gone to some unlicensed quack, probably."

"Donahure there?"

"Well I don't think Raminoff spent five minutes talking to the houseboy."

"Meet you at the corner of Fourth and Hawthorne. Ten minutes, maybe fifteen."

Ryder had arrived back at his table but had not yet sat down when pink pantaloons appeared again. "Another call, Mr. Green."

Ryder was back inside a minute. He sat and brought out his flask again.

"Two calls. The tail did, in fact, report back to Donahure. Going out there in a minute." Under Dunne's puzzled gaze Ryder gulped the contents of his refilled glass. "Second call was from John Aaron. You know him?"

"The *Examiner*? I know him."

"AP and Reuters are burning up the wires. Gentleman called them. You'd never guess the name he gave."

"Morro."

"Morro it was. Said he's engineered the San Ruffino break-in, which he was sure they knew nothing about. Gave in specific detail the amount of uranium-235 and plutonium that had been taken and asked any interested party to check with the power station. Also gave names and addresses of hostages and asked all interested parties to contact their relatives to check."

Dunne was calm. "No more than what you expected. Your phone must be ringing constantly at the moment. Any threats?"

"None. Just thought he'd let us know and give us time to consider the implications."

"Aaron say when the news is being released?"

"Be an hour at least. TV and radio stations are jittery as hell. They don't know whether it's a hoax or not and they don't want to appear the biggest fools in the West.
96

Also, even if it were true, they're not sure whether they'd be contravening national security regulations. Personally, I've never heard of any such regulations. They're apparently waiting confirmation and clearance from the AEC. If they get it, there'll be a simultaneous statewide release at eleven."

"I see. Well, it gives me plenty of time to get a man around to your Peggy."

"I'd much appreciate that. In the circumstances, most people would have forgotten all about a mere teen-ager."

"I told you. I have one. She doesn't think she's mere at all. You have your car?" Ryder nodded. "If you drop me off at my place I'll get hold of San Diego and have a couple of men on the job in ten minutes. No sweat." Dunne became thoughtful. "You won't be able to say that about the citizens of this state tomorrow. They'll be sweating buckets. Clever lad, this Morro. Mustn't underestimate him. He's craftily reversed the old maxim of better the devil you know than the devil you don't. Now it's a case of worse the devil you don't know than the devil you do. He'll have everyone in fits."

"Yes. The citizens of San Diego, Los Angeles, San Francisco, Sacramento wondering who's going to be the first for vaporization and each hoping to hell it's going to be one of the other three."

"You seriously think that, Sergeant?"

"I haven't really had time to think about anything. I'm just trying to imagine how other people would think. No, I don't seriously think so. Clever men like our friend Morro have an objective in mind and indiscriminate annihilation wouldn't be any way to achieve that. Threats would be enough."

"That's what I would think. But, then, it will take the public some time to realize—if they ever do—that we're up against a cunning and crafty person."

"And for such a person the mental climate is just right. For him, it couldn't be better." Ryder ticked off his fingers. "We've had the bubonic plague bugaboo. Didn't come to much, granted, but it scared half the people out of their wits. Then the swine flu—you could

97

say exactly the same about that. Now practically everybody in the state, especially those on the coast, has this obsessive and—what's the word—?"

"Paranoid?"

"I didn't get to college. Paranoid. This paranoid fear about when the next, the biggest and perhaps the last earthquake is going to come. And now this. The nuclear holocaust—you know, at least we think we know there isn't going to be any such thing. But try convincing people of that." Ryder laid money on the table. "At least it should take their minds off earthquakes for the time being."

Ryder met Jeff as arranged. They left their cars at the intersection and made their way on foot up Hawthorne Drive, a steep, narrow and winding lane lined with palms.

"The houseboy's back," Jeff said. "He came back alone so I should imagine Raminoff's either having his nose set or is being kept for the night in the emergency room. The houseboy and his wife don't sleep in the house—there's a little bungalow at the front of the garden. They're both inside there, for the night, I guess. Up this bank here."

They scrambled up a grassy bank, pulled themselves over a wall and parted some rose bushes. Donahure's house was built around three sides of an oblong swimming pool, with the center section, a long, low living room, brightly illuminated. The night had turned cool and steam over the pool hung motionless in the still night air, but not so opaque as to prevent the watchers seeing Donahure, glass in hand, pacing heavily up and down. The sliding glass doors were opened wide.

"Go down to the corner there," Ryder said. "Hide in the bushes. I'll get as close as I can to that living room. When I wave my arm, attract his attention."

They took up position, Jeff among the rose bushes, Ryder, on the other side of the pool, in the dark shadow between two yew trees—the Californians, unlike Europeans, do not relegate their yews and cypresses to graveyards. Jeff made a loud moaning sound. Donahure

98

stopped his pacing, listened, went to the opening between the sliding glass doors and listened again. Jeff repeated the sound. Donahure slipped off his shoes and
padded silently across the tiles, a gun in his hand. He had
taken only five steps when the butt of a Smith & Wesson
caught him behind the right ear.

They used a pair of Donahure's own handcuffs to secure him to the standpipe of a radiator, Scotch tape from
his desk to gag him and a table runner to blindfold him.

Ryder said: "The main entrance will be at the back.
Go down to the bungalow and check that the houseboy
and his wife are still there. When you come back, lock it
and if anyone rings, don't answer. Lock every door and
window in the house. Pull the curtains here, then start on
that desk. I'll be in his bedroom. If there's anything to be
found it will be in one of those two rooms."

"Still don't know what we're looking for?"

"No. Something that would make you lift an eyebrow
if you saw it in your house or mine." He looked around
the room. "No sign of a safe—and you can't have secret
wall safes in a wooden house."

"If I had as much on my conscience as you say he has
I wouldn't have anything in the house. I'd have it in a
bank safe-deposit. Well, at least you've got the satisfaction of knowing that he'll have a headache when he
wakes." Jeff thought. "He could have a study or office or
den—lots of these houses do."

Ryder nodded and left. There was no such study. The
first bedroom he came to was plainly unoccupied. The
second bedroom was Donahure's. Ryder used a pencil
flashlight, established that the curtains of both windows
were open, closed them and switched on overhead and
bedside lights.

The immaculate room clearly reflected the efficient
tidiness of the houseboy's wife, a tidiness that made
Ryder's task all that easier. Ryder was painstaking,
methodical, took all of fifteen minutes for his search and
found nothing for there was nothing to find. For all that,
he made an interesting discovery. One wall cupboard was
given over to a positive armory of weapons—revolvers,

automatics, shotguns and rifles with a copious supply of ammunition to match. There was nothing sinister in this, many American gun buffs had their own private armories, frequently setting aside an entire gun room to display them. But two particular weapons caught his attention—peculiarly-shaped lightweight rifles of a type not to be found in any gun store in America. Ryder took them both and a box of matching ammunition, then, for good measure, pocketed three of the splendid collection of handcuffs that Donahure had hanging from hooks on the side. All those items he laid on the bed while he went to examine the bathroom. There was nothing there that shouldn't have been. He picked up his newly acquired possessions from the bed and rejoined Jeff.

Donahure, chin slumped on his chest, appeared to be asleep. With the rifle barrel Ryder prodded him far from gently in the region of his expansive solar plexus. He was asleep. Jeff was sitting by the desk looking down into an opened drawer. Ryder said: "Anything?"

"Yes." Jeff looked pleased with himself. "I'm a slow starter but when I get going—"

"What do you mean, a slow starter?"

"Desk was locked. Took me some time to find the key—it was in the bottom of Fatso's holster." Jeff deposited a bundle of currency notes on the table. They were in eight separate lots, each secured with an elastic band.

"Hundreds of bills, all small denominations, looks like. What's Donahure doing with hundreds of bills?"

"What indeed? Got any gloves?"

"Now he asks me. Do I have any gloves? Masks—hoods, rather—because you told me. Now that I—and I suppose you—have smeared fingerprints all over the shop you ask for gloves."

"Our fingerprints don't matter. You think Donahure is going to report this matter and complain about the disappearance of all this money that we are about to take with us? I just want you to count the stuff and not smear up fingerprints. Old notes are no good, they could carry a hundred smears. Maybe some new notes. Count from the bottom left—most people and most tellers count from the top right."

100

"Where did you get those toys?"

"From Donahure's toy shop." Ryder looked at the two rifles. "Always wanted one of those. Thought you might want one too."

"You've got rifles."

"Not those. I've never seen one. I've seen a diagram."

"What are they?"

"You'll be surprised. Unobtainable in this country. We think we make the best rifles in the world. The British think they do and the Belgians think the same of their own NATO rifles. Well, we don't think, we say. But they all know that this is the best. Light, deadly accurate, can be stripped down in seconds and hidden in the pockets of your topcoat. Splendid weapon for terrorists—as the British soldiers in Northern Ireland have found out to their cost."

"The IRA have those?"

"Yes. It's called the Kalashnikov. If a person's hunting you at night with one of those fitted with infrared telescopic sights you might as well shoot yourself. Or so they say."

"Russian?"

"Yes."

"Catholics and Communists make strange bedfellows."

"The people who use those in Northern Ireland are Protestants. An extremist splinter group officially disowned by the IRA. Not that the Communists care very much who they associate with as long as they can stir up trouble."

Jeff took one of the rifles, examined it, looked at the unconscious Donahure and then at Ryder.

Ryder said: "Don't ask me. All I know about our friend's early background is that he's a first-generation American."

"From Northern Ireland?"

"From Northern Ireland. Fits in neatly. Probably fits in too neatly."

"Donahure—a Communist?"

"We mustn't look for a Red under every bush. No law against it—well, not since McCarthy departed this scene. I don't think so, anyway. He's too stupid and too selfish

101

to be interested in any ideology. That's not to say, of course, that he wouldn't accept their money. Count those notes and then check the rest of the desk. I'll go over the rest of the room."

Ryder looked while Jeff counted. After some minutes Jeff looked up, his face alight. "Boy, this is interesting. Eight packets of notes, each containing one thousand two hundred and fifty dollars. Ten thousand."

"So I was wrong. He's now got an eighth unofficial bank account. Very interesting I agree. But nothing to get excited about."

"No? There are several new notes in each packet. I've only made a quick check but as far as I can see they're in series. *And* they're the bicentennial two-dollar notes."

"Ah, this *is* interesting. The one the ungrateful American public turned their thumbs down on. The Treasury had carloads of the stuff printed but there's only a small percentage of it in circulation. If they really are in series, the FBI should be able to trace it without trouble."

Nothing more came to light and they left five minutes later after freeing a now stirring Donahure of his handcuffs, Scotch tape and blindfold.

Major Dunne was still in his office, handling two phones at the same time. When he'd hung up, Ryder said: "Not yet abed?"

"No. And I don't expect to be—not this night, anyway. I'll have plenty of company in my misery. Statewide alert, twenty-four-hour basis, for every agent who could walk. Description of Morro has been telexed, or is being telexed, throughout the country. I've arranged for this list of the organized weirdos but I won't have that until tomorrow. Your Peggy has been taken care of."

Jeff said to Ryder: "*Our* Peggy?"

"Forgot to tell you. The kidnapers have made a statement to AP and Reuters. No threats, just detailing what materials they've stolen and the names of the people they kidnaped. It will be released at eleven tonight." He looked at his watch. "Half an hour. I didn't want your
102

sister to have the shock of hearing of the kidnaping of her mother over the TV or radio. Major Dunne has kindly taken care of that."

Jeff looked from one man to another, then said: "It's just a thought. But has it occurred to you that Peggy might just possibly be in danger?"

"It is a thought and it has occurred." Dunne could be very precise and clipped in his speech. "It has also been taken care of." He peered at the rifles in Ryder's hand. "Late hour to go shopping."

"We borrowed them from your friend Donahure."

"Ah! How is he?"

"Unconscious. Not that there's much difference between that and his walking state. He knocked his head against the butt of an automatic."

Dunne brightened. "Disgraceful. You had reason for taking those? Something special?"

"I'm pretty sure. These are Kalashnikovs. Russian. Can you check with Washington, import controls, to see if any licenses have been issued to bring those in? I very much doubt it. The Russians just love to unload their arms on anyone with the cash to pay, but it's a fair guess they wouldn't part with the most advanced rifle in the business, which this is."

"Illegal possession? That would make him an ex-chief of police."

"Unimportant. He'll be that soon anyway."

"Communist?"

"Unlikely. Of course, he's capable of being an empty convert to anything if the money's good enough."

"I'd like to have those, if I may."

"Sorry. Finders keepers. You want to admit in court that you abetted breaking and entering? Don't be upset. Jeff's got a little present for you." Jeff placed the wad of bank notes on the table. "Ten thousand dollars exactly. All yours. How many consecutively listed brand-new two-dollar notes are there, Jeff?"

"Forty."

"Manna," Dunne said reverently. "I'll have the names of the bank, teller and drawer by noon tomorrow. Pity you weren't able to find out the name of the drawer."

"I told you. Donahure was asleep. I'll go back and ask him later on."

"Like that? May be pushing your luck, Sergeant."

"No. I've had the great misfortune to know Chief Donahure longer than you have. He's a bully—I know it's commonplace to say that all bullies are cowards, which is not at all true—but in his case it is. Take his face. A disaster, but the only one he has and he probably cherishes it. He saw what happened to his stake-out's face tonight."

"Mm." Dunne's momentarily beatific expression had been replaced by a frown and it wasn't because of anything that Ryder had said. He tapped the bundle of notes. "This. How am I to account for this, to explain it away? I mean, where did it come from?"

"Yes." It was Jeff's turn to frown. "I didn't think of that either."

"Easy. Donahure gave it to you."

"He what?"

"Despite the fact that he has about half a million in ill-gotten gains salted away under seven or eight forged names, we all know that he's basically a decent, upright, honorable man, deeply committed to the welfare of his fellow man, to upholding the rule of justice and ruthlessly crushing bribery and corruption wherever it raises its ugly head. He was approached by the syndicate responsible for the San Ruffino break-in and given this money in return for a blow-by-blow account of the steps being taken by the state and federal authorities in investigating this case. You and he worked out a plan to feed false and misleading information to the crooks. Naturally, he handed you this tainted money for safekeeping. You have to admire the man's unshakable integrity."

"Ingenious, but you've overlooked the obvious. All Donahure has to do is to deny it."

"With his fingerprints all over those notes—especially those new ones? He's either got to go with the story or admit that he had the notes cached away in the house, which would leave him the rather awkward task of ex-
104

plaining where he got them from. Which option do you think he'll elect?"

Dunne said admiringly, "You have a very devious mind."

"Set a thief to catch a thief?" Ryder smiled. "Maybe. Two things, Major. When you or whoever handle those notes don't touch the top right. Fingerprints, especially on the two-dollar bills."

Dunne looked at the notes. He said: "I'd estimate there's about two thousand bills there. You expect me to try them *all* for fingerprints?"

"I said you or whoever."

"Well, thanks. And the second thing?"

"Have you got a fingerprint set here?"

"Lots. Why?"

"Oh, I don't know." Ryder was vague. "You never know when those things come in handy."

Judge LeWinter lived in a rather splendidly impressive house as befitted one who was widely touted to become the next chief justice of the state supreme court. Within a few miles of the California coast is to be found a greater variety of home architecture than anywhere, but, even by such standards, LeWinter's home was unusual, a faithful replica of an Alabama antebellum house, gleaming white, with its two-story colonnaded porch, balconies, a profusion of surrounding magnolias and a plethora of white oak and long-bearded Spanish moss, neither of which seemed to find the climate very congenial. Within so imposing a residence—one couldn't call it a home—could only dwell, one would have thought, a pillar of legal rectitude. One could be wrong.

How wrong Ryder and his son found out when they opened the bedroom door without the courtesy of a prior knock and found the legal luminary in bed, but not alone—nor was he "not alone" with his wife either. The judge, bronzed, white-haired and white-mustached, the absence of a white winged collar and black string tie an almost jarring note, looked perfectly at home in the gilded Victorian iron bedstead, which was more than could be said for his companion, a sadly overpainted and sadly youthful demimondaine who looked as if she would have been much more at home in what could delicately be termed as the outermost fringes of society. Both wore startled and wide-eyed expressions as people tend to wear when confronted with two hooded men bearing guns, the girl's expression shading gradually into a guilty fear, the judge's, predictably, into outrage. His speech was equally predictable.

"What the devil! Who the devil are you?"

"We're no friends, you can be sure of that," Ryder said. "We know who you are. Who's the young lady?" He didn't bother to wait for the inevitable silence but turned to Jeff. "Bring your camera, Perkins?"

"Sorry."

"Pity." He looked at LeWinter. "I'm sure you would have loved us to send a snapshot to your wife to show that you're not pining too much in her absence." The judge's outrage subsided. "Right, Perkins, the prints."

Jeff was no expert but he was not long enough out of police school to have forgotten how to make clean prints. A deflated LeWinter, who clearly found the situation beyond him, offered neither objection nor resistance. When Jeff had finished he glanced at the girl and then at Ryder, who hesitated and nodded. Ryder said to her: "Nobody's going to hurt you, miss. What's your name?"

She compressed her lips and looked away. Ryder sighed, picked up a purse which could only be hers, opened it and emptied the contents on a dressing table. He riffled through those, picked up an envelope and said: "Bettina Ivanhoe, 888 South Maple." He looked at the girl, frightened, flaxen-haired, with high and rather wide Slavonic cheekbones: but for her efforts to improve on nature she would have been strikingly good-looking. "Ivanhoe? Ivanov would be nearer it. Russian?"

"No. I was born here."

"I'll bet your parents weren't." She made no reply to this. He looked through the scattered contents of the
106

purse and picked up two photographs, one each of the girl and LeWinter. That made her more than a one-time visitor. There had to be a forty-year gap in their ages. "Darby and Joan," Ryder said. The contempt in his voice was matched by his gesture of flicking the cards to the floor.

"Blackmail?" LeWinter tried to inject some contempt of his own but he wasn't up to it. "Extortion, eh?"

Ryder said indifferently: "I'd blackmail you to death if you were what I think you might be. In fact, I'd put you to death without any blackmail." The words hung chillingly in the air. "I'm after something else. Where's your safe and where's the key to it?"

LeWinter sneered, but there was—it could have been imagined—a hint of relief behind the sneer. "A petty heistman."

"Unbecoming language from the bench." Ryder produced and opened a penknife, then approached the girl. "Well, LeWinter?"

LeWinter folded his arms and looked resolute.

"The flower of southern chivalry." Ryder tossed the knife to Jeff, who placed the tip against LeWinter's second chin and pressed.

"It's red," Jeff said. "Just the same as the rest of us. Should I have sterilized this?"

"Down and to the right," Ryder said. "That's where the external jugular is."

Jeff removed the knife and examined it. The blade was narrow and only the top half inch had blood on it. To LeWinter, who had stopped looking resolute, it must have seemed that the arterial floodgates had burst. His voice was husky. "The safe's in my study downstairs. The key's in the bathroom."

Ryder said: "Where?"

"In a jar of shaving soap."

"Odd place for an honest man to keep a key. The contents of this safe should be interesting." He went into the bathroom and returned in a few seconds, key in hand. "Any servants on the premises?"

107

"No."

"Probably not. Think of the stirring tales they could tell your wife. Believe him, Perkins?"

"On principle, no."

"Me neither." Ryder produced three sets of handcuffs, all, until very recently, the property of the police chief. One set secured the girl's right wrist to a bedpost, the second LeWinter's left to the other bedpost, the third, passing behind a central headrail, secured their other two wrists together. For gags they used a couple of pillow slips. Before securing LeWinter's gag, Ryder said: "A hypocrite like you, who makes all those stirring speeches against the Washington gun lobby, is bound to have some lying around. Where are they?"

"Study."

Jeff began a meticulous search of the room. Ryder went below, located the study, located the gun cupboard and opened it. No Kalashnikovs. But one particular handgun, of a make unknown to him, took his attention. He wrapped it in a handkerchief and dropped it into one of his capacious coat pockets.

The safe was massive, six feet by three, weighing well over a quarter of a ton and built at some time in the remote past before safebreakers had developed the highly sophisticated techniques of today. The locking mechanism and key were woefully inadequate. Had the safe been freestanding Ryder would have opened it without hesitation. But it was set into a brick wall for a depth of several inches, a most unusual feature for that type of safe. Ryder returned upstairs, removed LeWinter's gag and produced his knife.

"Where's the cutoff switch for the safe?"

"What damned switch?"

"You were too quick in telling me where the key was. You wanted me to open that safe." For the second time that night LeWinter winced, more in apprehension than pain, as the knife tip punctured the skin of his neck. "The switch that cuts the alarm relay to the local sheriff's office."

LeWinter was more obdurate this time, but not
108

markedly so. Ryder returned downstairs and slid back a panel above the study door to expose a simple switch. Half of the safe was designed as a filing cabinet; the files, in the customary fashion, were suspended by metal lugs from parallel rails. Nearly all of those were given over to personal notes on court cases that had come before him. Two files were marked "Private Correspondence" but apparently weren't all that private, as some of them had been signed on his behalf by his secretary, a (Miss) B. Ivanhoe: clearly the young lady upstairs carried secretarial devotion to her boss to lengths above and beyond the call of duty. In the shelves above, only three things caught his attention and were removed. One was a list of names and telephone numbers. The second was a leather-bound copy of Sir Walter Scott's *Ivanhoe*. The third was a green and also leather-bound notebook.

As notebooks go, it was large—about eight inches by five—and secured by a locked brass clasp, a sufficient deterrent against the young or merely curious but of no avail against the ill-intentioned armed with a knife. Ryder sliced open the spine and riffled through the exposed pages, which told him nothing inasmuch as they were covered with neatly typed figures, not letters. He wasted no time on the notebook. He knew nothing of cryptography, which didn't worry him: the FBI had its own highly specialized department of code breakers who could decipher anything except the most highly sophisticated military codes and even that they could do if given enough time. Time. Ryder looked at his watch. It was one minute to eleven.

He found Jeff methodically going through the pockets of LeWinter's very considerable number of custom-made suits. LeWinter and the girl were still resting comfortably. Ryder ignored them and switched on a TV set. He didn't bother to select any particular station: the same program would be on every station. Ryder didn't bother to look at the screen. He didn't appear to be watching anything at all but, in fact, he didn't allow the couple on the bed to move out of peripheral vision.

The announcer, who might just coincidentally have

been dressed in a dark suit and tie, used his state funeral voice. He confined himself to the facts. The San Ruffino nuclear power reactor station had been broken into that late afternoon and the criminals had made good their escape, taking with them weapons-grade material and hostages. The precise amount of material taken was specified as were the names, addresses and occupations of the hostages. Neither the person giving this information nor the source from which it had come had been identified but the genuineness of the information was beyond dispute as it had been confirmed in detail by the authorities. The same authorities were carrying out an intensive investigation. The usual meaningless poppycock, Ryder thought; they had no leads to investigate. He switched off the set and looked at Jeff.

"Notice anything, Perkins?"

"The same thing you were noticing. What you can see of Casanova's face here didn't show much change in expression. Didn't show anything, in fact. Guilty as hell, I'd say."

"Good as a signed confession. That news was no news to him." He looked at LeWinter and appeared momentarily lost in thought before saying: "I've got it. Your rescuers, I mean. I'll send along a reporter and a photographer from the *Globe*."

"Isn't that interesting," Jeff said. "I do believe Don Juan has registered a slight change in expression."

LeWinter had, in fact, registered a marked change in expression. The bronzed skin had assumed a grayish hue and the suddenly protuberant eyes seemed bent on parting company with their sockets. One could enjoy the *Globe* without being able to read too well. It specialized in artistic portraits of unclad feminine illiterates who spent their evenings reading Sophocles in the original, in candid shots of newsworthys caught in apparently compromising or undignified situations and, for the intelligentsia among their readers, extensive muckraking couched in terms of holy crusades against shocked morality and, perforce, in the very simplest of prose: such was the intolerable pressure brought to bear through the demands imposed by the
110

clamorous urgency, the evangelistic immediacy and the socially important content of those journalist imperatives that the overworked editorial staff were frequently and reluctantly compelled to encapsulate, hold over or, most commonly, altogether forget, such trivia as the international news or, indeed, any but the most salaciously elevating items of the local news. One did not require telepathic aid to guess that the judge's mind was touching on such matters in general and, in particular, on page one, where the unretouched and considerably enlarged picture of himself and his handcuffed amorita would leave room only for the appalled caption.

Downstairs in the study Ryder said: "Glance through those court cases in the files. You may find something of interest, although I doubt it. I have a call to make." He dialed a number and, while waiting for his call to come through, glanced at the list of names and telephone numbers he had taken from the safe. His number answered and he asked for Mr. Jamieson. Jamieson was the night manager at the telephone exchange. He was on the line almost at once.

"Sergeant Ryder here. Important and confidential, Mr. Jamieson." Jamieson had delusions about his self-importance and liked to have those kept well stoked. "I have a number here and would be glad if you made a note of it." He gave the number, had it read back to him and said: "I think it's Sheriff Hartman's home number. Would you check and give me the address—it's not in the book."

"Important, huh?" Jamieson sounded eager. "Hush-hush?"

"You don't know how important. Heard the news?"

"San Ruffino? My God, yes. Just now. Bad, eh?"

"You better believe it." He waited patiently until Jamieson came back to him. "Well?"

"You got the right name, right number. Classified, God knows why—118 Rowena."

Ryder thanked him and hung up. Jeff said: "Who's Hartman?"

"Local sheriff. That safe is wired to his office. Missed something up there, didn't you?"

"I know."

"How?"

"If I hadn't missed it, you wouldn't mention it."

"You noticed how readily LeWinter parted with the key to that safe. What does that tell you about Sheriff Hartman?"

"Nothing much. Correction, nothing good."

"Yes. LeWinter would willingly be found in such a scandalous and compromising situation by very, very few people. But he knows that Sheriff Hartman wouldn't talk. So there's a bond between them."

"LeWinter *could* have a friend in this world."

"We're talking about the probabilities, not the near impossible. Blackmail? Unlikely. If the judge were blackmailing Hartman this would be a once in a lifetime chance for the sheriff to make sure that the blackmail ended here and now. LeWinter could be the victim but I can't see it that way. What I do see is that they are in some very profitable business together. Criminal business. An honest judge would never compromise himself by going into business with a lawman. Anyway, I know LeWinter is bent. I know nothing about this Hartman but he's probably the same."

"As honest—if unemployed—cops it's our duty to find out what Hartman's bent about. In what now appears to be the usual fashion?" Ryder nodded. "Donahure can wait?"

"He'll keep. Turned up anything?"

"Hell, no. All these 'whereases' and 'whereofs' and 'hereintofores' are too much for me."

"You can forget it. Even LeWinter wouldn't express his deepest thoughts—or criminal intentions—in legalese." Ryder again dialed a number, waited, then said: "Mr. Aaron? Sergeant Ryder here. Now, don't get me wrong but how would you like one of your photographers to take a picture of a prominent citizen caught in a compromising situation?"

Aaron's tone was uncomprehending. Not cold, just not

understanding. "I am surprised, Sergeant. You know the *Examiner* is not a yellow tabloid."

"Pity. I thought you were and would be interested in Judge LeWinter's peccadilloes."

"Ah!" LeWinter ranked with Chief Donahure at the top of the list of Aaron's targets for critical editorials. "What's that crooked old goat up to now?"

"He's not up to anything. He's lying down. He's with his secretary, who is young enough to be his grand-daughter. When I say 'with' I mean 'with.' He's hand-cuffed to her and they're both handcuffed to the bed."

"Good God!" Aaron made a coughing sound, probably trying to stifle laughter. "That intrigues me vastly, Sergeant. But I'm still afraid we couldn't publish—"

"No one asked you to publish anything. Just take a photograph."

"I see." There was a brief silence. "All you want is for him to know that such a picture has been taken?"

"That's it. I'd be glad if your boys would maintain the fiction I've told him—that I was sending people from the *Globe.*"

This time Aaron positively cackled. "That would make him happy."

"He's having fits. Many thanks. I'm leaving the hand-cuff keys on the study table."

Dunne, as he'd promised, was still in his office when they returned. Ryder said: "Progress?"

"None—almost impossible to make an outgoing call. Switchboard's been jammed since the news announce-ment. At least a hundred people have seen the crimi-nals—in, as usual, a hundred different places. You?"

"Don't know. You'll have to help us if you will. First off here's Judge LeWinter's fingerprints."

Dunne looked at him in disbelief. "He *gave* you his fingerprints?"

"Sort of."

"I warned you, Ryder. Tangle with that old bird and you step out of your class. Donahure has powerful friends locally but LeWinter has them where it counts—in Sac-ramento. Don't tell me you used violence again."

"Certainly not. We left him peacefully in bed and unharmed."

"Did he recognize you?"

"No. We wore hoods."

"Well, thank you very much. As if I haven't got enough on my hands. Do you know what kind of hornet's nest you'll have stirred up? And where will it all end up? In my lap." He closed his eyes. "I know who'll be the next caller on those damned phones."

"Not LeWinter. He's a bit restricted right now. Matter of fact we left him handcuffed to a bedpost and his secretary. They were there when we arrived. She's Russian."

Dunne closed his eyes again. When he'd assimilated this and steeled himself for whatever was to come, he said carefully: "And?"

"This is interesting." Ryder unwrapped the handgun he had taken. "I wonder what an upright judge is doing with a silenced automatic. Can you have it tested for fingerprints? Incidentally, the girl's fingerprints are already there. This is a notebook, coded. I imagine the key is in this copy of *Ivanhoe*. Perhaps the FBI can find out. Finally, this is his private list of telephone numbers. Some may or may not be significant and I've neither the time nor the facilities to find out."

Dunne was heavily sarcastic. "Anything else you'd like me to do for you?"

"Yes. A copy of the file you have on LeWinter."

Dunne shook his head. "FBI personnel only."

"Would you listen to him," Jeff said. "After all the legwork we do for him, after all the valuable clues we put in his hands—"

"Okay, okay. But I'm promising nothing. Where to now?"

"To see another lawman."

"He has my advance sympathies. Do I know him?"

"No. And I don't. Hartman. Must be new. Anyway, he's in Redbank. County division."

"What has this unfortunate done to incur your displeasure?"

114

"He's a pal of LeWinter's."

"That, of course, explains everything."

Hartman lived in a small and unpretentious bungalow on the outskirts of town. For a California house it was virtually a slum: it had no swimming pool. Ryder said: "His association with LeWinter must be pretty recent."

"Yes. He lets the side down, doesn't he? Door's open. Do we knock?"

"Hell, no."

They found Hartman seated at his desk in a small study. He was a large, heavily built man and must have stood several inches over six feet when he stood up: but Sheriff Hartman would never stand up again. Somebody had carefully cross-filed a soft-nosed bullet, which had entered by the left cheekbone: the dum-dum effect had taken off the back of his head.

It was pointless to search the house: whoever had been there before them would have made certain that nothing incriminating a third party—or parties—had been left behind.

They took the dead man's fingerprints and left.

FIVE

■ THAT was the night the earth shook. Not all of the earth, of course, but for a goodly portion of the residents of Southern California it might have been just that. The shock came at twenty-five minutes past midnight and the tremors were felt as far north as Merced in the San Joaquin Valley, as far south as Oceanside, between Los Angeles and San Diego, as far west as San Luis Obispo, close by the Pacific, to the southeast clear across the Mojave Desert and to the east as far as Death Valley. In Los Angeles, though no structural damage was done, the shake was felt by all who were awake and it was pronounced enough to wake many of those who were sleeping. In the other main centers of population—Oakland–San Francisco, Sacramento and San Diego—no tremors were felt but the earthquake, a very minor one at 4.2 on the Richter scale, was duly recorded on the delicate seismographs.

Ryder and Jeff, seated in the former's living room, both felt it and saw it—a ceiling lamp, traveling through an arc of not more than two inches at maximum, oscillated for about twenty seconds before coming to rest. Dunne, still in his office, felt it and paid no attention to it—he had been through many such tremors before and he had more important things on his mind. LeWinter, dressed now, as was his secretary, felt it through the open door of his safe, the remaining contents of which he was examining with some anxiety. Even Donahure, despite an aching occiput and a mind somewhat beclouded by his fourth consecutive large scotch, was dimly aware of it. And, although its foundations were firmly imbedded on the very solid rock of the Sierra Nevada, the Adlerheim felt it most acutely of all, for the excellent reason that the epicenter of the earthquake was no more

116

than a dozen miles distant: even more importantly, the quake registered strongly in the seismographical office installed in one of the caves—wine cellars—which Von Streicher had excavated out of the rock and on two other seismographs which Morro had foresightedly had installed in two private residences he owned, each about fifteen miles distant and in diametrically different directions.

And the shocks were registered, too, in institutes which, one would have thought, had considerably more legitimate interest in such matters than Morro. Those were the offices of the Seismology Field Survey, those of the California Department of Water Resources, in the California Institute of Technology and the U. S. Geological Survey's National Center for Earthquake Research. The last two, and probably most important of the four, were conveniently located where they would be the first to be demolished should a massive earthquake affect either Los Angeles or San Francisco, for the Institute of Technology was located in Pasadena and the Earthquake Research Center in Menlo Park. The nerve centers of all four institutes were in direct and permanent contact with each other and it had taken them only minutes to pin-point, with complete precision, the exact epicenter of the earthquake.

Alec Benson was a large calm man in his early sixties. Except on ceremonial occasions, which he avoided wherever and whenever possible, he invariably wore a gray flannel suit and a gray polo jersey, which went well enough with the gray hair that topped the tubby, placid and usually smiling face. Director of the seismology department, he held two professorships and so many doctorates and scientific degrees that, for simplicity's sake, his numerous scientific colleagues referred to him just as "Alec." In Pasadena, at least, he was regarded as the world's leading seismologist: while the Russians and Chinese may have disputed this it was noteworthy that those two countries were always among the first to nominate him as chairman of the not infrequent international seismological conferences. This esteem stemmed primarily from the fact

117

that Benson never made any distinction between himself and his world-wide colleagues and sought advice as frequently as he gave it.

His chief assistant was Professor Hardwick, a quiet, retiring, almost self-effacing scientist with a track record that almost matched Benson's. Hardwick said: "Well, about a third of the people in the state must have felt the shock. It's already been on TV and radio and will be in all the late editions of the morning's papers. At the least, there must be a couple of million amateur seismologists in California. What do we tell them? The truth?"

For once, Alec Benson wasn't smiling. He looked thoughtfully around the half-dozen scientists in the room, the vastly experienced nucleus of his research team, and studied their expressions, which were neither helpful nor unhelpful: clearly, they were all waiting for him to give a lead. Benson sighed. He said: "No one admires George Washington more than I do—but, no, we don't tell them the truth. A little white lie and it won't even rest uneasily on my conscience. What's to be gained if we tell the truth, other than scaring our fellow Californians even further out of their wits than they are now? If anything major is going to happen then it's just going to happen and there's nothing we can do about it. In any event, we have no evidence that this is a prelude to a major shake."

Hardwick looked doubtful. "No intimation, no warning, nothing?"

"What point would it serve?"

"Well, there's never been a quake in that spot in recorded history."

"No matter. Even a major quake there wouldn't be of great importance. Devastation of property and loss of life would be insignificant, because the area is so sparsely populated. Owens Valley, 1872, the largest recorded earthquake in California's history—how many people died there? Maybe sixty. The Arvin-Tehachapi quake of 1952, at 7.7 the largest in Southern California—how many died there? Perhaps a dozen." Benson permitted himself his customary smile. "Now, if this latest jolt had
118

happened along the Inglewood–Newport fault, I'd take a different view entirely." The Inglewood–Newport fault, which had been responsible for the Long Beach earthquake of 1933, actually ran under the city of Los Angeles itself. "As it is, I'm in favor of letting sleeping dogs lie."

Hardwick nodded. Reluctantly, but he nodded. "So we blame it on the poor old blameless White Wolf fault?"

"Yes. A calmly reassuring release to the media. Tell them again, briefly, about our EPSP, that we are cautiously pleased that it seems to be going according to plan and that the intensity of this shake corresponds pretty closely to our expected estimate of fault slippage."

"Release to the TV and radio stations?"

"No. General. Wire service. We don't want to lend anything that smacks of undue urgency or importance to our—ah—findings."

Preston, another senior assistant, said: "We don't let ethics creep into this, huh?"

Benson was quite cheerful. "Scientifically indefensible. But from the humanitarian point of view—well, call it justifiable."

It said much for the immense weight of Benson's prestige that the consensus was heavily on his side.

In the refectory hall in the Adlerheim, Morro was being equally cheerful and reassuring to the anxious hostages who had gathered there. "I can assure you, ladies and gentlemen, that there is no cause for alarm. I grant you, it was quite a nasty shake, the worst we have experienced here, but a shake of a thousand times that magnitude would leave us completely unharmed. Apart from the fact that you may probably have already learned from your TVs that there has been no damage throughout the state, you must all be intelligent enough and widely read enough to know that earthquakes spell danger only for those who live in dwellings on made-up filled land, marshy land whether drained or not and on alluvial soil. Damage rarely occurs to dwellings that have their foundations on rock—and we have our foundations on thousands of feet of rock. The Sierra Nevada has been here for millions of years—it is not likely to disappear overnight. It is unlikely that you could find any safer or more desirable—from the earthquake point of view—residence in the state of California." Morro glanced smilingly around his audience, nodding his approval when he saw that his words seemed to have had the desired calming effect. "I don't know about you people, but I have no intention of allowing this passing trifle to interfere with my night's sleep. I bid you all good night."

When Morro entered his private office the smile was markedly absent. Abraham Dubois was seated behind his, Morro's, desk, a phone in one hand, a pencil in the other, his huge shoulders hunched over a large-scale map of California. Morro said: "Well?"

"It is not well." Dubois replaced the phone and delicately pricked a pencil dot on the map. "Here. Exactly here." He used a rule, then set it against a mileage scale. "The epicenter, to be precise, is exactly eleven and a half miles from the Adlerheim. This is not so good, Mr. Morro."

"It's not so good." Morro lowered himself into an armchair. "Does it not strike you as rather ironic, Abraham, that we should pick the one spot in the state where an earthquake takes place outside our back door, so to speak?"

"Indeed. It could be an ill omen. I wish I could fault the triangulation, but I can't. It's been checked and rechecked." Dubois smiled. "At least we didn't pick an extinct volcano that has suddenly turned out not to be so extinct after all. What option do we have? There is no time, there is no alternative. This is our operating base. This is our perfectly secure cover. This is our weaponry. This is the only multiband radio transmitting station we have. All our eggs are in one basket but if we pick up that basket and try to walk away with it the chances are that we will fall and be left with only the ruined ingredients for an omelet."

"I'll go sleep on it, although I don't think I'll wake up feeling any differently from the way you do now." Morro pushed himself heavily to his feet. "We mustn't let what
120

could be only a once in a lifetime coincidence affect our thinking and planning too much. Who knows, there may not be another quake centered in this area for a hundred years. After all, there hasn't been one for hundreds, not at least that we know of or that has been recorded. Sleep well."

But Dubois did not sleep well for the excellent reason that he did not go to bed. Morro did sleep, but it was for only an hour or so. He awoke to find his light on and Dubois shaking his shoulder.

"My apologies." Dubois looked rather more cheerful than when last he had been seen. "But I've just made a videotape of a TV newscast and I think you ought to see it as soon as possible."

"The earthquake, I take it?" Dubois nodded. "Good or bad?"

"One could not call it bad. I think you might well turn it to your advantage."

The replay of the videotape lasted no more than five minutes. The newscaster, a bright and knowledgeable youngster who clearly knew enough about what he was talking about not to have recourse to a teleprompter, was remarkably brisk and fresh for one who was up and around at the unchristian hour of 3 A.M. He had a large relief map of California hanging on the wall behind him and wielded a slender cane with all the fluent dexterity of a budding Toscanini.

He began by giving concise details of what was known of the earthquake, the area over which it had been felt, the degree of apprehension felt in various areas and the amount of damage which it had caused, which was zero. Ht then went on to say: "From the latest authoritative statement, it would appear that this earthquake is to be regarded as a plus and not a minus, as a matter for some self-congratulation and not as a pointer toward some further calamity. In short, according to the state's top seismological sources, this may well be the first earthquake ever knowingly and deliberately brought about by man.

"If this is correct, then it must be regarded as a

121

landmark in earthquake control, the first success of the implementation of the EPSP. For Californians, this can only be good news. To remind you: EPSP stands for Earthquake Preventative Slip Program, which must be one of the clumsiest and most misleading titles thought up by the scientific fraternity in recent years. By 'slip' is meant simply the rubbing, sliding, jarring, earthquake-producing process which occurs when one of the eight, maybe ten, no one seems very sure, of the earth's tectonic plates, on which the continents float, push into, above, under or alongside each other. The title is misleading because it gives the impression that earthquakes may be brought under control by preventing this slip from taking place. In fact, it means precisely the opposite—the prevention of earthquakes, or at least major earthquakes, by permitting, indeed encouraging, this slipping factor to take place—but to take place in a gradual and controlled process in which there is a continuing and progressive easing of the strain between the plates by allowing them to slide comparatively smoothly past one another producing a series of minor and harmless quakes at frequent intervals instead of massive ones at long intervals. The secret, not surprisingly, is lubrication.

"It was purely a chance discovery that led to this possibility—which would now appear a strong possibility —of modifying earthquakes by increasing their frequency. Somebody, for reasons best known to themselves, injected waste water into a particularly deep well near Denver and discovered, to their surprise, that this triggered off a series of earthquakes, tiny, but unquestionably earthquakes. Since then there have been many experiments, both in the laboratory and under actual field conditions, that have clearly demonstrated that frictional resistance in a fault zone is lessened by decreasing the stress along the fault.

"In other words, increasing the amount of fluid in the fault lessens the resistance in the fault while withdrawing the fluid increases the resistance—if an existing stress is present between the faces of two tectonic plates it can be

122

eased by injecting fluid and causing a small earthquake, the size of which can be fairly accurately controlled by the amount of fluid injected. This was proved some years ago when Geological Survey scientists, experimenting in the Rangeley oil fields in Colorado, found that by alternately forcing in and then withdrawing fluids they could turn earthquakes off and on at will.

"To what may be to their eternal credit, seismologists in our state were the first to put these theories to practical use." The newscaster, who seemed to relish his role as lecturer, was now tapping the map on the wall. "From here to here"—he indicated a line that stretched from the Mexican border to the San Francisco Bay area— "massive drills, specifically designed for this task, have bored holes to an incredible depth of up to forty thousand feet in ten selected areas along this roughly southeast–northwest line. All of those boreholes are in known earthquake faults and all in areas where some of the most severe of recorded earthquakes have taken place."

Starting from the south, he tapped out a number of spots on the map. "Ten boreholes in all. The scientists are experimenting with various mixtures of water and oil for lubricating purposes. Well, not quite mixtures, for oil and water don't readily mix. First oil, then stuff they call mud, the whole pushed farther down and through cracks in the rocks by water under high pressure."

He stopped, looked at the camera for a dramatic five seconds, turned, placed the tip of the cane against a spot at the southern tip of the San Joaquin Valley, then, holding the cane in position, turned to face the camera again.

"And here—if I may coin a phrase—we seem to have struck oil at 1:25 A.M. today. Twenty, thirty miles southeast of Bakersfield. Exactly where a massive earthquake struck a quarter of a century ago. And exactly where the sixth borehole from the south is located. Ladies and gentlemen, I give you the villain of the piece—the White Wolf fault." The newscaster relaxed and smiled boyishly.

123

"And now, folks, you know as much about it as I do, which I'm afraid isn't very much. But have no fear—I'm sure the real seismological experts will be busy lecturing you on this for days to come."

Wordlessly, Dubois and Morro rose from their seats, looked at each other, then went to the map still spread on Morro's table. Morro said: "You are quite certain that the triangulation is correct?"

"Our three seismologists will swear to it."

"And our three bright boys place the epicenter in the Garlock fault not the White Wolf fault?"

"They should know. Not only are they highly experienced but we're practically sitting on top of the Garlock fault."

"The Seismology Field Survey, Cal Tech, the Geological Survey and God knows how many other scientific bodies—how could they all possibly—especially when they were all certainly working in collaboration—come up with the same mistake?"

"They didn't." Dubois was positive. "For earthquakes, this is the best monitored area in the world and those are among the world's top experts."

"They lied?"

"Yes."

"Why should they lie?"

Dubois was almost apologetic. "I've had a little time to think about this. I think there are two reasons. California is today obsessed with the fear, the almost certainty, that someday, maybe quite soon according to a few eminent earthquake researchers, the big one is going to strike, one that will make the San Francisco 1906 look like a firecracker; it's more than possible that state officials are trying to allay this fear by stating that this quake was man-made. Secondly, all those clever seismologists may be living with a brand-new fear which particularly affects themselves—that they may have been dabbling in murky waters, that they may not really have known what they were doing, that by messing around with those various faults they may have inadvertently
124

triggered off something they didn't expect—a movement in the Garlock fault where they *don't* have a borehole. But they do have a drilling rig sitting fair and square in the middle of the Tejon Pass on the San Andreas fault—and at Frazier Park, near Fort Tejon, the San Andreas and the Garlock faults intersect."

"I suppose it *is* a possibility. And if that were correct it might happen again, perhaps even on a major scale, and I don't think we'd like that at all." Morro compressed his lips then slowly smiled. "You *have* had more time to think about this than I have. I seem to recall your saying that we might just possibly turn this to our advantage." Dubois smiled in return and nodded. "Ten past three in the morning and what better time for a glass of that splendid Glenfiddich. Don't you agree?"

"For inspirational purposes."

"Indeed. You think perhaps we should relieve those prestigious seismological institutes of the fear that the public may come to associate unexpected earthquakes— quakes in the wrong place, that is—with their indiscriminate tampering with seismic faults? If the public were to know the truth, that is?"

"Something like that."

Morro smiled again. "I look forward to writing this communiqué."

Ryder wasn't smiling when he woke up. He cursed, quietly but with considered feeling, as he reached out for his bedside phone. It was Dunne.

"Sorry to wake you, Ryder."

"No sweat. I've had almost three hours' sleep."

"I've had none. Did you see that newcast shortly before three this morning?"

"The one about the White Wolf fault? Yes."

"There'll be another and even more interesting newscast in less than five minutes. Any channel should do."

"What's it this time?"

"I think the impact will be greater if you watch for yourself. I'll call you afterward."

125

Ryder replaced the receiver, lifted it again, told a querulous Jeff that there was something worth watching on TV, cursed again and went through to his living room. The newscaster—the same cheerful youngster whom he'd seen just over three hours previously—came to the point without preamble.

He said: "We have received a further communication from the same Mr. Morro who claimed last night to have been responsible for the break-in at the San Ruffino nuclear power station and theft of nuclear fuel. We had no reason to doubt that claim as the amounts claimed as stolen corresponded precisely to the amounts that were stolen. This station cannot guarantee the authenticity of this communication, that is to say, that it is from the same man. It may be a hoax. But as the various communications media received this message in exactly the same way as the previous one we regard this as prima facie evidence that the message is genuine. Whether the information it contains is also genuine is not, of course, for us to say. The message reads:

" 'The people of California have been subjected to a hoax in that they have been deliberately lied to by the state's leading seismological authorities. The earthquake which took place at 1:25 this morning did not, as so falsely alleged, take place in the White Wolf fault and I am sure this can easily be verified by consulting the owners of scores of privately owned seismographs throughout the state. None of them would alone dare challenge the authority of the state's official institutes but their combined testimony would make it clear that those state institutes are lying. I expect this statement to bring in massive confirmation of what I am saying.

" 'The reason why the institutes put out this untrue statement lies in their hope of allaying the people's increasing fear of imminent earthquake activity on an unprecedented scale and their own fear that the citizens of this state might come to associate fresh earthquakes, in areas other than those in which they are operating their EPSP plan, with their controversial attempts to tamper with the earth's crust.

126

" 'I can allay their latter fear. They were not responsible for this seismic shock. I was. The epicenter lay not in the White Wolf fault but in the Garlock fault, which, next to the San Andreas, is the largest in the state and is parallel and so close to the White Wolf fault that seismologists may easily have been deceived into believing that they had misread their instruments or that their instruments were in error.

" 'To be honest, I did not expect to trigger off this minor shock as there has been no earthquake in recorded history that would help explain the existence of this huge fracture. The small atomic device I exploded at 1:25 this morning was for purely experimental purposes to see, in effect, whether it worked or not. The results were gratifying.

" 'It is possible that there will be many in the state who will disbelieve my claim. There will be none in the state, or in the nation, who will have any doubts remaining when I explode a second nuclear device tomorrow at a place and time to be announced later. This device is already in position and is in the kiloton range of that which destroyed Hiroshima.'

"That's it, then." This time there was no trace of the boyish grin he'd permitted himself in the earlier newscast. "It *could* be a hoax. If not, the prospect is at best sobering, at worst chilling. It would be interesting to speculate on the effects and intentions of—"

Ryder switched off. He was quite capable of doing his own speculating. He made and drank several cups of coffee while he showered, shaved and dressed for what promised to be a very long day ahead.

He was into his fourth cup of coffee when Dunne rang and apologized for the delay in calling him back.

Ryder said: "The impact was guaranteed. There's only one question I can see—has the state, in the persons of our seismologists, been lying to us?"

"I have no idea."

"I have."

"Maybe so. Fact is, we have no closed line to Pasadena. But we have to our Los Angeles office. Sassoon is

127

very unhappy, not least about you, and wants to see us. Nine o'clock. Bring your son. As soon as possible."

"Now? It's only 6:40."

"I have things to tell you. Not over an open line."

"Tapping phones here, tapping phones there," Ryder complained. "Man's got no privacy left in this state."

Ryder and his son arrived at Dunne's office a few minutes after seven. Dunne, his alert, precise and efficient self, showed no trace of his sleepless night. He was alone.

Ryder said: "This room isn't bugged?"

"When I leave two suspects alone in it, yes. Otherwise, no."

"Where's the big white chief?"

"Sassoon's still in L.A. He's staying there. He is, as I said, unhappy. First, because this is happening in his own back yard. Second, the director of the FBI is winging his merry way from Washington. Third, the CIA has got wind of this and want into the act. As everybody must be very well aware, the FBI and the CIA are barely speaking to each other these days and even when they do speak you can hear the ice crackling."

"How did they get into the act?"

"I'll come to that in a moment. We're going on a short trip by helicopter soon. Pasadena. Nine A.M. the boss says, and we meet him exactly at that time."

Ryder was mild. "The FBI has no jurisdiction over a retired cop."

"I wouldn't even bother saying 'please.' Wild horses wouldn't stop you." Dunne shuffled some papers into a neat pile. "While you and Jeff have been resting lightly we, as usual, have been toiling all through the night. Want to make some notes?"

"No need. Jeff's my memory bank. He can identify over a thousand license plates within thirty miles of here."

"I wish it were only license plates we were dealing with. Well, now, our friend Carlton, the security deputy taken along with the nuclear fuel. A dossier of sorts. Captain, Army Intelligence, NATO, Germany. Nothing
128

fancy. No cloak-and-dagger espionage or counterespionage stuff. Seems he infiltrated a Communist cell among Germans working in the base camp. Unsubstantiated suspicion of having become too intimate with them. Offered transfer to regular tank battalion and refused. Resigned. He wasn't cashiered, he wasn't pressured to resign; let's say the Army didn't stand in his way. At least that's what they say. Probably correct. No matter how unjustified the suspicions that hang over a man, the Army understandably doesn't take chances. End of that line. When the Pentagon decides to clam up, that's it."

"Just a hint of a Communist tie-up?"

"That would be enough for the CIA. You can't move around the Pentagon without stepping on one of their agents. A whiff of a Red under the bed and they're reaching for their cyanide guns or whatever before you know it.

"His security references. Worked for an AEC plant in Illinois. Good record. Security chief checking on contacts. Then a reference from TVA's twin Brown's Ferry nuclear plants in Decatur, Alabama. But the man's never been there. Certainly not under that name, certainly not in security. Maybe some other capacity, some other name, but unlikely. Disastrous fire during the time, incidentally, but not caused by him. Technician looking for a leak with a lighted candle—he found it."

"How come the reference?"

"Forged."

Jeff said: "Wouldn't Ferguson, the security chief, have checked out the reference?"

Briefly, Dunne sounded weary. "He admits he didn't. Ferguson himself had been there and said that Carlton knew so many details about the place, including the details of the fire, that he thought a check-out pointless."

"How would he have known about the fire?"

"Unclassified. It's in the public domain."

Ryder said, "How long was he supposed to have been there?"

129

"Fifteen months."

"So he may just have dropped out of the scene for that time?"

"Sergeant Ryder, a man with the knowhow can go underground for fifteen years in this nation and never surface once."

"He may not have been in the country. He could have a passport at home."

Dunne looked at him, nodded and made a note. "Washington checked out with the AEC at 1717 H Street. They keep records there of those seeking information, those consulting card indexes and dockets on nuclear facilities. No one had ever checked information on San Ruffino—there was none to check. I got Jablonsky out of bed over this one. He was reluctant to talk. Usual threatening noises from the FBI. Then he admitted they have advanced plans for building a fast breeder reactor there. This comes under AEC control. Top secret. No records."

"So Carlton's our man?"

"Yes. Not that that's going to help much now that he's holed up with Morro." Dunne consulted another paper. "You wanted a list of all the organized and—'successful,' I think you said—cranks, weirdos, eccentrics or whatever in the state. This is it. I think I said two hundred. Actually, it's a hundred and thirty-five. Even so, I'm told it would take forever to investigate them all. Besides, if they're as clever and organized as they seem to be, they'll have an unbreakable cover."

"We can narrow it down. To start with, it'll have to be a large group. Also, a comparatively new group, formed just for this purpose. Say within the past year."

"Numbers and dates." Resignedly, Dunne made another note. "Don't mind how hard we have to work, do you? Next comes our friend Morro. Not surprisingly, nothing is known about him, as a man, a criminal with an eye patch and damaged hands, to us or to the police authorities."

Jeff looked at his father. "Susan's note. Remember she wrote 'American?' American, question mark?"

130

"And so she did. Well, Major, another little note if you please. Contact Interpol in Paris."

"So Interpol it is. Now the notes you took from Donahure. Easy—just meant waking up half the bank managers and tellers in the county. Local Bank of America. Drawn four days ago by a young woman with pebbled tinted glasses and long blond hair."

"You mean twenty-twenty vision and a long blond wig."

"Like enough. A Mrs. Jean Hart, 800 Cromwell Ridge. There is a Mrs. Jean Hart at that address. In her seventies, no account with the bank. Bank teller didn't count notes—just handed over ten banded thousands."

"Which Donahure split up eight ways for eight banks. We'll have to get his prints."

"We got them. One of my boys with the help of a friend of yours, a Sergeant Parker—who, like you, doesn't seem to care very much for Donahure—got them from his office about three this morning."

"You *have* been busy."

"Not me. I just sit here running up phone bills. But I've had fourteen good men and true working for me during the night—had to scrape the Southern Californian barrel to get them. Anyway, we've got some lovely clear specimens of Donahure's prints on those notes. More interestingly, we have some lovely clear specimens of LeWinter's, too."

"The paymaster. And how about the paymaster's automatic?"

"Nothing there. Not registered. Nothing suspicious in that—judges get threats all the time. Not used recently—film of dust in that barrel. Silencer probably a pointer to the type of man he is but you can't hang a man for that."

"The FBI file on him. Still reluctant to tell me about it?"

"Not now I'm not. Nothing positive. Nothing very good either. Not known to associate with criminals. His open list of telephone numbers would appear to confirm that. From that list he would appear to know every politician and city hall boss in the state."

"And you say he's not known to associate with criminals . . . ! What else?"

"Both we and the police are dissatisfied with some—more than some—of the sentences he has been handing out over the past years." Dunne consulted a sheet before him. "Enemies of known cronies getting unduly stiff sentences; criminal associates of cronies—repeat, he himself has no direct criminal associates—getting light, sometimes ludicrously light, sentences."

"Pay-off?"

"No proof, but what would you think? Anyway, he's not as naïve as his minion Donahure. No local accounts under false names—none that we know of, anyway. But we monitor—without opening—his correspondence from time to time."

"You're as bad as the KGB."

Dunne ignored this. "He gets occasional letters from Zurich. Never sends any, though. Keeps his tracks pretty well covered."

"Intermediaries feeding pay-offs into a numbered account?"

"What else? No hope there. Swiss banks will open up only in the case of a convicted criminal."

"This copy of *Ivanhoe* that LeWinter had in his safe? And the coded notebook?"

"Seems to be a mishmash of telephone numbers, mainly in this state and Texas, and what are beginning to look like meteorological reports. We're making progress. At least Washington is. There are no specialized Russian cryptographers in California."

"Russian?"

"Apparently. A simple variation—well, simple to them, I suppose—of a well-known Russian code. Reds lurking in the undergrowth again? Could mean anything, could mean nothing. Another reason, I suppose, for the keen interest being shown by the CIA. I imagine, without actually knowing, that the bulk of Washington cryptographers are on the CIA's payroll, one way or another."

"And LeWinter's secretary is Russian. Russian descent, anyway. A cypher clerk?"

"If this were any of a dozen countries in the world I'd have the fair Bettina in here and have the truth out of her in ten minutes. Unfortunately, this is not one of those dozen different countries." He paused. "And Donahure has—had—Russian rifles."

"Ah! The Kalashnikovs. Import permits—"

"None. So, officially, there are none of those rifles in the country. The Pentagon does have some but they're not saying where they got them. The British, I imagine—some captured IRA arms cache in Northern Ireland."

"And Donahure is, of course, a second-generation Irishman."

"God, as if I haven't got enough headaches." To illustrate just how many he had Dunne laid his forehead briefly on the palms of his hands then looked up. "Incidentally, what was Donahure looking for in your house?"

"I've figured that out." Ryder didn't seem to derive much satisfaction from the thought. "Just give me a lifetime and by the end of it I'll add up two and two and come pretty close to the right answer. He didn't come because Jeff and I hadn't been too nice to his stake-out and deprived him of a lot of his personal property, including his spy van—he'd never have dared connect himself with that. He didn't come for the evidence I'd taken from San Ruffino because he didn't know I'd taken any and, in the first place, he hadn't even had time to go to San Ruffino. By the same token he didn't have time to go to LeWinter's for a search warrant either. He wouldn't have dared to, anyway, for if he'd told LeWinter the real reason why he wanted the search warrant LeWinter might have considered him such a menace that he'd not only refuse a warrant but might have had him eliminated altogether."

Duanne wasn't looking quite so brisk and alert as when they had arrived. He said in complaint: "I told you I've got a headache."

"My guess is that a proper search of Donahure's home or office would turn up a stack of warrants already signed and officially stamped by LeWinter. All Donahure had

133

to do was to fill them in himself. I'd told him about the dossier I had on him. He'd come for that. So obvious that I missed it at the time. And I'd told him he was so bone-headed that he just had to be acting on his own. So he was, because it was something that concerned only himself personally."

"Of course it has to be that. The two of them might run for cover."

"Don't think so. They don't know the evidence is in *our* hands. Donahure, being a crook at heart, will automatically assume that only crooks would have stolen the money and the guns and they wouldn't be likely to advertise the fact. And I don't think that LeWinter will run either. He'll have been worried sick at first, especially at the thought of the stolen code book and the fact that his fingerprints had been taken. But when he finds out—if he hasn't already found out—that the picture of himself and his accommodating secretary has *not* appeared in the *Globe,* he'll have discreet inquiries made and find out that the two men who came to photograph him were *not* employed on the *Globe* and will come to the inevitable conclusion that they were blackmailers, perhaps out to block his appointment as chief justice of the state supreme court. You said yourself he had powerful friends—by the same token such a man must also have powerful enemies. Whatever their reason, he wouldn't be scared of blackmailers. Blackmailers wouldn't know a Russian code. True, fingerprints had been taken, but cops don't wear hoods and take your prints in bed. They arrest you first. And he could take care of blackmailers. California law is ruthless toward that breed—and LeWinter is the law."

Jeff said in injured reproach: "You might have told me all this."

"I thought you understood."

"You had all this figured in advance? Before you moved in on them?" Dunne said. Ryder nodded. "You're smarter than the average cop. Might even make the FBI. Any suggestions?"

"A tap on LeWinter's phone."

"Illegal. Congress is very uptight about tapping these days—chiefly, one supposes, because they're terrified of having their own phones tapped. It'll take an hour or two."

"You appreciate, of course, that this will be the second tap on his line."

"Second?"

"Why do you think Sheriff Hartman's dead?"

"Because he'd talk? A new recruit, still not deeply involved, wanting to get out from under before it was too late?"

"That, too. But how come he's dead? Because Morro had LeWinter's line tapped. I called the night telephone manager from LeWinter's house to get Hartman's address —he was unlisted but that's probably because he was fairly new to the area. Someone intercepted the call and got to Hartman before Jeff and I did. By the way, there's no point in recovering the bullet that killed him. It was a dum-dum and would have been distorted out of recognition and further mangled on imbedding itself in the brick wall. Ballistic experts are not wizards—you couldn't hope to match up what's left of that bullet with any gun barrel."

" 'Someone,' you said?"

"Perhaps Donahure—he was showing signs of coming to when we left him—or, just possibly, one of Donahure's underworld connections. Raminoff wasn't the only one."

"You gave your name over the phone?"

"Had to—to get the information I wanted."

"So now Donahure knows you were in LeWinter's house. So now LeWinter knows."

"No chance. To tell LeWinter that he'd have to tell him that he either had LeWinter's phone tapped or knew that it was tapped. By the same token, if my call to Aaron of the *Examiner* was tapped Donahure or whoever would still be unable to tell LeWinter. But unlikely that that second call was tapped—our eavesdropping friend

135

would have taken off like a bat after he'd heard mention of Hartman's name and address."

Dunne looked at him curiously, it might almost have been with respect. "To coin a phrase, you got all the angles figured."

"I wish I had. But I haven't."

One of the desk phones rang. Dunne listened in silence and his lips compressed as all trace of expression left his face. He nodded several times in silence, said "Yes, I'll do that," and replaced the receiver. He looked at Ryder in silence.

Without any particular inflection in tone, Ryder said: "I told you I didn't have all the angles figured. They've got Peggy?"

"Yes."

Jeff's chair crashed over backward. He was on his feet, face almost instantly drained of color, clenched fists ivory-knuckled on Dunne's desk. "Peggy! What's happened to Peggy?"

"They've taken her. As hostage."

"Hostage! But you promised us last night—so much for your damned FBI!"

Dunne's voice was quiet. "Two of the damned FBI, as you call them, were gunned down and are in the hospital. One is on the critical list. Peggy, at least, is unharmed."

"Sit down, Jeff." Still no inflection in the voice. He looked at Dunne. "I've been told to lay off."

"Yes. Would you recognize the amethyst she wears on the little finger of her left hand?" Dunne's eyes were bitter. "Especially, they say, if it's still attached to her little finger?"

Jeff had just straightened his chair. He was still standing, both hands holding the back bar as if he intended to crush it. His voice was husky. "Good God, Dad! Don't just sit there. It's not—it's not human. It's Peggy! Peggy! We can't stay here. Let's leave now! We can be there in no time!"

"Easy, Jeff, easy. *Where* in no time?"

"San Diego!"

136

Ryder allowed an edge of coolness to creep into his voice. Deliberately, he allowed it. "You'll never make a cop until you learn to think like one. Peggy, San Diego, they're just tangled up on the outside strand of the spider's web. We've got to find the spider at the heart of the web. Find it and kill it. And it's not in San Diego."

"I'll go myself, then! You can't stop me. If you want to sit around—"

"Shut up!" Dunne's voice was as deliberately harsh as Ryder's had been cool, but at once he spoke more gently. "Look, Jeff, we know she's your sister. Your only sister, your kid sister. But San Diego's no village lying out in the sticks—it's the second biggest city in the state. Hundreds of cops, scores of trained detectives, FBI—all experts in this sort of manhunt. You're not an expert, you don't even know the town. There're probably upward of a hundred men trying to find her right now. What could you hope to do that they can't?" Dunne's tone became even more reasonable, more persuasive. "Your father's right. Wouldn't you rather go kill the spider at the heart of the web?"

"I suppose so." Jeff sat in his chair but the slight shaking of the hand showed that blind rage and fear for his sister still had him in their grip. "I suppose so. But why you, Dad? Why get at you through Peggy?"

Dunne answered. "Because they're afraid of him. Because they know his reputation, his resolution, the fact that he never gives up. Most of all they're afraid of the fact that he's operating outside the law. LeWinter, Donahure, Hartman—three cogs in their machine, four if you count Raminoff—and he gets to them all in a matter of hours. A man operating inside the law would never have got to any of them."

"Yes, but how did they—"

"Simply with hindsight," Ryder said. "I said that Donahure would never dare tell I—we—were in LeWinter's place. But he told whoever ordered him to fix the tap. Now that it's too late I can see that Donahure is far too dumb to think of fixing a tap himself."

"Who's the whoever?"

"Just a voice on the phone, most likely. A link man. A link man to Morro. And I call Donahure dumb. What does that make me?" He lit a Gauloise and gazed at the drifting smoke. "Good old Sergeant Ryder. All the angles figured."

SIX

■ GOLDEN mornings are far from rare in the Golden
State and this was one of them, still and clear and calm
and beautiful, the sun already hot in a deep blue sky
bereft of cloud, the view from the Sierras across the mist-
streaked San Joaquin Valley to the sunlit peaks and
valleys of the Coastal Range quite breathtakingly lovely,
a vista to delight, to warm the hearts of all but the very
sick, the very near-sighted, the irredeemably misanthrop-
ical and, in this particular instance, those who were held
prisoner behind the grim walls of the Adlerheim. In the
last case, additionally, it had to be admitted that the
view from the western battlement, high above the courtyard, was rather marred, psychologically if not actually,
but the triple-stranded barbed-wire fence with its further
unseen deterrent of two thousand volts.

Susan Ryder felt no uplift of the heart whatsoever.
Nothing could ever make her anything less than beautiful
but she was pale and tired and the dusky blueness under
her lower lids had not come from any bottle of eye
shadow. She had not slept except for a brief fifteen-
minute period during the night from which she had
awakened with the profound conviction that something
was far wrong, something more terrible than even their
incarceration in that dreadful place. A heaviness of heart
is as much a physical as mental sensation and she was at
a loss to account for it. So much, she thought morosely,
for her reputation as the cheerful, smiling extrovert,
the sun who lit up any company in which she happened to
find herself. She would have given the world to have a
hand touch her arm and find herself looking into the
infinitely reassuring face of her husband, to feel his rock-
like presence by her side.

A hand did touch her arm, then took it. It was Julie Johnson. Her eyes were dulled and tinged with red as if she had spent a goodly part of the night ensconced behind the wet bar so thoughtfully provided by Morro. Susan put an arm around the girl's slender shoulders and held her. Neither said anything. There didn't seem to be anything to say.

They were the only two on the battlements. Five of the other hostages were wandering, apparently aimlessly, around the courtyard, none speaking to any of the others. It could have been that each wished to be alone with his or her personal thoughts or that they were only now beginning to appreciate the predicament in which they found themselves: on the other hand the inhibitory and intimidatory effects of those bleak walls were sufficient to stifle the normal morning courtesies of even the most gregarious.

The ringing of the bell from the door of the great hall came almost as a relief. Susan and Julie made their careful way down the stone steps—there was no guard rail—and joined the others at one of the long tables where breakfast was being served. It was a first-class meal that would have done justice to any hotel of good standing, but apart from Dr. Healey and Dr. Bramwell, who ate with a gusto becoming guests of long standing, the others did no more than sip some coffee and push pieces of toast around. In atmosphere, it was the early morning equivalent of the Last Supper.

They had just finished what most of them hadn't even started when Morro and Dubois entered, smiling, affable, courteous, freely bestowing good mornings and hopes that they had spent the night in peaceful and relaxing slumber. This over, Morro lifted a quizzical eyebrow. "I observe that two of our new guests, Professor Burnett and Dr. Schmidt, are absent. Achmed"—this to one of the white-robed acolytes—"ask them if they would be good enough to join us."

Which, after five minutes, the two nuclear scientists did. Their clothes were crumpled as if they had slept in them, which, in fact, was what they had done. They had unshaven faces and what was known to the trade as tartan eyes for which Morro had only himself to blame in having left refreshments so freely available in their suites; in fairness, he was probably not to know that the awesome scientific reputations of the two physicists from San Diego and U.C.L.A. were matched only by their awesome reputations in the field of bacchanalian conviviality.

Morro allowed a decent interval to elapse, then said: "Just one small matter. I would like you all to sign your names. If you would be so good, Abraham?"

Dubois nodded amiably, picked up a sheaf of papers and went around the table, laying a typed letter, typed envelope and pen before each of the ten hostages.

"What the devil is the meaning of this, you witless bastard?" The speaker was, inevitably, Professor Burnett, his legendary ill temper understandably exacerbated by a monumental hangover. "This is a copy of the letter I wrote my wife last night."

"Word for word, I assure you. Just sign it."

"I'll be damned if I will."

"It's a matter of utter indifference to me," Morro said. "Asking you to write those letters was purely a courtesy gesture to enable you to assure your loved ones that you are safe and well. Starting from the top of the table you will all sign your letters in rotation, handing your pens to Abraham. Thank you. You look distraught, Mrs. Ryder?"

"Distraught, Mr. Morro?" She gave him a smile but it wasn't one of her best. "Why should I?"

"Because of this." He laid an envelope on the table before her, address upward. "You wrote this?"

"Of course. That's my writing."

"Thank you." He turned the envelope face down and she saw, with a sudden dryness in her mouth, that both edges had been slit. Morro opened the edges, smoothed the envelope flat and indicated a small grayish squidge in the middle of the back of the envelope. "Paper was completely blank, of course, but there are chemical substances that bring out even the most invisible of writing. Now, even the most dedicated policeman's wife wouldn't carry invisible ink around with her. This little squiggle here has an acetic acid base, most commonly used in the making of aspirin but also, in some cases, nail polish. You, I observe, use colorless nail polish. Your husband is a highly experienced, perhaps even brilliant, detective and he would expect similar signs of intelligence from his wife. Within a few minutes of receiving this letter he would have had it in a police laboratory. Shorthand, of course. What does it say, Mrs. Ryder?"

Her voice was dull. "Adlerheim."

"Very, very naughty, Mrs. Ryder. Enterprising, of course, clever, spirited, call it what you like, but naughty."

She stared down at the table. "What are you going to do with me?"

"Do with you? Fourteen days' bread and water? I think not. We do not wage war on women. Your chagrin will be punishment enough." He looked around. "Professor Burnett, Dr. Schmidt, Dr. Healey, Dr. Bramwell, I would be glad if you would accompany me."

Morro led the way to a large room next to his own study. It was notable for the fact that it lacked any window and was covered on three sides by metal filing cabinets. The remaining wall—a side wall—was, incongruously enough, given over to rather repulsively Baroque paintings framed in heavy gilt—one presumed they had formed the prized nucleus of Von Streicher's art collection—and a similarly gilt-edged mirror. There was a large table in the center, with half a dozen chairs around it and, on it, a pile of large sheets of paper, about four feet by two, the top one of which was clearly a diagram of some sort. At one end of the table there was a splendidly equipped drink trolley.

Morro said: "Well, now, gentlemen, I'll be glad if you do me a favor. Nothing, I assure you, that will involve you in any effort. Be so kind as to have a look at them and tell me what you think of them."
142

"I'll be damned if we do," Burnett said. He spoke in his normal tone, that of defiant truculence. "I speak for myself, of course."

Morro smiled. "Oh, yes, you will."

"Yes? Force? Torture?"

"Now we are being childish. You will examine them and for two reasons. You will be overcome by your natural scientific curiosity—and surely, gentlemen, you want to know why you are here?"

He left and closed the door behind him. There was no sound of a key being turned in a lock, which was reassuring in itself. But, then, a push-button, hydraulically operated bolt is completely silent in any event.

Morro moved into his study, now lit by only two red lamps. Dubois was seated before a large glass screen, which was completely transparent. Half an inch from that was the back of the one-way mirror of the room where the four scientists were. From this gap the maximum of air had been extracted, not with any insulation purposes in mind but to eliminate the possibility of the scientists hearing anything that was said in the study. Those in the study, however had no difficulty whatsoever in hearing what the scientists had to say, owing to the positioning of four suitably spaced and cunningly concealed microphones in the scientists' room. Those were wired into a speaker above Dubois' head and a tape recorder by his side.

"Not all of it," Morro said. "Most of it will probably be unprintable—unrepeatable, rather—anyway. Just the meat on the bones."

"I understand. Just to be sure, I'll err on the cautious side. We can edit it afterward."

They watched the four men in the room look around uncertainly. Then Burnett and Schmidt looked at each other and this time there was no uncertainty in their expressions. They strode purposefully toward the drink trolley, Burnett selecting the inevitable Glenfiddich, Schmidt homing in on the Gordon's gin. A brief silence ensued while the two men helped themselves in generous

143

fashion and set about restoring a measure of tranquility to the disturbances plaguing their nervous systems.

Healey watched them sourly then made a few far from oblique references to Morro, which was one of the passages that Morro and Dubois would have to edit out of the final transcript. Having said that, Healey went on: "He's right, damn him. I've just had a quick glance at that top blueprint and I must say it interests me strangely —and not in a way that I like at all; and I do want to know what the hell we are doing here."

Burnett silently scrutinized the top diagram for all of thirty seconds and even the aching head of a top physicist can absorb a great deal of information in that time. He looked around at the other three, noted in vague surprise that his glass was empty, returned to the drink trolley and rejoined the others armed with another glass of the whiskey, which he raised to the level of his speculative eyes. "This, gentlemen, is not for my hangover, which is still unfortunately with me—it's to brace myself for whatever we find out or, more precisely, for what I fear we may find out. Shall we have a look at it then, gentlemen?"

In the study next door Morro clapped Dubois on the shoulder and left.

Barrow, with his plump, genial, rubicund face, ingenuous expression and baby-blue eyes, looked like a pastor —to be fair, a bishop—in mufti. He was the head of the FBI, a man feared by his own agents almost as much as he was by the criminals who were the object of his lifelong passion to put behind bars for as long a period as the law allowed and, if possible, longer. Sassoon, head of the California FBI, was a tall, ascetic, absent-minded-looking man who looked as if he would have been far more at home on a university campus, a convincing impression that a large number of convicted California felons deeply regretted having taken at its face value. Crichton was the only man who looked his part: big, bulky, tight-lipped, with an aquiline nose and cold gray eyes, he was the deputy head of the CIA. Neither he nor Barrow liked each

144

other very much, which pretty well symbolized the relationship between the two organizations they represented.

Alec Benson, Professor Hardwick by his side, bent his untroubled and, indeed, his unimpressed gaze on the three men, then let it rest on Dunne and the two Ryders in turn. He said to Hardwick: "Well, well, Arthur, we are honored today—three senior gentlemen from the FBI and one senior gentleman from the CIA. A red-letter day for the faculty. Well, their presence here I can understand—not too well, but I understand." He looked at Ryder. "No offense, but you would appear to be out of place in this distinguished company. You are, if the expression be pardoned, just ordinary policemen. If, of course, there are any such."

"Professor," Ryder said. "There are ordinary policemen, a great many of them far too ordinary. And we aren't even ordinary policemen—we're ex-ordinary policemen."

Benson lifted his brows. Dunne looked at Barrow, who nodded. "Sergeant Ryder and his son, Patrolman Ryder, resigned from the force yesterday. They had urgent and private reasons for doing so. They know more about the peculiar circumstances surrounding this affair than any of us. They have achieved considerably more than any of us, who have, in fact, achieved nothing so far, hardly surprising in view of the fact that the affair began only last evening. For good measure, Sergeant Ryder's wife and his daughter have both been kidnaped and are being held hostage by this man Morro."

"Jesus!" Benson no longer looked untroubled. "My apologies, certainly—and my sympathies, certainly. It may be we who haven't the right to be here." He singled out Barrow, the most senior of the investigative officers present. "You are here to ascertain whether or not Cal Tech, as spokesmen for the various other state institutes, and especially whether I, as spokesman for the spokesmen, so to speak, have been guilty of misleading the public—or, more bluntly, have I been caught lying in my teeth?"

145

Even Barrow hesitated. Formidable man though he was, he recognized another formidable man when he met one and he was aware of Benson's formidable reputation. He said: "Could this tremor have been triggered off by an atomic device?"

"It's possible, of course, but it's equally impossible to tell. A seismograph is incapable of deciding the nature of the source of shock waves. Generally, almost invariably, we are in no doubt as to the source. We ourselves, the British and the French, announce our nuclear tests—the other two members of the so-called nuclear club are not so forthcoming. But there are still ways of telling. When the Chinese detonated a nuclear device in the megaton range—a megaton, as you are probably aware, is the equivalent of a million tons of TNT—clouds of radiation gas drifted eventually across the United States. The cloud was thin, high and caused no damage, but was easily detected—this was in November 1976. Again, earthquakes, almost invariably, give off aftershocks.

"There was one classical exception—again, oddly enough, in November of 1976. Seismology stations in both Sweden and Finland detected an earthquake—not major, 4-something on the Richter scale—off the coast of Estonia. Other scientists disputed this, figuring that the Soviets had been responsible, accidentally or otherwise, for a nuclear detonation on the floor of the Baltic. They have been disputing the matter ever since—the Soviets, naturally, have not seen fit to give any enlightenment on the matter."

Barrow said: "But earthquakes do not occur in that region of the world."

"I would not seek, Mr. Barrow, to advise you in the matter of law enforcement. It's a minor area, but it's there."

Barrow's smile was at its most genial. "The FBI stands corrected."

"So whether this man Morro detonated a small nuclear device there or not I can't tell you." He looked at Hardwick. "You think any reputable seismologist in the state

146

would venture a definite opinion one way or another on this, Arthur?"

"No."

"Well, that's the answer to one question, unsatisfactory though it may be. But that, of course, is not the question you really want to ask. You wanted to know whether we—I, if you like—were entirely accurate in locating the epicenter of the shock in the White Wolf fault instead of, as Morro claims, in the Garlock fault. Gentlemen, I was lying in my teeth."

There was a predictable silence.

"Why?" Crichton was a man not noted for his loquacity.

"Because, in the circumstances, it seemed the best thing to do. In retrospect, it still seems the best thing." Benson shook his head in regret. "Pity this fellow Morro had to come along and spoil things."

"Why?" Crichton was also noted for his persistency.

"I'll try to explain. Mr. Sassoon, Major Dunne and the two policemen here—sorry, ex-policemen—will understand. For you and Mr. Barrow, it may not be so easy."

"Why?"

It seemed to Alec Benson that Crichton was a man of remarkably limited vocabulary, but he refrained from comment. "Because those four are Californians. You two are not."

Barrow smiled. "A state apart. I always knew it. Secession next, is that it?"

"It is a state apart, but not in that sense. It's apart because it's the only state in the union where, in the back—and maybe not so far back—of the mind of any reasonably intelligent person lies the thought of to-morrow. Not *when* tomorrow comes, gentlemen—*if* tomorrow comes.

"Californians live in a state of fear or fearful resignation or just pure resignation. There has always been the vague thought, the entertainment of the vague possibility, that one day the big one is going to hit us."

Barrow said: "The big one. Earthquake?"

"Of devastating proportions. This fear never really crystallized until as late as 1976—third time I've mentioned that year this morning, isn't it? 1976 was the bad year, the year that made the minds of people in this state turn to thoughts they'd rather not think about." Benson lifted a sheet of paper. "February 4, Guatemala—7.5 on the Richter scale. Tens of thousands died. May 6, northern Italy—6.5. Hundreds dead, widespread devastation, and later on in the same year another quake came back to wipe out the few buildings that were still left standing after the first one. May 16, Soviet Central Asia —7.2. Death rate and damage unknown—the Soviets are reluctant to discuss those things. July 27, Tangshan—8.2. Two thirds of a million died and three quarters of a million were injured—as this occurred in a densely populated area, large cities like Peking and Teintsin were involved. Then in the following month, the far south of the Philippines—8.0. Widespread devastation, exact deaths unknown but running into tens of thousands— this partly due to the earthquake, partly due to the giant *tsunami*—tidal wave—that followed because the earthquake had occurred under the sea. They had a lesser earthquake in the Philippines some way farther north on November 9—6.8. No precise figures released. In fact, November of that year was quite a month, with yet another earthquake in the Philippines, one in Iran, one in northern Greece, five in China and two in Japan. Worst of all Turkey—five thousand dead.

"And all those earthquakes, with the exception of the ones in Greece and Italy, were related to the movement of what they call the Pacific plate, which causes the so-called ring of fire around the Pacific. The section that mainly concerns us, as everyone knows, is the San Andreas fault, where the northeast-moving Pacific plate rubs against the westward-pressing American plate. In fact, gentlemen, where we are now is, geologically speaking, not really part of America at all but part of the Pacific plate and it hardly requires an educated guess to know that in the not too distant future we won't physically
148

be part of America either. Someday the Pacific plate is going to carry the western seaboard of California into the oceanic equivalent of the wild blue yonder, for where we're sitting at the moment lies to the *west* of the San Andreas fault—only a few miles, mind you; it passes under San Bernardino, just a hop, skip and jump to the east. For good measure, we're only about the same distance from the Newport–Inglewood fault to the west— that's what caused the Long Beach quake of 1933—and not all that much farther from the San Fernando fault to the north, which caused, as you may recall, that very nasty business back in February '72. Seismologically speaking, only a lunatic would choose to live in the county of Los Angeles. A comforting thought, isn't it, gentlemen?"

Benson looked around him. No one seemed to find it a comforting thought at all.

"Little wonder, then, that people's thoughts started turning inward. Little wonder that they increasingly wondered, 'When's our time going to come?' We're sitting fair and square astride the ring of fire and our turn might be any time now. It is not a happy thought to live with. And they're not thinking in terms of earthquakes in the past. We've only had four major earthquakes in our known past, two of them really big ones on the order of 8.3 on the Richter scale, Owens Valley in 1872 and San Francisco in 1906. But, I say, it's not those they're thinking of. Not in the terms of major earthquakes but of monster earthquakes, of which there have been only two recorded in history, both of the Richter order of 8.9, or about six times the destructive force of the San Francisco one." Benson shook his head. "An earthquake up to 10 on the Richter scale is theoretically possible but not even the scientific mind cares to contemplate the awfulness of it.

"Those two monster quakes occurred also, perhaps not coincidentally, in 1906 and 1933, the first in Ecuador, the second in Japan. I won't describe the effects to you two gentlemen from Washington or you'd be taking the

149

plane back East. Both Ecuador and Japan sit astride the Pacific ring of fire. So does California. Why shouldn't it be our turn next?"

Barrow said: "That idea about a plane is beginning to sound good to me. What *would* happen if one of those struck?"

"Assuming a properly somber tone of voice, I must admit I've given a great deal of thought to this. Say it struck where we're sitting now. You'd wake up in the morning—only of course the dead don't wake—and find the Pacific where Los Angeles is and Los Angeles buried in what used to be Santa Monica Bay and the San Pedro Channel. The San Gabriel Mountains might well have fallen down smack on top of where we are now. If it happened at sea—"

"How could it happen at sea?" Barrow was a degree less jovial than he had been. "The fault runs through California."

"Easterner. It runs out into the Pacific south of San Francisco, by-passes the Golden Gate, then rejoins the mainland to the north. A monster quake off the Golden Gate would be of interest. For starters, San Francisco would be a goner. Probably the whole of the San Francisco peninsula. Marin County would go the same way. But the real damage—"

"The *real* damage?" Crichton said.

"Yes. The real damage would come from the immense ocean of water that would sweep into the San Francisco Bay. When I say immense, I mean just that. Up in Alaska we have proof—earthquakes have generated water levels three and four hundred feet above normal. Richmond, Berkeley, Oakland, all the way down through Palo Alto to San Jose would be drowned. The Santa Cruz Mountains would become an island. And even worse—to anticipate, Mr. Crichton, there is worse—the agricultural heart of California, the two great valleys of San Joaquin and Sacramento—would be flooded, and the vast part of those valleys lie under an altitude of three hundred feet." Benson became thoughtful. "I hadn't really thought of it before but, come to that, I don't think I'd much care
150

to be living in the capital either at that time for it would be dead in line of the first great wall of water rushing up the Sacramento River Valley. Perhaps you are beginning to understand why I and my colleagues prefer to keep people's minds off such things?"

"I think I'm beginning to." Barrow looked at Dunne. "How do you—as a Californian, of course—feel about this?"

"Unhappy."

"You go along with this way of thinking?"

"Go along with it? If anything, I'm even ahead of it, I have the unpleasant feeling that Professor Benson is not only catching me up in my thinking but passing me by."

Benson said: "There are, I must admit, another couple of factors. In the past year or so people have begun delving into records and then wishing they hadn't delved. Take the northern part of the San Andreas fault. It is known that a great earthquake struck there in 1833 although, at the time, there was no way of calibrating its strength. The great San Francisco quake of 1906 struck there sixty-eight years later. There was one in Daly City in 1957 but at a magnitude of 5.3 it was geologically insignificant. There hasn't been, if I may use the term, a proper earthquake up north for seventy-one years. It may well be overdue.

"In the southern San Andreas there has been no major quake since 1857, one hundred and twenty years ago. Now, triangulation surveys have shown that the Pacific plate, in relation to the American plate, is moving northeast at two inches a year. When an earthquake occurs one plate jerks forward in relation to the other—this is called a lateral slip. Slips in 1906 of between fifteen and eighteen feet have been measured. On the two-inch-a-year basis, one hundred and twenty years could mean an accumulated pressure potential amounting to twenty feet. If we accept this basis—not everyone does—a major earthquake in the Los Angeles area is considerably overdue.

"As for the central area of the San Andreas, no major

quake has ever been recorded. Lord only knows how long that one may be overdue. And, of course, the big one may occur in any of the other faults, such as the Garlock, the next biggest in the state, which has been quiet for centuries." Benson smiled. "Now, that would be something, gentlemen. A monster lurking in the Garlock fault.

"The third thing that rather tends to preoccupy people's minds is that reputable scientists have begun to talk out loud—in print, radio and television—about the prospects that lie ahead of us. Whether they should talk out loud or not is a matter for their own principles and consciences—I prefer not to, but I'm not necessarily correct.

"A physicist, and a highly regarded one, Peter Franken, expects the next earthquake to be of a giant size, and he has openly predicted death-toll figures between twenty thousand and a million. He has also predicted that if it happens in the long quiescent central section of the San Andreas the severity of the shock waves would rock both Los Angeles and San Francisco and, in his own words, 'quite possibly wipe them out'; it is perhaps not surprising that, per head of population, California consumes more tranquilizers and sleeping tablets than any place on earth.

"Or take the San Francisco emergency plan. It is known that no fewer than sixteen hospitals in 'kit' form are stored in various places around the city ready to be set up when disaster strikes. A leading scientist commented somewhat gloomily that most of those, should a major earthquake occur, would probably be destroyed anyway, and if the city was inundated or the peninsula cut off the whole lot would be useless. San Franciscans must find this kind of statement vastly heartening.

"Other scientists posit a maximum of five years' existence for both Los Angeles and San Francisco. Some say two. One seismologist gives Los Angeles less than a year to live. A crackpot? A Cassandra? No. The one person they should listen to. A James H. Whitcomb of Cal Tech, the best earthquake forecaster in the business. He has
152

predicted before with an almost uncanny degree of accuracy. It won't necessarily be located in the San Andreas fault but it's coming very soon."

Barrow said: "Do you believe him?"

"Let me put it this way. If the roof fell in on us while we're sitting here I wouldn't raise an eyebrow—provided, that is, I had time to raise an eyebrow. I, personally, do not doubt that, sooner rather than later, Los Angeles will be razed to the ground."

"What were the reactions to this forecast?"

"Well, he terrified a lot of people. Some scientists just shrugged their shoulders and walked away—earthquake prediction is still in its infancy or, at best, an inexact science. Most significantly, he was immediately threatened with a lawsuit by a Los Angeles city official on the grounds that such reports undermined property values. This is on record." Benson sighed. "All part of the 'Jaws Syndrome,' as it has come to be called. Greed, I'd call it. Recall the film—no one who had commercial interests at stake wanted to believe in the killer shark. Or take a dozen years ago in Japan in a place called Matsushiro. Local scientists predicted an earthquake there, of such and such a magnitude at such and such a time. Local hoteliers were furious, threatened them with God knows what. But, at the predicted place, magnitude and time, along came the earthquake."

"What happened?"

"The hotels fell down. Commercial interests, commercial interests. Say Dr. Whitcomb predicted a quake on the Newport–Inglewood fault. One certain result would be the temporary closing of the Hollywood Park Race Track—it's almost smack on the fault and you can't have tens of thousands of people jammed into a potential death trap. A week goes by, two weeks, and nothing happens. Loss of profits might run into millions. Can you imagine how much Dr. Whitcomb would be sued for?

"And the Jaws Syndrome is just first cousin to the 'Ostrich Syndrome.' Put your head in the sand, pretend it's not there and it'll go away. But fewer and fewer people are indulging in that with the result that fear, in

153

many areas, is reaching a state dangerously close to hysteria. Let me tell you a story, not my story, but a very prophetic short story written some five years ago by a writer called R. L. Stevens.

"If I recall correctly, it was called 'The Forbidden Word.' There was a California Enabling Act which prohibited all reference to earthquakes in print or public. Penalty of five years. The state, apparently, had lost, by death or flight, fifty per cent of its population because of earthquakes. Roadblocks at state lines and people forbidden to leave. A man and girl were arrested for mentioning the word 'earthquake' in a public place. I wonder when we're going to have a real-life enabling act, when a mounting hysteria will drive us into a 1984 Orwellian situation?"

"What happened?" Barrow said. "In the story?"

"It's not relevant, but they got to New York, which was crowded by the millions of Californians who'd fled East and were arrested by the Population Control Board for mentioning the word 'love' in public. You can't win. The same as we can't win in this situation. To warn, to cry doom, the end of the world is nigh? Or not to warn, not to frighten them into a state of near panic? For me, there is one crucial factor. How can you evacuate three million people, as in Los Angeles, on a mere prediction? This is a free society. How in God's name can you close down coastal California, ten million, maybe more, and hang around for an indeterminate time while you wait for your predictions to come true? Where are you going to go, where are you going to put them? How can you *make* them leave when they know there is no place to go? This is where their homes are, their jobs are, their friends are. There are no homes anywhere else, no jobs anywhere else, no friends anywhere else. This is where they live, this is where they'll have to live, and, even though it's sooner rather than later, this is where they're going to have to die.

"And while they're waiting to die, I think they should be allowed to live with as much peace of mind, relative though that may be, as is possible. You're a Christian in
154

the dungeons in Rome and you know it's only a matter of time before you're driven into the arena where the lions are waiting. It doesn't help a great deal if you are reminded of the prospect every minute. Hope, however irrational, springs eternal.

"Well, that's my attitude and that's my answer. I have lied in my teeth and I intend to go on doing so. Any suggestions that we were wrong will be vehemently denied. I am not, gentlemen, committed to a lie—I am committed to a belief. I have, I think, made my position clear. Do you accept it?"

Barrow and Crichton looked briefly at each other, then turned to Benson and nodded in unison.

"Thank you, gentlemen. As for this maniac Morro, I can be of no help there. He's all yours, I'm afraid." He paused. "Threatening to explode an atomic bomb, or suchlike. I must say that, as a concerned citizen, I'd dearly love to know what he's up to. Do you believe him?"

Crichton said: "We have no idea."

"No inkling what he's up to?"

"None."

"Suspense, war of nerves, tension. Creating fear, hoping to panic you into precipitate and misguided action?"

"Very likely," Barrow said. "Only, we haven't got anything to act against yet."

"Well, just as long as he doesn't let it off under my seat or in any other inhabited area. If you learn the time and place of this proposed—ah—demonstration, may I request a grandstand seat?"

"Your request has already been granted," Barrow said. "We were going to ask you anyway. Would there be anything else, gentlemen?"

"Yes," Ryder said. "Would it be possible to borrow some reading material on earthquakes, especially recent ones?"

Everyone looked at him in perplexity. Everyone, that is, except Benson. "My pleasure, Sergeant. Just give this card to the librarian."

Dunne said: "A question, Professor. This Earthquake
155

Preventative Slip Program of yours. Shouldn't that delay or minimize the great quake that everyone seems to think is coming?"

"Had it been started five years ago, perhaps. But we're only just beginning. Three, maybe four years before we get results. I know in my bones that the monster will strike first. It's out there, crouched on the doorstep, waiting."

SEVEN

AT half-past ten that morning Morro re-entered his study. Dubois was no longer at the observation window but was sitting at Morro's desk, two revolving tape recorders in front of him. He switched them off and looked up.

Morro said: "Deliberations over?"

"Twenty minutes ago. They're deliberating something else now."

"How to stop us, no doubt."

"What else? I gave up listening some time ago, they couldn't stop a retarded five-year-old. Besides, they can't even speak coherently, far less think rationally."

Morro crossed to the observation window and switched on the speaker above his head. All four scientists were sitting—more accurately sprawling—around the table, bottles in front of them to save them the labor of having to rise and walk to the drink trolley. Burnett was speaking, his face suffused with alcohol or anger or both and every other word was slurred.

"Damn it to hell. All the way to hell. Back again, too. There's the four of us. Look at us. Best brains in the country, that's what we are supposed to be. Best *nuclear* brains. Is it beyond our capacity, gentlemen, beyond our intelligence, to devise a means whereby to circument—I mean circumvent—the devilish machinations of this monster Morro? What I maintain is—"

Bramwell said: "Oh, shut up. That makes the fourth time we've heard this speech." He poured himself some vodka, leaned back and closed his eyes. Healey had his elbows on the table and his hands covering his eyes. Schmidt was gazing into infinity, riding high on a cloud of gin. Morro switched off the speaker and turned away.

"I don't know either Burnett or Schmidt but I should

157

imagine they are about par for their own particular courses. I'm surprised at Healey and Bramwell, though. They're relatively sober but you can tell they're not their usual selves. In the seven weeks we've been here—well, they've been very moderate."

"In their seven weeks here they haven't had such a shock to their nervous systems. They've probably never had a shock like this."

"They know? A superfluous question, perhaps."

"They suspected right away. They knew for certain in fifteen minutes. The rest of the time they've been trying to find a fault, any fault, in the designs. They can't. And all four of them know *how* to make a hydrogen bomb."

"You're editing, I take it. How much longer?"

"Say twenty minutes."

"If I give a hand?"

"Ten."

"Then in fifteen minutes we'll give them another shock, and one that should have the effect of sobering them up considerably if not completely."

And in fifteen minutes the four men were escorted into the study. Morro showed them personally to their deep armchairs, a glass on a table beside each armchair. There were two other berobed acolytes in the room. Morro wasn't sure precisely what kind of reaction the physicists might provoke. The acolytes could have their Ingram submachine guns out from under their robes before any of the scientists could get halfway out of their chairs.

Morro said: "Well, now. Glenfiddich for Professor Burnett, gin for Dr. Schmidt, vodka for Dr. Bramwell, bourbon for Dr. Healey." Morro was a great believer in the undermining of confidence. When they had entered, Burnett and Schmidt had had expressions of scowling anger, Bramwell of thoughtfulness, Healey of something approaching apprehension. Now they all wore looks of suspicion compounded by surprise.

Burnett was predictably truculent. "How the hell did you know what we were drinking?"

"We're observant. We try to please. We're also thoughtful. We thought your favorite restorative might help you
158

over what may come as a shock to you. To business. What did you make of those blueprints?"

"How would you like to go to hell?" Burnett said.

"We may all meet there someday. I repeat the question."

"And I repeat the answer."

"You will tell me, you know."

"And how do you propose to set about making us talk. Torture?" Burnett's truculence had given way to contempt. "We can't tell you anything we don't know."

"Torture. Oh, dear me, no. I might—in fact, I shall be needing you later on. But torture? Hmm. Hadn't occurred to me. You, Abraham?"

"No, Mr. Morro." Dubois considered. "It is a thought." He came to Morro and whispered something in his ear.

Morro looked shocked. "Abraham, you know me, you know I don't wage war on innocents."

"You damned hypocrite!" Burnett's voice was a hoarse shout. "Of course that's why you brought the women here."

"My dear fellow—"

Bramwell said in a weary voice: "It's a bomb of some sort. That's obvious. It might well be a blueprint for a nuclear bomb, a thought that immediately occurred to us because of your propensity for stealing nuclear fuel. Whether it's viable, whether it will work, we have just no idea. There are hundreds of nuclear scientists in this country. But the number of those who can make, actually *make*, a nuclear bomb is severely restricted. We are not among the chosen few. As for those who can actually *design* a hydrogen bomb—well I, personally, have never met one. Our science is devoted to exclusively peaceful nuclear pursuits. Healey and I were kidnaped while working in a laboratory where they produced nothing but electricity. Burnett and Schmidt, as we are well aware, were taken in the San Ruffino nuclear reactor station. For God's sake, man, you don't build hydrogen bombs in reactor stations."

"Very clever." Morro was almost approving. "You do think fast on your feet. In your armchair, rather. Enough.

159

Abraham, that particular excerpt we selected. How long will it take?"

"Thirty seconds."

Dubois put a tape recorder on a fast rewind, his eye on the counter, slowed and finally stopped it. He pressed a switch, saying: "Healey first."

Healey's voice: "So we are in no doubt then?"

Schmidt's voice: "None. I haven't been since the first time I clapped eyes on those hellish blueprints."

Bramwell's voice: "Circuitry, materials, sheathing, triggering, design. All there. Your final confirmation, Burnett?"

There was a pause here, then came Burnett's voice, strangely flat and dead. "Sorry, gentlemen, I need that drink. It's the Aunt Sally, all right. Estimated three and a half megatons—about four hundred times the power of the bombs that destroyed Hiroshima and Nagasaki. God, to think that Willi Aachen and I had a champagne party the night we completed the design!"

Dubois switched off. Morro said: "I'm sure you could even reproduce those plans from your head, Professor Burnett, if the need arose. A useful man to have around."

The four physicists sat like men in a dream. They didn't look stunned, they just weren't registering anything. Morro said: "Come here, gentlemen."

He led the way to the window, pressed an overhead switch and illuminated the room in which the scientists had examined the blueprints. He looked at the scientists, but without satisfaction, gratification or triumph. Morro did not seem to specialize very much in the way of feelings.

"The expressions on your faces were more than enough to tell us all we wanted to know." If the four men had not been overcome by the enormity of the situation in which they found themselves, the ludicrous ease with which they had been tricked, they would have appreciated that Morro, who clearly had further use for them, was doing no more than establishing a moral ascendancy, inducing in them a feeling of helplessness and hopelessness. "But the recordings helped. That's the first thing I would have expected. Alas, outside your own arcane specialities, men with abnormally gifted minds are no better than little children. Abraham, how long does the entire edited version take?"

"Seven and a half minutes, Mr. Morro."

"Let them savor it to the full. I'll see about the helicopter. Back shortly."

He was back in ten minutes. Three of the scientists were sitting in their chairs, bitter, dejected and defeated. Burnett, not unexpectedly, was helping himself to some more of the endless supply of Glenfiddich.

"One further small task, gentlemen. I want each of you to make a brief recording stating that I have in my possession the complete blueprints for the making of a hydrogen bomb in the megaton range. You will make no mention whatsoever of the dimensions, no mention of its code name 'Aunt Sally'—what puerile names you scientists give those toys, just another sign of how limited your imagination is outside your own field—and above all, you will make no reference to the fact that Professor Burnett was the co-designer, along with Professor Aachen, of this bomb."

Schmidt said: "Why should those damn things be kept so secret when you'll let the world know everything else?"

"You will understand well enough inside the next two days or so."

"You've trapped us, fooled us, humiliated us and above all used us as pawns." Burnett said all this with his teeth clenched, no mean feat in itself. "But you can push a man too far, Morro. We're still men."

Morro sighed, made a small gesture of weariness, opened the door and beckoned. Susan and Julie came in and looked curiously around them. There was no apprehension or fear on their faces, just puzzlement.

"Give me that damned microphone." Without permission Burnett snatched it from the table and glared at Dubois. "Ready?"

"Ready."

Burnett's voice, though charged with emotion—pure,

161

black rage—was remarkably clear and steady, without a trace of the fact that he had, since his nonexistent breakfast, consumed the better part of a bottle of Glenfiddich, which said a great deal either for Professor Burnett or Glenfiddich.

"This is Professor Andrew Burnett of San Diego. It's not someone trying to imitate me—my voiceprints are in security in the university. This black-hearted bastard Morro has in his possession a complete set of plans for the construction of a hydrogen bomb in the megaton range. You had better believe me. Also you had better believe Dr. Schmidt and Drs. Healey and Bramwell—Drs. Healey and Bramwell have been held captive in this damned place for seven weeks. I repeat, for God's sake believe me. This is a step-by-step, fully composited, fully integrated plan ready to build now." There was a pause. "For all I know, the bastard may already have built one."

Morro nodded to Dubois, who switched off. Dubois said: "The third and last sentences, Mr. Morro—"

"Leave them in." Morro smiled. "Leave them. Eliminates the need for checking on voiceprints. They carry with them the normal characteristic flavor of the professor's colorful speech. You can cope, Abraham? Ridiculous question. Come, ladies."

He ushered them out and closed the door. Susan said: "Do you mind enlightening us? I mean, what *is* going on?"

"Certainly not, my dears. Our learned nuclear physicists have been doing a chore for me this morning. Not that they were aware of that fact—unknown to them I had their conversation recorded.

"I showed them a set of plans. I proved to them that I am indeed in possession of the secrets of the manufacture of hydrogen bombs. Now they are proving that to the world. Simple."

"Is that why you brought the scientists here?"

"I still have a further important use for them but, primarily, yes."

162

"Why did you bring us into that room, your study?"

"See? You are an inquisitive person. I was just satisfying your curiosity."

"Julie here is not an inquisitive person."

Julie nodded vigorously. For some reason she seemed close to tears. "I just want out of here."

Susan shook her arm. "What is it?"

"You know very well what it is. You know why he brought us in there. The men were turning balky. That's why *we* were brought up here."

"The thought hadn't escaped me," Susan said. "Would you—or that dreadful giant—have twisted our arms until we screamed? Or do you have dungeons—castles always have dungeons, don't they? You know, thumbscrews and racks and iron maidens? Do you break people on the wheel, Mr. Morro?"

"A dreadful giant! Abraham would be hurt. A kind and gentle giant. As for the rest? Dear me, dear me, dear me. Direct intimidation, Mrs. Ryder, is less effective than indirect. If people can bring themselves to believe something it's always more effective than having to prove it to them."

"Would you have proved it?" Morro was silent. "Would you have had us tortured?"

"I wouldn't even contemplate it."

"Don't believe him, don't believe him!" Julie's voice shook. "He's a monster and a liar."

"He's a monster all right." Susan was very calm, even thoughtful. "He may even be a liar. But in this case I believe him. Odd."

In a kind of despair, Julie said: "You don't know what you're saying!"

"I think I do. I think Mr. Morro will have no further use for us."

"How can you *say* that?"

Morro looked at Julie. "Someday you will be as wise and understanding as Mrs. Ryder. But first you will have to meet a great number of people and read a great number of characters. You see, Mrs. Ryder *knows* that the person

163

who laid a finger on either of you would have to answer to me. She knows that I never would. She will, of course, convince those disbelieving gentlemen we've just left and they will know I couldn't use this threat again. I do not have to. You are of no more use to me." Morro smiled. "Oh dear, that does sound vaguely threatening. Let us rather say that no harm will come to you."

Julie looked at him briefly, the fear and suspicion in her eyes undimmed, then looked abruptly away.

"Well, I tried, young lady. I cannot blame you. You cannot have heard what I said at the breakfast table this morning. 'We do not wage war on women.' Even monsters have to live with their monstrous selves." He turned and walked away.

Susan watched him go and murmured: "And therein lie the seeds of his own destruction."

Julie looked at her. "I—I didn't catch that. What did you say?"

"Nothing, Julie, nothing. I'm just rambling. I think this place is getting to me also." But she knew it wasn't.

"A complete waste of time." Jeff was in a black mood and didn't care who knew it. He had almost to raise his voice to a shout to make himself heard above the clamorous racket of the helicopter engine. "Nothing, just nothing. A lot of academic waffle about earthquakes and a useless hour in Sassoon's office. Nothing, just nothing. We didn't learn a thing."

Ryder looked up from the sheaf of notes he was studying. He said, as mildly as one could in a necessarily loud voice: "Oh, I don't know. We discovered that even learned academics can tamper with the truth when they see fit. We learned—at least I did—about earthquakes and this earthquake syndrome. As for Sassoon, nobody expected to learn anything from him. How could we? He knew nothing—how could he? He was learning things from us." He returned his attention to his notes.

"Well, my God! They've got Susan, they've got Peggy and all you can do is to sit there and read that load of old rubbish just as if—"
164

Dunne leaned across. No longer as alert and brisk as he had been some hours ago, he was beginning to show the effects of a sleepless night. He said: "Jeff. Do me a favor."

"Yes?"

"Shut up."

There was a pile of papers lying on Major Dunne's desk. He looked at them without enthusiasm, placed his brief case beside them, opened a cupboard, brought out a bottle of Jack Daniels and looked interrogatively at Ryder and his son. Ryder smiled but Jeff shook his head: he was still smarting from the effects of Dunne's particular brand of curtness.

Glass in hand, Dunne opened a side door. In the tiny cubicle beyond was an already made-up camp bed. Dunne said: "I'm not one of your superhuman FBI agents who can go five nights and days without sleep. I'll have Delage"—Delage was one of his juniors—"man the phones here. I can be reached any time but the excuse had better be a good one."

"Would an earthquake do?"

Dunne smiled, sat and went through the papers on his desk. He pushed them all to one side and lifted a thick envelope which he slit open. He peered at the contents inside and said: "Guess what?"

"Carlton's passport."

"Damn you. Anyway, nice to see someone's been busy around here." He extracted the passport, flipped through the pages and passed it to Ryder. "And damn you again."

"Intuition. The hallmark of the better-class detective." Ryder went through the pages, more slowly than Dunne. "Intriguing. Covers fourteen out of the fifteen months when he seemed to have vanished. A bad case of wander-bug infection. Did get around in that time, didn't he? Los Angeles, London, New Delhi, Singapore, Manila, Hong Kong, Manila again, Singapore, Manila yet again, Tokyo, Los Angeles." He passed the passport to Jeff. "Fallen in love with the mysterious East, it would seem. Especially the Philippines."

Dunne said: "Make anything of it?"

"Not a thing. Maybe I did have some sleep but it wasn't much. Mind seems to have gone to sleep. That's what we need, my mind and myself—sleep. Maybe when I wake up I'll have a flash of inspiration. Wouldn't bet on it, though."

He dropped Jeff outside the latter's house. "Sleep?"

"Straight to bed."

"First one awake calls the other. Okay?"

Jeff nodded and went inside. But he didn't go straight to bed. He went to the bay-fronted window of his living room and looked up the street. From there he had an excellent view of the short driveway by his father's house.

Ryder didn't head for bed either. He dialed the station house and asked for Sergeant Parker. He got through at once.

"Dave? No ifs, no buts. Meet me at Delmino's in ten minutes."

He went to the gas fire grate, tilted it forward, lifted out a polythene-covered green folder, went to the garage, pushed the folder under the Peugeot back seat, climbed in behind the wheel and backed the car down the driveway and into the road. Jeff moved as soon as he saw the rear of the car appearing, ran to his garage, started the engine and waited until Ryder's car had passed by. He followed.

Ryder appeared to be in a tearing hurry. Halfway toward the first intersection he was doing close to seventy, a speed normally unacceptable in a thirty-five-m.p.h. limit, but there wasn't a policeman in town who didn't know that battered machine and its occupant and who would ever have been so incredibly foolish as to detain Sergeant Ryder when he was going about his lawful operations. Ryder got through the lights on the green but Jeff caught the red. He was still there when he saw the Peugeot go through the next set of lights. By the time Jeff got to the next set they too had turned to red. When he did cross the intersection the Peugeot had vanished from sight. Jeff cursed, pulled over, parked and pondered.

Parker was in his usual booth in Delmino's when Ryder arrived. He was drinking a scotch and had one ready for Ryder, who remembered that he'd had nothing to eat so far that day. It didn't however, affect the taste of the scotch.

Ryder said without preamble: "Where's Fatso?"

"Suffering from the vapors, I'm glad to say. At home with a bad headache."

"Shouldn't be surprised. Very hard thing, the butt of a .38. Maybe I hit him harder than I thought. Enjoyed it at the time, though. Twenty minutes from now he's going to feel a hell of a sight more fragile. Thanks. I'm off."

"Wait a minute, wait a minute. *You* clobbered Donahure. Tell me."

Briefly and impatiently, Ryder told him. Parker was suitably impressed.

"Ten thousand bucks. Two Russian rifles. *And* this dossier you have on him. You have the goods on him all right—our ex-chief of police. But look, John, there's a limit as to how far you can go in taking the law into your own hands."

"There's no limit." Ryder put his hand on Parker's. "Dave, they've got Peggy."

There was a momentary incomprehension, then Parker's eyes went very cold. Peggy had first sat on his knees at the age of four and had sat there at regular intervals ever since, always with the mischievously disconcerting habit of putting her elbow on his shoulder, her chin on her palm and peering at him from a distance of six inches. Fourteen years later, dark, lovely and mischievous as ever, it was a habit she had still not abandoned, especially on those occasions when she wanted to wheedle something from Ryder, laboring under the misapprehension that this made her father jealous. Parker said nothing. His eyes said it for him.

Ryder said: "San Diego. During the night. They gunned down the two FBI men who were looking after her."

Parker stood up. "I'm coming with you."

"No. You're still an officer of the law. You'll see what me."

I'm going to do with Fatso and you'll have to arrest
"I've just turned blind."

"Please, Dave. I may be breaking the law but I'm still
on the side of the law and I need at least one person
inside the law I can trust. There's only you."

"Okay. But if any harm comes to her or Susan, I'm
out of a job."

"You'll be welcome in the ranks of the unemployed."

They left. As the door swung to behind them, a lean
Mexican youth with a straggling mustache that reached
his chin rose from the next booth, inserted his dime and
dialed. For a full minute the phone rang at the other
end without reply. The youth tried again with the same
result. He fumbled in his pockets, went to the counter,
changed a bill for loose change, returned and tried another
number. Twice he tried, twice he failed, and his mounting frustration, as he kept glancing at his watch, was
obvious: on the third time he was lucky. He started to
speak in low, hurried, urgent Spanish.

There was a certain lack of aesthetic appeal about the
way in which Chief of Police Donahure had arranged
his sleeping form. Fully clothed, he lay face down on a
couch, his left hand on the floor clutching a half-full
glass of bourbon, his hair in disarray and his cheeks
glistening with what could have been perspiration but
was, in fact, water steadily dripping down from the now
melting ice bag that Donahure had strategically placed
on the back of his head. It was to be assumed that the
loud snoring was caused not by the large bump that
undoubtedly lay concealed beneath the ice bag but from
the bourbon, for a man does not recover consciousness
from a blow, inform the office that he's sorry but he
won't be in today and then relapse into unconsciousness.
Ryder laid down the polythene folder he was carrying,
removed Donahure's Colt and prodded him far from
gently with its muzzle.

Donahure groaned, stirred, displaced the ice bag in
turning his head and managed to open one eye. His
original reaction must have been that he was gazing down
168

a long dark tunnel. When the realization gradually dawned upon his befuddled brain that it was not a tunnel but the barrel of his own .45, his Cyclopean gaze traveled above and beyond the barrel until Ryder's face swam into focus. Two things happened: both eyes opened wide and his complexion changed from its normal revolting puce to an even more unpleasant shade of dirty gray.

Ryder said: "Sit up."

Donahure remained where he was. His jowls were actually quivering. Then he screamed in agony as Ryder grabbed his hair and jerked him into the vertical. Clearly, no small amount of that hair had been attached to the bruised bump on his head. A sudden scalp pain predictably produces an effect on the corneal ducts and Donahure was no exception: his eyes were swimming like bloodshot goldfish in peculiarly murky water.

Ryder said: "You know how to conduct a cross-examination, Fatso?"

"Yes." He sounded as if he was being garroted.

"No you don't. I'm going to show you. It's not in any textbook and I'm afraid you'll never have an opportunity to use it. But, by comparison, the cross-examination you'll get on the witness stand in court will seem almost pleasant. Who's paying you off, Donahure?"

"What in God's name—" He broke off with a shout of pain and clapped his hands to his face. He reached finger and thumb inside his mouth, removed a displaced tooth and dropped it on the floor. His left cheek was cut both inside and out and blood was trickling down his chin: Ryder had laid the barrel of Donahure's Colt against his face with a heavy hand. Ryder transferred the Colt to his left hand.

"Who's paying you, Donahure?"

"What in the hell—" Another shout and another hiatus in the conversation while Donahure attended to the right-hand side of his face. The blood was now flowing freely from his mouth and dripping onto his shirt front. Ryder transferred the revolver back to his right hand.

"Who's paying you, Donahure?"

"LeWinter." A strangely gurgling sound; he must have

been swallowing blood. Ryder regarded him without compassion.

"What for?"

Donahure gurgled again. The ensuing croak was unintelligible.

"For looking the other way?"

A nod. There was no hate in Donahure's face, just plain naked fear.

"For destroying evidence against guilty parties, faking evidence against innocent parties?" Another nod. "How much did you make, Donahure? Over the years, I mean. Blackmail on the side of course."

"I don't know."

Ryder lifted his gun again.

"Twenty thousand, maybe thirty." Once more he screamed. His nose had gone the same way as Raminoff's.

Ryder said: "I won't say I'm not enjoying this any more than you are, because I am. I'm more than prepared to keep this up for hours yet. Not that you'll last more than twenty minutes and we don't want your face smashed into such a bloody pulp that you can't talk. Before it comes to that I'll start breaking your fingers one by one." Ryder meant it and the abject terror on what was left of Donahure's face showed that he knew Ryder meant it. "How much?"

"I don't know." He cowered behind raised hands. "I don't know how much. Hundreds."

"Of thousands?" A nod. Ryder picked up the polythene folder and extracted papers which he showed to Donahure. "Total of just over five hundred and fifty thousand dollars in seven banks under seven different names. That would be about right." Another nod. Ryder returned the papers to the polythene folder. If this represented only Donahure's rake-off, how much did LeWinter have safe and sound in Zurich?

"The last pay-off. Ten thousand dollars. What was that for?" Donahure was now so befuddled with pain and fright that it never occurred to him to ask how Ryder knew about it.

"Cops."

"Bribes to do what?"

"Cut all the public phones between here and Ferguson's house. Cut Ferguson's phone. Wreck his police band radio. Clear the roads."

"Clear the roads? No patrols on the hijack van's escape route?"

Donahure nodded. He obviously felt this easier than talking.

"Jesus. You are a sweet bunch. I'll have their names later. Who gave you those Russian rifles?"

"Rifles?" A frown appeared in the negligible clearance between Donahure's hairline and eyebrows, sure indication that at least part of his mind was working again. "*You* took them. And the money. You—" He touched the back of his head.

"I asked a question. Who gave you the rifles?"

"I don't know." Donahure raised defensive hands just as Ryder lifted his gun. "Smash my face to pieces and I still don't know. Found them in the house when I came back one night. Voice over the phone said I was to keep them." Ryder believed him.

"This voice have a name?"

"No." Ryder believed that also. No intelligent man would be crazy enough to give his name to a man like Donahure.

"This the voice that told you to tap LeWinter's phone?"

"How in God's name—" Donahure broke off not because of another blow or impending blow but because, swallowing blood from both mouth and nose, he was beginning to have some difficulty with his breathing. Finally he coughed and spoke in a gasp. "Yes."

"Name Morro mean anything to you?"

"Morro? Morro who?"

"Never mind." If Donahure didn't know the name of Morro's intermediary he most certainly didn't know Morro's.

Jeff had first tried the Redox in Bay Street, the unsavory bar-restaurant where his father had had his

171

rendezvous with Dunne. No one answering to either of their descriptions had been there, or, if they had, no one was saying.

From there he went to the FBI office. He'd expected to find Delage there, and did. He also found Dunne, who clearly hadn't been to bed. He looked at Jeff in surprise. "So soon. What's up?"

"My father been here?"

"No. Why?"

"When we got home he said he was going to bed. He didn't. He left after two or three minutes. I followed him, don't know why; I had the feeling he was going to meet someone, that he was stepping into danger. Lost him at the lights."

"Worry about the other guy," Dunne advised. "Some news for you and your father, not all that good. Both shot FBI men were under heavy sedation during the night, but one's clear now. He says that the first person shot last night was neither him nor his partner but Peggy. She got it through the left shoulder."

"No!"

"I'm afraid so, boy. I know this agent well. He doesn't make mistakes."

"But—but—if she's wounded, I mean medical attention, hospital, she must have—"

"Sorry, Jeff. That's all we know. The kidnapers took her away, remember."

Jeff made to speak, turned and left the office. He went to Delmino's, the station officers' favorite hang-out. Yes, Sergeants Ryder and Parker had been there. No, the barman didn't know where they had gone.

Jeff drove the short distance to the station house. Parker was there along with Sergeant Dickson. Jeff said: "Seen my father?"

"Yes, why?"

"You know where he is?"

"Yes. Again why?"

"Just *tell* me!"

"I'm not rightly sure I should." He looked at Jeff, saw the urgency and intensity. He said reluctantly: "He's at
172

Chief Donahure's. But I'm not sure—" He stopped. Jeff had already gone. Parker looked at Dickson and shrugged.

Ryder said, almost conversationally: "Heard that my daughter has been kidnaped?"

"No. I swear to God—"

"All right. Any idea how anyone might have got hold of her address in San Diego."

Donahure shook his head—but his eyes had flickered, just once. Ryder broke open the revolver: the hammer was lined up against an empty cylinder, one of two. He closed the gun, shoved the stubby finger of Donahure's right hand through the trigger guard, held the Colt by barrel and butt and said: "On the count of three I twist both hands. One—"

"I did, I did."

"How did you get it?"

"Week or two ago. You were out for lunch and—"

Ryder was contemplating Donahure speculatively.

"And I'd left my address book in my drawer so you kind of naturally wrote down a few names and addresses. I really should break your finger for this. But you can't sign a statement if I break your writing forefinger, can you?"

"A statement?"

"I'm not a law officer anymore. It's a citizen's arrest. Just as legal. I arrest you, Donahure, for larceny, corruption, bribery, the acceptance of bribes—and for murder in the first degree."

Donahure said nothing. His face, grayer than ever, had slumped between his sagging shoulders. Ryder sniffed the muzzle. "Fired recently." He broke open the gun. "Two bullets gone. We only carry five in a cylinder, so one's been fired recently." He eased out one cartridge and scraped the tip with a nail. "And soft-nosed, just like the one that took off Sheriff Hartman's head. A perfect match for this barrel I'll bet." He knew that a match-up was impossible, but Donahure either didn't know or was too far gone to think. "And you left your fingerprints on the door handle, which was a very careless thing to do."

173

Donahure said dully: "It was the man on the phone——"

"Save it for the judge."

"Freeze," a high-pitched voice behind Ryder said. Ryder had survived to his present age by knowing exactly the right thing to do at the right time and at the moment the right thing appeared to be to do what he was told. He froze.

"Drop that gun."

Ryder obediently dropped the gun, a decision which was made all the easier for him by the fact that he was holding the gun by the barrel anyway and the cylinder was hinged out.

"Now turn around nice and slow." He must have been brought up on a strict diet of B movies, Ryder reflected, but that didn't make him any less dangerous. He turned around nice and slow. The visitor had a black handkerchief tied below his eyes, wore a dark suit, dark shirt, white tie and, of all things, a black fedora. B movies, late 1930s.

"Donahure ain't going to meet no judge." He had the dialogue right, too. "But you're going to meet your maker. No time for prayers, mister."

"You drop that gun," said a voice from the doorway.

Obviously the masked man was considerably younger than Ryder for he didn't know the right thing to do. He whipped around and loosed off a snap shot at the figure in the doorway. In the circumstances it was a pretty good effort, ripping the cloth on the upper right sleeve of Jeff's coat. Jeff's reply was considerably more effective. The man in the mask folded in the middle like a collapsing hinge and crumpled to the floor. Ryder dropped to one knee beside him.

"I tried for his gun hand," Jeff said uncertainly. "Reckon I missed."

"You did. Didn't miss his heart, though." Ryder plucked off the handkerchief mask. "Well. What a shame. Lennie the Linnet has gone riding off across the great divide."

"Lennie the Linnet?" Jeff was visibly shaken.

"Yes. Linnet. A song bird. Well, wherever Lennie's singing now you can take long odds that it won't be to

174

the accompaniment of a harp." Ryder glanced sideways, straightened, took the gun from Jeff's lax hand and fired, all in seemingly slow motion. For the fifth time that night Donahure cried out in pain. The Colt he'd picked up from the floor spun across the room along with parts of his little and fourth fingers. Ryder said: "Do be quiet. You can still sign the statement. And to the charge of murder we'll now add one of attempted murder."

Jeff said: "One easy lesson, right?"

Ryder touched his shoulder. "Well, thanks, anyway."

"I didn't mean to kill him."

"Shed no sad tears for Lennie. A heroin pusher. You followed me?"

"Tried to. Sergeant Parker told me where you were. How did *he* get here?"

"Ah, now. If you want the detective sergeant at his brilliant best, ask him after the event. I thought our line was tapped so I phoned Parker to meet me at Delmino's. Never occurred to me they'd put a stake-out there."

Jeff looked at Donahure. "So that's why you didn't want me along. He ran into a truck?"

"Self-inflicted injuries. From now on, you're welcome along anytime. Get a couple of towels from the bathroom. Don't want him to bleed to death before his trial."

Jeff hesitated: he had to tell his father and actively feared for Donahure's life. "Some bad news, Dad. Peggy was shot last night."

"Shot?" The lips compressed whitely. Ryder's eyes switched to Donahure, the grip on Jeff's gun tightened, but he was still under his iron control. He looked back at Jeff. "Bad?"

"Don't know. Bad enough, I should think. Left shoulder."

"Get the towels." Ryder lifted the phone, got through to Sergeant Parker. "Come out here, will you, Dave? Bring an ambulance, Doc Hinkley"—Hinkley was the police surgeon—"and young Kramer to take a statement. Ask Major Dunne to come. And Dave—Peggy was shot last night. Through the shoulder." He hung up.

Parker passed on the requests to Kramer then went up to see Mahler. Mahler viewed him as he was viewing life at the moment, with a harassed and jaundiced eye.

Parker said: "I'm going out to Chief Donahure's place. Some trouble out there."

"What trouble?"

"Something that calls for an ambulance."

"Who said so?"

"Ryder."

"Ryder." Mahler pushed back his chair and rose. "What the hell is Ryder doing out there?"

"Didn't say. I think he wanted a talk with him."

"I'll have him behind bars for this. I'll take charge of this personally."

"I'd like to come, Lieutenant."

"You stay here. That's an order, Sergeant Parker."

"Nothing personal, Lieutenant." Parker put his badge on the desk. "I'm not taking orders anymore."

They all arrived together—the two ambulance men, Kramer, Major Dunne, Mahler and Dr. Hinkley. As befitted the occasion, Dr. Hinkley was in the lead. A small wiry man with darting eyes, he was, if not exactly soured by life, at least possessed of a profoundly cynical resignation. He looked at the recumbent figure on the floor.

"Good lord! Lennie the Linnet. A black day for America." He peered more closely at the white tie with the red-rimmed hole though it. "Heart damage of some kind. Gets them younger every day. And Chief of Police Donahure!" He crossed to where a moaning Donahure was sitting on his couch, his left hand tenderly cradling the blood-soaked towel around his right hand. None too gently, Hinkley unwrapped the towel. "Dear me. Where's the rest of these two fingers?"

Ryder said: "He tried to shoot me. Through the back, of course."

176

"Ryder." Lieutenant Mahler had a pair of handcuffs ready. "I'm placing you under arrest."

"Put those things away and don't make more a fool of yourself than you can help if *you* don't want to be charged with obstructing justice. I am making, I have made, a perfectly legal citizen's arrest. The charges are larceny, corruption, bribery, the acceptance of bribes, attempted murder and murder in the first degree. Donahure will admit to all of them and I can prove all of them. Also he's an accessory to the wounding of my daughter."

"Your daughter shot?" Oddly, this seemed to affect Mahler more than the murder accusation. He had put his handcuffs away. A disciplinary martinet, he was nonetheless a fair man.

Ryder looked at Kramer. "He has a statement to make but as he's suffering from a minor speech impairment right now I'll make it for him and he'll sign it. Give the usual warnings, of course, about legal rights, that his statement can be used in evidence, you know the form." It took Ryder only four minutes to make the statement on Donahure's behalf and by the time he had finished the damning indictment there wasn't a man in that room, Mahler included, who wouldn't have testified that the statement had been voluntary.

Major Dunne took Ryder aside. "So fine, so you've cooked Donahure's goose. You're doubtless aware that you've also cooked your own goose. You can't imprison a man without preferring charges and the law says those charges must be made public."

"There are times when I admire the Russian legal system."

"Yeah. So Morro will know in a couple of hours. And he's got Susan and Peggy."

"I don't seem to have many options open. Somebody has to do something. I haven't noticed that the police or the FBI or the CIA have been particularly active."

"Miracles take a little time." Dunne was impatient. "Meantime, they still have your family."

"Yes. I'm beginning to wonder about that. If they are in danger, I mean."

"Jesus! Danger? Course they are. God's sake man, look at what happened to Peggy."

"An accident. They could have killed her if they came that close. A dead hostage is no good to anyone."

"I suppose I could call you a cold-blooded bastard but I don't believe you are. You know something I don't?"

"No. You have all the facts that I have. Only I have this feeling that we're being conned, that we're following a line that they want us to follow. I told Jablonsky last night that I didn't think the scientists had been taken in order to force them to make a bomb of some kind. They've been taken for some other purpose. And if I don't think that then I no longer think that the women were taken to force them to build a bomb. And not for a lever on me either—why should they worry about me in advance?"

"What's bugging you, Ryder?"

"I'd like to know why Donahure has—had—those Kalashnikovs in his possession. He doesn't seem to know either."

"I don't follow you."

"Unfortunately, I don't follow myself."

Dunne remained in silent thought for some time. Then he looked at Donahure, winced at the sight of the battered face and said: "Who's next in line for your kindly ministrations? LeWinter?"

"Not yet. We've got enough to pull him in for questioning but not enough to hold him on the uncorroborated word of an unconvicted man. And unlike Donahure, he's a wily bird who'll give away nothing. I think I'll call on his secretary after an hour or two's sleep."

The phone rang. Jeff answered and held it out to Dunne, who listened briefly, hung up and said to Ryder: "I think you'll have to postpone your sleep for a little. Another message from our friends."

EIGHT

■ DELAGE was with a man the Ryders hadn't seen before, a young man, fair-haired, broad, wearing a gray flannel suit cut loose to conceal whatever weaponry he was carrying and a pair of dark glasses of the type much favored by Secret Service men who guard presidents and heads of state.

"Leroy," Dunne said. "San Diego. He's liaising with Washington on LeWinter's codes. He's also in touch with the AEC plant in Illinois, checking on Carlton's past contacts, and has a team working on the lists of the weirdos. Anything yet, Leroy?"

Leroy shook his head. "Late afternoon, hopefully."

Dunne turned to Delage. "So what didn't you want to tell me over the phone? What's so hush-hush?"

"Won't be hush-hush much longer. The wire services have it but Barrow told them to sit on it. When the director tells people to sit on something, it's sat on." He nodded to a tape recorder. "We recorded this over the direct line from Los Angeles. Seems that Durrer of ERDA was sent a separate recording."

He pressed a switch and a smooth educated voice began to speak, in English, but not American English. "My name is Morro and I am, as many of you will know by this time, the person responsible for the San Ruffino reactor break-in. I have messages to you from some eminent scientists and I suggest you all listen very carefully. For your own sakes, please listen carefully." The tape stopped as Dunne raised a hand.

He said: "Anyone recognize that voice?" Clearly no one did. "Anyone identify that accent? Would it give you any idea where Morro comes from?"

Delage said: "Europe? Asia? Could be any place. Could be an American with a phony accent."

179

"Why don't you ask the experts?" Ryder said. "University of California. On one campus or another, anywhere between San Diego and Davis, you'll find some professor or lecturer who'll recognize it. Don't they claim to teach every major and most of the important minor languages in the world somewhere in this state?"

"A point. Barrow and Sassoon may already have thought of it. We'll mention it." He nodded to Delage, who flipped the switch again.

A rasping and indignant voice said: "This is Professor Andrew Burnett of San Diego. It's not someone trying to imitate me—my voiceprints are in security in the university. This black-hearted bastard Morro—" And so Burnett continued until he had finished his wrathful tirade. Dr. Schmidt, who followed him on the tape, sounded just as furious as Burnett. Healey and Bramwell were considerably more moderate, but all four men had one thing in common—they were utterly convincing.

Dunne said to no one in particular: "We believe them?"

"*I* believe them." Delage's certainty was absolute. "That's the fourth time I've heard that played and I believe it more every time. You could tell they weren't being coerced, under the influence of drugs, physical intimidation, anything like that. Especially not with Professor Burnett. You can't fake that kind of anger. Provided, of course, that those four men are who they claim to be and they have to be—they'll be on TV and radio any time and there must be hundreds of colleagues, friends, students who can confirm their genuineness. A megaton? That's the equivalent of a million tons of TNT, isn't it? Downright nasty."

Ryder said to Dunne: "Well, that's part of the answer to what we were talking about back in Donahure's house. To confirm the existence of those plans and scare the living daylights out of us. Us and everybody in California. They're going to succeed, don't you think?"

Leroy said: "What gets me is that they haven't given the faintest indication as to what they're up to."

"That's what's going to get everyone," Ryder said.

180

"That's part of his psychological gambit. Scare hell out of everyone."

"And speaking of scaring, I'm afraid there is more to come." Delage flicked the "on" switch again and Morro's voice came through once more.

"A postscript, if you please. The authorities claim that the earthquake felt in the southern part of the state this morning came from White Wolf fault and, as I have already said, this is a lie. As already said, I was responsible. To prove that the state authorities are lying, I will detonate another nuclear device at exactly 10 A.M. tomorrow morning. The device is already in place in a site specially chosen so that I have it under permanent surveillance—any attempt to locate or approach this device will leave me no alternative other than to detonate it by radio control.

"People are advised not to approach within five miles of the site. If they do, I shall not be responsible for their lives. If they don't, but are still foolish enough not to wear specially darkened lenses, I shall not be responsible for their sight.

"The chosen site is in Nevada, about twelve miles northwest of Skull Peak, where Yucca Flat adjoins Frenchman's Flat.

"This device is in the kiloton range, of the approximate destructive power of those which destroyed Hiroshima and Nagasaki."

Delage switched off. After about thirty seconds' silence, Dunne said thoughtfully: "Well, that's a nice touch, I must say. Going to use the United States official testing ground for his purposes. As you ask, what the devil is the man up to? Does anyone here believe what we've just heard?"

"I do," Ryder said. "I believe it absolutely. I believe it's in position, I believe it will be detonated at the time he says it will, and I believe there is nothing we can do to stop him. I believe all you can do is to prevent as many rubber-necks as possible from going there and having themselves incinerated or radiated or whatever. A traffic problem of sorts."

Jeff said: "For a traffic problem you require roads. No major roads there. Dirt tracks, that's all."

"Not a job for us," Dunne said. "Army, National Guard, tanks, armored cars, jeeps, a couple of Phantoms to discourage air-borne snoopers—there should be no problem in cordoning the area off. For all I know everybody might be more interested in running in the other direction. All that concerns me is why, why, why. Blackmail and threats, of course, but again, what, what, what. A man feels so damned helpless. Nothing you can do, nothing you can go on."

"I know what I'm going to do," Ryder said. "I'm going to bed."

The Sikorsky cargo helicopter landed in the courtyard of the Adlerheim but none of those seated in the refectory paid it any attention: the helicopter, which ferried in nearly all the supplies for the Adlerheim, was constantly coming and going and one just learned to live with its deafening clatter. That apart, the few guards, the hostages, Morro and Dubois were considerably more interested in what was taking place on the big TV screen before them. The announcer, arms folded in a form of noble resignation and his features arranged in a solemn gravity appropriate to the occasion, had just finished the playing of the tape recordings of the four physicists and had embarked upon Morro's postscript. The pilot of the helicopter, clad in a red plaid mackinaw, entered and approached Morro but was waved to a seat: Morro was not concerned with listening to his own voice but appeared to derive interest and amusement from listening to the comments and watching the expressions of the others.

When Morro had finished his postscript, Burnett turned to Schmidt and said loudly: "Well, what did I tell you, Schmidt? The man's a raving lunatic."

The remark seemed to cause Morro no offense; nothing ever seemed to. "If you are referring to me, Professor Burnett, and I assume you are, that's a most uncharitable conclusion. How do you arrive at it?"

182

"In the first place you don't have an atom bomb—"

"And, even worse, that's a stupid conclusion. I never claimed it was an atom bomb. It's an atomic device. Same effect, though. And eighteen kilotons is not to be regarded lightly."

Bramwell said: "There is just your word—"

"At one minute past ten tomorrow morning you and Burnett will doubtless have the courtesy to apologize to me."

Bramwell was no longer so certain. "Even if such a thing did exist what would be the point in detonating it out in the desert?"

"Simple, surely. Just to prove to people that I have nuclear explosive power available. And if I can prove that, what is to prevent them from believing that I have unlimited nuclear armament power available? One creates a climate first of uncertainty, then of apprehension, then of pure fear, finally of outright terror."

"You have more of those devices available?"

"I shall satisfy the scientific curiosity of you and your three physicist colleagues this evening."

Schmidt said: "What in God's name are you trying to play at, Morro?"

"I am not trying, and I am not playing, as the citizens of this state and indeed of the whole world will soon know."

"Aha! And therein lies the psychological nub of the matter, is that it? Let them imagine what they like. Let them brood on the possibilities. Let them imagine the worst. And then tell them that the worst is worse than they ever dreamed of. Is that it?"

"Excellent, Schmidt, quite splendid. I shall include that in my next broadcast. 'Imagine what you like. Brood on the possibilities. Imagine the worst. But can you imagine that the worst is worse than you ever dreamed of?' Yes. Thank you, Schmidt. I shall take all the credit for myself, of course." Morro rose, went to the helicopter pilot, bent to listen to a few whispered words, nodded, straightened and approached Susan. "Come with me, please, Mrs. Ryder."

He led her along a passage. She said, curiously: "What is it, Mr. Morro? Or do you want to keep it as a surprise for me? A shock, perhaps? You seem to delight in shocking people. First you shock us all by bringing us here, then you shock the four physicists with your hydrogen weapon plan, now you shock millions of people in the state. Does it give you pleasure to shock people?"

Morro considered. "No, not really. The shocks I have administered so far have been either inevitable or calculated to further my own designs. But a warped and sadistic pleasure, no. I've just been wondering how to tell you. You *are* in for a shock, but not a serious one, for there's nothing serious to be worried about. I have your daughter here, Mrs. Ryder, and she's been hurt. Not badly. She'll be all right."

"My daughter! Peggy? Here? What in God's name is she doing here? And how hurt?"

For an answer, Morro opened a door in one side of the passageway. Inside was what looked like—and was—a small private hospital ward. There were three beds but only one was in use. The occupant was a pale-faced girl with long dark hair, in which point lay the only difference from her remarkable resemblance to her mother. Her lips parted and brown eyes opened wide in astonishment as she stretched out her right arm: the bandages around her left shoulder were clearly visible. Mother and daughter exchanged the exclamations, endearments, murmurs and sympathies which mothers and daughters might be expected to exchange in such circumstances while Morro considerately maintained a discreet distance, using his right hand mutely to bar the further progress of a man who had just entered: the newcomer wore a white coat, wore a stethoscope around his neck and carried a black bag. Even without the trappings, he had, indefinably, the word "doctor" written large upon him.

Susan said: "Your shoulder, Peggy. Does it hurt?"

"Not now. Well, a little."

"How did it happen?"

"I was shot. When I was kidnaped."

"I see. You were shot when you were kidnaped."

184

Susan squeezed her eyes shut, shook her head and looked at Morro. "You, of course."

"Mommy." The girl's face showed a complete lack of understanding. "What is all this? Where am I? What hospital—"

"You're not in the hospital. This is the private residence of Mr. Morro here. The man who broke into the San Ruffino reactor plant. The man who kidnaped you. The man who kidnaped me."

"You!"

Susan said bitterly, "Mr. Morro is not a piker. He doesn't do things on a small scale. He's holding eight others hostage too."

Peggy slumped back on her pillows. "I just don't understand."

The doctor touched Morro's arm. "The young lady is overtired, sir."

"I agree. Come, Mrs. Ryder, your daughter's shoulder requires attention. Dr. Hitushi here is a highly qualified physician." He paused and looked at Peggy. "I am genuinely sorry about this. Tell me, did you notice anything peculiar about either of your attackers?"

"Yes." Peggy gave a little shiver. "One of them—a little man—didn't have a left hand."

"Did he have anything at all?"

"Yes. Like two curved fingers, only they were made of metal, with rubber tips."

"I'll be back soon," Susan said and permitted Morro to guide her by the elbow out into the passageway where she angrily shook her arm free. "Did you have to do that to the poor child?"

"I regret it extremely. A beautiful child."

"You don't wage war on women." Morro should have shriveled on the spot but didn't. "Why bring her here?"

"I don't hurt women or permit them to be hurt. This was an accident. I brought her here because I thought she'd be better with her mother with her."

"So you shock people, you tell lies and now you're a hypocrite." Again Morro remained unshriveled.

"Your contempt is understandable, your spirit com-

185

mendable, but you're wrong on all three counts. I also brought her here for proper medical treatment."

"What was wrong with San Diego?"

"I have friends there, but no medical friends."

"I would point out, Mr. Morro, that they have fine hospitals there."

"And I would point out that hospitals would have meant the law. How many small Mexicans do you think there are in San Diego with a prosthetic appliance in place of a left hand? He'd have been picked up in hours and led them to me. I'm afraid I couldn't have that, Mrs. Ryder. But I couldn't leave her with my friends either because there she would be lonely with no one capable of looking after her wound, and that would have been psychologically and physically very bad for her. Here she has you and skilled medical attention. As soon as the doctor has finished treating her I'm sure he'll permit her to be wheeled to your suite to stay there with you."

Susan said: "You're a strange man, Mr. Morro." He looked at her without expression, turned and left.

Ryder awoke at 5:30 P.M., feeling less refreshed than he should have, because he had slept only fitfully, less because of worry about his family—he was becoming increasingly if irrationally of the opinion, it was no certainty, that they weren't in as grave danger as he had once thought—but because there were several wandering wisps of thought tugging at the corners of his mind which he couldn't identify for what they were. He rose, made sandwiches and coffee, consumed them while he plowed through the earthquake literature he had borrowed from Pasadena. Neither the coffee nor the literature helped him any. He went out and called up the FBI office. Delage answered.

Ryder said: "Is Major Dunne around?"

"Sound asleep. Is it urgent?"

"No. Let him be. Got anything that might interest me?"

"Leroy has, I think."

"Anything from 888 South Maple?"

"Nothing of interest. Local nosy neighbor, a rheumy-eyed old goat—I'm quoting, you understand—who would clearly like to know your Bettina Ivanhoe, if that's her name, better than he does, says that she hasn't been to work today, that she hasn't been out all morning."

"He's sure?"

"Foster—that's our stake-out man, spends most of his time around the back—says he believes him."

"Eternal vigilance, you'd say?"

"Probably with a pair of high-powered binoculars. She went out this afternoon, but walking—there's a super-market on the corner and she came back with a couple of shopping bags. Foster got a good look at her. Says he hardly blames the old goat. While she was out Foster let himself in and put a bug on her phone."

"Anything?"

"She hasn't used the phone since. More interesting, our legal friend was on the phone twice today. Well, only the second conversation was interesting. The first was made by the judge himself to his chambers. Said he's been stricken by a case of severe lumbago and could they get a deputy to stand in for him in court. The second was made *to* him. Very enigmatic. Told him to let his lumbago attack last for another couple of days and everything should be all right. That was all."

"Where did the call come from?"

"Bakersfield."

"Odd."

"What?"

"Close to the White Wolf fault where the earthquake was supposed to originate."

"How do you know that?"

"Education." Courtesy of the Cal Tech library, he'd learned the fact only ten minutes previously. "Coincidence. Pay phone, of course?"

"Yes."

"Thanks. Be down soon."

He returned to the house, called Jeff—he'd nothing to say to his son that a phone tapper would find of any interest—woke him and told him to call around but to

187

wear different clothes from those he had been wearing the previous night. While he was waiting, he himself went to change.

Jeff arrived, looked at his father's usual crumpled clothes, looked at his own well-pressed blue suit and said: "Well, no one could accuse you of entering the sartorial stakes. Are we supposed to be in disguise?"

"Sort of. For the same reason I'm going to call up Sergeant Parker on the way in and have him meet us at the FBI office. Delage says they may have something for us, by the way. No, we're going to have the pleasure of interviewing a lady tonight, although I doubt whether she'll regard it as such. Bettina Ivanhoe or Ivanov or whatever. She'll recognize the clothes we were wearing last night, which is more than we can say about her. She won't recognize our faces, but she would our voices, which is why I'm having Sergeant Parker briefed and having him do the talking for us."

"What happens if something occurs to you—even me—and we want Sergeant Parker to ask a particular question?"

"That's why we are going along—just in case that possibility arises. We'll arrange a signal, then she'll be told that we have to go out and check something with the station by the car radio-phone. Never fails to panic the conscience-stricken. Might even panic her into making a distress call to someone. Her phone's bugged."

"Cops are a lousy bunch."

Ryder glanced at him briefly and said nothing. He didn't have to.

"Let's start with Carlton," Leroy said. "The security chief at the reactor plant in Illinois never got to know him well. Neither did any of the staff there—the ones that are left, that is. That was two years or so ago and a good number have moved on elsewhere. Secretive kind of lad, it would appear."

"Nothing wrong with that," Ryder said. "Nothing I like better than minding my own business—in off-duty hours, that is. But in his case? Who knows? Any leads?"

188

"One, but it sounds more than fair. The security chief—name of Daimler—has traced his old landlady. She says Carlton and her son used to be very close, used to go away weekends quite a bit. Says she doesn't know where they went. Daimler says it's more likely that she didn't care where they went. She's well off—or was—her husband left her a good annuity but she takes in boarders because most of her money goes for gin and cards. Most of her time and interest too, it would appear."

"Sensible husband."

"Probably died in self-defense. Daimler offered—he wasn't too enthusiastic about the offer—to go and see her. I said thanks, we'd send one of our boys—an NFI card carries more weight. He's going there this evening—boy still lives at home.

"That's all. Except for his mother's comment about him —says he's a religious nut and should be put away somewhere."

"It's the maternal instinct. What else?"

"LeWinter's fancy codes. We've traced nearly all the telephone numbers—I think you've been told they were mainly California or Texas. Seem a respectable enough bunch—at least, preliminary inquiries haven't turned up anything about the ones investigated so far—but, on the face of it they would seem an odd group for a senior judge like LeWinter to be associated with."

"I've got a lot of friends—well, friends and acquaintances—who aren't cops," Jeff said. "But none of them, as far as I know, has ever seen the inside of a courtroom, much less a prison."

"Yes. But here's an eminent lawyer—or what a cockeyed world regards as an eminent lawyer—with a list of people who are primarily engineers, and not only that, but specialists in the engineering field. Specializing in petrochemicals and not only chemists, metallurgists, geologists, what you would expect to find, but also oilrig owners, drillers and explosives experts."

Ryder said: "A strange crew, agreed. Maybe LeWinter is figuring on moving into the oil exploration field—the old crook has probably accumulated enough in the
189

way of pay-offs to finance a stake in something of that nature. But I think that's too far-fetched. Much more likely that those names have something to do with cases that have come up before him. They could be people that have been called as expert witnesses."

Leroy smiled. "You wouldn't believe it, but we thought of that all by ourselves. We turned up a list of his civil, as distinct from criminal, court cases over the years and he has been involved in quite a number of lawsuits primarily involved with oil—exploration, leases, environmental pollution, marine trusts, lord knows what. Before he became a judge he was a defending counsel, and a highly successful one, as you would expect from such a devious character—"

"Assumption, assumption," Ryder said.

"So? You just called him an old crook. As I was saying, he made quite a reputation for himself for protecting the legal interests of various oil companies that had quite clearly transgressed the law until LeWinter proved otherwise. In fact, the amount of oil litigation that goes on in this fair state of ours is quite staggering. But it would seem that that's all irrelevant. To me, anyway. You, I don't know. But, one way or another, he's been swimming around in this oil business for close to twenty years, so I can't see how it bears on this present business."

"Neither do I," Ryder said. "On the other hand he could have been preparing for this day for all those years and is only now putting his knowledge to use. But, again, I think this is far-fetched. If there's any connection between oil prospecting or oil recovery I've never heard of it. How about this code-book-Ivanhoe thing? I was given to understand that the Washington Russian code breakers were making progress on that."

"They may well be. Unfortunately, they've gotten very coy. The center of their inquiries appears to have shifted to Geneva."

Ryder was patient. "Could you enlighten me, or did they choose to enlighten you, on just what the hell Geneva has to do with a nuclear theft in this state?"

"No, I can't enlighten you, because they clammed up. It's this damned interservice jealousy, if you ask me. 'Internecine' would be a better word."

Ryder was sympathetic. "You'll be telling me next that the damned CIA is shoving its oar in again."

"Has shoved, apparently. Bad enough to have them operating in friendly countries—allies, if you like—such as Britain and France, which they freely do without the permission of their hosts, but to start poking around in a strictly neutral Switzerland—"

"They don't operate there?"

"Of course not. Those agents you see lurking around the UNO, WHO and Lord knows how many international agencies in Geneva, are only figments of your imagination. Heady alpine air, or something like that. The Swiss are so sorry for them they offer them chairs in the shade, or under cover, depending on the weather."

"You sound bitter. Let's hope you'll resolve your differences in this particular case, and quickly. How has Interpol been doing with Morro?"

"They haven't. You have to remember that a good bit more than half the world has never even heard of the word 'Interpol.' It might help if we had the faintest clue as to where this pest comes from."

"The copies of the tapes of his voice? The ones that were to be sent out to our learned scholars?"

"There hasn't been time yet for any significant amount of comments to come in. We have had only four replies yet. One is positive that he has the voice of a Middle Easterner. In fact, he's positive enough to state categorically that the guy comes from Beirut. As Beirut is a hodgepodge of most of the nationalities in Europe, the Middle East, the Far East and a fair sprinkling of Africans, by which I mean people in African nations, it's hard to see what he's basing his conviction on. Another says, although not prepared to swear, that he's Indian. A third says he's definitely from the southeast of Asia. The last says that, as he's spent twenty years in Japan, he'd recognize Japanese-learned English anywhere."

Ryder said: "My wife described Morro as being a broad-shouldered six-footer."

"And Japanese answering to that description are not thick on the ground. I'm beginning to lose faith in the University of California." Leroy sighed. "Well, with the possible—and I'm now beginning to regard it as only faintly possible—exception of Carlton, we don't appear to have been making much headway. However, we may have something more encouraging for you in the way of those odd-ball organizations you wanted us to inquire about. You specified a year in existence and a large group. We're not saying you're wrong, but it did occur to us that it could conceivably be a smaller group, or one that has been in existence for a considerably longer period than a year and that may have been infiltrated or taken over by Morro and his friends. Here's the list. It's probably not a complete list; there's no state law that says you have to register yourself, or yourself and your like-minded friends, as a nut or nuts. But I'd guess it's as complete as we can get, certainly within the limited time available."

Ryder glanced at the list, handed it to Jeff, turned to say a few words to Sergeant Parker, who had just entered, then returned his attention to Leroy.

"List's fine as far as it goes, dates and existence, approximate numbers, but it doesn't tell me what they're nutty about."

"Could that be important?"

"How should I know?" Ryder was, understandably, a mite irritable. "Might give me an idea, even an inkling, just the shadow of a clue, just by looking at such a list. God knows I can't come up with one by myself."

With the air of a conjurer producing a rabbit from a hat, Leroy produced another sheet of paper. "And here we have what you want." He looked at the paper with some disfavor. "They're so damned long-winded about their reasons, their motivations for existence as groups, that it was impossible to get it all on one sheet. They tend to be a forthright, not to say garrulous, bunch about their ideals."

"Any religious nuts among them?"

"Why?"

"Carlton is said to be associated, or have associated, with one. Okay, so it's a far-out connection, but any straw for a drowning man."

"I think you're mixing your metaphors," Leroy said kindly. "But I see what you mean." He eyed the sheet. "Well, *most* of them are religious organizations. I think you'd expect that. But quite a number have been established too long—long enough to achieve a measure of respectability—to be classified as nuts. The followers of Zen Buddhism, the Hindu Guru groups, the Zoroastrians and some home-grown California groups—at least eight of those—you can't go around calling them nuts without having a lawsuit slapped on you."

"Call them what you want." Ryder took the sheet and examined it more in hope than expectation. He said in complaint: "Can't pronounce half of them, far less understand them."

"This is a very cosmopolitan state, Sergeant Ryder." Ryder looked at him in suspicion but Leroy's face was perfectly straight.

"Borundians," Ryder went on. "Corinthians. The Judges. The Knights of Calvary. The Blue Cross. The Blue Cross?"

"Not the hospital insurance people, Sergeant."

"The Seekers?"

"Not the singing group."

"1999?"

"That's the day the world ends."

"Ararat?"

"Splinter group of 1999. Where Noah's ark ended up. Working with a group called the Revelations, high up in the Sierras. Building a boat for the next flood."

"They could be right. According to Professor Benson of Cal Tech a large chunk of California is going to disappear into the Pacific. They may have to wait a bit though—million years, give or take. Ah, now. This is more like it. Group over a hundred strong. Established only eight months. The Temple of Allah."

"Muslims. Also operating out of Sierra Nevada but not quite so high up. Forget them. They've been checked out too."

"Still. Carlton's a religious nut—"

"You call a Muslim a nut, you have to call a Christian one too."

"Carlton's landlady's phrase. She probably thinks anyone who crosses a church door a nut. Morro *could* come from Beirut. Muslims there."

"And Christians. Spent 1976 wiping each other out. I've been up that blind alley, Sergeant. Morro could be Indian. Carlton's been in New Delhi. Hindu, not Muslim. Or Morro could be southeast Asian. So Carlton's been to Singapore, Hong Kong and Manila. First two —if anything—are Buddhist, third is Catholic. Or Japan —Carlton's been there, Morro may have been. Shintoism. You can't just pick the religion that fits your theory— and there's no record of Carlton ever having been in Beirut. I told you, this place has been checked out. Chief of police swears by them—"

"That's enough for an immediate arrest warrant."

"Not every police chief is a Donahure. This man— Curragh—is widely respected. The governor of California is their patron. They've given two million—I repeat, two million—to charity. Open to the public—"

Ryder held up a hand. "All right, all right. You made your point. Where does this bunch of paragons hang out?"

"Some kind of castle. Adlerheim, it's called."

"I know it. Been there, in fact. Brainchild of some wealthy crank called Van Streicher." He paused. "Muslim or not, anybody who lives there has to be a nut." He paused again, longer this time, made as if to speak, then clearly changed his mind.

Leroy said: "Sorry I can't help you more."

"Thanks. I'll take those lists if I may. Along with my earthquake studies, they're bound to lead me to point zero."

Parker led the way to the car. In a quiet voice, Jeff said to Ryder: "Come on, out with it. What were you about to say in there that you didn't?"
194

"When you consider the size of this state, the Adlerheim is only a stone's throw from Bakersfield. That's where LeWinter's mysterious phone call came from."

"Could mean something?"

"Could mean that I'm still in a far-fetched mood tonight. Be interesting to find out whether there's a direct line from the castle to Bakersfield."

On the way out to the suburbs Ryder briefed Parker as exhaustively as he could.

South Maple was short, straight, tree-lined, pleasant and quiet, all the houses of the pseudo Spanish-Moroccan architectural design so popular in the south. Two hundred yards short of his destination Ryder pulled up behind a black unmarked car, got out and walked forward. The man sitting behind the wheel glanced interrogatively at Ryder.

Ryder said: "You must be George Green."

"And you must be Sergeant Ryder. Office called me."

"Listen in to her phone all the time?"

"Don't have to. Very educated little bug." He tapped the square base of his telephone. "When she lifts her phone this little box goes tinkle-tinkle. Automatic recorder, too."

"We're going to have a word with her and going to find an excuse to leave her for a minute. She may put a panic call through in our absence."

"I'll have it for you."

Bettina Ivanhoe lived in a surprisingly nice house, small, not on the scale of Donahure's or LeWinter's homes, but large enough to provoke the thought that for a twenty-one-year-old secretary she was doing surprisingly well for herself or someone was doing surprisingly well for her. She answered the doorbell and looked a little apprehensively at the three men.

"Police officers," Parker said. "Could we have a word with you?"

"Police officers? Yes, I suppose so. I mean, of course."

She led the way to a small sitting room and tucked her legs under her while the three men took an armchair

195

apiece. She looked sweet and demure and proper, but that wasn't anything much to go by: she'd looked sweet and demure—if hardly proper—when she'd been lying chained to LeWinter in his bed.

"Am I—am I in any kind of trouble?"

"We hope not." Parker had a deep booming voice, one of those rare voices that could sound hearty, reassuring and ominous all at the same time. "We're just looking for any information that will help us. We're investigating allegations—they're more than that, I'm afraid—of widespread and illegal bribery involving foreigners and several high-placed individuals in public services in this state. A year or two back the South Koreans were giving away millions, seemingly out of the goodness of their hearts." He sighed. "And now the Russians are at it. You will understand that I can't be more specific."

"Yes. Yes, I understand." Clearly she didn't understand at all.

"How long have you lived here?" The hearty reassurance in his voice had gone all diminuendo.

"Five months." The apprehension was still there but it had been joined by a certain wariness. "Why?"

"Asking questions is my job." Parker looked around leisurely. "Very nice place you have here. What's your job, Miss Ivanhoe?"

"I'm a secretary."

"How long?"

"Two years."

"Before that?"

"School. San Diego."

"University of California?" A nod. "You left?" Another nod.

"Why did you leave?" She hesitated. "Don't forget, we can check all this out. Failed grades?"

"No. I couldn't afford to—"

"You couldn't afford to?" Parker looked around again. "Yet in two years, a secretary, a beginner, really, you can afford to live here. Your average secretary has to make do with a single room in the beginning. Or live
196

with her parents." He tapped his forehead lightly. "Of course. Your parents. Must be very understanding folk. Not to say generous."

"My parents are dead."

"I am sorry." He didn't sound sorry. "Then somebody must have been very generous."

"I haven't been charged with anything." She compressed her lips and swung her feet to the floor. "I won't answer another question until I've talked to my lawyer."

"Judge LeWinter is not answering the phone today. He's got lumbago." This got to her. She sank back against the cushions, looking oddly vulnerable and defenseless. She could have been acting but probably was not. If Parker felt a twinge of pity he didn't show it. "You're Russian, aren't you?"

"No. No. No."

"Yes, yes, yes. Where were you born?"

"San Diego."

"You'll have to do better than that. Your name is not in any birth register." Parker had no idea whether it was or not but it seemed a reasonable assumption. "Where were you born?"

"Vladivostok." She'd given up.

"Where are your parents buried?"

"They're alive. They went back to Moscow."

"When?"

"Four years ago."

"Why?"

"I think they were called back."

"They were naturalized?"

"Yes. A long time."

"Where did your father work?"

"Burbank."

"Lockheed, I suppose?"

"Yes."

"How did you get your job?"

"Classified ad. For an American secretary who could speak Russian and Chinese."

"There wouldn't be many of those around?"

"Only me."

"Judge LeWinter has private clients then?"

"Yes."

"Including Russian and Chinese."

"Yes. Sometimes they need a translator in court."

"Does he require any translation done for him out of court?"

She hesitated. "Sometimes."

"Military stuff. Russian, of course. In code."

Her voice was low now, barely above a whisper. "Yes."

"Anything about weather at any time?"

Her eyes were wide. "How do you know?"

"Don't you know it's wrong? Don't you know it's treason? Don't you know the penalty for treason?"

She put her forearm on the side of the couch and laid her blond head on it. She made no reply.

Ryder said: "You like LeWinter?" His voice didn't seem to register with her as the one she'd heard the previous night.

"I hate him! I hate him! I hate him!" The voice was shaking but the vehemence left no room for disbelief.

Ryder stood and jerked his head to the door. Parker said: "We're going to the car to call the station. Back in a minute or two." The three men went outside.

Ryder said: "She hates LeWinter and I, Dave, hate you."

"That makes two of us."

"Jeff, go see if the FBI man is intercepting a phone call. But I know I'm just wasting your time." Jeff left.

"Poor kid." Parker shook his head. "Imagine if that were Peggy."

"Just what I mean. Old man a spy, probably an industrial one. Called back to Russia to report and now being held over her head—along with her mother, probably. Being blackmailed to hell and back. One thing, we can probably tell our superspies in Geneva what they can do with themselves. She's intelligent. I'll bet she has total recall about this Russian weather report or whatever."

"Hasn't she had enough, John? And what will happen to her parents?"

198

"Nothing, I'd guess. Not if the report leaks out that she has been arrested or disappeared or held incommunicado. That's the way they'd act themselves."

"Not the way we act in our great American democracy."

"They don't believe in our great American democracy."

They waited until Jeff returned. He looked at them and shook his head.

"It figures," Ryder said. "Our poor little Bettina has no place left to go."

They went back inside. She was sitting straight again, looking at them without expectation. Her brown eyes were dulled and there were tear stains on her cheeks. The men didn't bother to sit down. She looked at Ryder.

"I know who you are."

"You have the advantage over me. I've never seen you before in my life. We are going to take you into protective custody, that's all."

"I know what that means. Protective custody. Spying, treason, a morals charge. Protective custody!"

Ryder caught her wrist, pulled her to her feet, and held her by the shoulders. "You're in California, not Siberia. Protective custody means that we're going to take you in and keep you safe and unharmed until this blows over. There will be no charges preferred against you because there are none to prefer. We promise that no harm will come to you, not now, nor later." He led her toward the door and opened it. "If you want to, you can go. Pack some things, take them to your car and drive off. But it's cold out there and dark and you'll be alone. You're too young to be alone."

She looked through the doorway, turned back, made a movement of the shoulders that could have been a shrug or a shriver and looked at Ryder uncertainly. He said: "We know a safe place. We'll send a policewoman with you, not a battle-ax to guard you but a young and pretty girl like yourself to keep you company." He nodded to Jeff. "I know my son here will take the greatest care, not to say pleasure, in picking out just the girl for you." Jeff grinned and it was probably his smile more than anything else that convinced her. "You will, of

199

course, have an armed guard outside. Two or three days, no more. Just pack enough for that. All we want to do is to look after you."

She smiled for the first time, nodded and left the room. Jeff grinned again. "I've often wondered how you managed to trap Susan but now I'm beginning to—"

Ryder gave him a cold look. "Green's all through here. Go and explain to him why."

Jeff left, still smiling.

Healey, Bramwell and Schmidt had forgathered in Burnett's sitting room after dinner, excellent as was all the food in the Adlerheim. It had been a somber meal, as most meals were, and the atmosphere had not been lightened by the absence of Susan, who had been eating with her injured daughter. Carlton had not been there either, but this had hardly been remarked upon, because the deputy chief of security had become a highly unsociable creature, gloomy, withdrawn, almost secretive: it was widely assumed that he was brooding over his own defects and failures in the field of security. After a meal eaten quickly and in funereal silence all had left as soon as they decently could. And now Burnett was dispensing his post-prandial hospitality—in this case an excellent Martell—with his customary heavy hand.

"Woman's not normal." Burnett was speaking and, as usual, he wasn't saying something, but was announcing it.

Bramwell said cautiously: "Which one?"

"Which woman is?" Burnett would have gone over big with women's lib. "But I was referring to Mrs. Ryder, of course."

Healy steepled judicious fingers. "Charming, I thought."

"Charming? To be sure, to be sure. Charming. Quite beautiful. But deranged." He waved a vague arm around. "All this, I suppose, did it. Women can't take it. Went along to see her after dinner, pay respects, commiserate with injured daughter, you know. Damn pretty young girl. Lying there all shot up." To listen to Burnett, one would
200

have assumed that the patient had been riddled with machine gun fire. "Well, I'm a pretty even-tempered fellow"—he seemed to be genuinely unaware of his own reputation—"but I must say I rather lost my temper. I said that Morro was at worst a cold-blooded monster that should be destroyed, at best a raving lunatic that should be locked up. Would you believe it, she didn't agree at all." He briefly contemplated the enormity of her error in character assessment, then shook his head at its being beyond normal comprehension. "Admitted that he should be brought to justice, but said he was kind, considerate and even thoughtful of others at times. An intelligent, I had thought highly intelligent, woman." Burnett shook his head again, whether in self-reproach at his own character assessment or because he was sadly figuring out what the rest of womankind might be like it was hard to say. He drank his brandy, clearly not savoring it at all. "I ask you, gentlemen. I simply ask you."

"He's a maniac, all right. That I grant you." Bramwell was being cautious again. "But not amoral as a madman should be. If he really wanted an impressive debut for this atom bomb of his—assuming he has one, and none of us here doubt it—he'd detonate it without warning on Wilshire Boulevard instead of with warning out in the desert."

"Balderdash. The extreme cunning of extreme madness. Wants to convince people that they're dealing with a rational human being." Burnett examined his empty glass, rose and made for the bar. "Well, he'll never convince me of that. I detest clichés but, gentlemen—mark my words."

They marked his words in silence and were still sitting in silence when Morro and Dubois entered. Morro was either oblivious of or ignored the thunder on Burnett's face, the gloom on that of the others.

"I am sorry to disturb you, gentlemen, but the evenings are a bit dull here and I thought you might care to see something to titillate your scientific curiosity. I do not want to sound like a showman in a circus, but I'm sure

201

you will be astonished—dumbfounded, I might almost say—by what Abraham and I are about to show you. Would you care to accompany me, gentlemen?"

Burnett wasn't going to pass up the opportunity to exercise his truculence. "And if we refuse?"

"Your privilege. And I mean yours, Professor. I somehow think your colleagues might be quite interested, and would take great pleasure in telling you afterward. Of course, you may all choose to refuse. I will bring no pressure to bear."

Healey rose. "I was born nosy. Your food is excellent but the entertainment factor is zero. Nothing on the TV—not that there ever is much—except the precautions being taken to keep people away from the Yucca Flat tomorrow and the rather fearful speculation as to what the next threat is going to be and what is the motivation behind it all. What *is* the motivation, Morro?"

"Later. Meantime, those of you who care—"

They all cared, even Burnett. Two white-robed acolytes were waiting in the passage. This didn't worry the four physicists, there was nothing new in this, nor in the certain knowledge that they would be carrying their Ingrams in the folds of their robes. What was unusual was that one of them was carrying a tape recorder. Burnett, as ever, was the first and principal objector.

"What's your devious mind planning on now, Morro? What's the damned recorder for?"

Morro was patient. "To make a recording. I thought you might like to be the first to inform your fellow citizens of what I have here and, by implication, what's in store for them. We will bring to an end what you, Dr. Healey, call their fearful speculations and let them know the dreadful reality. Their fears, almost certainly, will be replaced by a mindless panic such as a people have never known before. But it is justifiable. It is justifiable because it will enable me to achieve what I wish—and, more importantly from your point of view, to achieve it without the loss of the lives of perhaps millions of people. That loss is just conceivable—if you refuse to co-operate."

202

The quiet voice carried a total conviction but when a mind is confronted by the unconceivable it takes refuge in disbelief and nonacceptance.

"You are quite, quite mad." For once Burnett was neither furious nor truculent but he carried as much conviction as Morro had done. "If we refuse to, as you say, co-operate? Torture? The threat of the women?"

"Mrs. Ryder will have told you that they are safe from me. You really can be tedious at times, Professor. No torture, except that of your own consciences, the thought that will haunt you as long as you may live—you could have saved countless lives but have chosen not to."

Healey said: "What you are saying in effect is that while people might not believe you and take a chance that you are bluffing they would believe us and take no such chance."

Morro smiled. "It wounds what passes for my *amour-propre* but, yes, precisely."

"Let's go and see just how mad he is."

The lift was of a quite extraordinary construction. Its floor measured about four feet by six but, in height, it must have been at least fourteen feet. The faces of the four physicists reflected their puzzlement. As the lift whined down Morro smiled again. "It is peculiar, I admit. You will understand the reason for its unique design in a very few moments."

The lift stopped, the door opened and the eight men moved out into a large chamber about twenty feet square. The walls and roof were as they had been when cut from the solid rock, the floor of smooth concrete. On one side were vertically stacked sheets of steel, whether hardened or stainless it was impossible to judge; on the other were unmistakable sheets of aluminum. For the rest, it was no more or less than a comprehensively equipped machine shop, with lathes, machine presses, drills, power cutters, oxyacetylene equipment and racks of gleaming tools. Morro waved a hand.

"In an automobile plant, what you would call the body shop. Here we make the casings. I need say no more."

Running lengthwise along the roof of the chamber was

a heavy metal rail from which were suspended traveling chain blocks. This extended into the next compartment. Morro led the way in. There was a long table running the length of the chamber, a table fitted with circular metal clamps. On either side were racked storage compartments, wire-net fronted, both containing metal drums well separated at clearly calculated intervals.

Morro didn't even break stride. "Plutonium to the left, Uranium-235 to the right." He carried straight on to a smaller room. "The electrical shop, gentlemen. But that wouldn't interest you." He kept on walking. "But this next room should fascinate you. Again in auto manufacturing parlance, this is what you call the assembly shop."

Morro had made no mistake. The four physicists were, beyond any question, fascinated as they had never been in their lives. But not in the details of the assembly shop. What caught and held fast their disbelieving and horrified attention was the rack bolted to the right-hand wall. More precisely, what the rack held. Clamped vertically, side by side, were ten twelve-feet-high cylinders, each four and a half inches in diameter. They were painted matte black with the exception of two red bands, each an inch thick, that circled the cylinders one third and two thirds the way up their height. At the farther end of the row were two more sets of clamps which held nothing. Morro looked at each of the four physicists in turn. Each face held the same expression, a profound dismay coupled with a sick and shocked certainty. Morro's face registered nothing, no humor, no triumph, no satisfaction, nothing. The silence dragged on for a seemingly interminable time but, then, in circumstances sufficiently appalling, a few seconds cannot be measured in the normally accepted units of time. In the accepted units of seconds, twenty had passed before Healey broke the silence. His face was gray and his voice husky as he broke from his thrall and turned to look at Morro.

"This is a nightmare."

"This is no nightmare. From a nightmare you wake up. Not from this, for this is the dreadful reality. A waking nightmare, if you will."

204

Burnett was as hoarse as Healey had been. "The Aunt Sally!"

Morro corrected him. "The Aunt Sallies. Ten of them. You, Professor, are an excellent designer of hydrogen weapons. Your brainchild in its final physical form. One could wish that you could have seen it under happier circumstances."

There was something very close to hate in Burnett's eyes. "You, Morro, are an evil and vindictive bastard."

"You can save your breath, Professor, and for two reasons. Your statement is untrue for I derive no gloating pleasure from this; and, as you should know by now, I am impervious to insults."

With what must have been, for him, a Herculean effort, Burnett brought his temper and outrage under control and regarded Morro with an expression of suspicious thoughtfulness. He said slowly: "I have to admit they *look* like Aunt Sallies."

"You are suggesting something, Professor Burnett?"

"Yes. I'm suggesting this is a hoax, a gigantic bluff. I'm suggesting that all this fancy machinery you have down here, the steel and aluminum sheets, the nuclear fuel, the electrical shop, this so-called assembly shop, is just window dressing on an unprecedented scale. I suggest you are trying to trick my colleagues and myself into convincing the world at large that you really are in possession of those nuclear weapons whereas, in fact, they are only dummies. You could have those cylinders made in a hundred places in this state alone without arousing any suspicion. But you couldn't have the components, the very intricate and sophisticated components made without providing the very complex and highly sophisticated plans, and that *would* have aroused suspicion. I'm afraid, Morro, that you are no engineer. To make those components here you would have required highly skilled pattern cutters, template makers, turners and machinists. Such men are very hard to come by and are highly paid professionals who most certainly would not jeopardize their careers by working for a criminal."

Morro said: "Well spoken. Interesting but, if I may
205

say so, merely amusing observations. You have quite finished?"

When Burnett made no reply Morro crossed to a large steel plate let into one wall and pressed a button by its side. The steel plate slid sideways with a mute whine to reveal a square wire-meshed door. Behind the mesh were seated six men, two watching TV, two reading and two playing cards. All six men looked toward the mesh door. Their faces were pale and gaunt and held expressions of what could be called neither hatred nor fear but were compounded of both.

"Those may be the men you are looking for, Professor?" Again there was neither satisfaction nor triumph in Morro's voice. "One template maker, one pattern cutter, two lathe specialists, one machinist and one electrician or, should I say, a specialist in electronics." He looked at the six men and said: "Perhaps you would confirm that you are indeed the skilled practitioners of the arts that I have claimed you to be?"

The six men looked at him and said nothing, but their tightened lips and the loathing in their faces said it for them.

Morro shrugged. "Well, well. They do get like this occasionally—an irritating, if momentary, lack of co-operation. Or, to put it another way, they simply never learn." He crossed the chamber, entered a boothlike office and lifted a phone. His voice was inaudible to the watchers. He remained inside till a newcomer, a stranger to the physicists, entered the chamber. Morro met him and together they approached the waiting group.

"This is Lopez," Morro said. Lopez was a short tubby man with an appropriately chubby face, a low hairline, dark mustache and what appeared to be a permanently good-humored smile. He nodded and kept on smiling as Morro made introductions but said nothing.

"Lopez, I am just a little disappointed in you." Morro spoke severely but his smile matched Lopez's own. "And to think I pay you such a handsome salary."

"I am desolate, señor." If he was, he didn't look

it; the smile remained firmly in place. "If you would let me know in what way I have fallen short—"

Morro nodded at the six men behind the mesh. Fear, not hatred, was now the dominant expression in their faces. Morro said: "They refuse to talk to me."

Lopez sighed. "I do try to teach them manners, Señor Morro—but even Lopez is no magician." He pressed another button and the mesh gate slid open. He smiled with even greater good humor and beckoned. "Come, Peters. We'll go to my room and have a little talk, will we?"

The man addressed as Peters said: "My name is John Peters and I am a lathe operator." There was no mistaking the abject terror in his face and his voice shook. The four physicists looked at one another with a dimly comprehending shock on their faces.

A second man said: "I am Conrad Bronowski. I am an electrician." And, in a precisely similar fashion, each of the other four in turn gave his name and occupation.

"Thank you, gentlemen." Morro touched both buttons in succession and looked inquiringly at the four scientists as both gate and door closed. But they weren't looking at him, they were staring at Lopez.

Schmidt said: "Who is this man?"

"Lopez? Their guide and mentor. You could see how well they responded to his friendliness, his kindly good humor. Thank you, Lopez."

"My pleasure, Señor Morro."

With considerable difficulty Burnett removed his eyes from Lopez and looked at Morro. "Those men in there. They—they look like men I have seen in a concentration camp. Forced labor. And this man—he is their guard, their torturer. I have never seen such fear in men's faces."

"You are both unkind and unjust. Lopez has a deep concern for his fellow man. Those six men, I have to confess, are here under restraint but they will be—"

"Kidnaped, you mean?"

"As you will. But, as I was about to say, they will very shortly be returned unharmed to their families."

"You see?" Burnett turned to his three colleagues. "Just as Mrs. Ryder said. Kind, considerate and thoughtful of others. You're a goddamned evil hypocrite."

"Sticks and stones, Professor Burnett, sticks and stones. Now, perhaps, we can get on with this recording?"

"One minute." An expression of puzzlement had replaced the revulsion in Healey's face. "Accepting that those men in there are what they claim they are or what this monster made them claim to be"—Lopez continued to smile his genial smile, he was clearly as impervious to insults as Morro himself—"it's still impossible that they could have assembled this mechanism without the guidance of a first-class nuclear physicist. Which leads me to believe that those men in there have simply been brainwashed into saying what they have just said."

"Astute," Morro said, "but only superficially so. If I just wanted six men to say what those six just have then I would surely have rehearsed six of my own men who would have required neither persuasion nor incarceration to play the parts. Not so, Dr. Healey?" Healey's crestfallen expression showed that it was indeed so. Morro sighed resignedly. "Lopez, if you would be so kind as to remain in the office?" Lopez smiled, this time as if in anticipation, and walked across to the booth from which Morro had telephoned. Morro led the others to a second steel door, pressed a button to open it, then another to open the cage gate behind.

The cell was dimly lit but bright enough to show clearly an old man slumped in a tattered armchair, the only item of furniture there with the slightest suggestion of comfort. He had frizzy white hair, a haggard and unbelievably lined face and wore shabby clothes that hung loosely on a frame as emaciated as the face. His eyes were closed and he appeared to be asleep. Were it not for the occasional twitching of thin blue-veined hands he could equally well have been dead.

Morro gestured toward the sleeping man. "Recognize him?"

The four men studied him without recognition, then Burnett said contemptuously: "This your trump card?

This your mastermind behind the alleged nuclear weapons? You forget, Morro, that I know every top-ranking nuclear physicist in the country. I've never seen this man before."

"People can change," Morro said mildly. He shook the old man by the shoulder until he started and opened his eyelids to reveal clouded and bloodshot eyes. With a hand under a thin arm, Morro persuaded him to his feet and urged him out into the brighter light of the assembly room. "Perhaps you recognize him now?"

"What kind of put-on is this?" Burnett peered closely and shook his head. "I repeat, I have never seen this man."

Morro said: "It's sad how one can forget old friends. You know him very well, Professor. Imagine if he were, say, seventy pounds heavier. Imagine if the lines had gone from his face and his hair was as black as it now is white. Think, Professor, think."

Burnett thought. Suddenly his searching gaze changed to a stare, his face drained of expression just as his complexion drained of blood. He seized the old man by the shoulders.

"Jesus Christ Almighty! Willi Aachen! Willi Aachen! What in God's name have they done to you?"

"My old friend Andy!" The voice matched the appearance, a voice old and faint and quavering. "How good to see you again."

"What have they done to you?"

"Well. You can see. Kidnaped." He shivered and tried to smile at the same time. "They persuaded me to work for them."

Burnett flung himself toward Morro but didn't get halfway. Dubois' great hands closed on his upper arms from behind. Burnett was a powerful man and his fury gave him a momentarily berserker strength but he had no more chance of freeing himself from that monstrous grip than the wasted and shrunken Aachen would have had.

"It's no use, Andy." Aachen sounded sad. "No use. We are powerless."

Burnett stopped his futile struggling. Breathing heavily, he said for the third time: "What have they done to you? How? Who did it?"

Lopez, certainly in answer to some unseen signal from Morro, appeared at Aachen's elbow. Aachen saw him and took an involuntary step backward, flipping up an arm as if to protect a face suddenly contorted with fear. Morro, still holding him by the arm, smiled at Burnett.

"How naïve, how childlike and unthinking even the highest intelligences can be. There are, Professor Burnett, only two copies of plans for the Aunt Sally, drawn up by yourself and Professor Aachen, in existence and those are in the vaults of the Atomic Energy Commission. You must know that they are still there, so I could have obtained those plans from only two men in America. They are both with me now. Do you understand?"

Burnett was still having difficulty with his breathing. "I know Professor Aachen. I know him better than anyone. No one could have made him work for you. No one! No one!"

Lopez broadened his ever-genial smile. "Perhaps, Señor Morro, if I had a friendly little chat in my room with Professor Burnett here. Ten minutes would suffice, I think."

"I agree. That should be sufficient to convince him that anyone on earth would work for me."

"Don't, don't, don't!" Aachen was close to hysteria. "For God's sake, Andy, you've got to believe Morro." He looked in fearful loathing at Lopez. "This inhuman monster knows more awful, more unspeakable, more fiendish tortures than any sane man can conceive of, can imagine. In the name of heaven, Andy, don't be mad—this creature will break you as he broke me."

"I'm convinced." Healey had stepped forward and taken Burnett by the arm just as Dubois released his grip. He looked at Schmidt and Bramwell, then turned back to Burnett. "The three of us are convinced. Absolutely. What's the point of being broken on the modern equivalent of the rack if it's going to prove nothing? We *have* the proof. God's sake, you couldn't recognize an old friend you last saw ten weeks ago. Isn't that proof? And those six zombie technicians. Isn't that proof?" He looked at Morro. "There could, of course, be a final proof. If those Aunt Sallies are for real you must have some way of triggering them and the only way can be either by a time device or radio. It wouldn't be the former, because then you would have committed yourself to an irrevocable decision and I can't see a man like you committing yourself to the irrevocable—so I assume you have elected for a controllable radio impulse."

"Well, well." Morro smiled. "This time you have not been just superficially obtuse. You are correct, of course. Follow me, gentlemen."

He led the way to the small booth from which he had telephoned. Its inner wall held yet another steel door. There was no press button to open this. Instead, alongside the door, was a small brass panel, highly polished, measuring about ten inches by six. Morro placed his flat palm and fingers against it; the door slid smoothly open.

Inside was a tiny room, not more than six by six feet. On the wall opposite the door was a metal table which supported a simple radio transmitter, smaller than an attaché case, with calibrated dials and tuning knobs. On top of the case was a plastic-covered red button. Clamped to one side of the table was an eight-inch cylinder with a diameter about half that. At one end of the cylinder was a cranking handle; at the other end an insulated lead to a terminal in one side of the transmitter. There were two other terminals close by that one. From one, a lead reached down to a storage battery on the floor. The third terminal connected to a wall socket.

"An almost childishly simple device, gentlemen," Morro said. "A perfectly ordinary radio transmitter but one serving a most extraordinary purpose. It is programed with a specific code on a preset wave length. The chances of any-

211

one duplicating both the wave length and the code are so astronomically remote they can be said to be nonexistent. We have, as you see, guarded against any chance of a power failure—we have main current, battery and this hand-cranked generator." He touched the plastic-covered red button on top. "To operate, one simply unscrews the plastic dome, turns the button through ninety degrees and presses." He ushered them out, laid his hand against the brass panel and watched the door slide close. "One cannot very well have buttons for this purpose. Some careless person might accidentally lean against them."

Healey said: "Only your handprint can open that door?"

"You didn't imagine that plate was simply an elaborate press button? Well, gentlemen, the recording."

"One last thing," Burnett said. He nodded toward the row of Aunt Sallies. "There are two empty sets of clamps there. Why?"

"Well, now." Morro smiled his empty smile. "I thought you'd never ask."

The four physicists sat around the table in Burnett's room, contemplating both their brandies and the future with an understandably profound gloom.

"Well, I said it, didn't I?" Burnett said heavily. " 'Mark my words,' I said. Didn't I say that?"

No one said whether he'd said it or not. There didn't seem to be anything to say.

"Even that control room could have been part of a massive hoax." Schmidt was grasping at nonexistent straws.

No one said anything to that either and for the same reason.

"And to think that I said he wasn't amoral as a madman should be," Burnett said. "That if he were really mad he'd set off his atomic bomb on Wilshire Boulevard?"

No one had anything to say to that either. Burnett rose and said: "Back shortly, gentlemen."

Peggy was still in bed but looked considerably better
212

than she had on her arrival at the Adlerheim. Her mother sat in an armchair to one side. Burnett had a brandy glass in his hand. He hadn't brought his own with him; he'd gone straight behind Susan's bar the moment he had arrived. He was still behind it, his elbows on the counter, bending an apocalyptic gaze upon his audience and addressing them in apocalyptic tones. Armageddon, it was clear, was at hand, and the dark angel was there to announce the fact.

"You will not, ladies, doubt our unanimous conclusion that we are sitting atop enough nuclear explosive power to blast the biggest man-made crater of all time, enough to send us all into orbit—in a vaporized state, that is? The equivalent of thirty-five million tons of conventional explosive. It should cause quite a bang, don't you think?"

It was a night for silences, for unanswered questions. Burnett's doom-laden gaze homed in on Susan.

"Kind, gentle, humane, considerate—that's what you said Morro was. He may very well go down in history as the most cold-blooded, calculating monster ever. Seven broken men down in the vaults there whom he has tortured—or has had tortured—beyond the breaking point of screaming agony. Humane, considerate.

"And this kindly gentleman—where has he put the missing hydrogen bomb? It's a rather scaled-down version of the Aunt Sally—a trifling one and a half megatons, about seventy-five times as powerful as the ones that destroyed Hiroshima and Nagasaki. Released at a height of between ten and twenty thousand feet it could destroy half the population of Southern California. Those whom the blast didn't get, radiation and fire storms would. But as this bomb is already in position, it must be on or below ground level. The results will still be unimaginably dreadful. So, tell me, where do you think this gentle Christ-like figure placed this hydrogen device so that no harm will come to any of God's children?"

He was still looking fixedly at Susan but she wasn't looking at him. She wasn't avoiding his gaze; her mind, like those of the others, was numbed with shock and incomprehension: she just wasn't seeing anything.

"So must I tell you?"

It was still a night for silences.

"Los Angeles."

NINE

■ ON the following morning the absenteeism rate at work was the highest in the history of the state. The same almost certainly applied to the other states in the union and, to a somewhat lesser degree, through many of the civilized countries throughout the world, for the TV coverage of the projected—or threatened—atomic explosion in the Yucca Flat was being transmitted by satellite. Europe was hardly affected—though none the less concerned—for there the day's work was all over and most Europeans were home for the evening.

But in California the absenteeism was almost total. Even the corporations running the public and utilities services, the transport systems and police forces, had to operate with skeleton staffs. It could have been a great day for the criminals, particularly the robbers and burglars of California, were it not for the fact that they, too, had also stayed at home.

For reasons whether of prudence, sloth, the knowledge of the inaccessibility of Yucca Flat or the handy convenience of their TV sets, not one Californian in ten thousand made their way to the explosion site that morning. Those who did go—and there couldn't have been over two thousand of them—were outnumbered by members of the military, the National Guard and police, who found their task of keeping civilians at the mandatory five-mile distance almost ridiculously easy.

Among the spectators present were most of the ranking scientists in the state, especially and understandably those who specialized in the nuclear and earthquake fields. Why, precisely, they *were* there was difficult to see, for the blast, shock and radiation effects of an eighteen-kiloton atomic device had been known with sufficient precision for over thirty years. Most of them, admittedly,

215

had never seen an atomic explosion before, but the reason lay elsewhere. Blessed or cursed by that insatiable and rubber-necking curiosity that had been the driving force or bane of scientists since recorded history, they just wanted to see where the bomb would go off. They, too, could, of course, have stayed at home, but your true scientist is in the field or he is nothing.

Among those who stayed at home were Major Dunne in his office and Sergeant Ryder at his house. Even by helicopter the round trip was over five hundred miles, and that, for Dunne, represented a waste of valuable investigative time. For Ryder it represented a waste of thinking time, which he no longer regarded as being necessarily valuable but was better than not thinking at all. Jeff Ryder had originally wanted to go, but when coldly asked by his father how he hoped to help his family by spending what could be irreplaceable hours rubber-necking, he had readily agreed not to go, especially when Ryder had said that he wanted Jeff to help him. His father, Jeff thought, had a peculiar idea of what helping meant or, as far as he could see, his parent was doing absolutely nothing. He, Jeff, had been asked to type out every detail, however apparently insignificant, of the investigations that had been carried out till then, including, as far as possible, verbatim recollections of all conversations, and to this end he was employing his rather remarkable memory as best he could. From time to time he glanced rather resentfully at Ryder, who appeared to be doing nothing other than leafing idly through the pile of earthquake literature he'd picked up from Professor Benson.

About ten minutes before ten Jeff switched on the TV. The screen showed a bluish-tinged stretch of extremely unprepossessing desert, so unattractive a spectacle that the commentator was trying, and making extremely heavy weather of it, to compensate by an intense and breathless account of what was taking place, a gallant and fore-doomed effort, as nothing whatsoever was taking place. He informed the watchers that the camera was stationed
216

in Frenchman's Flat at a distance of five miles southwest from the estimated point of explosion, as if anyone cared from what direction his camera was pointing. He said that as the device was almost certainly buried to a considerable depth, there wasn't expected to be much in the way of a fireball, which everyone had been reminded of for hours past. They were, he said, using a color filter, which everyone who wasn't color-blind could readily see. Finally, he told them that the time was nine minutes to ten, as if he were the only person in California who owned a watch. He had, of course, to say something, but it was an extremely mundane build-up to something that might prove to be of historic significance. Jeff looked at his father in some exasperation: Ryder was certainly not looking and very probably not listening to anything that was going on. He was no longer leafing through the pages but was gazing, apparently unseeing, at one particular page. He laid down the literature and headed for the telephone.

Jeff said: "Dad, do you mind? There's just thirty seconds to go."

"Ah!" Ryder returned to his seat and gazed placidly at the screen.

The commentator was now speaking in that tense, breathless, near hysterical voice which commonly afflicts race-track commentators when they are endeavoring to generate some spurious excitement toward the end of a race. In this particular instance the tone was quite misplaced; a calm relaxed voice would have been much more appropriate: the imminent event carried in itself all the excitement that could be generated. The commentator had now started a countdown, starting at thirty, the numbers decreasing as the dramatic impact of his voice increased. The effect was rather spoiled because either his watch was wrong or Morro's was. The device exploded fourteen seconds ahead of time.

To a people who had long become accustomed to seeing atomic explosions on the screen, whether at home or in the cinema, to a people who had become blasé about and bored with the spectacle of moon rockets blasting off from Cape Canaveral, the effect, visually speaking, of this latest demonstration of science's resolute retrograde march was curiously—or perhaps not so curiously—anticlimactic. True, the fireball was considerably greater than predicted—the searing blue-white flash was of an intensity that caused many viewers to wince or even momentarily screw shut their eyes—but the column of smoke, fire and desert dust that streaked up into the blue Nevada sky, a blueness dramatically intensified by the camera filters, culminating in the mushrooming of the deadly radioactive cloud, faithfully followed the accustomed scenario. To the inhabitants of the central Amazon basin such a titanic convulsion would presumably have heralded the end of the world; to the more sophisticated peoples of the world it was passé, old hat, and had it occurred on some remote Pacific atoll the great majority of people wouldn't even have bothered to watch it.

But it hadn't happened on any remote Pacific atoll nor had it been Morro's purpose to provide the Californians with a diversionary spectacle to relieve the ennui of their daily lives. It had been intended, instead, to provide them with a chilling warning, an ominous threat, all the more frightening because unspecified, of impending evil, of some unimagined disaster that would surely strike at the whim of whoever had planted and triggered the atomic device. On a more mundane level it was intended to show that here was a man who meant what he said, who was not just there to play around and who had both the desire and ability to carry out whatever he had threatened. Had that been Morro's intention, and there obviously had been none other, then he had succeeded to a degree which perhaps even he had not realized was possible. He had struck fear into the hearts of the great majority of rational Californians and from that time on there was practically only one topic of conversation in the state: when and where would this unpredictable madman strike again and what in the name of all that

218

was holy—it wasn't expressed in quite that way—were his motivations. This topic, to be precise, was to last for only ninety minutes: then they were to be given something really definite and concrete to worry about or, more accurately, to reduce that part of California most directly concerned to a state of not unreasoning terror that was swiftly to shade off into panic.

Ryder rose. "Well, we never doubted that he was a man of his word. Aren't you glad you didn't waste your time going up to see that side show? For that's all it was. Well, it should at least keep people's minds off taxes and the latest shenanigans in Washington for a little."

Jeff didn't answer. It was doubtful if he'd even heard. He was still looking at the ever-expanding mushroom over the Nevada desert, still listening to the suitably awe-stricken voice of the commentator describing in great and wholly unnecessary detail what anyone with half an eye could see perfectly well for himself. Ryder shook his head and picked up the telephone. Dunne answered.

Ryder said: "Anything? You know this line is bugged."

"Some things coming in."

"Interpol?"

"Some things coming in."

"How long?"

"Half an hour."

He hung up, called Parker, arranged to have them meet in Dunne's office in half an hour, hung up, sat, briefly ruminated on the fact that both Dunne and Parker had taken the reality of Morro's threat so much for granted that neither of them had thought fit to comment on it, then resumed his reading. Fully five minutes passed before Jeff switched off the TV, glanced with some irritation at his father, sat down at his table, typed a few words and said acidly: "I hope I'm not disturbing you."

"Not at all. How many pages have you got down?"

"Six."

Ryder stretched out his hand and took them. "We're leaving in fifteen minutes to see Dunne. Something's come up—or is coming up."

"What?"

"You have forgotten, perhaps, that one of Morro's henchmen is wearing a headset tied into our phone?"

A chagrined Jeff resumed his typing while Ryder began a placid reading of Jeff's notes.

A much refreshed Dunne, who had obviously a good night's rest behind him, was waiting with Delage and Leroy when Ryder, Jeff and Parker arrived. Delage and Leroy were looking a good deal less rested: the assumption was that they did not have a good night's rest behind them. Dunne confirmed this, nodding at Delage and Leroy.

"A couple of devoted agents who think their boss is past it. Quite right too." He tapped a sheaf of papers in front of him. "Up all night—the devoted agents, I mean —collecting snippets of this and that. Some possibly useful information, some dead ends. What did you think of friend Morro's demonstration?"

"Impressive. What do you have?"

Dunne sighed. "The niceties of salon conversation, Sergeant Ryder, are not for all. Report from Daimler, remember him?"

"Security chief in the AEC reactor plant in Illinois?"

"Yes. Nothing wrong with your memory."

"Even less with Jeff's. I've just been reading some notes he typed out. Well?"

"He says that Carlton did associate with some far-out group. As I said, we preferred to have one of our boys do the direct legwork. Interviewed Carlton's landlady's son. He wasn't very forthcoming—he'd only attended two or three meetings then gave it up. Couldn't stand the mumbojumbo, he said."

"What were they called?"

"The Damascene Disciples. Nothing known of them. Never registered as a church or religious organization. Disbanded after six months."

"They had a religion? I mean, they preached, they had a message?"

"They didn't preach. They had a message, all right.
220

They advocated the eternal damnation of all Christians, Jews, Buddhists, Shintoists—in fact, as far as I can make out, everybody who wasn't a Damascene."

"Nothing original about that. Were the Muslims on their list, do you know?"

Dunne looked at a list. "Oddly enough, no. Why?"

"Curiosity. Could this landlady's son recognize any of them?"

"That would have been difficult. The Damascenes wores cloaks, masks and those pixie witches' hats affected by the Ku Klux Klan. Only this gang were dressed in black."

"Something in common, all the same—as I recall it the Ku Klux Klan aren't all that devoted to Jews, Catholics and Negroes. Anyway, no possible means of identification?"

"None. Except that this kid told our agent that one of them was the biggest man he had ever seen, a giant, maybe six-eight, and shoulders like a cart horse."

"This person didn't note anything peculiar about any of their voices?

"This person, according to our agent, just escaped being classified as a moron."

"But Carlton was no moron. Interesting, isn't it? What word about Morro?"

"Well, his accent. We've now had reports from—what shall we call them?—linguistic experts throughout the state. Thirty-eight so far, and more coming in every minute. All of them willing to stake their reputations, etc, etc. Point is, no less than twenty-eight plump for a southeast Asian origin."

"Do they indeed? Any attempt to pin-point the exact source?"

"That's as far as they will go."

"Again, still interesting. Interpol?"

"Nothing."

"You have a list of all the places they've contacted?" Dunne looked at Leroy, who nodded. "The Philippines, for instance?"

Leroy consulted a list. "No."

"Try Manila. Ask them to try around the Cotabato area in Mindanao."

"The what in what?"

"Mindanao is the large southern island in the Philippines. Cotabato is a seaside town. Manila may not be too interested in what goes on in Cotabato—it's at least five hundred and fifty miles away as the crow flies, maybe a thousand by road and ferry. Try, anyway."

"I see." Dunne paused. "You know something that we don't know?"

"No. Chances are I'm making a complete fool of myself, just a wild guess based upon ludicrous improbability. LeWinter?"

"Two things. The first one is extraordinarily odd. You will recall that in his telephone notebook he'd listed the numbers of all kinds of people with whom—outside his court cases, of course—LeWinter would not be expected to be on either social or professional terms. Engineers, drillers, oil-rig men. There were forty-four of those in all. Barrow, for reasons best known to himself, he's almost as close-mouthed as you, assigned a federal agent to interview each and every one of them."

"Forty-four. That's a lot of FBI agents."

Dunne was patient. "There are approximately eight thousand FBI men in the country. If Barrow cares to allocate one half of one percent of his men to a particular case, that's his privilege. He could allocate four hundred and forty if he wanted. Point is, twenty-six of those agents came up with the same puzzling—I'd call it astonishing—discovery—twenty-six of the men being investigated are missing. Wives, children, relatives, friends—none of them have any idea where they might be, none were given the slightest indication of their intention to depart. What do you make of that?"

"Well, that's interesting too."

"Interesting, interesting, interesting. Is that all you can say?"

"Well, as you say, it's damned odd."

"Look, Ryder, if you have any idea, if you're holding anything back—"

222

"Obstructing justice, you mean?"

"Just that."

"I thought I might be a complete fool, Dunne. Now I know you are." There was a silence, not long but extremely uncomfortable. "Sure I'm obstructing the course of justice. How many of *your* family is Morro holding hostage?" Another silence. "I'm going to talk to our friend LeWinter. Rather, he's going to talk to me. It's as plain as the hand in front of your face that he's supplied Morro with that list and that Morro has either had them bought or taken by force. Your twenty-six agents might be profitably engaged on checking on the criminal backgrounds, if any, of those twenty-six men. LeWinter will talk; I'll see to that—and not if I die in the attempt. He'll talk if *he* dies in *my* attempt."

The quietly spoken, cold ferocity in Ryder's voice had a chilling effect on everyone in the room. Jeff licked his lips and looked at a man he'd never seen before. Parker regarded the ceiling. Delage and Leroy looked at Dunne. Dunne looked at the hand before his face and used the back of it to smooth his brow.

Dunne said: "Maybe I'm not myself. Maybe we're not any of us ourselves. The apologies go without saying. Next you'll be accusing us of being a bunch of lily-livered incompetents. But, hell, Sergeant, there's a limit to how far you can step outside the law. Sure he has a list which included the twenty-six men who have disappeared. A dozen others may have similar lists and all for innocuous purposes. You're proceeding on the basis of assumptions. There isn't a shred of evidence, direct or otherwise, to link LeWinter and Morro."

"I don't need evidence."

Once again Dunne used the back of his hand. "You have just said, in the presence of three government officers, that you're prepared to use torture to obtain your information."

"Who said anything about torture? It'll look like a heart attack. You said you had two things to tell me about LeWinter. Well, that's one."

"Jesus!" Dunne wasn't smoothing his brow now, he

223

was mopping it. "Delage, you have the information. Me, I need time to think."

"Yes. Well." Delage didn't look any happier than his superior. "Miss Ivanhoe, if that's her name, well, LeWinter's secretary, has talked. There's a Geneva connection all right. It all sounds very much like something out of science fiction, but if it's even halfway true, then it's damn frightening. It must be if most of the nations of the world—major ones, that is, thirty to be precise—sit down at a disarmament conference in Geneva and talk about it."

"I have all morning," Ryder said.

"Sorry. Well, the lady talked and it didn't seem to make much sense so we contacted ERDA with the result that one of Dr. Durrer's senior assistants was called in, shown what Miss Ivanhoe said and had no trouble at all in making sense of it. He's an expert on the subject."

"I haven't got the afternoon too."

"Give me a break, will you? He wrote a condensed report. This is what he has to say."

"Classified?"

"Declassified. It's a bit formal, but here it is. He says: It has long been accepted that any nuclear war, even on a limited scale, would cause megadeaths. He puts in brackets, millions of deaths. The U.S. Arms Control and Disarmament Agency came to the conclusion a couple of years ago that megadeaths could arise from another agency which did not directly involve nuclear war. A large number of nuclear explosions, almost certainly in the megaton range, could damage the layer of ozone that shields the earth from the sun's lethal ultraviolet radiation.

"Most people are under the impression that ozone is what they sniff at the seaside. Ozone is an allotropic condition of oxygen, having three atoms instead of the normal two, and *can* be smelled at the seaside by the electrolysis of water and also after the discharge of electricity through the air, as occurs in a thunderstorm. But ozone in its natural state occurs almost solely in the
224

lower stratosphere at an altitude between ten and thirty miles.

"The intense heat given off by a nuclear explosion causes the oxygen and nitrogen molecules in the atmosphere to combine. Those form oxides of nitrogen which would be borne upward in the atomic cloud. Those would react with the ozone layer and by a well-understood chemical reaction convert the three atoms of ozone into two, that is, normal oxygen, which offers zero protection against ultraviolet radiation. This would effectively blow a hole in the ozone layer and would expose the earth underneath the hole to the direct effects of the sun.

"Two effects remain unclear. The first of those—"

Delage broke off as a telephone rang. Leroy picked it up, listened in silence, thanked the caller and hung up. He said: "I don't know why I thanked him for that call. From the local TV station. It seems that Morro wants to strike while the iron is hot. He has another statement to make. At eleven o'clock. That's in eight minutes' time. It will be carried on every TV and radio station in the state. For the rest of the states, too, I'd guess."

"Isn't that wonderful?" Dunne said. "A morning to remember. I wonder why it wasn't cleared with the FBI first—we would have heard, wouldn't we?"

Ryder said: "You blame them? After what the FBI did to stop the atomic blast in Nevada this morning? This is a matter for national concern now, not just for the FBI. Since when have you had the power to impose martial law? Their attitude, and probably the attitude of every citizen in the country, is that the FBI can go take a jump." He looked at Delage. "The first unclear effect?"

"You're a cold-blooded bastard, Ryder." Dunne undoubtedly meant what he said.

Delage looked unhappily at Dunne, but Dunne had his head in his hands. Delage returned to his notes.

"We just don't know what will happen. The consequences might be small, they might be catastrophic. We might just all end up becoming very heavily sun-tanned; or the ultraviolet could conceivably destroy all human,
225

animal and plant life. Subterranean and aquatic life might survive any conditions. We have no means of knowing." Delage looked up. "He *is* a cheery one, isn't he?"

"Let's take that up later," Ryder said. "Let's have the second unclear effect."

"Well. He says it is not known whether this hole in the stratosphere would remain localized and keep pace with the rotation of the earth. Worse, it is not known whether or not this hole can spread through the rest of the ozone layer. Chemical reactions at that level in the stratosphere are unknown and wholly unpredictable—there might well exist a form of breeder reaction, in which case large areas of the earth might well be devastated.

"The possibility must be taken into account that some nation may already have experimented in some remote and uninhabited region—"

Parker said: "Siberia?"

"He doesn't say. He goes on: It may have been established that such a hole can be blown through the ozone layer and has been found to be stable as to both location and extent. This, however, is pure conjecture.

"This introduces the Geneva connection. As long ago as September 3 of 1976, the thirty-nation disarmament conference there sent a draft treaty banning modification of the environment for military purposes to the United Nations General Assembly. The matter, not unexpectedly, is still under UNO's consideration.

"The treaty is designed, in the words of the communiqué, to prevent artificial induction by the military of such phenomena as earthquakes—"

"Earthquakes!" Ryder seemed jolted.

"Yes, earthquakes. He goes on: Tidal waves—"

"Tidal waves?" It was almost as if Ryder was beginning to comprehend something.

"That's what it says here. There's some more: ecological imbalance, alteration of weather and climate and changes in ocean currents, in the state of the ozone layer and the ionosphere, that is, the Appleton and Kennelly–Heaviside layers. Then he goes on to say that the United States delegate at Geneva, one Mr. Joseph Martin, believed that it would be a treaty amounting to a very strong practical inhibition against the hostile use of environmental modification techniques. He further comments that Mr. Martin appears to have forgotten or ignored the fact that the only effect of the Strategic Arms Limitation Talks was to encourage the Russians, in the sacred name of détente, to embark on a new and massive program of building a bigger and better generation of intercontinental ballistic missiles." Delage appeared to run his eye down the page. "He runs on a bit more but I'm afraid his scientific detachment gives way to a certain irony and bitterness. I would say that's about all—Miss Ivanhoe's rather vague ramblings in a coherent form."

"Switch on that TV," Dunne said. "A minute or so. Your sixty seconds' worth of observations, Sergeant Ryder?"

"Poppycock. Or if you want it in plain language—"

"That's plain enough. No Reds under the bed?" Dunne had a very disbelieving right eyebrow.

"I didn't say that. Neither do I say I disbelieve this story—theory, if you like—about blowing a hole through the ozone layer. I'm no scientist. All I'm saying is that I don't believe in its relevance in those circumstances. Russian secret codes." On the rare occasions that Ryder expressed contempt he came across very strongly. "You think the Russians—anyone—would use a young innocent, a marshmallow guaranteed to crack under the pressure of a fingertip, to decode a message or supposed secret that's been in the public domain for two years? The idea's preposterous."

"Laying a false scent, you would think?"

"Yes. No."

"You've forgotten 'perhaps.' "

" 'Perhaps' is what I mean. Morro's intention may lie elsewhere. On the other hand, it may not. Maybe he thinks the idea's so ridiculous that we'll dismiss it out of hand and so he'll go ahead and use that idea. Or not. Maybe the Russians *are* involved. Again, or not. It's the old story. Three ranchers are chasing a rustler who's disappeared up a canyon. Halfway up this canyon there is another canyon. Rancher A figures the rustler has gone hell for leather for the end of the canyon. Rancher B thinks he's smarter than A and that the rustler, figuring that's the way his pursuers will think, has taken the branch. C reckons that he's smarter than A and B, that the rustler will figure what B has figured and go to the end. No end to how long we could keep on outsmarting ourselves."

He paused. "There could, of course, be a second branch canyon that we know nothing about. Just as we know nothing about the first."

· "It's a rare privilege," Dunne said, "to see a detective's mind at work."

Ryder might not have heard him. *"Another* interesting thing. This expert from ERDA. A nuclear physicist, I assume. About blasting a hole through the ozone layer. If the Russians—or whoever—had carried out any such experiments with God knows how many hydrogen bombs we or one of our allies would have been bound to know of it. It would have made headlines—big, big headlines—throughout the world. But there haven't been any. Have there?"

No one said whether there had or hadn't.

"Well, so no experiments. Maybe the Russians—or again, whoever—are as scared of the outcome as we are. Maybe there never will be a nuclear war fought on land. Some people say it will be in space. Our friend in ERDA suggests—what did he say—subterranean or aquatic use of nuclear devices. How do we fancy getting our feet wet?"

"A rush on the stores for fishermen's waders?" Dunne turned toward the TV. "I'm sure our friend Morro is about to enlighten us on that one."

The newscaster, this time, was a much older man, which boded ill in itself. What boded worse was that he was dressed for a funeral in a suit of somber hue, a color in which the normal Californian newscaster would not normally have been found dead. What boded still worse was the doomsday expression customarily reserved for those occasions when the local gridiron heroes had been crushingly defeated by some out-of-state upstarts. The tone of voice accorded well with both clothes and expression.

"We have received another communication from this criminal Morro." The newscaster clearly held in contempt the fundamental tenet of Anglo-Saxon law that a man is presumed innocent until found guilty.

"It contains a dire warning, an unprecedentedly grave threat to the citizens of California and one that cannot be taken lightly in view of what occurred this morning in Yucca Flat. I have with me in the studio a panel of experts who will later explain the implications of this threat. But first, Morro."

"Good evening. This is a prerecorded message." As before, the voice was calm and relaxed, he could have been discussing some minor change in the Dow Jones Index. "It is prerecorded because I am completely confident of the outcome of my little experiment in Yucca Flat. By the time you hear these words you will know that my confidence has not been misplaced.

"This little demonstration of my nuclear resources inconvenienced nobody and hurt nobody. The next demonstration will be on a vastly larger scale, may well inconvenience millions and may well prove disastrous for an untold number of people if they are so stupid as to fail to appreciate the gravity of this warning. However, I am sure you would first like scientific confirmation, on the highest level, that I do have the means at hand. Professor Burnett?"

"He's got the means, all right, the black-hearted bastard." For a man of unquestionably brilliant intellect, Burnett was singularly lacking in resource when it came to the selection of suitable epithets. "I hate to use the word 'beg' in the presence of a monstrous lunatic but I do beg you to believe me that he has the resources he claims. Of that my fellow physicists and I are in no doubt. He has no fewer than eleven hydrogen nuclear devices here, any one of which could, say, turn Southern California into a desert as lifeless as Death Valley. They are in the three and a half megaton range—that is, each has the explosive potential of three and a half million

229

tons of TNT. You will appreciate the significance of what I mean when I say this bomb is about two hundred times as powerful as the one that destroyed Hiroshima. And he has eleven of those monsters.

"Correction. He has only ten here. The other is already in position. Where this crazy bastard intends to put it—"

Morro interrupted. "Revealing the location of the weapon is a privilege I reserve for myself. Dr. Schmidt, Dr. Healey, Dr. Bramwell, perhaps you would be so kind as to confirm your colleague's statement." With varying degrees of forcefulness, gravity and outrage, all three left listeners in no doubt as to the chilling genuineness of the threat. When Bramwell had finished, Morro said: "And now, the most telling confirmation of all, that of Professor Aachen, probably the country's leading nuclear weaponry physicist, who personally supervised every step in the building of the bombs. Professor Aachen, you may recall, vanished some seven weeks ago. He has been working with me ever since."

"Working with you? Working with you?" Aachen's voice held the high quavering note of senility. 'You monster! You—you—I would never work with you—" He broke into a weak sobbing and there was a brief silence.

"He's been tortured!" Burnett's voice was a shout. "Tortured, I tell you. He and six kidnaped technicians have been subjected to the most unspeakable—" His voice broke off in a peculiar gasp which sounded as if he was being strangled, which he probably was.

"How you do run on, Professor Burnett." Morro's tone was resigned. "Well, Professor Aachen. About the viability of those bombs?"

"They will work." The voice was low and still shaking.

"How do you know?"

"I built them." Aachen sounded desperately weary. "There are half a dozen nuclear physicists—if I were to give the design characteristics—"

"That will not be necessary." There was a brief silence, then Morro went on: "Well, that's it. All the confirmation that any but the most mentally retarded should ever require. One small correction. Although the
230

ten bombs remaining here are all of the three and a half megaton range, the one already placed in position is only of the one and a half megaton range because, frankly, I am uncertain of the effect of a three and a half megaton bomb which may unleash forces I do not wish unleashed—not, that is, as yet." Here he paused.

Dunne said with conviction: "He's quite crazy."

"Maybe," Ryder said. "One thing, he'd have made one hell of an actor. Pause for effect. Timing."

Morro said: "This bomb, a mere twenty inches by forty inches—it would fit into a car trunk—lies on the floor of the Pacific, off Los Angeles, roughly on the outskirts of Santa Monica Bay. When it is detonated, the resultant *tsunami*—tidal wave—will, it is calculated, be between fifteen and twenty feet high, although it may well reach twice this height when being funneled through the east-west streets of Los Angeles. The effects will be felt at least as far north as Point Arguello and as far south as San Diego. Residents in the Channel Islands— particularly, I should mention, Santa Catalina—should seek high ground. One unknown, I am afraid, is that it might trigger off the Newport–Inglewood fault, but then I would expect that area of the city to be evacuated anyway.

"I need hardly warn against any foolish attempt to locate this device. The device can be detonated at any time and will be if any attempt is made to interfere with it and if this should occur before any attempt is made to evacuate the area the results could not fail to be catastrophic. What I am saying is that any person or persons responsible for sending any aircraft or ships to investigate the area roughly between Santa Cruz Island and Santa Catalina will be directly responsible for the deaths of countless thousands.

"I have certain demands to make which will be announced at 1 P.M. If they are not met by midnight I will trigger the hydrogen bomb at 10 A.M. tomorrow morning. If, after that, the demands are still not met, the next bombs—not bomb but all the remaining bombs—will go

231

off at some time between dusk and dawn on Saturday night."

On this cheerful note Morro ended his message. The newscaster started to introduce his panel of experts but Dunne switched off the set with the observation that if Morro was uncertain as to the effects of the explosion then it was unlikely that the so-called experts had a clue. "Well, Ryder, consider yourself a prophet with honor. Inspired. We get our feet wet. Believe him?"

"Sure. Don't you?"

"Yes. What to do?"

"That's a matter for the authorities, whoever they might be. Me, I take to the hills."

Delage said: "I simply don't believe it."

"Bully for you," Dunne said. "The spirit that won the West. Tell you what. Leave me the details of your next of kin and stroll along the sea front at Long Beach tomorrow. Better still, take a deck chair on the Catalina ferry." He bent a cold glance on the unfortunate Delage, then turned to Ryder. "You would say that Los Angelinos are going to be rather preoccupied for the rest of the day?"

"Look on the bright side. The biggest break ever for the most neurotic city ever. The perfect excuse for giving full and public rein to all those hidden phobias and neuroses. The drug counters should be doing a roaring trade for the rest of the day."

Parker said: "He clearly doesn't expect this second warning to be sufficient or he wouldn't have all those back-up bombs. Jesus, his demands must be sky-high."

"*And* we don't know what those demands are yet." Dunne sighed. "Two hours yet. Evil bastard. He certainly knows how to turn the screw on psychological tension." He thought briefly. "I wonder why he didn't erase those references to torture. Rather spoils his image, no?"

"Did you believe it?" Ryder said. Dunne nodded. "That's it then. That was no act, that was for real. Conviction. Authenticity. What interests me more is that Morro *may* be growing careless or that he *may* be so sure of himself that he's talking too much. Why did he forbid
232

Aachen to give any specifications about the bombs and then gratuitously inform us that it was about twenty by forty inches or something of the kind? It was not in character. He's an economical speaker and that was unnecessary. If Aachen had given us details they would have been accurate. Granted, Morro didn't give us any specifications but I have a faint suspicion that the measurements given were inaccurate. If they were, why should he want to mislead us?"

"I don't follow," Dunne said. "What are you getting at?"

"I wish I knew. It would be instructive to find out what kind of bombs Aachen was in the habit of designing. I mean, if he didn't know about the design how could he supervise the construction? I wonder if you could find out."

"I'll phone the director and try. I wouldn't have much hope. That would be top secret and there are some people with whom the FBI has very limited powers of investigation. The Atomic Energy Commission is one of those."

"Even in a national emergency?"

"I said I'll try."

"And can you find out anything about Sheriff Hartman's background? Not police records. We can be sure that either LeWinter or Donahure or both had a hand in his installation in which case his records are bound to be faked. His *true* background."

"We're ahead of you, Sergeant. It's in hand."

"Well, thanks. In view of what we've just heard what do you feel now about my intentions of going to trample all over LeWinter's civic rights?"

"LeWinter? Who's LeWinter?"

"Indeed," Ryder said and left followed by Parker and Jeff.

They stopped off at the *Examiner* building. Ryder went inside, spoke briefly to Aaron, the editor, and emerged within two minutes, a buff envelope in his hand. Inside the car, he extracted a photograph and showed it to Parker and Jeff. Parker studied it with interest.

"Beauty and the Beast? April and December? How much do you think the *Globe* would give us for this masterpiece?"

LeWinter was at home and had the look of a man who didn't intend to leave it. If he was informed by the spirit of *joie de vivre* and good will toward his fellow man, he was concealing it well. In fact, he made no attempt to conceal his displeasure as the three policemen bustled him into his own luxurious living room. Parker did the talking.

"Police. We'd like to ask you a few questions."

"I'm a judge." The cold dignity came off in neither tone nor expression. "Where's your warrant?"

"You were a judge. 'Were' or 'are,' you're stupid. For questions, no warrant. Which leads me rather neatly into the first question. Why did you provide Donahure with signed blank search warrants? Don't you know that's illegal? You, a judge? Or do you deny it?"

"Most certainly I deny it."

"That was a foolish thing for a supposedly learned judge to say. Do you think we would make such an accusation unless we could substantiate it? We have them. You can see them down at the station. Well, that's for starters. We've established you're a liar. Henceforth, every statement you make will automatically be disbelieved unless we have independent corroboration. Still deny it?"

LeWinter said nothing. Parker had an excellent line in intimidation and demoralization.

Parker went on: "Found in his safe. We searched his house."

"On what grounds?"

"You're no longer a judge. He's under arrest."

LeWinter forgot he was no longer a judge. "On what grounds?"

"Bribery and corruption. You know, blackmail, taking dirty money and dishing it out to dishonest cops. Kept
234

most of it for himself, though." He looked reproachfully at LeWinter. "You should have taught him the basic tricks of the trade."

"What the devil do you mean?"

"How to stash away illegal money. Did you know he had half a million in eight accounts? He should have been sophisticated, shouldn't he? The clown stashed it away in local accounts. Switzerland's the place. Your numbered account in Zurich. We have it. Bank's been co-operative."

LeWinter's attempted look at outrage fell just short of the pathetic. "If you're insinuating that I, senior judge of the state of California, have been involved in any illegal financial transactions—"

"Shut up and save it for a real judge. We're not insinuating. We know. And perhaps you would care to explain how come that ten thousand dollars found in Donahure's possession had your prints all over them?"

LeWinter didn't care to explain. His eyes were moving restlessly from side to side but it couldn't have been because of any thought of escape in his mind: he could not bear to meet the three pairs of coldly accusing eyes.

Parker had LeWinter on the hook and had no intention of letting him get off it. "Not that that's the only thing that Donahure's been charged with. Oh, no. Unfortunately for you, oh, no. He also faces a rap and certain conviction for attempted murder *and* murder, witnesses *and* confession respectively. On the murder rap, you will be charged as an accessory."

"Murder? Murder!" In the course of his legal practice LeWinter must have heard the word a thousand times but it was long odds that it had ever affected him as it did now.

"You're a friend of Sheriff Hartman, aren't you?"

"Hartman?" LeWinter was caring less and less for the line the conversation was taking.

"So he says. After all, you do have an alarm connected from your safe to his office."

"Ah! Hartman."

"Ah, as you say, Hartman. Seen him recently?"

LeWinter had actually started wetting his lips, that
235

indication of corrosive anxiety to which he had succeeded in reducing hundreds of suspects over the years. "I can't remember."

"But you can remember what he looked like, I hope. You'd never recognize him now. Honestly. Back of his head blown off. It was downright uncivil of you to have your friend's head blown off."

"You're mad. You're crazy." Even the most newly qualified intern would have disapproved of LeWinter's peculiar complexion, which had acquired all the healthy vitality of that of a corpse. "You've no proof."

"Don't be so original. No proof. That's what they all say when they're guilty. Where's your secretary?"

"What secretary?" The latest switch in attack seemed to have a momentarily paralyzing effect on his thought processes.

"God help us." Parker lifted his eyes upward in temporary supplication. "Rather, God help you. Bettina Ivanhoe. Where is she?"

"Excuse me." LeWinter went to a cupboard, poured himself some bourbon and drank it in one gulp. It didn't seem to do him any good.

Parker said: "You may have needed that but that wasn't why you took it. Time to think, isn't that it? Where is she?"

"I gave her the day off."

"Whiskey didn't help. Wrong answer. When did you speak to her?"

"This morning."

"Another lie. She's been in custody since last night, assisting police with their inquiries. So you didn't give her a day off." Parker was quite without pity. "But it seems you gave yourself a day off. Why aren't you down in the court dispensing justice in your usual even-handed fashion?"

"I'm not well." His appearance bore him out. Jeff looked at his father to see if he would stop the ruthless interrogation but Ryder was regarding LeWinter with what appeared to be an expression of profound indifference.

"Not well? Compared to the way you're going to feel
236

very soon—when you're in your court being tried for murder—you're in blooming health. You're at home because one of your criminal accomplices, masters, more like, called you from Bakersfield and told you to lie low. Tell me, how well do you know Miss Ivanhoe? You know, of course, that her proper name is Ivanov?"

LeWinter had further recourse to his liquor cupboard. He said wearily, almost despairingly: "How long is this—this inquisition to go on?"

"Not long. If you tell the truth, that is. I asked a question."

"How well—she's my secretary. That's enough."

"No more than that?"

"Of course not."

Ryder stepped forward and showed LeWinter the photograph he'd collected from the *Examiner*'s office. LeWinter stared at it as if hypnotized, then got back to his lip licking.

"A nice kid." Ryder was being conversational. "Blackmail, of course. She's told us. Not with this end in view—this is just a spin-off. Principally, as we know, she came in handy for the translation of phony Russian documents."

"Phony?"

"Ah! So the documents do exist. I wonder why Morro wanted you to provide him with the names of engineers, drillers, oil-rig men. Even more, I wonder why twenty-six of them are missing."

"God knows what you're talking about."

"And you. Watched TV this morning?" LeWinter shook his head in a dazed and uncomprehending manner. "So perhaps you don't know he's detonating a hydrogen bomb in Santa Monica Bay or thereabouts at ten o'clock tomorrow morning." LeWinter made no reply and registered no expression, no doubt because he'd no expressions left to register. "For an eminent judge you do keep odd company, LeWinter."

It was a measure of LeWinter's mental distress that comprehension came so slowly. He said in a dull voice: "You were the man who was here last night?"

"Yes." Ryder nodded to Jeff. "And this is Perkins.

237

Remember Perkins? Patrolman Ryder. My son. Unless you're blind and deaf you must know that your friend Morro holds two of our family captive. One of them, my daughter—my son's sister—has been wounded. We feel kindly disposed to you. Well, LeWinter, apart from being as corrupt as all hell, a lecherous old goat, a traitor and accessory to murder, you're also a patsy, a sucker, a fall guy, scapegoat—call it what you will. You were conned, LeWinter, just as you thought you were conning Donahure and Miss Ivanov and Hartman. Used as a red herring to set up a nonexistent Russian connection.

"Only two things I want to know: who gave you something and to whom did you give something? Who gave you the money, the code book, the instructions to hire Miss Ivanov and to obtain the names and addresses of the now missing twenty-six men—and to whom did *you* give the names and addresses?"

LeWinter eventually registered an expression: he clamped his lips shut. Jeff winced as his father stepped forward, his expression, or lack of it, not changing, a gun swinging in his hand. LeWinter shut his eyes, flung up a protective forearm, stepped quickly back, caught his heel in a throw rug and fell heavily, striking the back of his head against a chair. He lay on the floor for ten seconds, perhaps longer, then slowly sat up. He looked dazed, as if having difficulty in relating himself to the circumstances in which he found himself and he .was clearly not acting.

He said in a croaking voice: "I've got a bad heart." Looking at and listening to him it was impossible to doubt it.

"I'll cry tomorrow. Meantime, you think your heart will last out long enough to let you get to your feet?" Slowly, shaking, using both a chair and a table, LeWinter got to his unsteady feet. He still had to hang on to the table for support. Ryder remained unmoved. He said: "The man who gave you all those things. The man to whom you gave the names. Was it the same man?"

"Call my doctor." LeWinter was clutching his chest. "God's sake, I've already *had* two heart attacks." His

238

face was registering an expression now. It was contorted in fear and pain; he clearly felt, and was probably right, that his life was in mortal danger and was begging to have it saved. Ryder regarded him with the dispassionate eye of a medieval headsman.

"I'm glad to hear it." Jeff looked at him in something close to horror but Ryder had eyes only for LeWinter. "Then I'll have nothing on my conscience if you die and there won't be a mark on you when the mortuary wagon comes to collect you. Was it the same man?"

"Yes." A barely audible whisper.

"The same man as called from Bakerfield?"

"Yes."

"What's his name?"

"I don't know." Ryder half lifted his gun. LeWinter looked at him in defeat and despair and repeated: "I don't know. I don't know."

Jeff spoke for the first time and his voice was urgent. "He *doesn't* know."

"I believe him." Ryder hadn't looked away from LeWinter. "Describe this man."

"I can't."

"Or won't."

"He wore a hood. Before God, he wore a hood."

"If Donahure got ten thousand dollars, then you got a lot more. Probably a great deal more. Give him a receipt?"

"No." LeWinter shuddered. "Just said if I would break my word he would break my back. He could have it done too. Biggest man I ever saw."

"Ha!" Ryder paused, seemed to relax, smiled briefly and went on far from encouragingly: "He could still come and do it. Look at all the trouble it would save the law and the prison hospital." He produced a pair of handcuffs and snapped them on LeWinter's wrists.

The judge's voice was weak and lacked conviction. "You have no arrest warrant."

"Don't be simple-minded and don't make me laugh. I don't want any vertebrae snapping. I don't want you getting on the wrong phone. I don't want any escape attempt. And I don't want any suicide." He looked at the

239

photograph he still held. "I'll be a long time forgetting. I want to see you rot in San Quentin." He led him toward the door, stopped and looked at Parker and Jeff. "Observe, if you will. I never laid a finger on him."

Jeff said: "Major Dunne will never believe it. Neither do I."

TEN

■ "YOU used us!" Burnett's face was white and bitter and he was shaking with such uncontrollable anger that his Glenfiddich was slopping over onto the floor of Morro's study, a shocking waste of which he was uncharacteristically oblivious. "You double-crossed us! You evil wicked bastard! A beautiful job, wasn't it, the way you spliced together our recordings and your own recording?"

Morro raised an admonitory finger. "Come, now, Professor. This helps no one. You really must learn to control yourself."

"Why the hell should he?" Schmidt's fury was as great as Burnett's but he had it under better control. All five physicists were there, together with Morro, Dubois and two guards. "We're not thinking just about our good names, our reputations. We're thinking about lives, maybe thousands of them, and if those lives are lost we're going to be held responsible. Morally at least. Every viewer, every listener, every reader in the state is going to be convinced that the hydrogen device you left off the coast is in the one and a half range. We know damn well it's in the three and a half. But because people will believe— they can't help believing—that it was all part of the same recording they're going to imagine that what you said was said with our tacit approval. You—you monster! Why did you do it?"

"Effect." Morro was unruffled. "Very elementary psychology. The detonation of this three and a half megaton device is going to have rather spectacular consequences and I want people to say to themselves: If this is the effect of a mere one and a half megaton what in the name of heaven will the cataclysmic effects of thirty-five megatons be like? It will lend persuasive weights to my demands,

241

don't you think? In the climate of terror all things are possible."

"I can believe anything of you," Burnett said. He looked at the shattered wreck of what had once been Willi Aachen. "Anything. Even that you are prepared to put thousands of lives at risk in order to achieve a psychological effect. You can have no idea what this *tsunami* will be like, what height it will reach, whether or not the Newport–Inglewood fault will trigger an earthquake. And you don't care. The effect is all."

"I think you exaggerate, Professor. I think that, where height is concerned, people will leave a very considerable margin of safety between the water levels I suggested and the worst they can fear. As for the Newport–Inglewood fault, only a madman would remain in the area at ten o'clock tomorrow morning. I do not visualize throngs of people heading for the Hollywood Park race track—if they head at that time of the morning, which I don't know. I think your fears are mainly groundless."

"Mainly! Mainly! You mean only a few thousand may drown?"

"I have no cause to love American people." Morro still maintained his monolithic calm. "They have not exactly been kind to mine."

There was a brief silence, then Healey said in a low voice: "This is even worse than I feared. Race, religion, politics, I don't know. The man's a zealot, a fanatic."

"He's nuts." Burnett reached for the bottle.

"Judge LeWinter wishes to make a voluntary statement," Ryder said.

"Does he now?" Dunne peered at the trembling fearful figure, a pale and almost unimaginable shadow of the imposing figure who had so long dominated the courts. "Is that the case, Judge?"

Ryder was impatient. "Sure it is."

"Look, Sergeant, I was asking the judge."

"We were there," Parker said. "Jeff and I. There was no coercion, no force, the only time Sergeant Ryder

242

touched him was to put on handcuffs. We wouldn't perjure ourselves, Major Dunne."

"You wouldn't." He turned to Delage. "Next door. I'll take his statement in a minute."

"One moment before he goes," Ryder said. "Any word about Hartman?"

Dunne permitted himself his first smile. "For once, some luck. Just came in. Hartman, it seems, has been living out there for some years. With his widowed sister, which accounts for the fact that his name was not in the phone book. Didn't spend much time there until a year or so ago. Traveled a lot. You'd never guess what his business is—well, was, till last year."

"Oil rigs."

Dunne said without heat: "Damn you, Ryder, you spoil a man's simplest pleasures. Yes. Boss roustabout. First-class record. How did you know?"

"I didn't. Who were his sponsors—you know, character endorsers?"

"Two prominent local businessmen and—well?"

"Donahure and LeWinter."

"Indeed."

Ryder looked at LeWinter. "You and Hartman made up that list of drillers and engineers together, you from your court cases and extensive briefs from the oil companies, Hartman from his field experience?"

LeWinter said nothing.

"Well, at least he doesn't deny it. Tell me, LeWinter, was it his job to recruit those men?"

"I don't know."

"To kidnap them?"

"I don't know."

"Well, then to contact them, one way or another?"

"Yes."

"And deliver them?"

"I suppose so."

"Yes or no."

LeWinter gathered together the shreds of his dignity and turned to Dunne. "I am being subjected to harassment."

"If that's what you choose to call it," Dunne said unsympathetically. "Proceed, Sergeant."

"Yes or no?"

"Yes, damn you, yes."

"So to be obvious, he must have known where to deliver those men after recruitment, voluntary or not. So, assuming it *was* Morro who was responsible for their disappearance, Hartman had a direct line to Morro or knew how to contact him. You must agree with that."

LeWinter sat down in a chair. He looked more like a cadaver than ever. "If you say so."

"And, of course, you and Donahure had the same line."

"No!" The denial was immediate and almost vehement.

"Well." Ryder was approving. "That's more like it."

Dunne said: "You believe him? That he had no line on Morro?"

"Sure. If he had, he'd be dead by now. A sweet lad, this Morro. Even playing the cards close to the chest he never lets his left hand know what the right is doing. Only Hartman knew. Morro thought that Hartman was totally in the clear. How was he to know, how was anyone to guess, that I'd trace him because of the alarm linking LeWinter's safe and Hartman's office? Morro certainly knew nothing about that. If he did, he'd never have exposed LeWinter and Donahure by planting misleading evidence on them. But Morro had taken no chances. He'd given strict orders to both LeWinter and Donahure that if anyone got a line on Hartman, the only man who had a line to him, then Hartman was to be eliminated. It's really all so simple, isn't it?" He looked consideringly at LeWinter, then back at Dunne. "Remove that pillar of justice, will you? He makes me sick."

When he'd gone, Dunne said: "A fair morning's work. I underestimated you, Sergeant Ryder. Not breaking his neck, I mean. I'm beginning to wonder if I could have done the same."

"You're either born with a heart of gold or you aren't. Any word from the boss man—Barrow, isn't it?—about what kind of bombs this Professor Aachen was designing when Morro snatched him?"

"I phoned him. He said he'd contact the AEC and call back. He's not a man to waste time. No reply from him yet. He was curious why we wanted to find out."

"Don't rightly know myself. I said I thought Morro was trying to mislead us, that's all. What you call an outside chance of nothing. And speaking of Morro—there wouldn't be any word from Manila?"

Dunne looked at his watch, then in a quietly exasperated patience at Ryder. "You've been gone exactly one hour and five minutes. Manila, I would remind you, is not just a couple of blocks down the road. Would there be anything else?"

"Well, since you're offering." Dunne momentarily closed his eyes. "Carlton's friend back in Illinois mentioned a very big man in the group of weirdos Carlton was flirting with. LeWinter has just mentioned, in a very very scared voice, a similar person who's threatened to break his back. Could be one and the same man. There can't be many eighty inchers around."

"Eighty inchers?"

"Six foot eight. That's what Carlton's pal said. Shouldn't be difficult to check whether anyone of that size has been charged or convicted at some time in this state. Nor should it be very difficult to find if such a character is a member of any of the oddball organizations in California. You can't *hide* a man that size and apparently this person doesn't go to much trouble to keep hidden. And then there's the question of helicopters."

"Ah."

"Not just any helicopter. A special helicopter. It would be nice if you could trace it."

"A trifle." Dunne was being heavily sarcastic. "First, there are more helicopters in this state than there are in any comparable region on earth. Second, the FBI is stretched to its limits—"

"Stretched to its limits! Look, Major, I'm in no mood for light humor this morning. Eight thousand agents

245

stretched to their limits and what have they achieved? Zero. I could even ask what they are doing and the answer could be the same. When I said a special helicopter, I meant a very special helicopter. The one that delivered this atom bomb to Yucca Flat. Or have your eight thousand agents already got that little matter in hand?"

"Explain."

Ryder turned to his son. "Jeff, you've said you know that area. Yucca and Frenchman's Flats."

"I've been there."

"Would a vehicle leave tracks up there?"

"Sure. Not everywhere. There's a lot of rock. But there's also shingle and rubble and sand. Chances are good, yes."

"Now then, Major. Would any of the eight thousand have been checking on tracks—trucks, cars, dune buggies —in the area of the crater—those, that is, that they didn't obliterate in their mad dash to the scene of the crime?"

"I wasn't there myself. Delage?" Delage picked up a phone. "Helicopters? An interesting speculation?"

"I think so. And I also think that if I were Morro that is the way I'd have dumped that hydrogen bomb in the Pacific. Cuts out all this tricky—and maybe attention-catching business—of trucking the bomb to the coast and then transferring it to a boat."

Dunne was doubtful. "There's still an awful lot of helicopters in the state."

"Let's limit it to the communes, the oddballs, the disenchanted."

"With a road transport system like we've got, who would want—?"

"Let's limit it to the mountains. Remember, we'd more or less decided that Morro and his friends have sought out high ground."

"Well, the more extreme the group, the higher they tend to go. I suppose some would require a chopper to get any place. But helicopters come expensive. They'd be hired on an hourly basis and you could hardly persuade a hired pilot to carry a hydrogen bomb—"

"Maybe the pilot isn't hired. Nor the helicopter. Then

246

there's the matter of a truck. Trucks. For the transport of weapons-grade material—the stuff taken from San Ruffino."

Dunne said: "You have that, Leroy?" Leroy nodded and, like Delage, reached for a telephone.

"Thanks." Ryder pondered briefly. "That's all. See you around—some time this afternoon."

Jeff looked at his watch. "Don't forget. Forty-five minutes. Morro will be on the air with his terms or demands or blackmail or whatever."

"Probably not worth listening to. Anyway, you can tell me all about it."

"Where are you going?"

"Public library. The study of contemporary history. I've fallen way behind in my reading."

"I see." Jeff watched the door swing to behind Ryder, then looked at Dunne. "I don't see. He's all right?"

Dunne was thoughtful. "If *he* isn't, what about us?"

Ryder arrived home some ninety minutes later to find Jeff and Parker drinking beer in front of the television. Ryder seemed in remarkably good spirits. He wasn't smiling broadly, far less laughing, nor was he cracking any jokes, for that was not his way. But for a man with two of his family held hostage and the threat of being drowned and vaporized far from being an impossibility, he was bafflingly composed and relaxed. He looked at the TV screen where literally hundreds of small craft, some with sails raised, were milling about in hopeless confusion, traveling at apparent random and ramming each other with a frequency that was matched only by a blind determination. It was an enclosed harbor with half a dozen piers thrusting out toward a central channel: the room to maneuver was minimal, the chaos absolute.

"Wow," Ryder said. "This is something. Like Trafalgar or Jutland. Those were very confused sea battles too."

"Dad." Jeff was heroically patient. "That's Marina del Rey in Los Angeles. The yachtsmen are trying to leave."

"I know the place. The boys of the California Yacht Club and the del Rey Yacht Club displaying their usual nautical composure, not to say stoicism. At this rate

247

they'll take a week to sort themselves out. What's the great rush? Incidentally, this will pose a problem for Morro. This must be happening at every harbor in Los Angeles. He said any vessel moving into the area between Santa Cruz Island and Santa Catalina would result in the detonation of the bomb. A couple of hours and there will be a couple of thousand craft in those waters. Careless of Morro. Anybody could have foreseen this."

Parker said: "According to the announcer, nobody intends to go anywhere near there. They're going to use the Santa Barbara and San Pedro channels and go as far north and south on the coast as possible."

"Lemmings. Even a small boat can ride out a tidal wave at sea. Not much more than a fast-traveling ripple, really. It's only when it reaches shallow water or estuaries that it starts to pile up into what people regard as a tidal wave. Why all this confusion, anyway?"

"Panic," Parker said. "The owners of smaller crafts are trying to lift them out of the water onto trailers and get them away but there are facilities available for only a few per cent at a time and those are so overloaded they keep breaking down. Diesel and gasoline supplies are almost exhausted and those that have been fueled are so hemmed in by boats looking for fuel that they can't get out. And then, of course, there are craft taking off under full power with their mooring lines still attached." Parker shook his head sadly. "I don't think urban Californians are really a sea-going race."

"That's nothing," Jeff said. "We're supposed to be *the* automobile race. You'd never know it. They've just been showing us street scenes in Santa Monica and Venice. Just a land-based version of what we're seeing here. Biggest traffic jams ever. Cars being used like tanks to batter a way through. Drivers jumping from their cars and knocking each other silly. Incredible."

"It would be the same the world over," Ryder said. "I'll bet Morro's glued to his screen in ecstasy. And everybody heading east, of course. City fathers issued any instructions yet?"

"Not that we've heard of."

248

"They will. Give them time. They're like all politicians. They'll wait to see what the majority of the people are doing then go ahead and tell them to do what they're already doing. Any food in this house?"

"What?" Jeff, understandably, was momentarily off balance. "Yes. Sandwiches in the kitchen."

"Thanks." Ryder turned to go then stopped abruptly as something on the screen caught his eye. "What an extraordinary coincidence. We can only hope that if it is a good omen then it's for us and not for Morro."

Jeff said: "We can wait forever."

"See that dock at the lower right of your screen? It's to the Southeast. The broad one. Unless I'm totally wrong, that's the source of all our troubles."

"*That* dock?" Jeff stared his incredulity.

"The name of it. Mindanao."

A minute later Ryder was taking his ease in an arm-chair, sandwich in one hand, beer in the other, half an eye on the screen. He focused both eyes on the screen and said: "That's interesting."

The picture was not without its interest. Three private planes, all twin-engined, had clearly been engaged in a multiple collision. The broken wing tip of one rested on the ground. The undercarriage of a second had crumpled while a lazy plume of smoke arose from the third.

"Land, sea and air." Ryder shook his head. "I know that place. Clover Field in Santa Monica. Apparently the air traffic controller has hightailed it for the Sierras."

"Honest to God, Dad!" Jeff was trying to contain himself. "You're the most infuriating, exasperating character that's ever walked. Haven't you got anything to say about Morro's ultimatum?"

"Well, no."

"Jesus!"

"Be reasonable. I've seen, heard and read nothing about it."

"Jesus!" Jeff repeated and fell into silence. Ryder looked inquiringly at Parker, who clearly steeled himself for the task.

"Morro was on time. As always. This time he really

249

was economical with his words. I'll make it even more economical. His ultimatum was simply this. Give me the locations and all the operating wave bands of all your radar stations on both the East and West coasts, your cruising radar bombers both here and in NATO and in all your spy satellites or I'll pull the plug."

"He said that, did he?"

"Well, quite a bit more, but that was the gist of it."

"Bull. Poppycock. I told you he wouldn't be worth listening to. I'd thought better of Morro than that. Babies along the Potomac and the Pentagon spinning around like a high-speed centrifuge."

"You don't believe it."

"If that's what you gather from my reactions, you're right."

"But look, Dad—"

"Look nothing. Rubbish. Maybe I'd better revise that snap judgment on Morro. Maybe he was well aware that he was making an impossible demand. Maybe he was well aware that it wouldn't be met. Maybe he didn't want it to be met. But just try convincing the American public—especially that section of it represented by this state—of that. It will take a long, long time and a long, long time is the one thing we don't have."

"Impossible demand?" Jeff said carefully.

"Let me think." Ryder chewed some more and drank some more while he thought. "Three things occur and none of them make sense and wouldn't to the Pentagon, which can't possibly be as retarded as the New York and Washington columnists say it is. First off, what's to prevent the Pentagon feeding him a long and highly convincing rigmarole of completely misleading information? What would lead him to suspect that it was misleading? And even if he did, how on earth could he possibly set about checking on the accuracy of the information? It's impossible. Second, the Pentagon would probably and quite cheerfully see California being wiped out rather than give away our first defense against nuclear attack. Third, if he's in a position to wipe out Los Angeles and San Francisco—and we must assume that he is—what's
250

to prevent him repeating the dose to New York, Chicago and Washington itself and so on until he achieved by direct means what he would achieve by indirect means by blinding our radar? It makes no kind of sense at all. But it all fits in."

Jeff digested this in silence. Parker said slowly: "It's all very well for you to sit there in—what kind of judgment do you call it?"

"Olympian?" Ryder said helpfully.

"That's it. It's all very well for you to sit there in Olympian judgment but you'd made up that crafty mind in advance that you weren't going to believe a word Morro said and you were also certain that he wouldn't say what you were convinced he couldn't say."

"Very shrewd, Sergeant Parker. Confusing, mind you, but shrewd."

"And you've just said it all fits in."

"I did say that."

"You know something we don't know?"

"I don't know any facts that you don't know, except for those I get from reading about earthquakes and contemporary history, a practice for which Jeff here thinks I need the services of a head shrinker."

"I never said—"

"You don't have to speak to say something."

"I have it," Parker said. "All good detectives come up with a theory. You have a theory?"

"Well, in all due modesty—"

"Modesty? So now the sun sets in the east. I don't even have to take time out for a reflective pause. Mindanao?"

"Mindanao."

When Ryder had finished, Parker said to Jeff: "Well, what do you make of that?"

"I'm still trying to assimilate it all." Jeff spoke in a kind of dazed protest. "I mean, I've just heard it. You've got to give me time to think."

"Come, come, boy. First impressions."

"Well, I don't see any holes in it. And the more I think—and if you would give me more time I could think

251

more—the fewer holes I can see. I think it *could* be right."

"Look at your old man," Parker said. "Can you see any sign of 'could' in his face?"

"That's just smirking. Well, I can't see any way in which it must be wrong." Jeff thought some more then took the plunge. "It makes sense to me."

"There you are now, John." Parker sounded positively jovial. "As near a compliment as you'll ever be likely to extract from your son. It makes a lot of sense to me. Come, gentlemen, let's try it out for size on Major Dunne."

Dunne didn't even bother saying it made sense. He turned to Leroy and said: "Get me Mr. Barrow. And have the helicopter stand by." He rubbed his hands briskly. "Well, well. Looks as if you're going to ruffle a few feathers in Los Angeles, Sergeant."

"You go and ruffle them. Top brass rub me the wrong way. Your boss seems almost human but that's more than I can say for Mitchell. You know as much about it now as I do and I'm only guessing anyway. The person I would like to see is Professor Benson. If you could fix that, I'd be grateful."

"Delighted. If you fly north."

"Blackmail." Ryder didn't sound too heated.

"Of course." Dunne regarded him over steepled fingers. "Seriously. Several things. First off, we could kill two birds with one stone—Pasadena is only ten minutes' helicopter hop from our offices up there. Again, if you don't turn up, both Barrow and Mitchell will automatically assume that you lack the courage of your own convictions. *You* can talk to them in a way that would get me fired on the spot. They can probe more deeply than I've done and ask questions that I couldn't answer—I know you've told me all that you regard as the essentials but there must be details that you consider irrelevant at the moment. What's the point in staying here—there's nothing more you can accomplish here and you know it—to convince the mandarins of your belief would be a major accomplishment." Dunne smiled. "Would you be so heart-
252

less as to deprive me of the pleasure of this—ah—encounter?"

"He's just scared of the big bad wolves," Jeff said. Ryder smiled.

Like all such rooms designed to give its occupants a proper sense of their own importance, the conference room was suitably impressive. It had the only mahogany-paneled walls in the building, behung with pictures of individuals who looked like the Ten Most Wanted but were, in fact, past and present directors and senior administrators of the FBI. It held the only mahogany oval table in the building, one that gleamed with that refulgent splendor rarely found among tables that have seen an honest day's work. Around it were grouped the only twelve leather and brass-studded chairs in the building. Before each chair was a leather-cornered blotter, indispensable for doodling but otherwise wholly superfluous, a brass tray for pens and pencils, a water jug and glass; the comprehensively stocked bar lay behind a sliding wooden panel. The over-all effect was slightly dimmed by the two stenographer's chairs that faced a battery of red, white and black telephones; those were covered in plastic leather. There were no stenographers there that afternoon; this was a top-secret meeting of the gravest national importance and the faces of most of the twelve seated men accurately reflected their awareness of this.

Nobody occupied the rounded head of the table: Barrow and Mitchell each sat an equidistant foot from the center line so that there could be no claimant for the chairman's position. The heavens might be falling but that would have to wait until protocol had been served. Each had three senior aides at the table—none of the six had been introduced—and all of them had brief cases and important-looking papers on the blotters before them. The fact that it had been deemed necessary to call the meeting clearly indicated that the contents of those papers were worthless, but at the conference table one has to have papers to shuffle or one is nothing. Mitchell opened the meeting; a toss of a coin had decided that.

253

He said: "To begin with I must request, in the politest possible way, that Sergeant Parker and Patrolman Ryder withdraw."

Ryder said: "Why?"

Nobody queried Mitchell's orders. He bent a cold eye on Ryder. "Given the opportunity, Sergeant, I was about to explain. This meeting is on the highest level of national security and those are not sworn men. Moreover, they are junior police officers both of whom have resigned their positions and therefore have no official capacity— they have not even been assigned to this investigation. That, I think, is a reasonable attitude."

Ryder considered Mitchell for a few moments, then looked across at Dunne, who sat opposite him. He said, in a tone of exaggerated disbelief: "You brought me all the way up here just to listen to this pompous and arrogant rubbish?"

Dunne looked at his fingernails. Jeff looked at the ceiling. Barrow looked at the ceiling. Mitchell looked mad. His tone would have frozen mercury.

"I don't think I can be hearing properly, Sergeant."

"Then why don't you vacate your position to someone who can? I spoke clearly enough. I didn't want to come here. I know your reputation. I don't give a damn about it. If you throw Mr. Parker and my son out then, by the same token, you have to throw me out. You say they have no official capacity—neither have you. You just muscled your way in. They have as much right to order you out as you have to order them out. You have no official jurisdiction inside the United States. If you can't understand that and stop antagonizing people who are doing an honest job of work, then it's time you yielded your chair to someone who can."

Ryder looked leisurely around the table. No one appeared disposed to make any comment. Mitchell's face was frozen. Barrow's was set in an expression of calmly judicial impartiality, a remarkable tribute to the man's self-control. Had he been eavesdropping and alone he would unquestionably have been rolling around holding his sides.

"So, having established the fact that there are no fewer than seven of us here in an unofficial capacity, let's look at the investigation. Mr. Parker and my son have already achieved a very considerable amount, as Major Dunne will confirm. They have helped solve the murder of a county sheriff, put a corrupt police chief behind bars on a charge of murder and also put behind bars, on a charge of accessory to murder, a judge widely regarded as the likely Chief Justice of the state supreme court. All three, including the murdered man, were deeply involved in the business at hand—this has provided us with extremely valuable information."

Mitchell had the grace to part his lips about half an inch. Barrow remained without expression. Clearly he'd been briefed by Dunne; equally clear was the fact that he hadn't bothered to pass on his information.

"And what has the CIA achieved? I'll tell you. It has succeeded in making a laughingstock of itself in general and its director in particular, not to mention uselessly wasting the taxpayer's money by sending its agents to pussyfoot around Geneva in search of so-called secret information that has been in the public domain for two years. Apart from that, what? An educated guess would say zero."

Barrow coughed. "Aren't you being needlessly intransigent?" He could have put more reproof into his voice if he'd tried, even a little.

"Needless intransigence is the only language some people seem to understand."

Mitchell's voice surfaced through layers of cracked ice. Your point is taken, Sergeant. You have come to teach us how to do our jobs."

Ryder wasn't quite through with being intransigent or letting Mitchell off the hook. "I am not a sergeant. I'm a private citizen and as such beholden to no one. I can't teach the CIA anything—I wouldn't know how to go about subverting foreign governments or assassinating their presidents. I can't teach the FBI anything. All I want is a fair hearing but it's really a matter of indifference whether I get it or not." His eyes were looking at

Mitchell's. "You can shut up and let me say what I've been brought here to say, against my better judgment, or not. I'd as soon leave. I find the atmosphere here uncomfortable, not to say hostile, and Major Dunne has all the essentials."

Mitchell said in a toneless voice: "We will hear you out."

"I don't like that expression either." Barrow winced. Despite his antipathy toward Mitchell, it was not hard to guess that, even although momentarily, he was putting himself in the other's position. "It's the term used by the chairman of the board when he's giving a carpeted executive the chance to justify himself before being fired."

"Please." Barrow turned the palms of his hands upward. "We get the point that you're a plain speaker. Please take our point that you haven't been brought here for nothing. We will listen carefully."

"Thank you." Ryder wasted no time on preamble. "You've all seen the streets around this block. As we came into your pad on the roof we saw a hundred streets like it. Blocked. Choked. The people are running scared. I don't blame them. If I lived here, I'd be running scared too. They believe that Morro is going to trigger off this bomb at ten tomorrow morning. So do I. I also believe that he will set off or is prepared to set off the other ten nuclear devices he claims to have. What I don't for a moment believe in is his demand. It's utter foolishness; he must know it is and we should recognize it for what it is— an empty threat, a meaningless demand that can't be met."

"Perhaps you should know," Barrow said. "Just before you arrived word came through that protests have been lodged by the Kremlin and Peking, and by their embassies in Washington, crying to high heaven that they are as innocent as the driven snow of this monstrous accusation against them—no one has accused them of anything but one gets their point—and that it's all part of a warmongering capitalist plot. First time in living memory that they've totally agreed with each other on anything."

"Not just the usual standard denial?"

"No. They're hopping mad."

256

"Don't blame them. The suggestion is ludicrous."

"You're sure the fact that you already seem to have discounted evidence pointing to some Communist connection has not influenced your thinking in this?"

"I'm sure. So are you."

Mitchell said: "I'm not so sure."

"You wouldn't be. Last thing you do every night is look under your bed."

Mitchell just stopped short of grinding his teeth. "If not that, what?" The words were innocuous enough but their tone left no doubt that he was prepared to fight to the death for his disbelief of every word Ryder was about to say.

"Bear with me. It all seems to start with the Philippines. I'm sure you all know how it is out there and I'm sure the last thing I am is a specialist in foreign affairs but I've been reading all about it in the library just a couple of hours ago. I'll briefly recap what I read, as much for my own sake as anybody else's.

"The Philippines are in a financial mess. Hugely ambitious development plans, mounting internal and external debts, heavy military expenditures—they're strapped. But like a good many other countries they know what to do when the kitty's empty—put the arm on Uncle Sam. And they're in an excellent position to apply pressure.

"The Philippines are the keystone of America's Pacific military strategy and the huge Seventh Fleet anchorage at Subic Bay and the strategically crucial Air Force base are regarded by the Pentagon as being indispensable and well worth the rent—many people regard it as a cross between ransom and extortion money—that they demand.

"The south of the Philippines—the island of Mindanao—is inhabited by Muslims. You all know that. Unlike Christianity, the Muslim religion has no moral laws against the killing of mankind in general—just against the killing of Muslims, period. The concept of a holy war is an integral part of their lives and this is what they're doing right now—carrying out a holy crusade against President Marcos and his predominantly Catholic government. They regard it as a religious war being

257

waged by an oppressed people. Whether it's a justifiable war or not is—well, it's none of my business. In any event, it is an intensely bitter war. I think all this is well known.

"What is, perhaps, not quite so well known is that they feel almost equally bitter toward the United States. It's not hard to understand. Although Congress raises its hand in holier-than-thou horror at Marcos' long-term track record on civil liberties, they still cheerfully, as I said, ante up the rent for our bases to the tune of several hundred million dollars a year in military aid, no small amount of which is put to what the Philippine Government regards as being perfectly good use in crushing the Muslims.

"Even less known is the fact that the Muslims aren't all that much fonder of Russia, China and Vietnam. Not, as far as is known, that those countries have caused them any harm—it's just that the Philippine Government has established cordial—and diplomatic—relations with those three countries and countries that reciprocate the Philippines Government's overtures are automatically classified by the Mindanaon Muslims as belonging to the enemy camp.

"What the Muslims desperately lack is arms. Provided that they were armed to the same standards as the government's well-equipped eighty field battalions—well-equipped, mainly, by the courtesy of Uncle Sam—they could give a good account of themselves. Until last year what little supplies they received came from Libya—until Imelda Marcos went there and sweet-talked Colonel Gadhafi and his foreign minister, Ali Tureiki, into cutting off the Mindanaon Muslims' last lifeline.

"So what were they to do? They couldn't obtain or manufacture their own arms in the Philippines. Even if they didn't hate America there was no way the Americans would supply arms to insurgents against the Philippine Government. They weren't even speaking to the Communists. And their own fellow Muslims had turned against them. So the Muslim rebels came up with the only answer. Any big armament firm in the world will supply arms to
258

anyone—if the money is right and on the barrelhead, irrespective of race, creed and politics. Why shouldn't they? Governments do it all the time—America, Britain and France are the worst offenders. All they had to do was to find the cash to put on the barrelhead.

"The solution was simple. Let the enemy provide. In this case the unfortunate provider was to be Uncle Sam. All the better if you can wound him in the process. Rob him blind, hurt him and—to kill two birds with one stone—discredit the U.S.S.R. and China by using them as a smoke screen. That's what I believe is happening in California here and now. And the frightening thing about it is that we have to remember that the Koran gives a Muslim a conscience-free hand to knock off anyone who isn't a Muslim. And if your conscience is free, what's the difference between one and one million? If all's free in love and war, what's it like in a holy war?"

"It's an interesting hypothesis," Mitchell said. His tone implied that he was a courteous man tolerantly listening to another theorizing about how the moon is made of green cheese. "You have evidence to back this up, of course?"

"Nothing that you would regard as positive evidence. Elimination, circumstantial evidence, all perhaps better than nothing. In the first place it's the only theory that explains the situation in which we find ourselves now."

"But you said they're after cash. If that's so, why didn't they blackmail the government for cash?"

"I don't know. I have the glimmerings of an idea but I know what you would do with a glimmering. Second, speech experts place Morro's area of origin as southeast Asia—which includes the Philippines. Third, it is certain —there is no question about this—that he is in criminal association with Carlton, the supposedly kidnaped San Ruffino deputy of security, and there is also no question that Carlton has been in Manila several times. Fourth, if Morro has a weakness, it seems to be that it tickles his ironic fancy to give himself an alias associated with the operation he is conducting. The first stage of his operation here was concerned with nuclear fuel so he may well

259

have purposely chosen to call himself after the nuclear station at Morro Bay. Fifth, that's not the only name pronounced that way—there's another in the Philippines, called Moro Gulf. Sixth, this is in Mindanao and is the focus of the Muslim insurgent movement. Seventh, last year, Moro Gulf was the scene of the greatest natural disaster in Philippine history. An earthquake at the mouth of the gulf—the interior bay is crescent-shaped—caused a gigantic tidal wave that took over five thousand lives and left seventy thousand homeless, all along the shores. A tidal wave we're promised for tomorrow. I'll take long odds that we'll be promised an earthquake on Saturday. I think that this may be Morro's Achilles' heel. I think it would mightily tickle his fancy to have his name associated with nuclear weapons, tidal waves and earthquakes."

"You call this evidence?" Mitchell's tone was nasty, but it could have been nastier.

"No proof, I agree. Indicators, that's all. But they're all important. In police work you can't look anywhere until you have *some* indication of where to look. You start hunting where the hound dog points. Put it another way. I'm looking for a lodestone and I set down a compass. The needle swings and steadies. That *might* indicate the direction of the lodestone. I put down a second compass and it points in the same direction. That could be coincidence, although a remarkable one. I put five more and they *all* point the same way. I stop thinking about coincidences. I have seven needles here and they all point toward Mindanao." Ryder paused. "I'm convinced. I understand, of course, that you gentlemen would require some sort of proof."

Barrow said: "I think I'm convinced if only for the reason that I can't see any needle pointing any other damned way. But some proof would be nice. What would you call proof, Mr. Ryder?"

"For me, any one answer to any one of, oddly, seven questions." He took a sheet of paper from his pocket. "What is Morro's place of origin? Where can we locate a six-foot-eight giant who must be a senior lieutenant of

Morro's? What kind of bomb did this Professor Aachen design? I think Morro lied about its dimensions for the simple reason that he didn't have to mention it at all." He looked reproachfully at Barrow and Mitchell. "I understand the AEC has put the shutters on this one. If you two gentlemen can't make them open up, who can? Then I want to know if there are any private organizations up in the mountains using their own helicopters. Any using their own private vans. Major Dunne is working on those two. After that, I'd like to know if Morro is going to threaten us with an earthquake on Saturday. I've said I'm sure he is. Lastly, I'd like to know if the post office can discover whether there's a radiophone link between Bakersfield and a place called the Adlerheim."

"Adlerheim?" Mitchell had lost some of his intransigence: it was reasonable to assume that he hadn't become director because his aunt's cousin knew some stenographer in a CIA typing pool. "What's that?"

"I know it," Barrow said. "Up in the Sierra Nevada. Von Streicher's Folly, they call it, isn't it?"

"Yes. I think that's where we'll find Morro. Anyone mind if I smoke?"

Not only did nobody object, nobody even seemed to have heard his request. They were busy. They were busy studying the insides of their closed eyelids, or the papers before them, or infinity. Ryder was almost an inch down on his Gauloise before Barrow spoke.

"That's quite a thought, Mr. Ryder. Having heard what you've had to say so far I don't think anyone is going to dismiss it out of hand." He made a point of not looking at Mitchell. "Wouldn't you agree, Sassoon?"

Sassoon spoke for the first time. "I've heard enough not to make a fool of myself. You will, of course, have your pointers, Mr. Ryder." He smiled as he said it.

"None that you don't all have. In that rather cryptic note my wife left when she was kidnaped, she said that Morro referred to their destination as having bracing air and a place where they wouldn't get their feet wet. Mountains. It's been taken over by a group of Muslims, quite openly—this would be typical of Morro's effrontery—and
261

his overconfidence. It's called the Temple of Allah or some such now. It's got official police protection to ensure its privacy—a fact which would again appeal to Morro's ironic—if warped—sense of humor. It's virtually impregnable to outside assault. It's close to Bakersfield, where LeWinter had a telephone contact. I should think the chances are high that they have a helicopter—we'll soon know. A guess, you might say, and too damned obvious. The clever investigator overlooks the obvious. Me, I'm stupid—I'd go for the obvious, which is the last thing that Morro would expect us to do."

Barrow said: "You don't actually *know* this Morro?"

"Unfortunately, no."

"You seem to have got inside his mind pretty well. I only hope you haven't taken any wrong turnings."

Parker said in a mild tone: "He's quite good at getting inside minds, actually. No pun intended, but ask anyone inside. Ryder's put away more felons than any detective in this state."

"Let's hope his luck doesn't run out. That all, Mr. Ryder?"

"Yes. Two thoughts. When this is all over you might make out a citation to my wife. If she hadn't thought she'd seen a black eye patch and *suspected* there was something wrong with his hands we'd still be back in square one. We still don't know for certain if she was right. The second thought is just amusing and irrelevant except that it probably again has a bearing on Morro's twisted sense of humor. Anyone know why Von Streicher built the Adlerheim where he did?"

Nobody knew.

"I'll bet Morro did. Von Streicher had a phobia about tidal waves."

Nobody said anything because, for the moment, they had nothing to say. After some time, Barrow stirred and pressed a bell twice. The door opened, two girls entered and Barrow said: "We're thirsty." The girls moved to one wall and slid back a wooden panel.

A few minutes later Barrow laid down his glass. "I wasn't really thirsty. I just wanted time to think. Neither the time nor the scotch has helped any."

"We go for the Adlerheim?" Mitchell's aggression was in abeyance: this was just a doubtful suggestion put up for discussion.

"No." Ryder gave a negative shake of the head in a very positive way. "I think I'm right; I could be wrong. Either way I wouldn't give a damn about proof and legality and I don't think anyone else here would either. But it's both the hostages and the physical factor. You can't storm the place. I told you it's impregnable. If Morro's there he'll have it guarded like Fort Knox. If we did attack the place and there was armed resistance then we'd know for sure he's there. What then? You can't use tanks and artillery up a mountainside. Planes with rockets, missiles, bombs? What a lovely idea with thirty-five megatons of hydrogen bombs in there."

"It would be a bang," Mitchell said. He seemed almost human. "And what a bang. How many dead? Tens of thousands? Hundreds? Millions? With the radioactive fallout all over the western states? Yes, millions."

Ryder said: "Not to mention blasting a hole through the ozone layer."

"What?"

"Nothing."

"It's out of the question, anyway," Barrow said. "Only the Commander-in-Chief could authorize such an attack and whether he's motivated by political cynicism or humanity no President is going to let himself go down in history as the man directly responsible for the deaths of millions of his fellow citizens."

"That apart," Ryder said, "I'm afraid we're all missing the point, which is that those bombs will be triggered by radio wave and Morro will be sitting up there all the time with his thumb on the button. If he has the bombs sited—which he could well have by now—he has only to press that button. They could be in transit—and he has still only to press that button. Even if he's sitting on top of the damn things he'd still do the same. It would be a splendid way to pay the Americans back for the billion or more dollars and military aid they've given Marcos' government to use to crush the Muslims. American lives are nothing to them and, in a holy war, neither are theirs. They can't lose—the gates of Paradise are standing wide."

There was a long pause, then Sassoon said: "It's getting a bit chilly in here. Anyone join me in a scotch or bourbon or something?"

Everyone, it seemed, was conscious of a drop in the temperature. There was another, and equally long, pause, then Mitchell said, almost plaintively: "How do we get at those damn bombs?"

"You can't," Ryder said. "I've had more time than you to think this out. Those bombs will be under constant surveillance all the time. Go anywhere near any of them and it'll blow up in your face. I wouldn't fancy having a three and a half megaton bomb blow up in my face." He lit another cigarette. "Well, I don't know. No worry, really. In my vaporized state I wouldn't be likely to know much about it. Forget the bombs. We want to get to that button before Morro presses it."

Barrow said: "Infiltration?"

"How else?"

"How?"

"Using his overconfidence and colossal arrogance against him."

"How?"

"How?" Ryder showed his first irritation. "You forget that I'm just an unofficial interferer."

"As far as I'm concerned—and, in these United States of ours, I'm the only one who *is* concerned—you're now a fully accredited, paid-up and charter member of the FBI."

"Well, thanks very much."

"How?"

"I wish to God I knew."

The silence was profound. By and by Barrow turned to Mitchell. "Well, what are we going to do?"

"That's the FBI all over." Mitchell was scowling heavily but not at anyone in particular. "Always trying to beat us to it. I was about to ask you the same question."

"I know what I'm going to do." Ryder pushed back his chair. "Major Dunne, you will recall that you promised me a lift out to Pasadena."

A knock came at the door and a girl entered, an envelope in her hand. She said: "Major Dunne?" Dunne stretched out an arm, took the envelope, withdrew a sheet of paper and read it. He looked across at Ryder.

"Cotabato," he said.

Ryder pulled his chair back in. Dunne rose, walked to the head of the table and handed the letter to Barrow, who read it, handed it across to Mitchell, waited until he had finished, took it back and began to read aloud.

"Manila. Chief of police, also countersigned by a General Huelva, whom I know. It says: 'Description referring to person called Morro exactly tallies with that of a wanted criminal well known to us. Confirm he has two badly damaged hands and the sight of only one eye. Injuries sustained when one of group of three participating in aborted attempt to blow up presidential holiday retreat. One accomplice—a man of enormous stature and known as Dubois—unscathed. The third, a small man, lost left hand. Shot way out.' " He paused and looked at Ryder.

"A small world. Our large friend again. The other is probably the lad with the prosthetic appliance who put the arm on my daughter in San Diego."

" 'Morro's real name is Amarak. Inquiry confirms our belief that he is in your country. Enforced exile. There is one million US. dollars on his head. Native of Cotabato, focal point for Muslim insurgents in Mindanao.

" 'Amarak is the head of the MNLF—Moro National Liberation Front.' "

ELEVEN

■ "ONE sometimes despairs of mankind," Professor Alec Benson said sadly. "Here we are, twenty miles from the ocean, and still they go marching steadily east—if cars moving at an average of a mile per hour can be said to be marching. They're as safe from a tidal wave here as they would be if they lived in Colorado but don't suppose any of them intend stopping until they pitch camp atop the San Gabriel Mountains." He turned away from the window, picked up a cane and pressed a switch to illuminate a nine-by-eight wall chart of the state of California.

· "Well, gentlemen, to our Earthquake Preventative Slip Program—EPSP. Where we have selected certain locations for drilling and why. The where and the why are really one and the same thing. As I explained last time, the theory, in essence, is that by injecting lubricating fluid along certain fault lines we will ease the frictional resistance between tectonic plates and so—hopefully— cause them to slide past each other with a minimum of fuss and bother—a series of tiny earthquakes at frequent intervals instead of major earthquakes at long intervals. If the frictional coefficient is allowed to build up until the lateral stress becomes intolerable then something has to go and one plate jerks forward, perhaps anything up to twenty feet, in relation to the other. That's when we have a big one. Our sole purpose—perhaps I should say our hope—is to release this frictional coefficient gradually." He tapped the chart with the cane. "I'll start from the bottom—the south.

"This is actually the first borehole we started digging, the first of what we call our trigger spots. It's in the Imperial Valley, between Imperial and El Centro. We had an earthquake here in 1915, 6.3 on the Richter scale; another in 1940, a fairly big one of 7.6; and a small one in 1966. This is the only known section of the San Andreas fault near the U.S.–Mexican border." He moved his cane.

"We've drilled this one here near Hemet. There was a heavy earthquake here in 1899—no seismological recordings of it—in the area of the Cajon Pass, another of 6.8 in 1918 in the same fracture—this is the San Jacinto fault.

"This third drill hole is the nearest to where we are now—in the San Bernardino area. Latest earthquake there was seventy years ago and that was only 6 on the scale. We have a strong feeling here that this may be a sleeper with a slip overdue—but that may be because we are living so close to the damn thing."

Barrow said: "What effects would such earthquakes have if they did occur? Big ones, I mean."

"Any one of the three would certainly make the citizens of San Diego unhappy, and the second and third would offer a direct threat to Los Angeles." He moved the pointer again. "The next borehole lies in a fault which *was* a sleeper until 1971—6.6 in the San Fernando Valley. We hope that easing the pressure here might take some of the strain off the Newport–Inglewood fault, which, as you know, lies directly under the city of Los Angeles and had its own earthquake of 6.3 in 1933. I say 'hope.' We don't know. We don't know how the two faults are connected. We don't even know *if* they're connected. There's an awful lot we don't know and is guesswork, hopefully inspired, probably not. But it's no guess that a big one there could hurt Los Angeles badly—after all, the community of Sylmar, the worst-hit area in the shock, actually lies inside the Los Angeles city boundaries." The point of the cane moved again.

"Tejon Pass. This one has us worried. Long overdue activity here and the last one—a hundred and twenty years ago—was a beauty, the strongest in Southern California history. Well, it wasn't as great as the massive earthquake that hit Owens Valley in 1873—that was the biggest in recorded California history—but we're a parochial lot hereabouts and don't regard Owens Valley as being in Southern California. A big slip here would very definitely give the Los Angelinos something to think about—if I knew about it in advance I, personally, would get out of town. Tejon Pass is on the San Andreas fault, and it's close by here, at Frazier Park by Fort Tejon, that the San Andreas and Garlock faults intersect. There's been no major earthquake in the Garlock that is known of—whether that recent small shake was caused by our friend Morro or not we have no means of telling—and none is expected—but then, no one expected the 1971 business in San Fernando." The cane moved on.

"Here we have our—let me see—sixth drilling hole. It's on the White Wolf fault. It was the scene—"

He broke off as the phone rang. One of his assistants answered, looked around the seated men. "Which one of you is Major Dunne, please?"

Dunne took the phone, listened briefly, thanked the caller and hung up. He said: "The Adlerheim has quite a transport fleet. Not one but two helicopters, two unmarked plain vans and a jeep." He smiled at Ryder. "Two more pointers you can tick off, Sergeant." Ryder nodded; if he experienced any satisfaction he didn't show it; more probably, he had been so convinced in advance of what Dunne had just said that the confirmation of his conviction hardly called for comment.

Benson said: "What's all this about pointers."

"Routine investigative checks, Professor."

"Ah. Ah, well, I suppose it's none of my business. I was saying—yes, the White Wolf—7.7, 1952, the biggest in Southern California since 1857. The epicenter was somewhere between Arvin and Tehachapi here." He paused and looked at Ryder. "You frown, Sergeant? Quite heavily, if I may say so."

"Nothing, really, Professor. Passing thoughts. Please carry on."

"Well. This is a very tricky area. It's all conjecture, really. Anything happening in the White Wolf could affect

268

both the Garlock fault and the San Andreas at Tejon. We don't know. There could be a link with the Santa Ynez, Mesa and Channel Islands faults. Very attractive earthquake area, reports going back to the beginning of the nineteenth century, last big one at Lompoc in 1927. It's all so uncertain. Any major disturbance in the Santa Ynez area would certainly cause a major disturbance in Los Angeles." He shook his head. "Poor old Los Angeles." Benson wasn't smiling. "It's ringed by earthquake centers—apart from having its own private and personal one at Long Beach. Last time I saw you I talked about the monster earthquake. If it were to hit San Jacinto, San Bernardino, San Fernando, the White Wolf, Tejon Pass, Santa Ynez—or, of course, Long Beach itself—the Western Hemisphere would be one major city less. If our civilization vanishes and another rises, then that new one will be talking about Los Angeles as we today talk about the lost city of Atlantis."

Barrow said: "You are in a jovial mood today, Professor."

"Alas, events happening around me and people asking me the questions do tend to make me less than my optimistic sunny self. Forgive me. Next, up here in the central San Andreas, we are digging an interesting hole between Cholame and Parkfield. We know we're smack on the San Andreas there. Very active area, lots of shaking and banging going on most of the time but, again ominously, no great earthquake has ever been recorded in this area. There was a pretty big one some way to the west, back in the eighties, at San Luis Obispo, which could have been caused by the San Andreas or the Nacimiento fault paralleling the coast west of the San Andreas." He smiled without any particular mirth. "A monster striking in either fault would almost certainly dump the Morro Bay nuclear reactor station into the sea.

"Farther north, we've drilled deep down between Hollister and San Juan Bautista, a few miles to the west, partly because this is another dormant area—again there have only been comparatively minor shakes in this area—

269

and because it's just south of Hollister that the Hayward fault branches off to the right to go to the east of San Francisco Bay, cutting up through or close by Hayward, Oakland, Berkeley and Richmond then out under the San Pablo Bay. In Berkeley, the fault actually runs under the university football stadium, which can't be a very nice thought for the crowds of people who attend there regularly. There have been two very big earthquakes along this fault, in 1836 and 1868—until 1906 San Franciscans always referred to the latter as 'the great earthquake'—and it's there that we've drilled our ninth hole by Lake Temescal.

"The tenth one we put down at Walnut Creek in the Calaveras fault, which parallels the Hayward. Our suspicions about this fault are in the inverse proportion to what we know about it, which is almost zero."

Barrow said: "That makes ten and that, I take it, is all. You spoke a few minutes ago about poor old Los Angeles. How about poor old San Francisco?"

"To be thrown to the wolves, it would seem, the orphan left out in the snow. San Francisco is, geologically and seismologically, a city that waits to die. Frankly, we are terrified to tamper with anything up there. The Los Angeles area has had seven what you might call historic quakes that we know of; the Bay area has had sixteen and we have no idea in the world where the next, the monster, may hit. There was a suggestion—frankly, it was mine—that we sink a borehole near Searsville Lake. This is close by Stanford University, which had a bad time of it during the 1906 earthquake, and, more importantly, just where the Pilarcitos fault branches off from the San Andreas. The Pilarcitos, which runs into the Pacific some six miles south of the San Andreas, may, for all we know, be the true line of the San Andreas and certainly was some millions of years ago. Anyway, the 1906 shake ran through many miles of unpopulated hill regions. Since then, unscrupulous property developers have built virtual cities along both fault lines and the consequences of another 8-plus earthquake are too awful to contemplate.
270

I suggested a possible easement there but certain vested interests in nearby Menlo Park were appalled at the very idea."

Barrow said: "Vested interests?"

"Indeed." Benson sighed. "It was in 1966 that the U.S. Geological Survey's National Center for Earthquake Research was established there. Very touchy about earthquakes, I'm afraid."

"Those boreholes," Ryder said. "What diameter drills do you use?"

Benson looked at him for a long moment then sighed again. "That had to be the next question. That's why you're all here, isn't it?"

"Well?"

"You can use any size within reason. Down in Antarctica they use a twelve-inch drill to bore through the Ross Ice Shelf, but here we get by with a good deal less, five, perhaps six inches, I don't know. Find out very easy enough. So you think the EPSP drillings are a double-edged weapon that's going to turn in our hands? There's a limit to what you can achieve by tidal waves, isn't there? But this is earthquake country, so why not harness the latent powers of nature and trigger off immense earthquakes, and where better to pull the triggers than in the very EPSP sites we've chosen?"

Barrow said: "Is it feasible?"

"Eminently."

"And if—" He broke off. "Ten bombs, ten sites. Matches up a damn sight too well. If this were to happen?"

"Let's think about something else, shall we?"

"If it *were?*"

"There are so many unknown factors—"

"An educated guess, Professor."

"Goodbye California! That's what I would guess. Or a sizable part of it—bound to affect more than half of the population. Maybe it will fall into the Pacific. Maybe just shattered by a series of monster earthquakes—and if you set off hydrogen bombs in the faults monster earthquakes are what you are going to have. And radiation, of course,

271

would get those the sea and the earthquake didn't. An immediate trip back east—and I mean immediate—suddenly seems a very attractive prospect."

"You'd have to walk," Sassoon said. "The roads are jammed and the airport is besieged. The airlines are sending in every plane they can lay hands on but it's hardly helping—they're stacked heaven knows how many deep just waiting for a chance to land. And, of course, when a plane does land there's a hundred passengers for every seat available."

"Things will be better tomorrow. It's not in human nature to stay permanently panic-stricken."

"And it's not in an aircraft's nature to take off in twenty feet of water, which is what the airport might be under tomorrow." He broke off as the phone rang again. This time Sassoon took it. He listened briefly, thanked the caller and hung up.

"Two things," he said. "The Adlerheim does have a radiotelephone. All quite legal. The post office doesn't know the name and address of the person who answers it. They assume that we wouldn't want to make inquiries. Secondly, there *is* a very big man up in the Adlerheim." He looked at Ryder. "It seems you were not only right but right about their arrogant self-confidence. He hasn't even bothered to change his name. Dubois."

"Well, that's it, then," Ryder said. If he was surprised or gratified, no trace of those feelings showed. "Morro has kidnaped twenty-six drillers, engineers—anyway, oil men. Six are being used as forced labor in the Adlerheim. Then he'll have a couple of men at each of the drilling rigs —they'll have guns on them but he has to have experienced men to lower those damn things. I don't think we need bother the AEC any more to find out about Professor Aachen's design—whatever nuclear device he's constructed it's not going to be more than five inches in diameter." He turned to Benson. "Do the crews on those rigs work on weekends?"

"I don't know."

"I'll bet Morro does."

Benson turned to one of his assistants. "You heard. Find out, please."

Barrow said: "Well, we know for sure now that Morro lied about the dimensions of the bomb. You can't stick something twenty inches in diameter down a five or six-inch borehole. I think I have to agree that this man is very dangerously overconfident."

Mitchell was glum. "He's got plenty to be confident about. All right, we know he's up in his fancy castle and we know, or are as certain as can be, that he has those nuclear devices up there. And a lot of good that knowledge does us. How do we get at him or them?"

An assistant spoke to Benson. "The drilling crew, sir. They don't work weekends. A guard at nights. Just one. Gentleman says no one's likely to wheel away a derrick on a wheelbarrow."

The profound silence that followed was sufficient comment. Mitchell, whose splendid self-confidence had vanished off the bottom of the chart, said in a plaintive voice: "Well, what in the hell are we going to do?"

Barrow broke the next silence. "I don't think that there's anything else that we can do. By that, I mean the people in this room. Apart from the fact that our function is primarily investigative, we don't have the authority to make any decisions on a national level."

"International, you mean," Mitchell said. "If they can do it to us they can also do it to London or Paris or Rome." He almost brightened. "They might even do it to Moscow. But I agree. It's a matter for the White House, Congress, the Pentagon. Personally, I prefer the Pentagon. I'm convinced that the threat of force—and if this isn't a threat of force I've never known of one—can be met only by force. I'm further convinced that we should choose the lesser of two evils, that we should consider the greatest good for the greatest number. I think an attack should be launched on the Adlerheim. At least the damage, though catastrophic, would be localized. I mean, we wouldn't have a half of the damn state being devastated." He paused, then a thought struck him.

273

"By God, I believe I have it! We're not thinking. What we require is a nuclear physicist here, an expert on hydrogen bombs and missiles. We're laymen. What do we know about the triggering mechanisms of those devices? For all we know they may be immune to—what's it called—sympathetic detonation. If that were the case, a fighter-bomber or two with tactical nuclear missiles—and poof!—all life would be immediately extinct. Instant annihilation for everyone in the Adlerheim."

Archimedes in his bath or Newton with his apple couldn't have shown more revelationary enthusiasm.

Ryder said: "Well, thank you very much."

"What do you mean?"

Dunne answered him. "Mr. Ryder's lack of enthusiasm is understandable, sir. Or have you forgotten that his wife and daughter are being held hostage there, not to mention eight others, including five of the country's outstanding nuclear physicists?"

"Ah! Oh!" Much of the missionary zeal vanished. "I'm sorry, no, I'm afraid I'd forgotten that. Nevertheless—"

"Nevertheless, you were going to say, the greatest good for the greatest number. Your proposal would almost certainly achieve the opposite—the greatest destruction of the greatest number."

"Justify that, Mr. Ryder." Mitchell cherished his brain children and no one was going to take his baby away if he could help it.

"Easily. You are going to use atomic missiles. The southern end of the San Joaquin Valley is quite heavily populated. It is your intention to wipe those people out?"

"Of course not. We evacuate them."

"Heaven send me strength," Ryder said wearily. "Didn't it occur to you that from the Adlerheim Morro has an excellent view of the valley and you can bet he has more than a scattering of spies and informants down there? What do *you* think *he* is going to think when he sees the citizens of the plain disappearing *en masse* over the northern and southern horizons? He's going to say to himself: 'Ha! I've been rumbled'—and apart from any-

thing else that's the last thing we want him to know—
'I must teach those people a lesson for they're clearly
preparing to make an atomic attack on me.' So he sends
one of his helicopters down south to the Los Angeles
area and another up north to the Bay area. Six million
dead. I should think that's a conservative estimate. Is
that your idea of military tactics, of reducing casualties
to a minimum?"

From the crestfallen expression on his face it didn't
seem to be. Clearly, it wasn't anybody else's either.

Ryder went on: "A personal opinion, gentlemen, and
offered for what it's worth, but this is what I think. I
don't think there *are* going to be any nuclear casualties
—not unless we're stupid enough to provoke them ourselves." He looked at Barrow. "Back in your office some
little time ago I said that I believed Morro is going to
trigger off this bomb in the Bay tomorrow. I still do.
I also said I believed he would set off or would be
prepared to set off the other ten devices on Saturday
night. I've modified that thinking a bit. I still think that
if he's given sufficient provocation he'd still be prepared
to trigger his device, but I now don't believe that he'll do
it on Saturday night. In fact, I would take odds that
he won't."

"It's odd." Barrow was thoughtful. "I could almost
believe that myself. Because of his kidnaping of nuclear
physicists, his theft of weapons-grade material, our knowledge that he does have those damned nuclear devices,
his constant nuclear threats, his display in Yucca Flat
and our conviction that he is going to explode this device
in the Bay tomorrow morning, we have been hypnotized,
mesmerized, conditioned into the certainty of the in-
evitability of further nuclear blasts. God knows we have
every reason to believe what this monster says. And yet—"

"It's a brainwash job. A top-flight propagandist can
make you believe anything. Our friend should have met
Goebbels in his heyday—they would have been blood-
brothers."

"Any idea what he *doesn't* want us to believe?"

"I think so. I told Mr. Mitchell an hour ago that I had a glimmering but that I knew what he would do with a glimmering. It's a pretty bright beacon now. Here's what I think Morro will be doing—or what I would do if I were in Morro's shoes.

"First, I'd bring my submarine through the—"

"Submarine!" Mitchell had obviously—and instantly—reverted to his earlier opinion of Ryder.

"Please. I'd bring it through the Golden Gate and park it alongside one of the piers in San Francisco."

"San Francisco?" Mitchell again.

"It has better and more piers, better loading facilities and calmer waters than, say, Los Angeles."

"Why a submarine?"

"To take me back home." Ryder was being extremely patient. "Me and my faithful followers and my cargo."

"Cargo?"

"For God's sake, shut up and listen. We'll be able to move with complete safety and impunity in the deserted streets of San Francisco. No single soul will be there because no hour was specified as to when the hydrogen bombs will be detonated during the night and there'll be nobody within fify miles. A gallant pilot six miles up will be able to see nothing because it's night and even if it's a completely suicidal low-flying pilot he'll still be able to see nothing because we know where every breaker for every transformer and power station in the city is.

"Then our moving vans will roll. I'll have three and will lead them down California Street and stop outside the Bank of America, which as you know, is the largest single bank in the world containing loot as great as that of the federal vaults. Other vans will go to the Transamerica Pyramid, Wells Fargo, the Federal Reserve Bank, Crockers and other interesting places. There will be ten hours of darkness that night. We estimate we will require six at the outset. Some big robberies, such as the famous break-in to a Nice bank a year or two ago, took a whole leisurely weekend, but gangs like those are severely handicapped because they have to operate in silence. We shall use as much high explosive as need be and for difficult cases will use a self-propelled 120-mm. tank gun firing armor-piercing shells. We may even blow some buildings up but this won't worry us. We can make all the noise in the world and not care—there'll be nobody there to hear us. Then we load up the vans, drive down to the piers, load the submarine and take off." Ryder paused. "As I said earlier, they've come for cash to buy their arms and there's more cash lying in the vaults of San Francisco than all the kings of Saudi Arabia and maharajas of India have ever seen. As I said before it takes a simple and unimaginative mind to see the obvious and in this case, for me at least, it's so obvious that I can't see any flaws in it. What do you think of my scenario?"

"I think it's damned awful," Barrow said. "That's to say, damned awful because it's so inevitable. That has to be it, first, because it's so right, and second, because it just can't be anything else." He looked around at the company. "You agree?"

Everyone, with one exception, nodded. The exception, inevitably, was Mitchell. "And what if you're wrong?"

"Must you be so damnably pigheaded and cantankerous?" Barrow was irritated to the point of exasperation.

Ryder didn't react, just lifted his shoulders and said: "So I'm wrong."

"You must be mad! You would take the burden of the deaths of countless fellow Californians on your hands?"

"You're beginning to bore me, Mitchell. In fact, not to put it too politely, you do bore me and have done so for some time. I think you should question your own sanity. Do you think I would breathe a word of our conclusions—with you being excepted from our conclusions—outside this room? Do you think I would try to persuade anybody to remain in their homes on Saturday night? When Morro knew that people had ignored the threat and had heard, as he inevitably would, the reason why—namely, that his scheme was known—the chances

277

are very high that in his rage and frustration he'd just go ahead and press the button anyway."

The singularly ill-named Café Cleopatra was a watering hole of unmatched dinginess but on that hectic, frenetic and stifling evening it possessed the singular charm of being the only such establishment open in the blocks around Sassoon's office. There were dozens of others but their doors were rigorously barred by proprietors who, when the opportunity was open to them, were lugging their dearest possessions to higher levels or who, when such opportunity was denied them, had already joined the panic-stricken rush to the hills.

Fear most certainly was abroad that evening but the rush was purely in the mind and heart: it was most certainly not physical for the cars and people who jammed the street were almost entirely static. It was an evening for selfishness, ill temper, envy, argument, and antisocial behavior ranging from the curmudgeonly to the downright bellicose. Phlegmatic the citizens of the Queen of the Coast were not.

It was an evening for those who ranged the nether scale from the ill-intentioned to the criminally inclined as they displayed in various measure that sweet concern, Christian charity and brotherly love for their fellow man in the hour of crisis by indulging in red-faced altercation, splendidly uninhibited swearing, bouts of fisticuffs, purse snatching, wallet removal, mugging and kicking in the plate-glass windows of the more prosperous-looking emporiums. They were free to indulge their peccadilloes unhindered: the police were powerless as they, too, were immobilized. It was a night for pyromaniacs, as many small fires had broken out throughout the city although, in fairness, many of those were caused by the unseemly speed of the departure of householders who left on unconsidered cookers, ovens and heating appliances. Again, the fire brigades were powerless, their only consolation being the faint hope that significant numbers of the smaller conflagrations would be abruptly extinguished at ten o'clock the following morning. It was not a night
278

for the sick and the infirm: elderly ladies, widows and orphans were crushed against walls or, more commonly, deposited in unbecoming positions in the gutter as their fitter brethren pressed on eagerly for the high land. Unfortunates in wheel chairs knew what it was to share the emotions of the charioteer who observes his inner wheel coming adrift as he rounds the first bend of the Circus Maximus. Especially distressing was the case of thoughtless pedestrians knocked down by cars, driven by owners concerned only with the welfare of their families, which mounted the pavement in order to overtake the less enterprising who elected to remain on the highway; where they fell, there they remained, for doctors and ambulances were as helpless as any. It was hardly an edifying spectacle.

Ryder surveyed the scene with a jaundiced and justifiably misanthropic eye although, in truth, he had been in a particularly ill humor even before arriving to sample the sybaritic pleasures of the Café Cleopatra. On their return from Cal Tech he had listened to, without participating in, the endless wrangling as to how best they should counter and hopefully terminate the evil machinations of Morro and his Muslims. Finally, in frustration and disgust, he had announced that he would return within the hour and had left with Jeff and Parker. There had been no attempt to dissuade him: there was something about Ryder, as Barrow, Mitchell and their associates had come to appreciate in a very brief period of time, that precluded the very idea of dissuasion and, besides, he owed neither allegiance nor obedience to any man.

"Cattle," Luigi said with a splendid contempt. He had just brought fresh beers to the three men and was now surveying the pandemoniac scenes being enacted beyond his unwashed windows. Luigi, the proprietor, regarded himself as a cosmopolitan par excellence in a city of cosmopolitans. Neapolitan by birth, he claimed to be a Greek and did his undistinguished best to run what he regarded as an Egyptian establishment. From his slurred speech and unsteady gait it was clear that he had been his own best customer for the day. *"Canaille!"* His few words of French served, as he fondly imagined, to enhance his cosmopolitan aura. "All for one and one for all. The spirit that won the West! How true. The California gold rush, the Klondike. Every man for himself and the devil take the rest. Alas, I fear they lack the Athenian spirit." He swung a dramatic arm around him and almost fell over in the process. "Today, this beautiful establishment—tomorrow, the deluge. And Luigi? Luigi laughs at the gods for they are but mannequins that masquerade as gods else they would not permit this catastrophe to overtake those mindless infants." He paused and reflected. "My ancestors fought at Thermopylae." Overcome by his own eloquence and the alcohol-accentuated effects of gravity, Luigi collapsed in the nearest chair.

Ryder looked around at the incredible dilapidation which was the outstanding characteristic of Luigi's beautiful establishment, at the vanished patterns on the cracked linoleum, the stained Formica table tops, the aged infirmity of the bentwood chairs, the unwashed stuccoed walls behung with sepia daguerreotypes of pharaonic-profiled bas-reliefs, each with two eyes on the same side of the face, portraits of so unbelievable an awfulness that the only charitable thing that could be said about them was that they tended to restore to a state of almost pristine purity the unlovely walls which they desecrated. He said: "Your sentiments do you great credit, Luigi. This country could do with more men like you. Now, please, would you leave us alone? We have important matters to discuss."

They had, indeed, important matters to discuss and their discussion led to a large and uncompromising zero. The problems of what to do with the apparently unassailable inhabitants of the Adlerheim seemed insuperable. In point of fact, the discussion was a dialogue between Ryder and Parker, for Jeff took no part in it. He just leaned back, his beer untouched, his eyes closed as if he were fast asleep or had lost all interest in solving the unsolvable. He appeared to subscribe to the dictum laid down by the astronomer J. Allen Hynek: "In science it's against the rules to ask questions when we have no way of approaching the answers." The problem on hand was not a scientific one: but the principle appeared to be the same.

Unexpectedly, Jeff stirred and said: "Good old Luigi."

"What?" Parker stared at him. "What's that?"

"And Hollywood only a five-minute hop from here."

Ryder said carefully: "Look, Jeff, I know you've been through a hard time. We've all been through—"

"Dad?"

"What?"

"I have it. Mannequins masquerading as gods."

Five minutes later Ryder was on his third beer, but this time back in Sassoon's office. The other nine men were still there and had indeed not stirred since Ryder, Jeff and Parker had left. The air was full of tobacco smoke, the powerful aroma of scotch and, most disquietingly, an almost palpable aura of defeat.

Ryder said: "The scheme we have to propose is a highly dangerous one. It possibly verges on the desperate but there are degrees of desperation and it's by no means as desperate as the circumstances in which we find ourselves. Success or failure depends entirely on the degree of co-operation we receive from every person in this nation whose duty is in any way concerned with the enforcement of the law, those not concerned directly with the law, even those, if need be, outside the law." He looked in turn at Barrow and Mitchell. "It's of no consequence, gentlemen, but your jobs are on the line."

Barrow said: "Let's have it."

"My son will explain it to you. It is entirely his brainchild." Ryder smiled faintly. "To save you gentlemen any cerebral stress, he even has all the details worked out."

Jeff explained. It took him no more than three minutes. When he had finished the expressions around the table ranged from the stunned, through incredulity, then intense

281

consideration and, finally, in Barrow's case, the tentative dawning of hope where all hope had been abandoned.

Barrow whispered: "My God! I believe it could be done."

"It has to be done," Ryder said. "It means the instant and total co-operation of every police officer, every FBI officer, every CIA officer in the country. It means the scouring of every prison in the country and even if the man we require is a multiple murderer awaiting execution in death row he gets a free pardon. How long would it take?"

Barrow looked at Mitchell. "The hell with the hatchets. Bury them. Agreed?" There was a fierce urgency in his voice. Mitchell didn't answer, but he did nod. Barrow went on: "Organization is the name of the game. This is what we were born for."

"How long?" Ryder repeated.

"A day?"

"Six hours. Meantime, we can get the preliminaries under way."

"Six hours?" Barrow smiled faintly. "It used to be the wartime motto of the Seabees that the impossible takes a little longer. Here, it would appear, it has to take a little shorter. You know, of course, that Muldoon has just had his third heart attack and is in Bethesda hospital?"

"I don't care if you have to raise him from the dead. Without Muldoon we are nothing."

At eight o'clock that evening it was announced over every TV and radio station in the country that at ten o'clock Western standard time—the times for the other zones were given—the President would be addressing the nation on a matter of the utmost national gravity which concerned an emergency unprecedented in the history of the republic. As instructed, the announcement gave no further details. The brief and cryptic message was guaranteed to ensure the obsessive interest and compulsory viewing of every citizen in the republic who was neither blind nor deaf nor both.

282

In the Adlerheim, Morro and Dubois looked at each other and smiled. Morro reached out a hand for his bottle of Glenfiddich.

In Los Angeles, Ryder showed no reaction whatsoever, which was hardly surprising in view of the fact that he had helped draft the message himself. He asked Major Dunne for permission to borrow his helicopter and dispatched Jeff to pick up some specified articles from his, Ryder's, home. Then he gave Sassoon a short list of other specified articles he required. Sassoon looked at him and said nothing. He just lifted a phone.

Exactly at ten, the President appeared on TV screens throughout the country. Not even the first landing on the moon had attracted so vast a viewing—and listening—audience.

He had four men with him in the studio and those he introduced as his Chief of Staff and the Secretaries of State, Defense and the Treasury, which seemed largely superfluous as all of them were nationally and indeed internationally known figures. Muldoon, the Secretary of the Treasury, was the one who caught the attention of everyone. Color TV showed him for what he was, a very sick man indeed. His face was ashen and, although not particularly tall, he was a man of enormous girth and, as he sat, his great pot belly seemed almost to touch his knees. He was said to weigh 330 pounds but his precise weight was irrelevant. What was truly remarkable about him was not the unsurprising fact that he had had three heart attacks but the fact that he had managed to survive any of them.

"Citizens of America." The President's deep, resonant voice was trembling, not with fear but with an outraged fury that he made no attempt to suppress. "You all know the great misfortune that has befallen, or is about to befall, our beloved state of California. Although the government of these United States will never yield to coercion, threats or blackmail, it is clear that we must employ every means in our power—and in this, the greatest country in the world, our resources are almost

283

infinite—to avert the impending doom, the threatened holocaust that looms over the West." Even in the moments of the greatest stress, he was incapable of talking in other than presidential language.

"I hope the villainous architect of this monstrous scheme is listening to me, for, despite the best efforts—and those have been immense and indefatigable—of hundreds of our best law enforcement officers, his whereabouts remain a complete secret and I know of no other means whereby I can contact him. I trust, Morro, you are either watching or listening. I know I am in no position to bargain or treat with you"—here the President's voice broke off on an oddly strangled note and he was forced to have recourse to several gulps of water—"because you would appear to be an utterly ruthless criminal wholly devoid of even the slightest trace of humanitarian scruples.

"But I suggest that it might be to our mutual advantage and that we might arrive at some mutually satisfactory arrangement if I, and my four senior governmental colleagues with me here, were to parley with you and try to arrive at some solution to this unparalleled problem. Although it goes violently against the grain, against every principle dear to me and every citizen of this great nation, I suggest we meet at a time and a place, under whatever conditions you care to impose, at the earliest possible moment." The President had quite a bit more to say, most of it couched in ringingly patriotic terms which could have deceived only those mentally retarded beyond any hope of recovery. But he had, in fact, said all that he had needed to.

In the Adlerheim, the normally impassive and unemotional Dubois wiped tears from his eyes.

"Never yield to coercion, threats or blackmail! No condition to bargain or treat with us. Mutually satisfactory arrangement! Five billion dollars to begin with, perhaps? And then, of course, we proceed with our original plan?" He poured out two more glasses of Glenfiddich, handed one to Morro.

284

Morro sipped some of the whiskey. He, too, was smiling but his voice, when he spoke, held an almost reverent tone.

"We must have the helicopter camouflaged. Think of it, Abraham, my dear friend. The dream of a lifetime come true. America on its knees." He sipped some more of his drink then, with his free hand, reached out for a microphone and began to dictate a message.

Barrow said to no one in particular: "I've always maintained that to be a successful politician you have to be a good actor. But to be a president, you must be a superlative one. We must find some way to bend the rules of the world of the cinema. The man must have an Oscar."

Sassoon said: "With a bar and crossed leaves."

At eleven o'clock it was announced over TV and radio that a further message from Morro would be broadcast in an hour's time.

At midnight, Morro was on the air again. He tried to speak in his customary calm and authoritative voice, but beneath it were the overtones of a man aware that the world lay at his feet. The message was singularly brief.

"I address this to the President of the United States. We"—the "we" had more of the royal than the editorial about it—"accede to your request. The conditions of the meeting, which will be imposed entirely by us, will be announced tomorrow morning. We shall see what can be accomplished when two reasonable men meet and talk together." He sounded genuinely aware of his incredibly mendacious effrontery.

He went on in a portentous voice: "This proposed meeting in no way affects my intention to detonate the hydrogen device in the ocean tomorrow morning. Everybody, and that includes you, Mr. President, must be convinced beyond all doubt that I have the indisputable power to carry out my promises.

"With reference to my promises, I have to tell you

285

that the devices I still intend to detonate on Saturday night will produce a series of enormous earthquakes that will have a cataclysmic effect beyond any natural disaster ever recorded in history. That is all."

Barrow said: "Well, damn you, Ryder, you were right again. About the earthquakes, I mean."
Ryder said mildly: "That hardly seems to matter now."

At 12:15 A.M. word came through from the AEC that the hydrogen bomb, code-named Aunt Sally, designed by professors Burnett and Aachen, had a diameter of 4.73 inches.
That didn't seem to matter at all.

TWELVE

■ AT eight o'clock the next morning Morro made his next contact with the anxiously and—such is mankind's morbidly avid love of vicarious doom and disaster—vastly intrigued world. His message he delivered with his now accustomed terseness.

He said: "My meeting with the President and his senior advisers will take place at eleven o'clock tonight. However, I insist that the presidential party arrive in Los Angeles—if the airport is functioning, if not, San Francisco—by six o'clock this evening. The meeting place I cannot and will not specify. The travel arrangements will be announced late this afternoon.

"I trust the low-lying regions of Los Angeles, the coastal regions north to Point Arguello and south to the Mexican border, in addition to the Channel Islands, have been evacuated. If not, I will accept no responsibility. As promised, I shall detonate this nuclear device in two hours' time."

Sassoon was closeted in his office with Brigadier General Culver of the U.S. Air Force. Far below, a deathly hush lay over the totally deserted streets. The low-lying regions of the city had indeed been evacuated, thanks in large part to Culver and over two thousand soldiers and national guardsmen under his command who had been called in to help the hopelessly overworked police restore order. Culver was a ruthlessly efficient man and had not hesitated to call in tanks in number close to battalion strength, which had a marvelously chastening effect on citizens who, prior to their arrival, had seemed hell-bent not on self-preservation but on self-destruction. The deployment of the tanks had been co-ordinated by a fleet of police, coast guard and army helicopters, which had pin-pointed the major traffic bottlenecks. The empty streets were littered with abandoned cars, many of which bore the appearance of having been involved in major crashes, a state of affairs for which the tanks had been in no way responsible: the citizens had done it all by themselves.

The evacuation had been completed by midnight, but long before that the fire brigades, ambulances and police cars had moved in. The fires, none of them major, had been extinguished, the injured had been removed to far-away hospitals and the police had made a record number of arrests and forced evacuation of hoodlums whose greed in taking advantage of this unprecedented opportunity had quite overcome their sense of self-preservation and were still looting away with gay abandon when police-men with drawn guns had taken a rather less than a paternal interest in their activities.

Sassoon switched off the TV set and said to Culver: "What do you make of that?"

"One has to admire the man's colossal arrogance."

"Overconfidence."

"If you like. Understandably, he wants to conduct his meeting with the President under cover of darkness. Obviously the travel arrangements, as he calls them, are linked with the deadline for the plane arrival. He wants to make good and sure that the President has arrived before he gives instructions."

"Which means that he'll have an observer stationed at both San Francisco and Los Angeles airports. Well, he has three separate phones with three separate numbers in the Adlerheim and we have them all tapped."

"They could use short-wave radio communication."

"We've thought of that and discounted the possibility. Morro is convinced that we have no idea where he is. In which case, why bother with unnecessary refinements? Ryder has been right all along—Morro's divine belief in himself is going to bring him down." Sassoon paused. "We hope."

"This fellow Ryder. What's he like?"

"You'll see for yourself. I expect him within the hour.
288

At the moment he's out at the police shooting range practicing with some fancy Russian toys he took away from the opposition. Quite a character. Don't expect him to call you 'sir.' "

At eight-thirty that morning a special news broadcast announced that James Muldoon, Secretary of the Treasury, had had a relapse in the early hours of the morning and had had to have emergency treatment for cardiac arrest. Had he not been in the hospital and with the cardiac arrest unit standing by his bedside, it was unlikely that he would have survived. As it was, he was off the critical list and swearing that he could make the journey out to the West Coast even though he had to be carried aboard Air Force One on a stretcher.

Culver said: "Sounds bad."
"Doesn't it though? Fact is, he slept soundly the whole night through. We just want to convince Morro that he's dealing with a man in a near critical condition, a man who clearly must be treated with every gentle consideration. It also, of course, gives a perfect excuse for two additional people to accompany the presidential delegation—a doctor and a Treasury undersecretary to deputize for Muldoon in the event of his expiring as soon as he sets foot in the Adlerheim."

At nine o'clock an Air Force jet lifted off from Los Angeles airport. It carried only nine passengers, all from Hollywood and all specialists in their own arcane crafts. Each carried a suitcase. In addition, a small wooden box had been loaded aboard. Exactly half an hour later the jet touched down in Las Vegas.

A few minutes before ten Morro invited his hostages along to his special screening room. All the hostages had TV sets of their own but Morro's was something special. By a comparatively simple magnification and back-projection method he was able to have a screened picture some six feet by four and a half, about four times the

289

width and height of a normal twenty-one-inch set. Why he had invited them was unclear. When not torturing people—or, more, precisely, having them tortured—Morro was capable of many small courtesies. Perhaps he just wanted to watch their faces. Perhaps he wanted to revel in the magnitude of his achievement and the sense of his invincible power and the presence of an audience always heightened the enjoyment of such an experience, but that last was unlikely as gloating did not appear to be a built-in factor in Morro's mental make-up. Whatever the reason, none of the hostages refused the invitation. In the presence of catastrophe, even though such catastrophe be at second hand, company makes for comfort.

It was probably true to say that every citizen in America, except those engaged in running absolutely essential services, was watching the same event on their screens: the number watching throughout the rest of the world must have run into hundreds of millions.

The various TV companies filming the incident were, all too understandably, taking no chances. Normally all outdoor events on a significantly large scale, ranging from *grand prix* racing to erupting volcanoes, are filmed from helicopters, but here they were dealing with the unknown. No one had even an approximate idea of what the extent of the blast and radiation would be and the companies had elected against the use of helicopters—which was prudent of them in more ways than one as the camera crews would have refused to fly in them anyway. All the companies had elected the same type of site for their cameras—on the tops of high buildings at a prudent distance from the ocean front: the viewers in the Adlerheim could see the blurred outline of the city abutting the Pacific in the lower segment of their screens. If the nuclear device was anywhere near where Morro had said it was—between the islands of Santa Cruz and Santa Catalina—then the scene of action had to be at least thirty miles distant, but the telescopic zoom lenses of the cameras would take care of that with ease. And at that moment the zoom lenses were fully
290

extended, which accounted for the out-of-focus blurring of the city front.

The day was fine and bright and clear with cloudless skies, which, in the circumstances, formed an impossibly macabre setting for the convulsion the watchers were about to witness, a circumstance that must have pleased Morro greatly for it could not but increase the emotional impact of the spectacle. A storm-wracked sky, lowering clouds, driving rain, fog, any face of nature that showed itself in a somber and minor key would have been far more in keeping with the occasion—and would have lessened the impact of the spectacle of the explosion. There was only one favorable aspect about the weather. Normally, at that time of the day and at that time of year the wind would have been westerly and onshore. Today, because of a heavy front pressing down from the northwest, the wind was slightly west of southerly and in that direction the nearest land mass of any size lay as far distant as the Antarctic.

"Pay attention to the sweep-second hand on the wall clock," Morro said. "It is perfectly synchronized with the detonating mechanism. There are, as you can see, twenty seconds to go."

A pure measure of time is only relative. To a person in ecstasy it can be less than the flicker of an eyelid; for a person on the rack it can be an eternity. The watchers were on no physical rack but they were on an emotional one and those twenty seconds seemed interminable. All of them behaved in precisely the same way, their eyes constantly flickering between the clock and the screen and back again at least once in every second.

The sweep second reached sixty and nothing happened. One second passed, two, three and still nothing. Almost as if by command the watchers glanced at Morro, who sat relaxed and apparently unworried. He smiled at them.

"Be of good faith. The bomb lies deep and you forget the factor of the earth's curvature."

Their eyes swiveled back to the screen and then they

saw it. At first it was no more than a tiny protuberance on the curve of the distant horizon, but a protuberance that rose and swelled with frightening rapidity with the passage of every second. There was no blinding white glare of light; there was no light whatsoever of any color, just that monstrous eruption of water and vaporized water that rose and spread, rose and spread until it filled the screen. It bore no resemblance whatsoever to the mushroom cloud of an atomic bomb but was perfectly fan-shaped in appearance, much thicker in the center than at the edges, the lowermost sides of which were streaking outward just above and almost parallel with the sea. The cloud, had it been possible to see it from above, must have looked exactly like an inverted umbrella, but from the side it still looked like a gigantic fan opened to its full 180 degrees, much more dense in the center presumably because there the blast had had the shortest distance to cover before reaching the surface of the sea. Suddenly the giant fan, which had run completely off the screen, shrank until it occupied no more than half of it.

A woman's voice, awed and shaky, said: "What's happened to it? What's happened to it?"

"Nothing's happened to it." Morro looked and sounded very comfortable. "It's the camera. The operator has pulled in his zoom to get the picture inside the frame."

The commentator, who had been babbling on almost incoherently, telling the world what they could see perfectly well for themselves, was still babbling on.

"It must be eight thousand feet high, now. No, more. Ten thousand would be nearer it. Think of it, just think of it! Two miles high and four miles across the base. Good God, is the thing never going to stop growing?"

"I think congratulations are in order, Professor Aachen," Morro said. "Your little contraption seems to have worked quite well."

Aachen gave him a look which was meant to be a glare, but wasn't. A broken spirit can take a long time to heal.

For about the next thirty seconds the commentator stopped commentating. It was no instance of a gross dereliction of duty, he was probably so awe-struck that he could find no words to describe his emotions. It was not often that a commentator had the opportunity to witness the terrifying spectacle unfolding before his eyes: more precisely, no commentator had ever had the opportunity before. By and by he bestirred himself. "Could we have full zoom, please?"

All but the base of the center of the fan disappeared. A tiny ripple could be seen advancing lazily across the ocean. The commentator said: "That, I suppose, must be the tidal wave." He sounded disappointed; clearly he regarded it as an altogether insignificant product of the titanic explosion he'd just seen. "Doesn't look much like a tidal wave to me."

"Ignorant youth," Morro said sadly. "That wave is probably traveling something about four hundred miles an hour at the moment. It will slow down very quickly as it reaches shallower water but its height will increase in direct proportion to its deceleration. I think the poor boy is in for a shock."

About two and a half minutes after the detonation a thunderous roar, which seemed as if it might shake the TV to pieces, filled the room. It lasted about two seconds before it was suddenly reduced to a tolerable level. A new voice cut in.

"Sorry about that. We couldn't reach the volume control in time. Whew! We never expected a deafening racket like that. In fact, to be quite honest, we didn't expect any sound at all from an explosion so deep under the water."

"Fool." Liberal as ever, Morro had supplied refreshment for the entertainment and he now took a delicate sip of his Glenfiddich. Burnett took a large gulp of his.

"My word, that was a bang." The original commentator was back on the air. He was silent for some time while the camera, still on full zoom, remained fixed on the incoming tidal wave. "I don't think I like this too much. That wave might not be so big but I've never seen anything moving so fast. I wonder—"

The viewers were not to find out what he was wondering

about. He gave an inarticulate cry, there was an accompanying crashing sound and suddenly the tidal wave on the screen was replaced by an empty expanse of blue sky.

"He's been hit by the blast shock wave. I should have warned them about that, I suppose." If Morro was covered with remorse, he was hiding it well. "Couldn't have been all that bad or the camera wouldn't still be functioning."

As usual, Morro was right. Within seconds the commentator was on the air again but was clearly so dazed that he had forgotten the fact.

"Jesus Christ! My head!" There was a pause, punctuated by a fair amount of wheezing and groaning. "Sorry about that, viewers. Mitigating circumstances. Now I know what it's like to be hit by an express train. If I may be spared a feeble joke, I know the occupation I'd like to have tomorrow. A glazier. That blast must have broken a million windows in the city. Let's see if this camera is still functioning."

It was functioning. As the camera was lifted back to the upright the blue sky was gradually replaced by the ocean. The operator had obviously advanced the zoom for the fan was once again in the picture. It had grown no larger and appeared to be in the first beginnings of disintegration because it had become ragged and was gradually losing its shape. A faint grayish cloud, perhaps two miles high, could be seen faintly drifting away.

"I think it's falling back into the ocean. Can you see that cloud drifting away to the left—to the south? That can't be water, surely. I wonder if it's a radioactive cloud."

"It's radioactive, all right," Morro said. "But that grayness is not radioactivity, it's water vapor held in suspension."

Burnett said: "I suppose you're aware, you lousy bastard, that cloud is lethal?"

"An unfortunate by-product. It will disperse. Besides, no land mass lies in its way. One assumes that the competent authorities, if there are any in this country, will warn shipping."

294

The center of interest had now clearly changed from the now dispersing giant fan to the incoming tidal wave because the camera had now locked on that.

"Well, there she comes." There was just a hint of a tremor in the commentator's voice. "It's slowed but it's still going faster than any express train I've ever seen. And it's getting bigger. And bigger." He paused for a few seconds. "Apart from hoping that the police and army are a hundred per cent right in saying that the entire lower area of the city has been evacuated, I think I'll shut up for a minute. I don't have the words for this. Nobody could. Let the camera do the talking."

He fell silent and it was a reasonable assumption that hundreds of millions of people throughout the world did the same. Words could never convey to the mind the frightening immensity of that massive onrushing wall of water—but the eyes could.

When the tidal wave was a mile away it had slowed down to not much more than fifty miles an hour, but was at least twenty feet in height. It was not a wave in the true sense, just an enormously smooth and unbroken swell, completely silent in its approach, a silence that served only to intensify the impression that here was an alien monster, evil, malevolent, bent upon a mindless destruction. Half a mile away it seemed to rear its evil head and white showed along the top, like a giant surf about to break, and it was at this point that the level of the still untroubled waters between the tidal wave and the shore perceptibly began to fall as if being sucked into the ravenous jaw of the monster, as indeed they were.

And now they could hear the sound of it, a deep and rumbling roar which intensified with the passing of every moment, rising to such a pitch that the volume controller had to turn down the sound. When it was fifty yards away, just as it was breaking, the waters by the foreshore drained away completely, leaving the ocean bed showing. And then, with the explosive sound of a giant thunderclap directly overhead, the monster struck.

Momentarily, that was all there was to it as all

visual definition was lost in a sheet of water that rose a hundred vertical feet and spray that rose five times that height as the wave smashed with irresistible power into the buildings that lined the waterfront. The sheet of water was just beginning to fall, although the spray was still high enough to obliterate the view of the dispersing fan of the hydrogen explosion, when the tidal wave burst through the concealing curtain and laid its ravenous claws on the numbly waiting city.

Great torrents of water, perhaps thirty to forty feet high, seething, bubbling, white like giant maelstroms, bearing along on their tortured surfaces an infinity of indescribable—in that they were wholly unidentifiable—debris, rushed along the east–west canyons of the area, sweeping along in their paths the hundreds of abandoned cars that lay in their paths. It seemed as if the city was to be inundated, drowned and remain no more than a memory, but, surprisingly, this was not to be so, largely, perhaps, because of the rigid building controls that had been imposed after the Long Beach earthquake of 1933. Every building lining the front had been destroyed: the city itself remained intact.

Gradually, with the rising lift of the land and the spending of their strength, the torrents slowed, their levels fell away and, finally exhausted, began with an almost obscenely sucking sound and its appetite slaked, to return to the ocean whence they had come. As always with a tidal wave there was to be a secondary one, but, although this, too, reached into the city it was on such a comparatively minor scale that it was hardly worth the remarking.

Morro, for once, bordered almost on the complacent. "Well, I think that possibly might give them something to think about."

Burnett began to swear, with a fervor and singular lack of repetition that showed clearly that a considerable part of his education must have been spent in fields other than the purely academic, remembered belatedly that he was in the presence of ladies, reached for the Glenfiddich and fell silent.

Ryder stood in stoical silence as a doctor removed splinters of glass from his face: like many others, he had been looking out through the windows when the blast had struck. Barrow, who had just suffered the attentions of the same doctor, was mopping blood from his face. He accepted a glass of some stimulant from an aide and said to Ryder: "Well, what did you think of that little operation?"

"Something will have to be done about it and that's a fact. There's only one thing to do with a mad dog and that is to do away with it."

"The chances?"

"Better than even."

Barrow looked at him curiously. "It's hard to tell. Do you look forward to gunning him down?"

"Certainly not. You know what they call us—peace officers. However, if he even starts to bat an eye—"

"I'm still unhappy about this." Brigadier General Culver's expression bore out his words. "I think this is most inadvisable, most. Not that I doubt your capabilities, Sergeant. God knows you're a proven man. But you have to be emotionally involved. That is not a good thing. And your fiftieth birthday is behind you. I'm being honest, you see. I have young, fit, highly trained—well, killers if you want. I think—"

"General." Culver turned as Major Dunne touched his arm. Dunne said gently: "I'll give you my personal affidavit that Sergeant Ryder is probably the most emotionally stable character in the state of California. As for those superfit young assassins in your employ— why don't you bring one of them in here and watch Ryder take him apart?"

"Well. No. I still—"

"General." It was Ryder and still showing no emotion. "Speaking with my accustomed modesty, *I* tracked Morro down. Jeff, here, devised the plan for tonight. My wife is up there, as is my daughter. Jeff and I have the motivation. None of your boys has. But much more im-

297

portantly, we have the right. Would you deny a man his rights?"

Culver looked at him for a long moment, then smiled and nodded acceptance. "It is perhaps a pity, I think, that you're about a quarter century beyond the age for enlistment."

As they were leaving the viewing room, Susan Ryder said to Morro: "I understand that you are having visitors tonight?"

Morro smiled. As far as it was possible for him to form an attachment for anyone, he had formed one for Susan. "We are being honored."

"Would it—would it be possible to just see the President?"

Morro raised an eyebrow. "I would not have thought, Mrs. Ryder—"

"Me? If I were a man instead of the lady I pretend to be, I would tell you what to do with the President. Any president. It's for my daughter—she'll talk about it forever."

"Sorry. It's out of the question."

"What *harm* would it do?"

"None. One does not mix business with pleasure." He looked curiously at her. "After you've seen what I've just done—you still talk to me?"

She said calmly: "I don't believe you intend to kill anyone."

He looked at her in near astonishment. "Then I'm a failure. The rest of the world does."

"The rest of the world hasn't met you. Anyway, the President might ask to see us."

"Why should he?" He smiled again. "I cannot believe that you and the President are in league."

"I wouldn't like to be either. Remember what he said about you last night—an utterly ruthless criminal wholly devoid of even the slightest trace of humanitarian scruples. I don't for a moment believe that you intend any harm to any of us but the President might well ask to view the bodies as a preliminary to negotiations."

"You are a clever woman, Mrs. Ryder." He touched her once on the shoulder, very gently. "We shall see."

At eleven o'clock a Lear jet touched down at Las Vegas. Two men emerged and were escorted to one of five waiting police cars. Within fifteen minutes four other planes arrived and eight men were transferred to the four other police cars. The police convoy moved off. The route to their destination was sealed off to all traffic.

At four o'clock in the afternoon three gentlemen arrived at Sassoon's office from Culver City. They were warned upon arrival that they would not be allowed to leave until midnight. They accepted the news with equanimity.

At four forty-five Air Force One, the presidential jet, touched down at Las Vegas.

At five-thirty Culver, Barrow, Mitchell and Sassoon entered the small anteroom off Sassoon's office. The three gentlemen from Culver City were smoking, drinking and had about them an air of justifiable pride. Culver said: "I've just learned about this. Nobody ever tells me anything."

Ryder now had brown hair, brown mustache, brown eyebrows and even brown eyelashes. The well-filled cheeks now had pouches in them and there were slight traces of a long-healed double scar on the right cheek. His nose was not the one he'd had that morning. Susan would have brushed by him in the street without a second glance. Nor would her son or Parker have merited a second glance either.

At five-fifty Air Force One touched down at Los Angeles International airport. Even a tidal wave has no effect on the massively reinforced concrete of a runway.

At six o'clock Morro and Dubois were seated before a microphone. Morro said: "There can be no mistake?" It was a question but there was no question in his voice.

"Presidential seal, sir. They were met by two unmarked
299

police cars and an ambulance. Seven men disembarked. Five of them were the men we saw on TV last night. Bet my life on that. Mr. Muldoon seems to be in very poor shape. He was helped down the steps by two men who took him to the ambulance. One was carrying what I took to be a doctor's bag."

"Describe them."

The observer, obviously a very highly trained one, described them. Down to the last detail his description tallied exactly with the way both Jeff and Parker looked at that moment.

Morro said: "Thank you. Return." He switched off, smiled and looked at Dubois. "Mumain is the best in the business."

"He has no equal."

Morro picked up another microphone and began to dictate.

At seven-thirty the next and last message came through from Morro. He said: "It is to be hoped that there was no loss of life this morning. As I have said, if there was, the fault was not mine. One regrets the considerable physical damage inevitable in the circumstances. I trust that the display was sufficiently impressive to convince everyone that I have in my power the means to implement my promises.

"It will come as a surprise to no one to know that I am aware that the presidential party landed at ten minutes to six this evening. They will be picked up by helicopter at exactly nine o'clock. The helicopter will land in the precise center of Los Angeles airport, which will be fully illuminated by searchlights or whatever means you care to employ. No attempt will be made to trace or follow the helicopter after take-off. We will have the President of the United States aboard. That is all."

At nine o'clock the presidential party duly boarded the helicopter. Considerable difficulty was experienced in hoisting Muldoon aboard but it was finally achieved
300

without precipitating another heart seizure. For air hostesses they had two guards, each equipped with an Ingram submachine gun. One of them went around and fitted each of the seven men with a black hood which was secured at the neck by drawstrings. The President protested furiously and was ignored.

The "President" was actually Vincent Hillary, widely regarded as the best character actor Hollywood had ever produced. Even to begin with, he had borne a remarkable resemblance to the President. By the time the make-up artist had finished with him in Las Vegas the President himself would have stood in front of a plate of transparent glass and sworn that he was looking into a mirror. He had a remarkable capacity for modulating his voice so as to imitate a remarkably wide range of people. Hillary was expendable and was cheerfully prepared to acknowledge the fact.

The Chief of Staff was a certain Colonel Greenshaw, lately retired from the Green Berets. Nobody knew the number of deaths that lay at his door and had never cared to enumerate. It was widely said that the only thing he really cared about was killing people and he was unquestionably very good at this.

The Defense Secretary was one called Harlinson, a man tapped to be one of the choices to succeed Barrow as head of the FBI. He looked almost more like the Defense Secretary than the Defense Secretary did. He was said to be very good at looking after himself.

The Secretary of State was, of all things, a remarkably successful attorney at law who had once been an Ivy League professor. Johannsen had nothing in particular to recommend him—he wouldn't even have known how to load a gun—except the intense patriotism of a first-generation American and his uncanny resemblance to the real Secretary. But his own private make-up men had improved even on that.

The Assistant Treasury Secretary, one Myron Bonn, also had some pretensions toward being a scholar and uncannily bore out a statement earlier made by Ryder. He was at present in the throes of writing a thesis for his

Ph.D., and remarkably erudite it was, but then the thesis was about prison conditions and the suggested ameliorations thereof, upon which he was an undoubted expert as the thesis was being written in a cell in death row, where he was awaiting execution. He had three things going for him. Being a criminal does not necessarily make a man less a patriot. His original resemblance, now perfected, to the Assistant Secretary, had been astonishing. And he was widely regarded by the police as being the most lethal man in the United States, behind bars or outside them. He was a multiple murderer. Oddly, he was an honest man.

Muldoon, the Treasury Secretary, was unquestionably the *pièce de résistance*. Like Hillary, he was an actor—both of them were to give performances that night worth platinum Oscars. It had taken the unremitting efforts of no less than three of the best special-effects make-up men in Hollywood six hours of work to transform him into what he was. Ludwig Johnson had suffered in the process and was still suffering, for even a man weighing two hundred pounds to begin with does not care to carry another unnecessary sixty pounds around with him. On the other hand, the make-up men had made that sixty pounds look like one hundred and thirty, and for that he was reasonably grateful.

So, purely by chance and not from necessity, three of them were men of unquestionable action while three would not have said boo to the proverbial goose. Ryder would not have cared if all six were in the latter category. But so the cards had fallen.

THIRTEEN

■ THE helicopter hedge-hopped its way due east, no doubt to fly under the radar which the pilot may have mistakenly imagined was following him. After a certain distance he turned sharply to the northwest and set his craft down near the town of Gorman. At this point they were transferred to a minibus which stopped just south of Greenfield. Here they were transferred to another helicopter. Throughout, Muldoon's sufferings were heart-wrenching to behold. At eleven o'clock precisely, the helicopter set them down in the courtyard of the Adlerheim. Not that anyone was to know that. Their blindfolds were not removed until they were inside the refectory-cum-prayer-hall of the castle.

Morro and Dubois greeted them. There were others in the unofficial welcoming committee but they hardly counted as all they did was to stand around watchfully with Ingram submachine guns in their hands. They were in civilian clothes. To have worn their customary robes would have been to wear too much.

Morro was unexpectedly deferential. "You are welcome, Mr. President."

"Renegade!"

"Come, come." Morro smiled. "We have met together to negotiate, not recriminate. And as a non-American, how can I be a renegade?"

"Worse! A man who is capable of doing today what you did to the Los Angeles area is capable of anything. Capable, perhaps, of kidnaping the President of the United States and holding him to ransom?" Hillary laughed contemptuously and it was more than possible that he was even enjoying himself. "I have put my life at risk, sir."

"If you care, you may leave now. Call me what you

303

wish—renegade, rogue, criminal, murderer, a man, as you say, totally without any humanitarian scruples. But my personal integrity, even though it may be that of what you would term an international bandit, my word of honor, is not in question. You could not be safer, sir, in the Oval Room."

"Ha!" Hillary went slowly red in the face with anger, an achievement which the world would have regarded as a remarkable Thespian feat and for which he was widely renowned: in fact, many people can do just that by holding their breath and expanding the stomach muscles to the maximum extent. Slowly, imperceptibly, Hillary relaxed his muscles and began, again unobtrusively, to breathe again. His color returned to normal. "Damned if I couldn't even begin to believe you."

Morro bowed. It wasn't much of a bow, an inch at the most, but it was nevertheless a token of appreciation. "You do me an honor. The photographs, Abraham."

Dubois handed across several blown-up pictures of the presidential party. Morro went from man to man, carefully scrutinizing both man and picture in turn. When he was finished he returned to Hillary. "A word apart, if you please?"

Whatever emotion Hillary felt, his thirty-five years' acting experience concealed it perfectly. He had not been briefed for this. Morro said: "Your Assistant Treasury Secretary. Why is he here? I recognize him, of course, but why?"

Hillary's face slowly congealed until both it and his eyes were positively glacial. "Look at Muldoon."

"I take your point. You have come, perhaps, to discuss, shall we say, financial matters?"

"Among other things."

"That man with the brown hair and mustache. He looks like a policeman."

"Damn it to hell, he *is* a policeman. A Secret Service guard. Don't you know that the President always has a Secret Service guard?"

"He didn't accompany you on the plane today."

"Of course he didn't. He's the head of my West Coast Secret Service. I thought you'd be better informed than that. Don't you know that in flight I never—" He broke off. "How did you know—"

Morro smiled. "Perhaps my intelligence is almost as good as yours. Come, let us rejoin the others." They walked back and Morro said to one of the guards: "Bring the doctor."

It was a bad moment. Morro could have sent for the doctor, Ryder thought, to check on Muldoon. No one had thought of this possibility.

Morro said: "I am afraid, gentlemen, that it will be necessary to search you."

"Search *me?* Search the President?" Hillary did his turkey-cock act again, then unbuttoned his overcoat and coat and flung them wide. "I have never been subjected to such damnable humiliation in my life. Do it yourself."

"My apologies. On second thought it will not be necessary. Not for the other gentlemen. Except one. Ah, Doctor." The physician had appeared on the scene. He pointed to Jeff. "This young man is alleged to be a physician. Would you examine his case?"

Ryder breathed freely again and was quite unmoved when Morro pointed a finger at him. "This, Abraham, is the President's Secret Service agent. He might, perhaps, be a walking armory."

The giant approached. Unbidden, Ryder removed his coat and dropped it to the floor. Dubois searched him with an embarrassing thoroughness, smiling at the sight of Ryder's tightly clenched fists, even going to the lengths of poking inside his socks and examining his shoes for false heels. He looked at Morro and said: "So far so good."

He then picked up Ryder's coat and examined it with excruciating thoroughness, paying particular attention to the linings and the hem. Finally, he returned it to Ryder, keeping only the two ballpoints he had taken from the coat's breast pocket.

During the time of this examination, Morro's physician was examining Jeff's case with a thoroughness that matched Dubois' examination of Ryder.

Dubois crossed to Morro, took a photograph, pulled a particularly unpleasant gun from his waist, reversed the photograph, handed one of the pens to Ryder and said: "The point is retracted. I do not care to press the button. People can do all sorts of things with ballpoints these days. I mean no offense, of course. Perhaps you would care to write something. My gun is on your heart."

"Jesus!" Ryder took photograph and pen, pressed the button, wrote, retracted the point and handed both back to Dubois. Dubois glanced at it and said to Morro: "This is not a very friendly message. It says: 'The hell with you all.' " He handed the other pen to Ryder. "My gun is still on your heart."

Ryder wrote and handed the photograph back to Dubois, who turned to Morro and smiled. " 'In triplicate,' he says." He handed both pens back.

Morro's physician returned and handed the case back to Jeff. He looked at Morro and smiled gently. "Someday, sir, you will supply me with a medical case as superb as this one."

"We can't all be the President of the United States."

The doctor smiled, bowed and left.

Hillary said: "Now that all this needless tomfoolery is over may I ask you if you know something about the late evening habits of the President? I know we haven't all night, but surely there is time—"

"I am aware that I have been most remiss in my hospitality. But I had to observe certain precautions. You must know that. Gentlemen."

Settled in Morro's private office suite, the company might have been sampling the sybaritic comforts of some exclusive country club. Two of Morro's staff, incongruously—for them—in black-tie evening suits, moved around with drinks. Morro kept his usually impassive, but occasionally smiling, calm. It could have been the greatest moment of his life but he wasn't letting it show. He was sitting beside Hillary.

Hillary said: "I *am* the President of the United States."

"I am aware of that."

"I am also a politician and, above all, I hope, a statesman. I have learned to accept the inevitable. You will appreciate that I am in a dreadfully embarrassing position."

"I am aware of that also."

"I have come to bargain." There was a long pause. "A famous British Foreign Secretary once demanded: 'Would you send me naked to the conference table?' "

Morro said nothing.

"One request. Before I commit myself publicly, even to my cabinet, may I talk to you privately?"

Morro hesitated.

"I bear no arms. Bring that giant with you if you will. Or do I ask too much?"

"No."

"You agree?"

"In the circumstances, I can do no less."

"Thank you." An irritable note crept into Hillary's voice. "Is it necessary that we have *three* armed guards to watch eight defenseless men?"

"Habit, Mr. President."

Muldoon was slumped forward in his chair—his massive back was almost to them—and Jeff, a stethoscope hanging from his neck, was holding a glass of water and some tablets in his hand. Hillary raised his voice and said: "The usual, Doctor?"

Jeff nodded.

"Digitalis," Hillary said.

"Ah! A heart stimulant, is it not?"

"Yes." Hillary sipped his drink, then said abruptly: "You have hostages here, of course."

"We have. They have come to no harm, I assure you."

"I can't understand you, Morro. Highly civilized, highly
307

intelligent, reasonable—yet you behave as you do. What drives you?"

"There are some matters I prefer not to discuss."

"Bring me those hostages."

"Why?"

"Bring them or, as sure as God's in heaven, I will not deal with you. I may be making the mistake of taking you at your face value. You may—I only say *may*—be the inhuman monster you're said to be. If they are dead, which God forbid, you may take the life of the President before he will deal with you."

Some time passed, then Morro said: "Do you know Mrs. Ryder?"

"Who is she?"

"One of our hostages. It sounds as if you were in telepathic communication with her."

Hillary said: "I have China to worry about. I have Russia to worry about. I have the European Common Market. The economy. The recession. A man's mind can accommodate only so many things. Who is this—her name?"

"Mrs. Ryder."

"*If* she is alive, bring her. If she's all that telepathic I could replace my Vice-President. And the others."

"I knew beforehand—and the lady knew—that you would make such a request. Very well. Ten minutes." Morro snapped his fingers at a guard.

The ten minutes passed swiftly enough, much too swiftly for the hostages, but it was time and to spare for Ryder. Morro, with his customary hospitality, had offered each hostage a drink and warned them that their stay would be brief. The center of attraction was inevitably Hillary, who, wearily but charmingly, out-presidented any President who had ever lived. Morro did not leave his side. Even an inhuman monster had his human side: it is not given to every man to present a President to his people.

Ryder, glass in hand, wandered around, spending an inconsequential word with those whom he met. He approached one of the hostages, who was perhaps the fifth or sixth person he'd chatted to, and said: "You're Dr. Healey."

"Yes. How did you know?"

Ryder didn't tell him how he knew. He'd studied too many photographs too long. "Can you maintain a deadpan face?"

Healey looked at him and maintained a deadpan face. "Yes."

"My name is Ryder."

"Oh yes?" Healey smiled at the waiter who refilled his glass.

"Where's the button? The switch?"

"To the right. Elevator. Four rooms, fourth along."

Ryder wandered away, spoke to one or two others, then accidentally ran into Healey again.

"Tell no one. Not even Susan." This, he knew, would establish his credibility beyond any doubt. "In the fourth room?"

"Small booth. Steel door inside. He has the key. The button's inside."

"Guards?"

"Four. Six. Courtyard."

Ryder wandered away and sat down. Healey happened by. "There are steps beyond the elevator." Ryder didn't even look up.

Ryder observed, without observing, that his son was doing magnificently. The dedicated physician, he did not once leave Muldoon's side, didn't once glance at his mother or his sister. He was due, Ryder reflected, for promotion to sergeant, at least. It never occurred to him to think about his own future.

Two minutes later Morro courteously called a halt to the proceedings. Obediently, the hostages filed out. Neither Susan nor Peggy had as much as given a second glance to either Ryder or his son.

Morro rose. "You will excuse me, gentlemen. I am going to have a brief and private talk with the President. A few minutes only, I assure you." He looked around the

309

room. Three armed guards, each with an Ingram, two waiters, each with a concealed pistol. Carrying security to ridiculous lengths—but that was how he survived, had survived all those long and hazardous years. "Come, Abraham."

The three men left and moved along the corridor to the second door on the right. It was a small room, bare to the point of bleakness, with only a table and a few chairs. Morro said: "We have come to discuss high finance, Mr. President."

Hillary sighed. "You are refreshingly—if disconcertingly—blunt. Do you mean to tell me you have no more of that splendid scotch left?"

"Heaven send—or should I say Allah send—that we should show any discourtesy to the leader of—well, never mind. You mentioned the inevitable. It takes a great mind to accept the inevitable." He sat in silence while Dubois brought a glass and a bottle of what appeared to be the inevitable Glenfiddich to the small desk before Morro. He watched in silence while Dubois poured, then raised his glass. It was not to be in a toast. He said: "The negotiating point?"

"You will understand why I wished to talk in private. I, the President of the United States, feel that I am selling out the United States. Ten billion dollars."

"We shall drink to that."

Ryder, glass in hand, wandered slowly, aimlessly, around the room. In his coat pocket he had, as instructed, pressed the button of his ballpoint six times and, as promised, the writing tip had fallen off at the sixth time. Harlinson was standing close to one of the waiters. Greenshaw had just ordered another drink.

Muldoon—Ludwig Johnson—had his back to the company. He shuddered and made a peculiar moaning noise. Instantly, Jeff bent over him, hand on his pulse and stethoscope to his heart. Jeff's face could be seen to tighten. Jeff pulled back his coat, undid the massive waistcoat and proceeded to do something that none of the guards could see.

One of them said: "What is wrong?"

"Shut up!" Jeff was very curt indeed. "He is very very ill. Heart massage." He looked at Bonn. "Lift his back up."

Bonn bent to do so and as he did there came a faint zipping noise. Ryder cursed inwardly. Plastic zips were meant to be noiseless. The guard who had spoken took a step forward. His face was a blend of suspicion and uncertainty. "What was that?"

The nearest guard was only three feet from Ryder. Even with a pen, it was impossible to miss at that range. The guard made a weird sighing noise, crumpled and fell sideways to the floor. The two guards turned and stared in disbelief. They stared for almost three seconds, which was a ludicrously ample time for Myron Bonn, the legal luminary from Donnemara, to shoot them both through the heart with a silenced Smith & Wesson. At the same instant Greenshaw chopped the man bending over him with a drink and Harlinson did the same for the other waiter standing in front of him.

Johnson had worn a double-thickness zipped bodice under his shirt. Below that he had worn a cover of foam rubber, almost a foot thick where the lower part of his stomach ought to have been. Next to his skin he had worn another sheet of foam rubber almost but not quite as thick, which was why it had taken three special make-up men six man-hours to fit him out to Muldoon's physical specifications. Between the two layers of rubber lay three rubber-wrapped pistols and the disassembled parts of two Kalashnikov machine rifles. It took Ryder and his son less than a minute to reassemble the Kalashnikovs.

Ryder said: "Bonn, you're the marksman. Stay outside the door. Anybody comes along the corridor, either side, you know what to do."

"I get to finish my thesis? A doctorate, no less?"

"I'll come to your graduation ceremony. Jeff, Colonel Greenshaw, Harlinson—there are armed guards out in the courtyard. I don't care how much noise you make. Kill them."

"Dad!" Jeff's face was white and shocked and beseeching.

"Give that Kalashnikov to Bonn. Those people would have killed a million, millions, of your fellow Californians."

"But God! Dad!"

"Your mother—"

Jeff left. Greenshaw and Harlinson followed. Bonn and Ryder moved out after them into the corridor and it was then that Ryder made his first mistake since his grouchy lieutenant had called him at home to inform him of the San Ruffino break-in. It wasn't a mistake, really, he had no idea where Morro and Dubois had taken Hillary. It was just that he was very very tired. He normally would have taken into account the possibility that Morro had gone to a room between where he stood and the elevator to the caverns below. But he was very very tired. To all the world he looked like a man of indestructible iron. But no man is indestructible. No man is made of iron.

He listened to the stuttering bark of the Kalashnikovs and wondered whether Jeff would ever forgive him. Probably not, he thought, probably not, and it was little consolation to know that millions of Californians would. If. Not yet. The time was not yet.

Fifteen feet down the corridor to his right Dubois, gun in hand, came out, followed by Morro dragging Hillary with him. Ryder lifted his Kalashnikov and Dubois died. It was impossible to see where the bullet had struck and Ryder had not pressed the trigger. The future doctor of philosophy was still earning his degree.

Morro was moving away, dragging his human shield with him. The elevator gate was less than fifteen feet away.

"Stay here," Ryder said. His voice was strangely quiet. "Watch out to the left." He switched the Kalashnikov to single-shot and squeezed the trigger. He didn't want to do it, he hated to do it, Hillary had cheerfully admitted that he was expendable, but he still remained, as he had proved that night, a strangely likable human
312

being. Brave, cheerful, courageous and human—but so were millions of Californians.

The bullet hit Morro's left shoulder. He didn't shriek or cry, he just grunted and kept on dragging Hillary to the elevator. The gate was open. He thrust Hillary in and was disappearing himself when the second bullet struck him in the thigh, and this time he did cry out. Any ordinary man with a smashed femur either passes into unconsciousness or just waits for an ambulance to come, for after the initial impact of a serious wound there is no great pain, just a numbed shock: the pain comes later. But Morro, as the world now knew, was no ordinary man. The elevator gate closed and the sound of its whining descent was proof enough that Morro still had the awareness to find the descent button.

Ryder reached the blanked face of the shaft and stopped. For a second, two, three, all he could think of was Morro making his way toward the apocalyptic button. Then he remembered what Healey had said. Stairs.

They were only ten feet away and unlit. There had to be a light but he did not know where the switch was. He stumbled down the first flight in total darkness and fell heavily as he struck a wall. There were flights of stairs. He turned right, found the next flight and this time was careful enough to anticipate the end of them. Automatically, as many people do, he had counted the number of steps to a flight. Thirteen. The third flight he negotiated with all the careful speed at his command. The fourth was easy, for it was awash with light.

The lift was there, its door open, a dazed Hillary sitting against one side and massaging the back of his head. He didn't see Ryder and Ryder didn't see him. Ahead were a series of what appeared to be caverns. The fourth, Healey had said, the fourth. Ryder reached the fourth and then he saw Morro inside the little plywood booth hauling himself to his feet. He must have been dragging himself along the floor like a wounded animal, for his leg was useless and the agonizing progress he had made was clearly limned by the track of blood.

Morro fumbled with the brass panel and had the door open. He lurched inside, an insane dreamer in an insane dreamer's world. Ryder lifted his Kalashnikov. There was no dramatic urgency. There was time.

Ryder said: "Stop, Morro, stop! Please stop."

Morro was dreadfully injured. By that time, his mind must have been in the same way. But, even if he had been well both in body and mind he would probably have acted in the same way for, sick or in health, for the mercifully few of the Morros in the world, fanaticism is the sole sustaining power, the wellspring of their being.

Morro had incredibly reached a calibrated, dialed metallic box and was beginning to unscrew a transparent plastic cover that housed a red knob. Ryder was still ten feet away, too far away to stop him.

He switched the Kalashnikov's slide from single-shot to automatic.

Susan said: "How can you bear to drink that dreadful man's whiskey?"

"Any port in a storm." Susan was both crying and shaking, a combination Ryder had never seen before. He tightened his arm around his daughter, who was sitting on the other arm of his chair, and nodded across Morro's office where Burnett was conducting a seminar. "What's good enough for a professor—"

"Do be quiet. You know, I rather like the way you look. Maybe you should stay that way."

Ryder sipped some more Glenfiddich in silence.

She said: "I'm sorry in a way. Okay, he was a fiend. But he was a kindly fiend."

Ryder knew how to treat the one person in his world. He kept silent.

"End of a nightmare," Susan said. "Happy ever after."

"Yes. The first chopper should be here in ten minutes. Bed for you ladies. Happy ever after? Maybe. Perhaps we'll be as lucky as Myron Bonn there and have a stay of execution. Perhaps not. I don't know. Somewhere out there in the darkness the monster is still crouched on the doorstep, waiting."

314

"What on earth do you mean, John? You never talk like that."

"True. Something a professor at Cal Tech said. I think maybe we should go and live in New Orleans."

"What on earth for?"

"They've never had an earthquake there."

Edward S. Aarons

"Assignment Series"

☐ ASSIGNMENT AFGHAN DRAGON	14085-7	$1.75
☐ ASSIGNMENT AMAZON QUEEN	13544-6	$1.25
☐ ASSIGNMENT BLACK GOLD	P3354	$1.25
☐ ASSIGNMENT BLACK VIKING	14017-2	$1.75
☐ ASSIGNMENT BUDAPEST	13785-6	$1.25
☐ ASSIGNMENT CEYLON	13583-7	$1.50
☐ ASSIGNMENT THE GIRL IN THE GONDOLA	13897-6	$1.50
☐ ASSIGNMENT GOLDEN GIRL	13801-1	$1.50
☐ ASSIGNMENT HELENE	13955-7	$1.50
☐ ASSIGNMENT LILI LAMARIS	13934-4	$1.50
☐ ASSIGNMENT MANCHURIAN DOLL	P3449	$1.25
☐ ASSIGNMENT MOON GIRL	13856-9	$1.50
☐ ASSIGNMENT QUAYLE QUESTION	13823-2	$1.50
☐ ASSIGNMENT SILVER SCORPION	13615-9	$1.50
☐ ASSIGNMENT SHEBA	13696-5	$1.50
☐ ASSIGNMENT STAR STEALERS	13944-1	$1.50
☐ ASSIGNMENT SULU SEA	13875-5	$1.50
☐ ASSIGNMENT 13TH PRINCESS	13919-0	$1.75
☐ ASSIGNMENT TIGER DEVIL	13811-9	$1.50
☐ ASSIGNMENT TREASON	13913-1	$1.50
☐ ASSIGNMENT UNICORN	13998-0	$1.50
☐ ASSIGNMENT ZORAYA	13909-3	$1.50

Buy them at your local bookstores or use this handy coupon for ordering:

John Updike

W0123-W

☐ THE CENTAUR	22922-X	$1.75
☐ COUPLES	C2935	$1.95
☐ MARRY ME	23369-3	$1.95
☐ A MONTH OF SUNDAYS	C2701	$1.95
☐ THE MUSIC SCHOOL	23279-4	$1.75
☐ PICKED-UP PIECES	23363-4	$2.50
☐ PIGEON FEATHERS	23951-9	$1.95
☐ THE POORHOUSE FAIR	23314-6	$1.50
☐ RABBIT REDUX	23247-6	$1.95
☐ RABBIT, RUN	23406-1	$1.95
☐ OF THE FARM	30822-7	$1.50